MADNESS

MADNESS

ESOMNOFU EBELENNA

Abibiman
Publishing
New York & London

First published in the United Kingdom in 2023
by Abibiman Publishing.
www.abibimanpublishing.com

Abibiman Publishing is registered under
Hudics LLC in the United States
and in the United Kingdom.

ISBN: 978-1-7392675-2-0

Cover design by Stephen Embleton

Printed in the United Kingdom by Clays Ltd.

DEDICATION

For my lovely parents, Chinwedu Andrew Esomnofu and Ngozi Edith Esomnofu. My university education was a depressing experience, but you made sure I did not get drowned. May God continue to bless you, my heroes.

FIRST YEAR

CHAPTER 1

The plane begins its descent into Lagos International Airport, and Nkem Obi, a Heineken University of Education first-year student, wonders if the elderly man seated next to him is mad. The pink-faced American's regular but egg-encrusted teeth arouse suspicion, he tells himself. The unintelligible accent, the set of owlish eyes, the ears that are bat-like and mottled, the hair that bends out in all directions like the white bristles of an overused toothbrush. The cream-coloured polo, which says *Helping Nigeria, Helping Africa*, and the ludicrous drawings of snakes, of elephants, and of mosquitoes beneath the writing.

"As I was saying, I obey all the Ten Commandments in the Holy Bible, pay my tithe and worship God all the time, so that when I die I will not go to a Nigerian university," the man says as the plane taxies down the tarmac under a milky June sky of golden clouds and hovering birds. "There're decent ones, though. Like yours. My Nigerian niece attended your prestigious university and, after impressive five years, she almost learned how to spell 'bread'."

He furrows his brows, adjusts the lapel of his white shirt and his orange bowtie, and shifts closer to the window to marvel at the sky's gorgeous purple. But "bread"? The word cannot dissolve from his mind. This graduate who cannot spell "bread", he hopes, is not named Chioma. He thinks she is probably made-up, but he knows, and knows that the white man knows, that the story is certainly plausible. He thinks his university, like many other universities here, is A Theatre of the Absurd, but fire burns his chest when a non-Nigerian attacks the disgraceful institution. What wouldn't he give to protect the image of his country among foreigners?

A pebble of tension in him dissolves as they the passengers on board are not plunged into the icy waters of the Atlantic Ocean. The thing that perturbs him now is no longer his seatmate's criticism, but his aggressiveness, his tirelessness. He visualizes himself collecting an invisible hammer from the window and hitting it at the back of the man's head. But his mother's sanctimonious voice—*Love your enemies and pray for them even if they slap you seventy times* — floats to him, shakes his imaginary weapon off his unsteady grip, and then leaves with it.

It's his magazine's headlines that encourage this American's campaign to besmirch Nigerian universities. *A Nigerian Student Forces His Lecturer's Head into a Dirty Toilet,* the elderly man reads out loud with a childish enjoyment. *ASUU Strike Called Off & Students Bark to Campuses. The Nigeria's Minister of Education Caught in a Californian Brothel, Playing Lawn Tennis with 9 Naked Harlots.* The elderly man laughs so much that he breaks into a fit of phlegmy coughing while calling the magazine a Pulitzer-worthy masterpiece of our generation in which no dogs but students *bark*.

Like a dog, he wonders, and takes the magazine from the elderly man. But, God, by this word "bark" is pun intended? Not a nice thing to write after six months of ASUU strike, but some of his classmates might find it funny. His heart thuds with the delightful images of them and their lecturers, of his serene Else-Shall-Die hostel, of his long sequestered campus. Soon he will satirize the editors' lack of discernment with some of his professors; soon his economic theories will dazzle these professors within the offices, within the lecture rooms, within the conference halls. Dictionary is what his mother calls him whenever he sets the house on fire with his grammar corrections or his economic theories. Dictionary is what she calls him when he tells her it's his desire to graduate valedictorian of his class. Dictionary, the nickname, stuck the day he, an irreligious thorn in his mother's neck, was impelled to lead in the morning prayers. Dictionary told God, in a solemn tone, that he would be *shushed*, *hushed* and *crushed* if he failed to leave the university with a first-class degree, failed to hear a song of himself in the leading newspapers, failed to receive an appointment letter from his university. Yet he didn't mention to the kneeling family members that Chioma, the girlfriend whom he loves more than all of them bound together, is one of his strongest motivations to be exceptional.

"If I were you, I'd dodge all my lectures and stay at home to watch TV," the man says, his voice grave and loud over the wolf-like barks of the engine. "Nothing excites me more than seeing a Nigerian student I love being expelled from his university. I wish I could expel you, my dearest. Is there any way I can help you to fail?"

"Your speech was amazingly beautiful; it has changed my life, obviously."

He expects the man to call him an egotistical eccentric, as many elderly people, particularly his professors, often say; but the foe rolls his eyes and blushes. The foe fishes out his smartphone from his trouser pocket and types swiftly: *Just landed in africa. . .*

He averts his gaze and pushes his Harry Potter glasses up his nose to look more bookish, more snobbish.

But where are his parents? They rang him up after Uncle Sobechi had hugged him goodbye at the New York airport and promised him a safe flight. They promised to meet him at the Lagos airport. They promised to shuttle him home in his father's car: a Peugeot 504 Ifenna Nzekwu, his roommate and friend, once called *metal rubbish* with a provoking snigger. "But don't come close to strangle me, darling," Ifenna added. "My neck is powdered, and I don't want any angry hand to wipe off my expensive Baby powder. But why are you *always* angry? All the students, including me, say it's because you think you're too brilliant and too handsome to be punished with broke parents. You're also pompous and anti-religion, but Chioma and I can throw our *poorer* parents into a dustbin for you."

"Who wouldn't throw their poor parents into a dustbin for me?" he retorted, and threw the huge Oxford Advanced Learner's Dictionary he was studying at Ifenna because the boy said the obvious.

Now, however, he regrets that he failed to deny this truth with polite words because he likes Ifenna a lot. He would like Ifenna, or Chioma, to await his arrival, and not his father, not his mother. Not even his twin siblings, Joseph and Josephine. He wishes he could confess to Chioma, this singing love of his life, that she's the flower that brings him home as lilies bring butterflies to their white petals. The flower that made him reconsider continuing his education in the bushy town. But he neither informed her about his homesickness nor about his homecoming: because surprises, he believes, are the gardeners that water the flowers of relationships. He believes she'll be boisterously excited when he hugs her from behind and whispers, "Blessed wine."

At the arrival lobby, he sights his parents. He's surprised they're chatting with an emerald-coated man who seems affluent and narcissistic like a movie star. He's surprised that his father, tallish and tiny in a shabby green suit that looks like a patchwork of vegetables, is chewing something he hopes is not gum. He hopes, also, that his father's sand-coloured fedora bearing a picture of a flying banana did not amuse Chioma.

And his mother, diminutive and lean, even looks worse: she's dried up by perpetual fasting, chalk-coloured by unanswered prayers. A slouchy gown, a creased handbag, a leopard-patterned headscarf that is wilted. Did her priest, a thick-lipped stammerer with an oversized head, advise her to dress like this? He raises his hand when their eyes meet, and then smiles as they approach with wearied gaits and enclose him in a clumsy embrace, the stench of crayfish-filled food filling his nostrils. This smile of excitement, he knows, is dimmed by the sudden tautening in his face as his mother bursts into a gospel song (*"What will I give the Creator who lives above for what He has done for us…?"*), and his witty father, grinning and turning, asks passing passengers to join them with drums.

"Dictionary, you look healthier but unfathomably unhappy. I doubt you ever went to church in America."

His mother says this to him in her reedy voice in the Peugeot as the car rattles in its trek east. He sits up on the backseat to see how his father, the driver next to his mother in the front, has received this remark. "Faith, I'm glad our son, well-fed in the United States for six months, looks three days younger than his age," his father says in Igbo.

"Jude, Jude, I beg you, don't make me jump out of this window and walk home!" his mother says, and tucks a fluttering wisp of dark hair from her face. "And, Dictionary, Sobechi failed to drag you to a church? Tell me the truth."

He leans back, the word *church* stamping in his chest like a soldier's boot, stamping, echoing, and the journey's still young. "The truth is that Uncle Sobechi's a bookish professor," he says. "I was telling you about the books on the semicolon, which the genius bought for me."

Her eyes in the rearview mirror are now asquint in the sudden gush of wind, but she says, in reproach, "My body's so hot it can roast potatoes, so don't fan my embers with the story of Semicolon, or any other white man. My brother should be taking his nephew to God, and not to Semicolon. Is this Mr. Semicolon a Christian? If he's a born-again, and not one of those millions of Americans that promote disgusting things, did he take you to church?"

"Dear Mum, semicolon is a punctuation mark that joins two related independent clauses of equal emphasis," he says. Then, to his humming father: "My sweet mother really wants me to go to heaven."

"But you want to go to your secret girlfriend's hostel," his father teases, steers the roaring car with his hairy hands and it sends up a shower of ashen dust in this tranquil but anonymous town of a pineapple smell and lush greenery. "She used to sing for me whenever your mother was away until your mother found out and knocked the cigarette-smelling girl out with a huge Bible."

"The registrar's daughter, who spent only five weeks in California, returned yesterday smelling of sinful cigarettes, but she can now speak through her nose," his mother says, her voice thick with envy. "She saw me and said, "I lav yah san's brain. Oh Gad, he doesn't nou me, but iz he bek?' Her vowel sounds were so beautiful... I mean, *beautiful*, that I hugged her immediately!"

He leans forward and says, to change the topic, "The Nigeria's Minister of Education was discovered in California playing lawn tennis with nine naked prostitutes from Brazil. An angry Nigerian with a camera saw him, and he screamed, dropped the racket, and escaped through a window. The cameraman only succeeded in capturing the Minister's torn trousers. This news is in the papers."

His father honks at a rusty lorry that is inches away from the bumper of their Peugeot. It's packed full with cows and sheep, this lorry, and the air is unbreathable with the billowing black smoke from its exhaust.

"Who won the tournament? his father asks, his eyes on the quivering red hand of the defective speedometre. "Hope our Minister's torn trousers didn't prevent him from winning the tournament for our dear country. Or the cameraman, who I suspect is one of your lecturers his government refused to pay for months, seized the tennis?"

"How are Joseph and Josephine, Mom?" he asks her with an exaggerated American accent to enliven her, but she mumbles, "The twins are good", and looks out the window.

"Your siblings are still in the boarding school," his father says. "Your mother told them they're *beauuuuriful* as we drove them back to the school. One day their teacher will pronounce beau*ri*ful as beau*ti*ful and your mother will write frantic letters to the the dean of studies, the Commissioner for Education, and the Minister of Education, imploring them to torture the teacher with thirty leather belts before kicking her out like an old bucket that has become leaky and useless — or arrest her with the police."

They laugh at this prophecy, he and his father. They laugh at his muted mother. They continue in this jovial manner until he finds, hours later, their car spluttering up the tree-lined alleyway that leads to Heineken University of Education.

Dad and Mum did not solicit, nor did they demand, the skylit staff quarters on that red hill; they knew then, as they know now, that they don't deserve that gift: Dad is a clerk, but he often sees Dad whistling on the way home to sleep. Mum is a porter, but he often sees Mum preaching on the way home to sleep. The family reside there because they and the white-haired registrar are from the hometown of Oba. The registrar helped them remove the occupant who was a freshly retired professor of Political Science, helped them secure the two-bedroom flat despite the strident protests of deserving lecturers, helped them bribe the Admissions Office for him, and helped them with a free matriculation gown.

The granite-coloured entrance, he notices with glee, has been straightened, repainted and festooned with red roses. Cars trundle in and trundle out, and the dust they raise engulfs students who are milling about. Butterflies hover above the periwinkles clustered on carpet grass; this weed girds a gurgling fountain of an elephant half-obscuring the sunset.

Behind his magazine he shuts his eyes and imagines himself curled up like a foetus in a womb; he doesn't want Chioma or any of their classmates to catch him, the university's Nelson Mandela, in the cheap vehicle. He hums Dirty Money's "Coming Home" until he hears the car belch to a stop at their quarters.

Inside the living room, a photograph-infested rectangle ablaze with fluorescents, a chaos of nasty things welcomes him: oil-stained bulletins on the floor, ragged towels strewn on battered sofas and Okoye's nugatory textbooks on a food-stained table:

Understanding this Course.

The Economic Importance of Cow Dung in West Africa.

The Negative Effects of Cigarettes Importation in Nigeria Prior to Independence in 1960.

Long before the ASUU strike, the books gave Chioma the ruse and, in a whisk, his heart opened like a door for her in the university library that idyllic Monday morning. He would be delighted to tell this story: how he wore his Harry Potter glasses on the bridge of his nose. How he underlined the books' outrageous inaccuracies with a red pen he picked from the marbled floor. How she plodded in, this fearless character, and tried to attract his attention, as she usually attracts people's attention, by stretching, yawning, coughing. How he lowered his head to give her the impression that he was determined to keep his attention out of her reach; that he was absorbed in his studies; that he had no time for conversation. But how she strode straight to him and seized the books.

You paid that squalid drunkard for compiling his ignorance and publishing it in books, she said in evidently rehearsed English. Books in which he, the author, secretly wrote the advertisement on their covers. *What a great economics book from Africa!* — *Professor Andrew Longneck, Harvard University, UK.* Two: *Utterly remarkable and infinitely helpful to all economic students* —*The New York Times.* And three: *Any student of economics who doesn't buy Dr. Okoye's sumptuously written book is hopeless*—*Vanguard.* Fine boy, Okoye's mad!

Mesmerized by her courage, he let his eyes dart up and down her petite body.

The worst is *The Economic Importance of Cow Dung in West Africa,* he said. What importance? Which countries in West Africa? Whose cows? Which bloody dung? I really want to set fire to all of them.

You know you're the most intelligent guy in Economics and on this campus?

Oh yes, obviously. I even know how to use a semicolon.

She tutted and nudged him. Rainbowed beads of sweat, collected on her eyelashes, dropped and burst on his fingers.

Chioma Emenike's my name, she said. Chioma Emenike's like you: just Economics, just first year. Look, if you have a girlfriend, dispose her like a plastic cup: I will stalk into your room with my luggage and musical instruments.

She penned her phone number on the first pages of the three books amidst brief interludes of titters. These sounds, he recollects, were interspersed with birdsong from the sun-reddened windows flung open by sudden winds, but he could not shun her: he was still with astonishment. This stillness encouraged her to hand the books back to him with a wink. This stillness encouraged her to give him a loud kiss on the cheek before turning away with a coquettish smile.

This lovely girl is into weed, he thought. This lovely girl probably smoked some blunts smuggled in from a Caribbean island, but what a butch-looking beauty: a warrior with nine gold rings glistening round each ear. Hair dyed the colour of fire, a guitar sketched across her chocolate-coloured arm. A striking dressing—black t-shirt, black jeans, black canvases.

He moped at her as she sidled to the row of seats in the front, her movements purposefully manly, her back pocket revealing the tip of a hunting knife—a weapon she'd later describe as her "radical feminist" against misogynists who harassed women on campus. How did this dangerous object escape the notice of these bespectacled librarians?

Now, as he reflects about The Girl with a Hunting Knife, he remembers that later on the day, at quarter past five or quarter past six, she described this instrument of attack while they sat, alone and close, on a marble-topped pew. It's egg-shaped, this pew, this *loveseat*, and sentinel to a deserted basketball court abandoned behind a rainbow-tinged swimming pool. He remembers he simulated a laugh as she pontificated about this knife. As she threatened, playfully, to break his Harry Potter glasses which made him irresistibly sexy. As she confessed that she merely hurried into the library to meet him, and not any book, as she had met her ex-boyfriend named Mathew Onwudinjo: a tramplike nerd in their class and in their lives. A boy whose fellow students mocked after he missed all his exams as he couldn't pay the tuition fees. A boy several students saw, a week before the strike, dangling lifeless from a cashew tree off campus. He and Chioma spent thirty-something minutes talking about the suicide and the dues, and about his novel reviews and booze. The chilly winds made his teeth chatter as they chatted, and flocks of bats flew overhead until the translucent sky faded into the colour of charcoal. It wasn't ample, the time they spent together, but he held her hand, under that dark canopy of stars, and smiled with her to Else-Shall-Die hostel.

El-Shadai! he corrected the semi-illiterate landlord who was not even there, and led his unapologetically smoking sweetheart into his white-walled self-contained apartment that smelt of watercolour paint. There was power outage, as always, but they were shrouded in celestial light seeping in through a heart-shaped hole in the latched window. There was beer in the fridge, but he chose a Coke, sipped the Coke, and she smoked another cigarette. The song could have been Bob Marley's, could have been Frankie Valli's, could have been R. Kelly's, but he let "Please Don't Chew My Love Like Gum", her recently released track, play continuously on her smartphone because the girl was fun. The song sounded to him like naughty children aggressively beating their mothers' pans and buckets with sugarcanes while the poor woman wailed behind them, but he stiffled laughter and inquired after her parents' livelihoods. She turned off the music and told him that her Daddy is a private school driver, but Mummy? Nothing, nothing at all.

Nothing at all, he thought, and nodded as though he's impressed, but said nothing. He said nothing even as she waded into the kitchen with his torchlight, even as she praised his cleanliness, devoured his jollof rice, drank his yoghurt. And back in the bedroom, she replayed that music, tickled him, called him an irresistible sin she'd like to commit by all means, and he laughed and got up to dance with her; they drifted along in it, gyrating round a heap of novels and textbooks which colonized the rose-coloured rug, until she stopped him, pulled him to herself, and kissed him on the lips.

He was giggling when she took off their clothes and when she pushed him down on the foam. But the giggles soon gave way to silent moans. He was arched above her, tender and slow-moving, like The Gentleman. The Gentleman, he remembered as the pleasure intensified, is a hero in a French romance novel that won several awards. *I'll review this great book*, he thought, to delay ejaculation, but was shocked as he toppled over off the foam and took the lamp on his side table with him.

You didn't damage the lamp, I hope? She sat up and lit her third cigarette of the evening. Angry? Come on, funny Sugar. Get dressed, and tell me who Oscar Wilde is. You've a lot of her books.

He picked his boxer shorts and the lamp.

Blessed wine, if you respect me, go and research *him*, he said.

Later, in her hostel, she phoned to inform him that she researched nobody but Nkem Obi. A text followed the call: *can u be my boyfriend immediately?*

There was something appealing about the modest urgency of her proposal, so he wrote back in pastel sentences: *To say no is to choose to drown. How can fish possibly say goodbye to water, blessed wine?*

But now, months after their first date, he gathers the textbooks, trots to the lavatory and dumps them in a dustbin. It's better they stay in the lavatory as Joseph and Josephine laughingly suggested. He'd like the twins to conserve their toilet paper and use the books to clean their noses and buttocks.

As he returns he hums a Hitler Youth song as if he

has just emerged from a Nazi book burning in pre-war Germany, but stops as his eyes are riveted by his last birthday present—a gold-coloured picture painted by Ifenna — nailed to the wall: beardless, fatless, but not at all cheerless. Oh God, I'm gaspingly gorgeous, he thinks: nice cherry lips, nice athlete's physique, nice basketball height, nice hair that curls and ripples and shines.

In the living room, he rereads *Go Tell It on the Mountain* until the sky turns grey and pigeons begin cooing in their garden. He ignores the music of the birds, ignores the enthusiasm of his parents who're chattering about America on the phone with Uncle Sobechi, and glides into the bedroom to write a sonnet he'll send to Chioma. The poem will reassure her of his love, inform her that he's back, and ask her to meet him in Okoye's office at sunrise. Can a single poem achieve all these?

With a wary chuckle, he pins a DO NOT DISTURB sign on the mahogany door of the bedroom, locks it, and sits crossed-legged at his reading table. "To a Blessed Wine" is what he titles the poem before he types it, edits it and sends it to her on WhatsApp. Every minute, he modifies and resends it, and yet there's no reply. Calling her has become urgent, but her phone is switched off.

The first thing he does at sunrise is redial her number, but it's still unavailable. The second thing he does is grab his white T-shirt, on which SEMICOLON is written in black, and buttons it with his quivering fingers as he grumbles to her A-shaped one-storey bulding with dilapidated windows. But he does not find any student. A note on the rusted entrance says *Renovation in Progress. Opens Next Weak.*

He leaves with the wrongly spelt word whistling in his head. The whistling ebbs as he approaches the front steps of the Faculty of Social Sciences main building, where he expects to meet Okoye, and his phone beeps with Chioma's WhatsApp reply: *Sorry, sugar. Will you ever forgive me?*

A poor attempt at humour, is it? This cryptic composition might not be designed to tease or frighten him, but what is she apologizing for?

He phones her: it rings but ends unanswered. He tries again. No answer. No message. Nobody should tell him this isn't a sign that she has got married. Or perhaps a practical joker is in possession of her phone?

He pockets his phone, knocks on the half-closed door and pushes it open with gentle hands.

Inside, Okoye is, to his mild surprise, seated behind the desk and reading a magazine with no girl beside him. The bald head, the wrinkled forehead, the white brows: aren't they testaments to Okoye's age of retirement? No wonder it's rumoured that most faculty members who're too old to retire are only in their 40s and 50s at Heineken University, but are in their 60s and 70s in their respective hometowns. Before the strike, Okoye once intimated to him that he's 46 on this campus, but his bricklaying brother, who's two years younger than him, is 56. Before the strike, Okoye vowed that he'd be given additional ten years like "other dinosaurs."

He moves closer to the desk, as the magazine's ridiculous title (*Let These Ripe Breasts Be Mine, Oh Lord*) appalls and galls him, and says in a strangled tone, "Good morning, blessed wine."

But the magazine-reader doesn't look up. The magazine-reader is analysing the pink-coloured nipples in the magazine for another doctorate degree or what? To kick that filthy publication out of the smile-filled, wrinkled face of that old bastard will probably pacify him, the angered visitor, but he's not wearing any mask. He can merely make a strangled owl's face, and then he startles the nipple-studying academic with a gunshot of a cough. This unhibitable incivility instantly ends the big-eyed scrutinisation of European nipples. How the book, as he steps back in shouted apologies, flies off its owner's hand like a plate of burning plantains and displaces an empty can of Heineken beer from the desk will always strike him as applaudably impressive.

He lets the word *sorry* tumble out of his mouth as he outstretches his hand to be fondly shaken or cartoonishly stabbed with a pen. But the lecturer ignores it and says, in a husky alto thick with a spurious geniality, "Ladies and gentlemen, may we all rise to welcome the long-awaited honourable Chief Semicolon Hyphen."

27

He gives Okoye a bark of phoney laugher, hugs the man, and makes a salt-licking face: the reek of cigarettes, mixed with the odour of beer, has assailed his nostrils; but he cannot complain. He cannot say it's fear that restrains him, for he likes to think he's a lion, for he likes to think Okoye's the most approachable and tolerant lecturer. But what's the deterrence? The word, *respect*, floats on his mind like a leaf on placid water, but he suspects there are more accurate terms.

After they have slouched into tattered swivel chairs, Okoye says, smiling, "It's indeed a pleasant surprise that we survived the strike and met again. Honestly, Semicolon, I thought it was my wife coming to search my drawers, briefcase and trouser pockets for hidden girlfriends. But it's you, fortunately. Or unfortunately, for you're not a girl. Boys are useless, you know, but I won't throw you out if you promise me you'll not attack my Benson & Hedges cigarettes, or any other imported property of great importance."

"Sir, I'm surprised you find it funny when this country's really sinking economically", he says, squinting at the bright mid-morning light now streaming in through the window. "The populace eats Chinese rice, use Indian toothpicks, carry American umbrellas in rainy seasons, don Turkish underwear, put sham Brazilian hairs on their empty heads, rub bloody French bleaching creams on their skins..."

"Stop crying and have something. I think you deserve a presidential reception, but I have ferried all my juices and cakes to orphanage homes. As a nerd, would you like to have a copy of *Let These Ripe Breasts Be Mine, Oh Lord*?"

Christ, is Okoye struggling to be funny? He waits until the distasteful words drift away like choking cigar buffs before he proceeds. "This economic slavery maddens me. I craved America, but I couldn't abandon my education. And my Chioma, obviously. But let's talk about your lectures, blessed wine."

"That singer is creative in bed with you?" Okoye sounds genuinely keen and coltish at once, and does not wait for his answer. "When will you finish using her so that others can use? I wish she were my property. Rose, who you know as my own property, is a pigheaded hairstylist with the compulsively slappable mouth of a parrot."

His own property: what a phrase! Isn't this unabashed objectification one of the reasons Chioma roams the campus with a hunting knife in her handbag?

He crosses his legs, gives the foreign-looking ceiling a quick frown but releases no deluge of disapproval to drown the shimmering image of Rose's "compulsively slappable" mouth.

"The lecture, blessed wine," he says. "I would like us to go to the class."

"Where did you pick this 'blessed wine'? In a novel?"

"Sir, the wine. . .?" he falters, unable to recollect, unable to segue from the topic to the pedagogy of economics.

Okoye says, "I'm expecting a girl, chief, and I'm sure you want to go to the library to study your books. You may go: there's a girl, not your Chioma, who promised to . . .You understand? I'm not an English professor, but I will make that girl produce vowel sounds in my bed."

He stares at Okoye, whose tears of merriment plead for a laugh, or at least a tender grin, for this risque witticism, but he wrinkles his nose and says, "The six-month ASUU strike cost us students, obviously. I humbly suggest lecturers push all these girls aside and concentrate on their lectures."

Okoye leans back to say he finds the wasted period of the ASUU strike irrecoverable and the government unpardonable. But does Nkem suggest that large-breasted girls from the bedrooms of the Minister of Education be given to all male lecturers in Nigeria as gifts of forgiveness?

He stares at the grinning man in pained silence; hot water, which has filled his chest, rises through his throat to his mouth, but he restrains himself from pounding the desk with a fist and storming out. The water cools, returns to his chest, and his mind, despite his attempts to stop it, circles back to Chioma. He pictures her beside him, humming, smoking, stubbing out her cigarette on Okoye's baldness. He stops when Okoye bows his head to snore.

The students, he thinks: they could be asleep, too. They could be awake while Chioma reposes or sings or plays her guitar. They could be in the classroom watching as Chioma teaches other feminists martial arts for self-defence.

Unable to stay for another minute, he gets up, stuffs his hands into his pockets to assume a donnish air, and shambles away.

At the Department of Economics block, he peeps in through the window, his breath fogging the cracked glass. How the whiteboard is so cleaned of words, the ceiling fans fallen off or stolen, the rows of rickety chairs wobbling with some expectant folks on them: studious students, chatty students, dozing students, flirtatious students. But there's no Chioma. "The Semicolon won't step in," he hears a familiar female voice say in Igbo. "An egotist, but Chioma worships him. A puerile pedant."

A puerile pedant. He has remembered the girl. Kambili, her name, is also the name of the loveable girl in *Purple Hibiscus*. She's a final-year student of Economics, twenty-two, slightly taller, but he remembers he walked up to her with his hands in his pockets and told her he liked her because he had read *Purple Hibiscus* and had liked her namesake in it. He remembers the tender rain falling on the roof, the blueish luminance of the flourenscence that clarified her figure as she bent in the deserted classroom, the jewelled hand with which she raised her indigo skirt. He remembers the grunt that escaped his mouth when his name, finally, was erased from the Book of Virgins. Was it regrettable that she tittered while he moaned? Yes, somehow, it was; somehow, *every* man, not only he, not only the proud, would find it humiliating. Not only he, not only the proud, would quickly do what he did: end the relationship. He did what he did not only because of her disrespectful amusement but also because she whined that she couldn't see why human beings read that novel or any novel at all.

Chioma is equally indifferent to literature, but he will not break up with her. He steps out into the sun and dials her number. A robot's voice says: *The number you're trying to call is currently switched off.* He phones Uncle Sobechi to thank him for "that snowy but memorable vacation in New York", sends Ifenna a laconic text — *I'm back, obviously* —and returns to Okoye's office.

The lecturer faces the ceiling that drips water now, snoring like a truck, flies using his O-shaped mouth as their latrine. An experimental cough from him makes Okoye blink his eyes open like twin torches with renewed batteries, yawn wildly, plunge back into sleep.

You must teach us, he thinks. You must teach us or you and I will continue dawdling away the day. He imagines tearing off Okoye's trousers with a razor, scarpering off with it; but Okoye finally awakens and asks him to follow him to a classroom where he possibly mislaid the lecture note.

He obeys but confesses that he cannot be happy: he cannot see Chioma, or his roommate, or any lecturer who's cager to teach them.

As they amble along the rowdy corridor that is mingled with the odours of shoes and dizzy perfumes belonging to students and their professors who are hastening toward the exit, Okoye does what annoys him: the man pulls up the black tie he uses as a belt to hold up his trousers and tells him that he, Nkem Obi, is wasting his time in the university because there's no job after graduation.

"I'm not discouraged," he says, looking over his shoulder at a sleek girl who's crooning a song about diamonds in the sky in a cacophonous voice that recalls Chioma's. "My certificate cannot be immaterial, obviously."

Okoye lapses into silence. But when they're out of the building into the air made blue with fumes from car exhausts the reluctant lecturer says, "An essay tittled 'The Youth and their Animalistic Optimism' should be written."

Before them are moving cars and hurrying students. Above them is a fierce sun. The winds are dust-coated and whistling. "What next, sir?" he asks.

Okoye turns and begins waddling back to his office. "Your obsession with lectures is worrisome. If you continue like this, you might end up being the best graduating student and those wicked buffoons will punish you by making you a lecturer. The only advantage is that you'll sleep with girls from all the east's local governments before your retirement."

He holds his tongue and follows Okoye, his eyes scanning the throng of students on the stairs for Chioma, and when they get back in Okoye's office, he eases himself into a chair and says, "I really want to earn a first class degree."

Okoye parts his lips to encourage him, or discourage him, but the door opens with a loud creak. Rose, Okoye's girlfriend, says hi to them, saunters in with mysterious giggles and closes the door. "The Nigerian army cover the airport with flowers for you to walks on them, the great Semicolon?" she says.

He gives her a close-lipped smile for the poor grammar, but frowns as she sits next to him. A gentle breeze brings a sheet of paper down to her figure-hugging vermillion skirt. She picks it, sniffs it, and he sees that bleaching creams have transformed her fingers into fried plantains.

"Rosie, how was the lecture with Professor Israel?" Okoye asks to win her attention, but she's scrutinizing the one from America. "Rosie?"

"My Prince Nkem, you look hot!" she says. "See your cheeks, fresh and big like two apple, and not like Ifenna your roommate's, who wore your girlfriend's skirt to a party and it was teared by Izu. Have you arrest Izu? And how's the skirt feeling now? Have you take it to a doctor? A tailor, I mean. But when do you returned?"

"Yesterday, my princess." He stresses the peculiar appellation to drive Okoye wild with jealousy and envy, but the lecturer puts his glasses back on and gives her a faint smile of subtle disapproval.

He shakes his head, again and again, thinking: Okoye my lecturer is the fool who bought all the smells in this office: the girl's smell of body lotion, of talcum powder, of hair cream in a blonde wig.

"Sir, can you believe this boy write a letter to the Vice Chancellor, telling him to chase away students who eats foreign rice and wears foreign clothes?" she says.

Okoye stares at her. "You're falling in love with him because he theorizes that the rising level of imports and the growing trade deficit has a negative effect on our country's exchange rate?"

"You sounds sad," she says. "Look into my handbag and be happy again. See? These customers travel to one polytechnic for night parties; they cannot take your tests. Here's the money for you and me to help them."

Okoye leans forward to tell her, "The regular customers, I know. I'm sure Ifenna Nzekwu's name is there. That's great news, Rosie."

"But give Ifenna a C, not an A because he see my beautiful gown yesterday but don't compliment it." She returns to her previous chair to hand Okoye a swollen sepia-coloured envelope from her handbag. "Give Maryann an A because her boyfriend is beating her. Let's console that girl and make her happy. Their names is on that envelope. . . Please, baby, they say you shouldn't rush off with their money to drink beer at Children of God beer parlour and forget to help them."

He averts his hot head, but from the corner of his eye, he watches as Okoye slips his left hand under her skirt and rubs the side of her thigh. "They should also ask for receipts. Customers, they say, are always right; but I can afford to lose these blockheads. You're the only beautiful student. . ."

"Behind every beautiful university girl in expensive clothes, there's a corrupt lecturer," she says, tearing off Okoye's hand. "Ah! Wait, wait, baby, you'll tear my underwear!"

Okoye withdraws his hand, turns to him and winks. "You want to read a book in the library, Nkem?"

I will slap you, he thinks with fury. I will slap you and slap you until you get it into your head that it's my duty to be here and stop whatever you intend to do. I will slap you until you decide to go to the class where you are paid to be. I will slap you if you refuse to teach the knowledge-starved students. I will slap you if your hand touches the girl's thigh again. I will slap you after the three of us in this office have rendered today meaningless with these senseless conversations. I will slap you if you ask me why I slapped you.

"I want you to read a book in the library," Okoye continues, his hand sneaking into Rose's skirt again like a thief at night. "No, I'm not dragging you out. You're like a son to me and that's why I insist you study your books in a library right now."

"Don't go," Rose says, then faces Okoye in mock indignation. "You wants him to go so you can start begging me to breastfeed you?"

Okoye tilts his head at him with a suppressed chuckle. "Rosie told me Chioma your love says I'm the most incredibly corrupt lecturer in Africa. I'm flattered, but don't believe anything she tells you."

Rose titters and tears Okoye's hand, which is skulking into her skirt the third time, off her body, and says, "Please kindly give Shadrach, Meshach and Abednego some marks; they buyed me milk and Ofoma bread when I'm hungry."

And his eyes open; he gapes at Okoye who faces him with eyes luscious with amusement.

"Rosie is exploiting your role model because she's a she," Okoye says. "I'm your role model, right?"

He tries to give Okoye an insincere smile, but his face is stiff with sudden exasperation.

"I almost forget I catched Professor Eziokwu and the HOD under that mango tree, where Professor Ayodele once say that its fruits are round, or my breasts?" Rose says, changing the topic. "Maybe it's the fruit, the mangoes, and not my breasts, but I'm sure Eziokwu's telling postgraduate students that he can't understand why you extort money from we students and sends it to orphanage homes."

Okoye nods three times like a giant lizard. "With the Vice Chancellor? Wait... a minute."

From Okoye's trouser pocket, he sees a packet of Dorchester cigarettes drop, its contents scattering on the floor.

Rose's lips part as though she wants to notify its departing owner, but he pins her down with a warning frown until the door is closed behind Okoye.

"You're hating the *philantopic* because he used Chioma when you're in America?" she asks, and glances back at the door like a criminal. "It's business. Ifenna and Chioma wants to pass Okoye's course and my baby want to suck breasts. So Ifenna give him Chioma and he promise them an A each. After enjoying and rewarding Chioma, my baby show Ifenna his gratitude with an A, a packet of Cabin biscuits and bread. My baby don't even butter the bread. Maybe he send his butter to the orphanage home. My baby like orphans. I lie that I'm an orphan, so he's paying all my school fees. And the bread, I eat some of it, and I'm sorry."

This is the time to slap her mouth, but he does not, he cannot. The news sounds histrionic and dismissible, but it renders him motionless, and a massive blackness engulfs him.

"Investigate or threaten Chioma to give you the photos," she says. "She think you'll not come back to Nigeria."

Now he admits he shouldn't have come back, knows it's prudent to migrate to Uncle Sobechi's America. He knows WAEC withholds his literature result and his literature result will be requested when he applies to study Literature in America. He knows it's time to run from economics, from girlfriend-stealing lecturers, from Chioma, from Ifenna, from Rose, from everybody here. But what will he do to Okoye as a punishment? Writing a letter to the Vice Chancellor sounds like a good idea, but he will not. He will not be civil. He will do something that will be shocking and unforgettable in the university's history. Nobody's going to know this plan. Nobody's going to stop him.

He grasps his bag from the desk, brushes Rose aside and flings the door open: the windows rattle and a heavy object rolls off the shelf and explodes on the ground. A frog-eyed professor limping across the passage drops her handbag like it's a snake and whirls around to flee. He stamps past her and clatters down the stairs littered with banana peels and groundnuts.

CHAPTER 2

OKOYE moves his stomach away from his reading table and envisions himself running through flames, through mobs, and through states. How the loud voices of Nkem and Chioma chase after him. Each stone he dodges, each roadblock he scales, each human he runs to tries to catch him. He shakes off these imagined scenes and the bedroom door creaks but remains ajar. The Legend Extra stout he has already imbibed churns in his belly. But he's listening to the entrance, an oil-stained wooden door that, at the moment, seems to hide someone.

A few guesses: Chinenye, the lovable daughter. Ebuka, the unlovable son, the self-acclaimed Rastafarian. Or Dorothy their mother and—he gnashes his teeth—his wife and "adviser."

But it's the morning wind lifting the dirty white curtain. Ebuka-shaped silhouette burgeons on the floor, and then on the door, like a sly ghost in a movie as the entrance opens wide. He gulps his Hero beer, lowers the emptied bottle on the ground, and nods at his vacant Guinness crate and then at his briefcase—his two reliable weapons.

Ebuka flounders into the bedroom with bread, singing about Emancipation and rubbing at his pimpled neck where the word FUCK is unapologetically tattooed. The dreadlocked Jamaican savouring a gherkin-sized blunt on Ebuka's black-and-red singlet seems to be staring at him, Okoye, with eyes reddened by marijuana, mocking him, daring him to do his worst.

What an ugly mug, he thinks. This thing is really my biological son? He doesn't like Ebuka's nose, which looks like a horse stepped on it; and Ebuka's shapeless face that's riddled with scars. It half-amuses him that the brat's his first child, his only son. "But I'd gladly exchange the 14-year-old abomination with a crate of beer," he likes to say with semi-seriousness that shocks all his girlfriends except Rose who finds it funny.

Now, however, he speaks to him with sincere affection: "Chief, my only chief. Please don't forget to lock the gate when I leave."

"Zikora's daddy bought him a smartphone and added him on Facebook," his son says in Igbo. "Now Janet is liking all Zikora's posts and pictures on Facebook. But my own father took some of my clothes to orphanage homes, so that people would say he's a good man. And he's asking me to close a rusty gate. Stop it, man!"

The words are cutting, but he'll not flinch. He will continue being a tolerant father and fighting off the thoughts to disinherit Ebuka in the hope that "the evil spirits" his wife says possessed the brat will jump out of him.

At the sound of a car horn, he turns away from Ebuka and gazes out the window: an orange sun looms on the horizon. Behind glinting rooftops of the several buildings sprinting from sun-streaked hill, there's a swaying pear tree that houses buzzing bees and chirping birds. "As you already know, I lost both my parents in the Nigerian-Biafran war," he says. "As an orphan, I sold cassava and palm nuts to train myself in this university. You have a father in me, but you're not appreciative. I'm not helping all the orphans I see in order to look good in the eye of the public. I only sympathize with their plight."

"But you don't want to sympathize with my own plight?" His son seizes the Blue Band butter on the reading table that is a podium for emptied bottles of beer and cigarette ashes, and dusts its cover with the mien of a cobbler examining a broken but expensive-looking shoe. Satisfied with its new semi-neatness, he twists it open, gives a half-smile of triumph, and begins to butter his bread. A howling wind bangs the door shut.

He eases his chair back and rises to seize the butter, but the door opens with a sigh to reveal Dorothy his wife.

If I were fat, she's a commercial refrigerator, he tells himself as Dorothy watches him with rabbity eyes, then waddles into the bedroom, sneezing and chewing. Garlic? Onion? Onion and garlic? In her hand is their palm-sized mirror: an object that always fills him with shame and the feverish feeling of malaria. He detests her because she's usually mischievous or foolishly insensitive with that damn mirror. He detests all the mirrors in the house; they are positioned to show him his wrinkles, to show him his saggy belly. They will be smashed soon.

"Your clothes," she says, her Igbo words clotted with sorrow. "Is this not a lipstick stain on the collar? The way you go round this university town with the girls in your class is degrading me. All my colleagues know about it and cannot stop laughing. I can't lift my face in the staffroom any longer. My face is always hidden behind either a *Vanguard* newspaper or *The Daily Sun*, as if I'm reading. Because of your shameful affairs I have bought almost thirty newspapers, but your girls still kiss you. Isn't this a lipstick stain?"

He shakes his head and imagines himself opening her head with a magical breadknife to bring out a coconut stored in it.

She says, "You want me to keep hiding my face in newspapers, right? Do you know how much I have spent on newspapers?"

Now, he's tempted to remind her that she's dumb and immature, but he doesn't want to be soaked with tears; he inhales, shakes his head again, and wonders why she persistently brushes English off her tongue even at Heineken University Secondary School, where she teaches biology, or thinks she teaches biology. It's true her English is as embarrassing as a trumpeting fart in a silent church, but he has seen worst speakers.

He says, "It's quarter past seven, Dorothy. Or do you want to go to the school late again and win the Best Teacher of the Year Award?"

"Ebuka's post on Facebook says there's a lipstick stain on your shirt," she says, disregarding his derision. "Whose lipstick, Ezi?"

He has warned her, begged her, to desist from calling him Ezi, which is the abridged version of his name, and she has promised to stop it. Ezinwa is the complete version, but many people he knows prefer the former. What kind of utter laziness, what infantile mischievousness, what insensitive playfulness makes them condescend to this? But he does not shout: my name is not a task, for Christ's sake. He does not shout: Ezinwa translates to "a good child" whereas Ezi means "Pig."

He waits for his son to exit the room before he says, "Lock all the doors; I dreamt that one of my angry students sneaked into this house, burnt our TV, our beds and all the buckets."

"Oh, it's a marker stain," his wife says, and heaves. "But how you handle markers! And green bottles!"

"And brown bottles. Some of the beers I drink have brown bottles. Budweiser, for example."

She stares at him with her mouth slack as if she were gulping the air, or drowning in it, but no syllable escapes.

The sounds of footsteps, the beep of a phone, and then Chinenye, their light-skinned daughter, appears at the door clutching a Danielle Steele novel, her white wig tinted with the morning sunlight. Her liver-coloured school uniform, which has three cigarette holes, makes him wonder when he smoked near her wardrobe. Or was it Ebuka who did it for fun?

"Ebuka says that Rose, your student and his Facebook friend, told him she asked you to guess the soap she uses to bathe and stand a chance of bathing with her," his daughter says. "And you answered quickly but correctly."

"And then he breakdanced into her bathroom to bathe with her?" his wife asks their daughter. "Ezi, I didn't hear about this soap-guessing competition which you won."

"I have won other prestigious competitions but

forgot to celebrate with you," he says, and his wife frowns.

But their daughter, to his surprise, fails to catch the sarcasm in his tone. "Which other competitions? Drinking or smoking? These competitions, if they are actually real and true, shouldn't be celebrated, Daddy."

"But I'm celebrating them, darling."

"That post has gone viral." His daughter extracts her smartphone from her schoolbag, peers into it, and shakes her head. "647 comments, 915 likes and 438 shares. Force Ebuka to delete it."

Dorothy looks at their daughter with narrowed eyes and strolls toward him. "Don't let Ebuka's repulsive behaviour depress you. And, please, no beer today."

"Yes, no beer, no beer, and thanks." He whistles as he wears his shoes, as he ties his stout-stained lemon tie. A bloated cockroach flies off the curtain and lands on his rumpled black trousers; his daughter moves closer to him to bat the insect off with her novel, but he thanks her, brushes it away with his left hand. And as his wife looks round in search of the roach, he picks his briefcase from the bed and escapes.

He'll not teach any human being today; it's a day to ponder about his clingy wife who believes that adulterous women should be slaughtered and not animals, and about his Facebook-crazed son who steals his cigarettes to smoke or peddle, and about his novel-reading daughter who assists her mother in hiding his alcohol. A day he will phone three or four big-bosomed girls who flunked his course and persuade them to dole out some naira notes. A day he will visit the orphanage homes with ill-gotten money, and with some of his tins of milk and some of his tins of detergent. After doing this, he will cruise downtown to drink chilled beer, eat catfish and mope at women's bottoms. After doing this, he will select the biggest bottom and ask the girl to follow him to the cheapest bedroom in a motel and have a nice time.

On the Campus Road, a hoarse voice bawls his name, but he has to drive into the Car Park in the TETFund Complex and march the brake. *Dr. Okoye the Best Businessman*, advertises the red ink on the roof of the car. *I deal in all kinds of high quality grades – A, B, C, D. Buy my goods at affordable prices.* Alarmed, he wipes it off with his palm and turns at the sound of approaching footsteps.

"Wait or I will shoot you, the greatest Igbo man of our time!" Professor Ayodele his friend says with mock petulance. He's blundering toward him, his breasts flapping in his sybaritic shirt that's adorned with tiny glistening stars and starched, and impeccably white. "The greatest Igbo man of our time!"

The greatest dog of our time, he would like to retort. Dear uncastrated dog, stop bristling in your obsessive neatness. A jolly "Christian" with a fascinating past, this Professor Ayodele guy. A jolly "Christian" and jolly "Muslim". A jolly criminal. The second chapter of his highly acclaimed book, *How to Learn: Seminal Works in Educational Psychology*, is lifted from the dissertation of one of his erstwhile students in an undisclosed state-owned university in western Nigeria. Professor Ayodele had to resign and come east: because the Vice Chancellor banned the book, because the boy (a notorious cultist named Opeyemi or Adeyemi) routinely confronted him off campus and beat him brutally with firewood. He recalls that Professor Ayodele told him, over a chilled bottle of Martinellis one downcast Sunday evening in a pub, that "the young monster" he plagiarized copied a large portion of the thesis from a girl who copied from a boy who copied from a girl who copied from a boy, and he cannot puzzle out why he was so determined to murder him with firewood. If ever he finds this Ayodele Tormentor, he will give the little hero a hug and a warm handshake because he did something he rather admires.

"We professors are paid peanuts here, but the Minister of Education flies to America every week to play lawn tennis with prostitutes," Professor Ayodele remarks. "Or so the newspapers say. Aside *Let These Ripe Breasts Be Mine, Oh Lord*, do you have any other recent paper I can read?"

"No," he lies, and shakes his friend's outstretched

hand. "No newspaper in my briefcase, only bottle openers for my beers."

He hasn't used any of the busty girls and women in the man's guidance and counselling class, or drunk any beer provided by the man, or smoked any cigarette bought by the man, and yet they're still friends. Why is he still a friend of a man who's parsimonious, short-legged, and always behaves as if he desires to identify with children?

"Talking about beer openers and such indispensable teaching aids, what's it with you Cabin biscuits?" Professor Ayodele asks with a mirth in his voice. "Cabin biscuits may be instructional materials in this country, but why did you gift one of your male students Cabin biscuits and a good grade for his roommate's girlfriend?"

He glances at the nearby stagnated water, greenish and gleaming with the morning sunlight, and spits as sudden winds spray it with bits of papers and leaves, filling his nostrils with the odour of the mangoes rotting all around them. He wonders, spitting into the water again, why his conversations with this man always circle back to girls.

"And bread," he says with a sneer. "Why did the idle gossip who informed you fail to include bread? I also fed the boy with bread."

Professor Ayodele chortles. "I wish I were your student so I would be eating bread and Cabin biscuits every day."

"Please, Ayo, don't shed tears here. It's never late; your parents can enroll you in my class." He doesn't want to see how his friend receives this speech, so he glances at his watch and coughs. "No lecture this morning?"

"You're not aware that the Vice Chancellor removed my name from the list of professors running for the position of the Head of Psychology of Education? I wrote a letter to him, querying his decision for my disqualification. And his reply was 'How many Igbo people are heads in Yoruba universities?' I was stupefied. Being Ayosky, I wanted to force a convocation gown into his mouth and leave this town. But the thought of all these curvy girls here at Heineken held me with two firm hands. They always hold me, especially that garrulous one you're currently enjoying. What's her name again?"

"You mean Lady (Chief) Oguagbaka Mgbeke, the white-haired, hunchbacked professor of Medieval History? You want to make love to her? I can help you."

Professor Ayodele's face stretches into a sincere smile. "As my nearest intimate and a philanthropist, you ought to give your Rose to me on a higher purchase. . ."

His briefcase slips from his hand and lands on the red-brown sand. His friend picks it for him with the prompt humility of a mendicant. He despises this faux modesty so much that he once told Rose that Professor Ayodele died of AIDS and the girl, to his utter amazement, rolled her eyes and fainted. Because she hated to see any lecturer dead or because she slept with the lecturer, that's the question. Perhaps he should tell her that Professor Ayodele has syphilis and gonorrhea. Or maybe staphylococcus?

"There are prettier girls in your class," he says.

"The presentable ones fear God and the plain ones have tiny mangoes on their chests, which are nothing to write home about."

"I'd love to have that girl you're currently using tonight. Kayode my son is back to the UK and my wife's still in the village. So I can bring the girl home. Hotel rooms are expensive now."

"Adultery is painfully expensive, Papa Kayode."

"Drop that 'Papa Kayode' nonsense. Call me Ayo, or Ayosky as the students do."

"But you're Papa Kayode, Papa Kayode."

"Look, if you call me Papa in the presence of my babes, I will strangle you!"

"Don't worry, Ayosky."

They laugh: a reverberating croupy noise in the serene environment. A dust-coloured he-goat wandering on the road not far from them stops as if offended, stares at them, and continues his journey. A van carrying about one hundred noisy fowls rattles past, leaving white feathers, black smoke and obnoxious odour of dung behind, and startling the he-goat into a nearby bush.

"A joke, my man." Professor Ayodele pauses to

adjust his glistening gold cufflinks. "You espouse One Nigeria, and that's commendable. You're the greatest Igbo man of our time."

"You extol me as if I've just solved a global problem like racism or tribalism."

"An Igbo man giving a Yoruba man a naked Igbo girl to use in his bedroom is the first serious step in eradicating tribalism in Nigeria. You've amplified my love for Igbo people." He turns to leave. "I'll phone you later today for beer."

He dusts his briefcase and lumbers on. He does not return any of his students' greetings until he gets to his office, and finds Chioma at the door. Why is she waiting for him?

Her wig is crooked, her pink lipstick smudged. "My dearest Chioma, you want to share the word of God with me, I presume?" he asks.

But she doesn't smile. Her white polo, which says *JESUS SAVES* in italics, has an open collar and no buttons. He's grateful to the clothes because it's now possible for him to see the tattoo of two hands playing a piano on the top of her left breast. But what's the message? What is a piano doing on a breast?

Finally, she speaks. "Good morning, *Ezi*."

He stares at her and wrinkles his forehead because the name Ezi is stressed. This subtle jibe is unusual and unexpected: she used to call him Sweet Daddy with an entrancing smile, and not Ezi, and not Dr. Okoye, and not even the conventional Sir. She used to come to him, singing his approachability, singing his amiability, and usually greeted him with what he liked to describe as a distinctly harmless hug of a daughter. An innocent daughter, he tells himself, but the irony clutches his throat: father and daughter have chased each other round a hotel room naked, laughing and fighting playfully with their undies, towels and pillows. Perhaps gossipy students have heard about their affair. But who the hell could it be? Only two students, he believes, know about his romping with this musical girl: Ifenna, the one who arranged the furtive affair; and Rose, the one who bumped into them at the hotel where he was drinking and smoking with the girl. He believes it cannot be Rose because he placated her with things she likes: pepper soup, seven brassieres (brand new and designed in Indonesia), extra marks in his course. He believes it cannot be anybody but Ifenna. He believes it must be the exposure of his affairs with Chioma, and not the problem of a failed course; he always helps the girls he takes into hotel rooms better than all his colleagues. Perhaps Ifenna confessed to her, and now she has marched to the office with eyes reddened by anger and a mouth swollen with sarcastic blame. Experience tells him he must treat her carefully, as if she were a lit candle in the wind. But can his eyeballs, which like to stay on her chest, behave well today?

Inside, he says, "I'm excited to see you again, Chioma. I'm very, very excited to see… to see. . ."

"I know what you're excited to see."

Her Igbo words flash past his ear, a fire-coloured arrow. He scratches his scalp and says, with divided attention, "I was teaching Eco 101 yesterday and… and… The door is locked? Yes, Eco 101. . . Today's bright and beautiful…"

"Just like these two identical places where your eyes are."

"I was merely reading the words on your polo!" He quickly lifts his left hand like a traffic officer stopping a fast-moving lorry. "Jesus saves, I agree. He really saves. . . Please sit down and tell me everything about your music career. Have you remixed some of your dreary masterpieces?"

Her eyes register no delight. Perhaps she knows it's clear to him that her songs are frightful nonsense and he's being nice in an attempt to have her in his bed again. He wishes he didn't leave his sunglasses at home; he wears them whenever he wants to survey the boobs or the backsides of his female students and his female colleagues. The sunglasses make it virtually impossible for the so-called feminists to catch his eyeballs and know where he's looking. He has successfully objectified more than three hundred women at Heineken University since he bought the sunglasses from Professor Ayodele eleven months ago.

Chioma's indignant voice jostles him back to the world of reality: "Respectfully, my music is not your business because your crates of beer are not my business."

Is this blatant insult a proof that she's in possession of something that's capable of sending him packing?

He says, wrinkling his nose, "Your language is quite polite. I see you're well-brought up."

"Nkem doesn't think so. He phoned to call me *cheap* because you used *the* girl who was well-brought up. He used the sexist word *used* because your girlfriend Rose, who revealed our secret, used the word. Why did you discuss us with your girlfriend? Why did you obliterate my perfect relationship?"

"Your boyfriend threw you out because of the rubbish my girlfriend allegedly spewed? My student: not my girlfriend. I'm married, Chioma."

She rubs her eyes as though she's on the brink of tears. "But your *pencil* doesn't know you're married. I think your girlfriend advised my boyfriend to show the Vice Chancellor our pornographic photos and videos."

"I hope those are the ones displaying where I put on my best performace? I want the Vice Chancellor to be impressed. But of course there're no videos and the photos to show."

"You think I'm unserious? You think. . . Stop staring at my chest!"

He looks away at the ground, then at the cracked window, then at the ceiling, and thinks: Why don't

I have the temerity to rebuke my own student? His honest answer, to himself, sounds bland: it's because of our familiarity, our propinquity, our fumbles under duvets. How he wishes he didn't sleep with her. How he wishes he could fix this crushing problem of sex and stop stomaching his female students' affronts. Should he castrate himself? But castration sounds excruciating, inordinate. Castration makes him wonder if he ought to walk into a conservative church, become born again, become pure. Castration reminds him of his Christian colleagues with whom he drinks or smokes; these Christian colleagues have three or four girlfriends each except Professor Ayodele who has eight, excluding married women and widows. This tyranny of lust has got to go on.

He rivets a probing gaze on the girl. "What's the evidence? Nkem climbed into our hotel room through the window with a camera?"

"Don't push me into bringing out my hunting knife, Ezi!"

He lumbers over to her chair and takes her hands. "Someone really videod us? I beg you, don't shout. We'll settle this amicably. I'm sorry, but I didn't rape you. We both enjoyed ourselves. I thought you're a feminist."

"Don't ever juxtapose feminism and your obnoxious affairs... Leave my hand!"

Leave her hand and be a little playful? But is humour the most expedient way to approach career-threatening matters like this? Slowly, cautiously, he tickles her cheeks, pets her ears, and she shifts and closes her eyes.

"I can't leave you, Chioma," he jokes, encouraged by her sudden placidness, her passiveness. "You're irresistible. You've the finest nipples in this department. May I see them again? You know God cursed me with women's nipples."

Morbidly he expects a quick laugh or a chuckle, but she pelts his head with her handbag and the neck of her polo tears, exposing her bra strap. Cars roar by on the road below and she springs up with eyes fiery like those of a wild animal. A knock on the door stiffens her.

"Ah!" she says, covering her chest with both hands. "What should I do?"

"You tore it yourself?" he says, in a panicked whisper. "Hide behind the shelf, please!"

But she grasps her handbag, dashes to the window and hides behind a fluttering curtain. *Don't speak, please*, he mouths and faces the door, his face a sunned watermelon, his hands two trembling ladles. He cannot button his shirt; he cannot pull up his tie-belt. "Who's that? I'm coming." He whistles to the door and opens it.

Ifenna lumbers in, a multicoloured umbrella under his armpit as though it's raining outside.

Absurd, he thinks: Ifenna, an African boy, is perambulating with an umbrella to protect his skin against the sunshine? His daughter won't even touch an umbrella unless it's raining. It's true Ifenna knows his secrets and can use them against him, it's true Ifenna brings students who buy his grades, but he's tired of students' disrespectful eccentricities, tired of friendships across generations. How can he dismiss this Umbrella Clown with effeminate pouting lips, a glistening nose ring and a feathered hat on hair supposedly plaited by Rose? The gum Ifenna's chewing is, to him, way too noisy, way too dramatic.

"Awesome morning, Professor," Ifenna says.

A apart of Ifenna's book in soaked. But in what? Sweat and beer, maybe: he reeks of alcohol and cigarettes. Has the drag queen begun to hang around tough guys? He hopes so.

"What do you want, boy? I meant girl. He or she?"

Ifenna snickers at the nouns and the pronouns. "I was reading your textbook at Children of God beer parlour, but the terms in it are not in any dictionary. Maybe they are misspelt?"

"Almost all the words in that book are misspelt." He looks over his shoulder at the curtain. "Please go back to the beer parlour, I will refund you."

"Business, Professor. Some of us customers want to buy good grades."

The voices of approaching lecturers in conversation freeze his blood. He tightens his belt and catches the drunk boy's neck as though he were a large pigeon. Then he pulls him into the office and locks the door. "I don't need customers now, chief!"

"Professor, I swear, my father wants me to come out with a first-class degree so I can work in a bank or be an economic adviser. . . " He sways forward with his umbrella. "I cried, knelt and told him that I prefer drawing fruits and painting human beings and animals, but he hit my neck violently with a live fish. Let's help that man because his son has helped you in multiple ways: I scrubbed your office, I bought you Christmas shoes, I gave you Chioma who satisfied you in bed. And I bought another shoes for you. And singlets."

He sits back, his eyes on his peeling donkey-coloured shoes. Only God knows what Chioma is doing behind the quivering curtain. Only God knows if she's phoning somebody. Only God knows if this is a set-up.

"How many bottles of beer did you drink, Nzekwu? The security guards didn't see you staggering?"

Ifenna belches. "My friends bought bedsheets for you, Professor."

I'm not a professor, you nemesis, he wants to say but does not. He does not even think he will ever be a professor. He does not know why Ifenna is calling him a professor. Calling him a professor to remind him that he isn't one? Calling him a professor to amuse himself? How can he get rid of the inebriated thorn without pricking himself, without creating a scene?

"Thanks for the girl, the shoes, the singlets and the bedsheets," he says in English. "But what you solicit I absolutely decline to give."

Ifenna sits and then flies up as though his chair were magically splayed with red-hot charcoals. "But you've enjoyed the girl! And you promised me and Class Rep twenty marks when I gave you the shoes. Rose asked me to collect the shoes because you didn't help us. But I trust you, and that's why I asked my friends to buy bedsheets. . ."

A sibilant sound behind the curtain. The wind? The usual rodent? The girl?

"Nzekwu, someone's coming to see me." He clutches the boy's hand and leads him to the door. "Come back later with the bedsheets."

"Professor...?"

"Come back later with the bedsheets!"

After the door is shut, he wheels to the quivering curtain. "Come out, my singer," he says.

Chioma comes out, eyes narrowed, hair awry. He holds his breath as she limps to the desk, as she sits with her face creased, as beads of sweat roll down her face.

"Your boyfriend-in-chief's roommate is a dipsomaniac," he says.

"That's none of my business!" she replies with poison in her tone. "My business is to endeavor to take an A from you misogynistic patriarch every semester."

"You think I must tolerate your awful manners because I ... Take yourself out of my office!"

Her merciless eyes of a falcon distend. "I won't

receive another A from you bedsheet-collecting, beer-smelling toad this semester? I'll expose you if you don't comply. You were photographed and videoed while we were in a hotel bed fighting playfully with pillows. I'm here to humble you and I've succeeded. Now a woman is in attack and you're a man in defence. Take my term paper with this hand you use to collect bedsheets and shoes. You'll give me an A, or Ifenna and I will go to your house and collect your shoes and bedsheets and then show the HOD the video and these photos; they'll see your small *pencil*."

His head bows, and his legs, miraculously boneless, start shaking rhythmically as though he were rehearsing some African cultural dance.

"Are you not this large guy who's sucking at my breasts like a baby? You think my automatic camera didn't capture us?"

He lifts his head and peers at the photographs she's showing him with tremulous hands.

Picture One shows he's tangled in bed with her, naked with her, twisting her nipples as if he were searching for a radio station.

Picture Two shows she's also in bed with her but in a yellowing singlet and rumpled boxer shorts; he's sipping a glass of beer and rewriting the answers in a fresh examination answers booklet with his left hand, while she laughs and smokes.

He doesn't have to look at the other photographs; the ones he has perused are exceedingly unethical and strong enough to volley him—and her, of course—over the campus algae-covered fence into that dark abyss called depression. But is she not rational? Is this girl so irrational that she cannot see she's treading on her admission, squashing it like a clay pot? Or perhaps she's paid by the Management to be a net catching lecturers like fishes? Perhaps she's merely warring against him because his girlfriend poured fuel on her relationship, threw a lit match on it, and stepped back to watch it burn to ashes. "You know you're my favourite singer, right?" he says with a fake smile.

"Stay where you are... my hunting knife is still in my handbag."

"Please don't let the HOD or other lecturers see the pictures. I can do anything to raise your grade if you immolate the pictures. Let's go to a picturesque place and talk business. I suggest Children of God beer parlour; the doughnuts are wonderfully mellow and oily, wonderfully sweet."

Tears—or sweat? —sluice down her cheeks. "I'm not here to eat doughnuts! You extinguished Nkem's love for me, and now you're asking me to go and eat oily doughnuts with you. Come here, Ezi! I said, Come here!"

He surprises himself by approaching her with great humility. "Please don't shout."

"Kneel down, you bedsheets-collector!" she snaps, and he drops to his knees with the swiftness of a nursery pupil who has accidentally spilled chocolate on his unpaid teacher's lesson note. A cartoon, he thinks. I'm behaving like a silly cartoon because of a girl who's young enough to be my daughter. His head droops and his glasses drop from his sweaty nose and shatter on the gritty floor.

"Good boy," she says. "Now mollify me by taking my term paper and promising me an A. Or I'll dance to the HOD's office with these photos. I've nothing to lose. I've more of our pornographic photos in my hostel. I'm on your neck and I'm enjoying it!"

"I'll give you both an A this semester if you burn the photos, my *kindest* student."

"Of course I am being kind to you."

"God bless you," he mumbles with a rising sense of fatuity, and staggers up. "We will resolve this neatly. Thanks."

As she extracts the photographs from her handbag, his heart lurches. But she tears them to shreds. Then she forces her hand into his trouser pocket, takes the last packet of cigarettes he has scheduled to smoke at sunset and boasts she has accepted to save his nauseating reputation from complete ruin; boasts he cannot help but give her an A; boasts that anything less than a distinction for her means she will enlarge all his nude photos in her hostel and whistle excitedly to the HOD's office. "And I will help the university to look for one of my aunties who will replace you," she adds before turning to the door.

After she's gone, he picks his irreparably damaged glasses and plods round the office, pondering who sent her.

A knock bangs on the door. A cleaner, a colleague, a student? Probably one of these lecture-crazed students who imagine that *only* an impressive result can procure a job in an air-conditioned office for them immediately after graduation? Or Chioma again? "Who's that?" he asks.

"*The* student," a surly boy's voice answers.

"The student? Whoever you are or whatever you are, send your problem to my Gmail."

"Sir, I want to see you," the voice says. "It's Semicolon, obviously."

He feels like a disarmed hunter in a forest running from a tigress to find himself confronted by a tiger. Does Nkem have some of the pornographic photos?

He brings his hands together like a praying mantis, lowers his noise-filled head to the desk and closes his eyes: a silent prayer to Jehovah to burn down the loverboy for him.

"Sir!" The voice is loud and angry. "Sir? Sir!"

He dials the Security Office, and when the telephone is picked, he says with breathless urgency: "Office Number 9, Department of Economics! There's a bloodthirsty cultist struggling to knock down my door and knife my stomach. . ."

CHAPTER 3

IFENNA doesn't like that the Security Office is filled with the heavy odour of tobacco. He doesn't like that through the unclosed entrance, through the uncurtained glass that's the window, comes a light breeze with no scent of lilacs or the purple flowers he can see in the garden across the bumpy road. He has always argued that the most irksome thing is the fact that most people do not prioritize elegance. He has always argued that security officers and even police officers should afford to do without guns and without batons, but not without flowers and gold-painted ceilings. Not even without glamorous men and glamorous women. He has always argued that he can be bold enough to ask why the university filled the security office with inelegant people, but now fear has gripped his tongue.

Before the arrest, the word "fear" was the intriguing motif in some of Nkem's probing questions, which was usually: "Blessed wine, you draw and paint fantastically, and I suppose you don't want to quit Economics for Fine and Applied Arts because you fear your *deadbeat* father?"

Or: "Fear is what restrains you from wearing these funny flowered skirts you bought and hid in our wardrobe?"

Or: "You like girls, obviously, but the fear of a quick rebuff is the hindrance?"

He would giggle. He would throw things at him. He would say, "Sometimes I wonder what a brilliant genius like you is doing with a staggering idiot who drinks *whiskey* and says it's it *risky*. I will never disappoint or betray you, Semicolon."

But here he is with Chioma, for the roommate in whose heart his name stands among words like *traitor*, *hypocrite* and *foe* as weeds. They are like two statues, he and Chioma, standing still before a desk littered with bread crumbs and ants. They have drunk his whiskey for courage. They have listened to her militant songs with semi-seriousness. They have the things they suppose Nkem needs: a flask of stew and rice, a bottle of water, a collection of Oscar Wilde's poetry, a Chinua Achebe novel. "We wan' see Semicolon," he says in pidgin English, and takes off his pink hat.

The three security guards around the desk blink in

amazement. The one standing behind them smiles; the one standing in front of them does not. There's only one woman in the office, but she's snoring at her small table, her misaligned eyes half-open to the rattling ceiling fan.

"Not a punctuation mark," Chioma clarifies. "A human being called Nkemdilim Obi."

"All human beings but students are permitted to advance into the detention room," a pale-faced officer at the door informs them in astonishingly graceful English. The name tag, he notices, says Mr. Timothy Johnson. No Igbo name: this must have throttled Nkem.

Chioma shakes her head, dusts a leaf-green plastic bench and perches on it with uncharacteristic carefulness. "We need to see him."

"I swear, my new hairstyle will brighten his day," he jokes in Igbo, his eyes on Chioma's unzipped handbag for buns or doughnuts. But the things in it are a hunting knife, a packet of cigarettes, a cigarette lighter, a dog-eared textbook, a rechargeable torch. Because she's different from other girls, because she has a musical ambition, Nkem let her wheedle into his heart. The odd thing about Nkem: he likes odd people. Nkem says he befriends him because he, Ifenna, has Oscar Wilde's characteristics: the femininity, the secrecy, the outlandish dressing, the wit. But can this be the truth, the only truth? He'll ask Nkem this question as soon as this cage is opened and the detained scholar, like a bird, is allowed to fly home.

"Throwing a victim into this bloody cave is a cowardly act!"

He winces as this aggressive voice of Nkem comes from the room within the building. The voice again: "You don't want me to explain and you don't want me to read my novels here! This is preposterous, obviously!"

"Since you can't give him his novels to read, let him eat the rice," Chioma says, and he grins at the fearless irritability in her voice. "Let him eat the rice."

"The girlfriend?"

He looks sideways at the small table and finds the speaker, who minutes ago impressed him with her musical snoring. Funny she's jarred awake by their voices and is now a smiling woman. He likes that she's portly, likes that she's pregnant. He likes her mouth, round and pink and elongated like a toy trumpet, but surprisingly reminiscent of Professor—the earless piglet his father gifted him when he won the Best Painter and Artist of the Year in a row in secondary school. He likes her skin, for it's dotted with reddish pimples, for it's grilled by cut-rate bleaching creams, for it makes him think of the caricatures of the legendary Boris Artzybasheff.

"The girlfriend?" the woman says again. "Ask my colleagues. We offered him your flask. He opened it, frowned and said it's imported rice. The nationalist is hungry, but angry with you for bringing him foreign rice. Your boyfriend's funny. Is he an aspiring actor?"

Chioma arches her brows, but in a voice free of

acid, she asks them to inform Nkem that the rice is not foreign, and they should act fast as her boyfriend would rather die than touch foreign rice for economic reasons.

"Yet you couple use imported disposables in bed?" a white-haired officer with some missing teeth asks in rural Igbo, vibrating with throaty laughter and straightening up. "Don't you also shirk from foreign disposables for economic reasons?"

"Dearest Grandpa, we don't even use local disposables." Chioma's voice, now thick with sarcasm, bounces around the office and settles on the cream-coloured marbled floor, which is broken by time and tattooed by sand-coated boots. "As a consequence, I've bungled thirty-nine abortions. But it's *my* own womb, isn't it, dearest Grandpa?"

The officers in the office exchange glances. "Now, get out," says the white-haired officer with some missing teeth. "Dr. Okoye and the Dean of Students' Affairs have asked us to free him. Out!"

Together they slip out into the chilly air. Above the sky is so white he says he wishes he could paint it, but Chioma hums some blues to discourage conversation.

Outside the campus, they part ways: she to Children of God beer parlour to smoke cigarettes, he to Classic Women's Hair Dressing & Salon to wash his hair, polish his nails and drink the whiskey the establishment offers its "male customers". He loves to be full of alcohol, melodramatic, flippant, petulant but strikingly elegant before whistling to Uncle Elijah's Poverty Bye-Bye Ministry to check on this prophet of God.

When he arrives at the church with his odour of alcohol, the sun has turned to the colour of rose and gone down beyond palm trees. The winds comb the elephant grass that surrounds the sign-post reading POVERTY BYE-BYE MINISTRY.

These painted words are his first artistic joke here, his first unpaid work. It used to be POVER-TEA, the original word; but one of the few lettered folks in the church scolded and corrected him.

But I will still bring TEA, he tells himself. I will bring MILK. I will bring beverages the same way Uncle Elijah likes to bring Nkem to God, to church, to himself. Uncle Elijah wants Nkem because he wants English. He calls Nkem when he discovers a fancy word, he jokes with Nkem when the congregants are wowed by the fancy word. Nkem Obi: a river where Uncle Elijah journeys to wash away muddy sentences, drink clean sentences, and so why is he, Ifenna Nzekwu, startled when he finds Nkem seated on the doorway with Uncle Elijah, in the tenebrous crescent of frangipani trees, eating mangoes, sipping bottled water and watching two fighting fowls? Perhaps it's my guilty conscience, he reasons, and his pace slackens. How is he going to deal with the odd duo?

He takes off his hat and coughs to draw their

attention, but they're engrossed in the fowls' "mortal kombat," as Uncle Elijah now puts it in English. There's an Oxford Advanced Learner's Dictionary in the lap of the Anglophile; he takes it virtually everywhere he goes.

When their eyes finally meet, Uncle Elijah's face congeals with annoyance, and he faces Nkem to continue their conversation. It annoys him that their voices are now lowered and solemn, now confidential.

He puts on his hat with a heightened sense of amusement, shakes his head and thinks: Nkem and Uncle Elijah. Call it the congress of the supercilious and the docile. Call Nkem the unbeliever, call Uncle Elijah the believer. Think what they could be whispering about. How he exchanged his roommate's girlfriend with an A, Cabin biscuits and bread? When did Uncle Elijah convert his ministry into a court of law? Nkem and Uncle Elijah have met and dined before, bared their dreams, bared their secrets, and yet he's amazed that their mismatched friendship is not yet ashed.

Hurriedly, Uncle Elijah rises without the plates of mangoes and limps into the L-shaped bungalow. Nkem follows the prophet, brown leaves from an unseen tree spinning and drifting above their heads. On the back of Nkem's black polo, there's a customized question in red: *Can you marry a woman who does not know how to use a semicolon?*

Yes, he believes he can, even if she doesn't know

how to use the full stop, the question mark and the bracket. But does he really need a girl now, or a wife, like Nkem his jealous roommate?

He selects the ripest mango from the plate and sucks its delicious juice as he smiles into the church.

In the perfumed hall, he halts and takes off his hat. All around the building are young women, middle-aged women, and old women: some rolling on the dusty floor, some speaking in tongues, some shaking their heads, some shouting Jesus in maniacal voices. He wishes he could produce loud monkey sounds to stop their noisemaking, hit them with the church's plastic chairs and ask them to get out and face their businesses. But he fears they might mistake him for the Devil's Agent and pound him so mercilessly with enormous Bibles and hymn books until he vomits all the alcohol in his system.

In his trouser pocket, his phone vibrates. He suspects it's Uncle Elijah, but when he brings the device out and peers at its screen, he finds it's Okoye. He will not answer Okoye. He is sure Okoye longs to know if he's the one who divulged his affair with Chioma to Nkem. But where's the lecturer calling from? A beer parlour, most likely. The lecturer must be at Children of God beer parlour with another student's girlfriend. The lecturer should leave green bottles, stride to his girlfriend Rose's hostel and interrogate her. But will she deny it?

The call has ended unanswered. He pockets the device and saunters into Uncle Elijah's incense-smelling counselling room with a grin. The grin, he feels, vanishes the moment he sights a white bucket on a desk littered with candles. The white bucket says, in pale mauve ink, **Olive Oil: For Barren Women and Unmarried Women, For Jobless Men and Cursed Men.**

It's his oil, not Uncle Elijah's. He remembers telling his uncle, after one of those clockwinding grammar lessons with Nkem in their apartment, that he bought the oil because he prefers to fry stolen chickens in olive oil. He remembers telling his uncle that he would not sell it and he would not give it out. The questions he'd like to ask Uncle Elijah: Uncle Elijah, can't you make do with groundnut oil? Uncle Elijah, why did you visit us, steal my oil, which you're now selling to your flock of sheep? Or did Nkem bring the oil to the church because it was "*made in Switzerland*"? But it was clearly made in Abakaliki. The word, "Switzerland", he ought to explain to Nkem, is a marketing strategy. But not now.

They all settle into swivel chairs and exchange greetings in lowered tones. "Listen, Ifenna," Uncle Elijah says. "You know Judas is Carrot constituted suicide after betraying Jesus?"

He aches to draw attention to Uncle Elijah's chronic malapropism, but that might sound offensive. "I didn't know that carrots commit suicide."

Uncle Elijah and Nkem exchange glances as if to confirm that marijuana or some cheap substance has fried his brain like *akara*. "Why did you betray your best friend?"

He giggles. "Uncle, never befriend someone who will be wicked enough to refuse to betray you at least once every two weeks."

"You talk a lot of rubbish, you remorseless ignoramus!" Nkem says in an almost-choked voice. "How dare you submit my Chioma like a term paper to that filthy freak? You drank alcohol, so that you wouldn't tremble before me, obviously. Why don't you tremble before me?"

A cold tone, a cold boy. A cold boy with the greenish veins craquelured on that bulging neck of his. He gazes at the gold-framed photograph of Christ and His twelve apostles hung on the turquoise wall. "I only fear our miraculous Jesus who fed the multitude with five loaves of bread and two fish," he says. "Turn the water in this jug here on this desk into wine or beer, and I will begin to fear you too. Should I give you the jug?"

Uncle Elijah lets out a whoop of laughter, his shoulders and stomach shaking like Okoye's. But what's so funny, he wants to ask but does not. Through the open window, he watches butterflies flitting among pink flowers. He pops him into his mouth and chews it noisily, smilingly, as he wrestles the urge to look at

Uncle Elijah or Nkem—two women-obsessed arses, he tells himself. But my uncle is a nicer arse.

He likes Uncle Elijah's secret girlfriends and wines, his undersized head on a swollen neck, his "Moses beard," his bow legs. "I'm forty-two years old, but I enjoy being a bachelor," Uncle Elijah often says in Onitsha dialect. "I'm madly in love with four biological sisters who are married and I think God wants me to marry one of them."

"Your *cucumber*, not God," he once corrected Uncle Elijah. He hungers to tell this to Nkem to cheer him up, but the Semicolon Boy is glaring at the heart-shaped clock on the wall as though he's afraid to face him. Or perhaps he's trying to discover if it was manufactured outside Nigeria. If he discovers it was imported from China, will he, like a demented cartoon, smash it on somebody's head?

Into the stuffy silence, he says, "Semicolon, I swear, I don't know how my Uncle Elijah lures all these young women in his church into his bed; his stomach is so big he struggles to button his shirts."

Uncle Elijah wipes his watery eyes with his palm and glances at the entrance. "Please speak continentally," he says in a muffled voice, and smirks. "I once told you you'll grow just as fat if you let yourself slip into Pentecostal evangelism, preach, heal or prophesy. But that's not why we are here. You betrayed your roommate, and we need to know why…"

"Uncle, I drank whiskey, so I need *a blessed wine* to heal me." He purses his lips because Nkem, the owner of the absurd expression, blinks and then his face buckles. Surprisingly, Nkem adjusts his Harry Potter glasses, and not pull them off for a fight, and lets no insult fly out of him. Because, perhaps, he has been reading some writer whose novel or poem condemns vulgarity?

"Uncle Elijah's real name is Azikiwe, as I suppose he has told you," he continues, as bats swoop past the windows. "Since he left Onitsha, where our ancestral home is, the name, like cigarette smoke blown into gentle winds, gradually disappeared, and he christened himself Elijah."

"Stop changing the topic," Uncle Elijah says, stifling laughter.

He stands, spinning his hat on his finger, and circles the office. "We're changing the topic? No, the only thing we have succeeded in changing here is Nkem's facial expression. He has forgiven me, though, and will never burn the crate of beer Dr. Okoye promised to give me—or the dog I promised to buy for myself. A very happy puppy, but it's very stumpy, very grumpy, lumpy, and not at all frumpy like some of our girlfriends. You should see this happy puppy who, as I said, is grumpy, lumpy and frumpy!"

Nkem rushes at him and grabs the collar of his sunflower shirt with both hands. "Now why did you exchange my girl with bloody Cabin biscuits, unbuttered bread and an A?"

"The bread was actually buttered, but wait first… wait! Take my *hat* because I broke your *heart*." He takes off the hat as Nkem's hands, unbelievably, let go of his shirt but the eyes staring at him with wonder are so large he imagines them bursting like balloons. He puts the hat on Nkem's head and steps backwards in case he needs to dodge a military punch.

Nkem bites his lip, grasps the shirt again and opens his mouth but says nothing.

"Say something," he tells Nkem, and gives Uncle Elijah a secret wink. "I swear, you look beautiful in the hat like a character in a novel –or a poem, my dear Semicolon?"

Uncle Elijah looks away to hide his smiling face. Nkem watches them with popping eyes and then, quite suddenly, grabs the collar of his shirt, drags him like a sacrificial lamb to the bucket of olive oil and forces his head into it. The head struggles and struggles in the bucket for its life like a trapped animal, and he yells for help, while swallowing oil and pounding the desk: candles and other religious objects he cannot see jump off and land on the floor. He hears Uncle Elijah, who has been laughing, rush forward forward to separate them.

Footsteps: several, heavy, quick. A hand taps at the door. A female voice calls Prophet Elijah in a frantic dialect he cannot place, and a hush falls. The knob turns and rattles, somebody pounds on the door three times in swift succession, and then Uncle Elijah says, in irritated English, "Akpan? Don't bother: There's no problem."

"Vely good, Plophet," Akpan says.

They retreat with murmurs, while he and Nkem take their seats and gaze at Uncle Elijah. The prophet pulls his drawer open and retrieves a white handkerchief, then approaches him, with a face brightened by this brief but satisfactory entertainment, to clean the olive oil on his face, scalp, neck, ears.

After his appearance has been cleaned to some degree of respectability and everybody's settled down, he thinks about their family and the office darkens. Why can't his father remember him? Why can't his father ever phone him and ask him how he's faring on campus? Why can't his father be good, funny and generous like Uncle Elijah? To amuse Nkem into forgiveness, he clears his throat and asks his uncle why he hasn't told the Great Nkem about the Nzegwu family. About the late Uncle Ifeanyi, a banker and motivational speaker, who graduated from Heineken University seven years ago by buying his lecturers bedsheets after examinations. About Auntie Usonwa, a crayfish supplier at Onitsha Main Market, who does not take his calls but tells people that he's also buying bedsheets for his lecturers. About Grandpa Obanye, a bullet-spotted Biafran soldier and son of Nzekwu, who frowned and slumped to his death the day Auntie Usonwa got married to a cheerful Yoruba lawyer named Obafemi and nicknamed Obafemi Awolowo. About Mrs. Golibe Nzekwu, the mother of "stupid Ifenna", who eloped with a moustached Japanese contractor to China—or a moustached Chinese contractor to Japan? —and her "numerous affairs with men." About Mr. Nzekwu Nzekwu(junior), her "good-for-nothing" husband and his father, who abandoned his whiskey shop and escaped to Calabar to avoid all the people he owed in Onitsha. About Chubaego, his "almost forgotten marshed potato of a brother", who joined their father because he heard the youth learn Internet scam faster in the city and he already had two white "clients" in the UK, two black "clients" in the US, and two brown "clients" in India. About Uncle Elijah himself, the annointed man of God, who after hearing that he buys his lecturers bedsheets and shoes for good grades and gives them people's girlfriends, still pays his tuition fees with smiles. About Grandma Nnukwunwanyi's maid, Afoma, who once tried to strangle a ten-year-old Ifenna behind a kitchen cupboard because he wore her curry-smelling shirt and high-heeled shoes.

The name, Afoma, seems to amuse the blinking Uncle Elijah, who bought the skirt and the shoes(and, if Grandma's story is to be trusted, the girl's bra and pants), and so he asks the man of God about the maid.

Uncle Elijah laughs and throws a half-burnt candle at him. He wants to pick the candle, but a church member, whom he suspects is mad, or semi-mad at least, screams in tongues in the hall.

"That's Brother Akpan," Uncle Elijah says in Igbo. "He left the Catholic Church for this house of God the day Sister Wandoo started worshipping with us. He always sits behind, and not beside, her."

He returns to his chair and combs his thick eyebrows. "Brother Akpan claims he can walk on water. The other day, he asked me to sow the money you gave me for my school fees as seeds in his pocket. But I whizzed away: I want to pay my school fees and graduate. I swear, I only strive to make a decent grade (without studying, of course) so that Papa will not disinherit me via SMS".

Brother Akpan screams again.

"Please go and check if the man of God's hovering around Sister Wandoo," Uncle Elijah tells him.

"Don't be jealous, Uncle Elijah. He'll not escape with any of the women."

Another scream from Brother Akpan and frightened fowls begin squawking somewhere. The aphasic tone of Brother Akpan drowns it:

Lock of ages
Creft foh meee
Ret meee haaid…

As the song fades, Nkem sits up. "You had the

courage to exchange my girlfriend with Cabin biscuits and bread and then put a pink hat on my head?"

His mouth opens, but he finds, to his surprise, that he can no longer prevaricate. Uncle Elijah's eyes on him are watery with concern, pleading his remorse, pleading his confession, but he is visualizing himself painting their cheeks and their noses with his favourite colours: red, green, yellow, white, pink, purple. Like masquerades, like clowns.

Into the strained silence, Brother Akpan sings about the Liver Jordan, about Paul and Siras, about the Heavenry Lace. Plaintive piano sounds accompany this disjointed singing. Brother Akpan screams, claps, whistles. The drums reach their crescendo and a lady's voice begins to warble "What a Marvellous God."

After the longish pause Uncle Elijah addresses him in Igbo. "You've to kneel down and apologize to your roommate whose girlfriend you helped your lecturer strip naked, grabbed her breasts. . ."

"Stop, stop, your description is turning me on," he says.

Uncle Elijah laughs and turns to Nkem, who says, "You're aroused, Ifenna? You and that self-acclaimed philanthropist eviscerated my Chioma, and now the description is giving you an erection?" Nkem rises, gathers his books from the desk and trots to the door. "Ifenna, if I ever forgive you, call me a bastard."

CHAPTER 4

NKEM peers at the misted screen of his ringing phone and anger flies up in his chest like an overheated burner. The phrase on the screen, MY IFENNA, fades, appears, fades, as if to tease him, to mock him. First he deletes the possessive adjective, then the name, then the number. He will block the number if Ifenna calls again, or sends a text message. He will burn the traitor's photographs, track him down and smash him with a steel bludgeon.

The worst roommate, the worst mistake, he tells himself, and continues trekking on the pedestrians' side of the town's major road, a tea-coloured path that is bumpy and lined with timeworn car tyres, palm fronds and crushed beer cans. Above him, the sky is a white blanket on which blood and grey-blue paint are spilled, the clouds are frayed pillows drifting across this stained bleeding sky, and the winds fragrant but dust-laden. Beside him, behind a boy behind him, there are two identical groups of green-painted students who are walking and talking and laughing. Before him, a horde of girls: they are in multicoloured clothes; they are forcing their hands into a chuckling boy's trouser pockets, tickling him, pecking him, touching him.

He pockets his phone, hurries past them and branches into the leaf-carpeted road leading to the campus where, he's certain, there will be other groups of rowdy students to behold and to avoid.

It's Rag Day.

On campus, there are students with emptied tins of milk and tea, entreating for alms. There are students in ragged polos and ragged jeans, entreating for alms. There are students in dyed wigs, students in scary masks and walking sticks, students in inside-out clothes, students on rusted bicycles, students in brassieres on their tops, students dressed like tramps and beggers, students reeling in painted shirt-shaped cartoons like happy drunkards. Unlike these students and most people he knows, he finds Rag Day inelegant and utterly unexciting. A perverse joy overflows in his heart as he recollects his attack on Rag Day this morning: He hid Ifenna's flowered skirt and extra-large brassiere in the cupboard in their kitchen, partly because they were made in Indonesia and not in Nigeria, partly because numerous cultists poured fuel on two male professors from Sociology Department during the last Rag Day and threw burning handkerchiefs on them. The two men, he recalls with a shudder, were burning and running and screaming until they fell into a gutter littered with rotten food and drowned in the soupy waters.

A girl with a synthetic beard scurries past him with her money-filled tin, past a cheering group of boys, past Professor Ayodele's approaching Toyota Camry.

Ayosky has slept with her, he thinks, and tightens his grip on his schoolbag swollen with economic notebooks, textbooks, handouts. Everything that isn't connected to his studies must wait for twenty-four hours. The novels. The poems. The girlfriend. Has she realized how cheap she is? How disgraceful. How he wishes he could yank her out of his mind because this is the time to study harder, the time to fill up the holes his stay in America dug in his patchy education.

"Hold on a minute, Obi," someone calls from behind.

Oh God, no! he shouts inside his head. This must be a person from his department, a person who feeds on gossips, a person who must have heard something from Rose. He makes a crying baby face before he wheels around.

The sight of the unexpected man who has just

halted his progress makes him want to kick things and shatter glasses. The man's name is Sir Israel. The man's the head of Economics Department. The man's clothes are usually ironed English suits, but today he's wearing only a white Turkish shirt that's rumpled, and a pair of black trousers that looks suspiciously French.

He makes another crying-baby face as the man approaches him, his cucumber-coloured tie flapping in the powdery breeze.

Tall, stooped, white-haired and thin like a stick. He thinks: it's a miracle that the winds have not blown away this hungry-looking killer of African economy. This killer of African names, African culture, African pride. He thinks: why would a Nigerian who's not a moron keep bearing Israel, his idiotic parent-given name, when there's no Israeli called Nigeria in Israel? He dislikes Sir Israel and his family with British names, British education, British foods, British clothes.

"Good morning, sir," he says with yet another crying-baby face.

Sir Israel regards him through magnifying glasses, and then says, in a tart but homiletic tone, "Your unaccountable rebelliousness is distasteful and hell-leading. Anger is a deadly sin. The Ancient of Days abhors strife and egotism: the parents of anger. In the Holy Bible, Moses did not enter the Promised Land because of his anger, remember? You don't remember, Obi?"

He knows this man has the ability to frame him and influence his expulsion, but the urge to attack is irresistible. "Yes, blessed wine, obviously."

"Blessed wine? The Holy Communion? What do you mean?"

He glances at Sir Israel's hair, tinted with morning light and quivering in the sultry winds, and thinks: Stop asking me senseless questions, you 70-year-old ancestor. Stop wasting our time. Go back to your church, where you belong. Or kindly retire.

"It's quite unfortunate that you're an infinitely priggy young man," Sir Israel continues with aggravating disapprobation. "Your haughtiness finally permitted you to write a letter of apology to our philanthropist, Mr. Nwoye?"

Mr. Nwoye. So Sir Israel doesn't even know the name of his colleague? He fights down the temptation to shoot him a humbling correction. An orange-belied bird swoops past them and his eyes follow it toward a decrepit auditorium, toward a dove fountain vomiting blue water, and toward a swaying frangipani tree where it hides.

"May I have the reason why you've elected not to perform this crucial duty? You exhibited unashamed philistinism which I found extremely bizarre and disgraceful. Were you intoxicated?"

There's no response.

"Splendid," Sir Israel says, and turns to leave. "You will have to write a letter of apology to Mr. Nwoye."

Why did they appoint this bastard the HOD, he wonders. Because he can quote Paul's Letters to the Galatians and can discuss the Book of Leviticus? It's preposterous to ask me to write a letter of apology when I am right. It's unjust to compel me to do that. It's a command the old fellow is going to forget. It's going to be ghastly, this day: the curious eyes of lecturers and students, the teasing boys, the teasing girls.

But the day goes well: the tutorials are brief but understandable; the lecturers and the students pretend they didn't hear any farcical story, the librarians aren't self-righteous, discourteous. The fire-coloured sunlight of midafternoon burns his eyes as he saunters back to Else-Shall-Die hostel.

Waiting for him at his hostel door is Chioma. She is crouched, eyes closed, nodding rhythmically to the waveband of diverse songs in other apartments. Bliss and disrespect: that's what he thinks this posture means. Bliss and disrespect. But doesn't that denote carelessness, fearlessness? Doesn't that denote she's just having fun? Why is she having fun while he burns? The loaf of bread in her left hand, which she bites from time to time, fuels his anger; but he will not be the first to speak. He will not turn back. He will keep listening to the whisper of leaves outside until the hot water in his chest is cooled.

But what about her own temper? Does she feel disgraced by his unprecedented attack on Okoye's office door, which broke the entrance into the warehouse where her immoral deeds are packed like banned goods?

When Chioma looks up and sees him, she drops the bread and rises with a dim smile of remorse.

"What the hell are you doing here, Mary Magdalene?" he says.

Chioma edges closer to maybe give him a hug and a rub, but halts. "Sugar, if you've no sin, cast a stone at me. That was what Jesus told them, right? Jesus knows I love you wildly and irreversibly. I love everything about you."

"It's evident you love everything about me, including my slippers. Who wouldn't love me? But do I still love you? No, obviously. Will I ever love you? No, obviously. What do I want? Your instant disappearance from my face." He elbows her out of his way, unlocks the entrance, flounders into the powder-smelling apartment and bolts the door with a hand trembling from irritation.

The peeling walls of the room have been repainted the colour of a calm sea and decorated with artificial sunflowers, peacock feathers and the sculptures of the moon and the stars in a basket of gold. Despite the circumstance, he stands motionless, marvelling at Ifenna's aesthetic works until he hears Chioma race to the window and slap the metal frame.

"In Gustave Flaubert's classic novel, *Madame Bovary*

(1859), the protagonist cheats on her husband and you know what happens to her?" he says, tottering to the window. "You know how the novel ends?"

"Sugar, but we're not in any novel!" she says. "Please burn that stupid book and listen to me! And give me one more chance. I will be faithful this time. I will be as humble as an orphan, or a waif. I'm a feminist, but I'll see you as my lord: I will polish all your shoes and wash all your clothes, including your boxer shorts and singlets. And your socks. Sugar, I will iron all of them. I will dust your radio and TV and I will cook for you. I'm a changed girl, Sugar. I've learnt to iron shirts without getting them burnt; ask my roommates. Let's bury the past and move on. If I cheat on you again, let me accidentally swallow my soap, and may the soap never digest."

"Thirty-five Lux soaps will easily digest in your gluttonous stomach!" He shuts the window and its frame rattles.

Still, she continues speaking outside, in a voice so demented and loathsome: "Your ego is bigger than Aso Rock! What do you even think you are? Just because you've sexy pink lips, a few classic novels and semicolons in your small head does not give you the right to call me a glutton, you disdainful nationalist! Men cheat on women all the time and our patriarchal society doesn't care. But now I let Okoye make thirty-second love to me and everybody's throwing stones at me because I'm a woman. May God punish all of you men! May God punish you and your semicolons!"

"Which of the gods, blessed wine?" he says. "There are innumerable gods in this world. But then, how would you know? Do you even know how to use the semicolon you're cursing? You only know how to parrot your unabashed misandry, how to stuff your stomach with fast food, how to smoke cheap cigarettes and how to put your nipple into a lecturer's smelly mouth. That's not the lifestyle of a true feminist."

He expects her to strike the window with the hunting knife in her handbag, but she scoffs at him and calls him a stone. Calls him an arrogant bastard.

He opens his mouth to retort, but his phone beeps with a WhatsApp message from Prophet Elijah: *splendid aftanoon senicolon. Pls former letters hav 3 adreses right?* No, *they've 4 addresses,* he replies in annoyance, pockets the device, and glances at Chioma.

"But earnestly speaking, Sugar, you're hurting me," she says. "I will replace you with a finger—my finger—or look for my fully charged vibrator, and you'll learn to be humble. I don't like your inability to be humble."

"I don't like your inability to use a semicolon! And I cannot marry a woman who doesn't know how to use a semicolon."

Silence from her.

Silence again.

His heart races as questions form: Did she drop her phone? Or maybe she flopped? Did she pause to dry the tears in her eyes? Or maybe she slumped? Did she put the call on hold and sit back to hear him drown? He hears her footsteps leaving, bites his cheek and sinks into the foam that smells of paint and flowers. Almost immediately, he gets up, totters to his reading table, where a leaf-green diary containing the maudlin sonnets he wrote for her lies open. Outside: a boy, nine or ten, is riding an orange-coloured bicycle and screaming, "We should all quit school and focus on the great Cristiano Ronaldo!" He nods, as if in agreement, and looks at the sihouetted landscape to make a brief travel out of the excruciating world of reality. His eyes are closed as he begins to feel adrift. Still closed as he floats unhinged on the stormy waters he has so beautifully imagined and given the colour blue, still closed as he assures himself that his love and respect for Chioma are now mere ashes which time will eventually scatter into the winds. Still closed as this flowing river, or this flowing sea, ferrying him like a washed-up bottle to a glimpsed island, climbs and dips and climbs and dips. And he shivers. And shivering he blinks the eyes open: the splendid but tortuous visions curl away from his lashes like skeins of rainbow-coloured smoke. Despite his lordly frown upon the melodramatic, he finds himself hitting the windowpane with the flat of his palm and saying, out loud or in his swimming head: Ah, I threw away the love of my life, the fire in my life that burnt my life, but these ashes will rise with the sun.

But can he ever let it rise again? Can he carry on? Can he let her step back into his life if he discovers he cannot live without her? He would rather choose to drown.

The next morning, as the fire-coloured light of dawn streams in through the window, his mother startles him with a phone call. He holds the device with an unsteady hand, staring at the screen ("Sweet Mum"), biting his lip, glowering, pondering: is Mummy calling to tell him she heard about his detention and then reproach him? To know if Mezie, his first campus friend, a big-nosed creative photographer and first-year student of Biology who journeyed to Ivory Coast during the ASUU stike to rent a studio, has returned to resume his education? That'll be strange because he has told her the photographer stole Ifenna's paintings, their jewelry, their artworks, their clothes, and will never step into Heineken University. He has told her to stop asking him about the photographer or anybody except Chioma and Ifenna, his only "platonic", true chums. Now he will tell her to also rip these two quislings out of her heart, he will tell her he'll never make friends, male or female, ever again even if a machine-gun is put to his face. He will tell her not to ask him why.

The call has ended unanswered; he calls her back and says, fighting back tears, "Mummy, how's home?"

"Home's ashamed of you, Dictionary!" she says. "My colleague, Sister Martha from our church, told me you've a girlfriend. You're chasing the girls and fighting lecturers who're chasing the girls you're chasing and fighting the lecturers for sleeping with the girls you want to be sleeping with. Shame on you! I can't believe I nurtured you. You're a big disgrace to the Obi family. . ."

"Momma, wait, wait, I wanna explain this motherfucking bullshit," he says in a phoney American accent to placate and amuse her, soften her. "I'm gonna explain, momma. Just give ya Dictionary some minutes to explain this motherfucking bullshit."

But she ends the call, and the apartment, suddenly airless and rotatory, transforms into a black casket in which he imagines himself being lowered into a grave.

CHAPTER 5

OKOYE has a lecture on Econometrics with post-graduate students, but he cannot find his drunkenly prepared lecture note. Maybe he didn't write anything while drinking that chilled Baron Romero three days ago. Maybe he did but lost it at the last orphanage home he visited with a bag of rice. Maybe it was here, at the thatch-roofed bar of the popular Children of God beer parlour, the previous day with Rose?

He closes his eyes and the past, bright and colourful like a movie on a TV, comes back to him: he sees himself, in the first scene, slurping Goldberg beer with his right hand while squiggling the note with his left hand. He sees himself, in the second scene, listening as Rose asks him to push the "rubbish" aside or put it into his briefcase. He sees her spitting condescending comments on his ambidextrousness: his handwriting on the pages were, in the noisy girl's Igbo words, "quite clumsy, baby, like the lines a ravenous hen scrabbles with her claws on water-soaked soil while searching for food."

He would like to summon all the barboys and interrogate them; but they are outside the building, near the main road, offloading fresh crates of beer from a lorry the size of a bungalow. The phrase, "Nigerian Breweries", is inscribed in green above the big head of a man drinking a Hero beer with his eyes closed in ecstasy.

In a few strides, he is at the Gulder Beer refrigerator pushed to the knife-scarred wall on which the bottle of Budweiser beer is deftly drawn. He takes one cold bottle of 3-3 beer, installs himself in a Life Beer chair and smiles at the alcohol in his hand as though it were a pretty woman. It's his wish that the barboys' offloading business will be over before he finishes his beer. But can the job be done in the next five hours? He cannot stake a bottle of beer on this, but he's certain that, in most of these drinkers'estimations, there are about two hundred and fifty crates of beer in that vehicle. And before the week wanes, he knows, all the beers will be finished by fat and thin lecturers, poor and rich students, some townsmen, some townswomen. It's reported that over one thousand crates of beer are consumed in the university town on a daily basis.

Okoye the Alcoholic contributes substantially to this impressive statistics, he tells himself with a proud smile of accomplishment, and brings his half-filled glass to his waiting lips again.

Half-hour later, he's drinking Heineken beer because Gulder beer has finished in the fridge. He drinks another Heineken and smokes someone else's forgotten cigarette. A shouty rap song starts as he staggers off, accidentally kicking a green bottle abandoned on the ground and sending it flying to the stomach of an approaching fat boy in a discoloured tiger-painted caftan. The bottle ricochets off the stomach and shatters on the ground. Some drinkers mistake the earsplitting noise for a gunshot and run helter-skelter; others watch with their mouths agape. Eyes rolling, body wobbling, the overweight fellow falls backward with a loud cry of agony like a wild animal gunned down in a schoolchildren's end-of-the-year's party drama, but he bypasses the victim, thinking: what a very nice sound! I love it. But the idiot, the owner of the interesting sound, is my student, who once snatched my girl and has never bought me beer. Let him keep crying like a baby there. Let him find the lecture note I was looking for and use it to wipe his tears: because there'll be no lecture today. I will cancel that uselessness. He will cancel that *uselessness*, because he has remembered that today is his daughter's birthday, because he has promised to buy all the foodstuff: his wife always fights the idea of cooking with crayfish, cooking with fish, cooking with meat. To her, butchering any animal, butchering any living thing, is gross callousness, and people should try to allow mosquitoes to bite them. He will go to the office of the most hated Chiamaka, a jet-black muscular woman with a beard and tawny teeth who he secretly thinks primordial, to procure tomatoes before sauntering down to the market to buy meat and a cake. The weird woman has promised to bring the tomatoes into the university specially for him. They both know she brings her tomatoes into the university for cooks, students, lecturers and any living thing with money, but he was wise enough not to draw her attention to the ridiculous mendacity.

The usually squalid office, he discovers with fury when he arrives, is obsessively cleaned, obsessively perfumed. Perhaps she, and not her students, scrubbed and used the best deodorizers in the vegetable-filled office because he's coming. Perhaps it was lurid with scattered books. Lurid with the odours of rotten pineapples, of rotten guavas. Perhaps she's in love with him. A woman who, according to Rose, dropped from a mango tree and landed on her head is in love with him? A woman who, according to Rose again, visits a neurosurgeon to examine that vegetable-filled head of hers, is in love with him? How dare this thing fall in love with him when she has such a beard, such a voice, such unpresentable large feet?

They exchange their dishonest cordialities, and she gets up.

Probably useable in a small way, he thinks, and steps

backwards to take a survey of her buttocks as she bends over to count the plum tomatoes in a coffin-shaped lime bowl. Is there enough money in my briefcase? He touches his trouser pockets, touches his breast pocket, and finding no money in them, only condoms, TomToms, concludes that he's improvident. Concludes that his going to Children of God is an unwise doing. This doing, drinking not one and not two but three bottles of beer, has ruined his daughter's birthday. But he hopes to exit Chiamaka's office, or "farm", as she likes to call it, without spending one naira.

"The head of department doesn't complain about these tomatoes?" he asks, to break the silence.

"Put them into a Bagco bag, cover with two or three huge Bibles, and he will hug you," she says. "My friend, Dr. Tina Okereke, once came here to take free tomatoes from me. Sir Israel floundered in to show us some errors in the students' published results, and we both threw Bibles and hymnbooks into the bag to conceal the tomatoes. He peeped, yes, and saw the Bible: he says, '*Otito diri Jesu*! Praise be to Jesus!' and we hugged. Later, Dr. Tina had to pay me for the tomatoes. Very understanding woman, that Tina. My best friend, yes. How's your own best friend? I haven't seen him or any of his thirty-nine girlfriends since last week."

"I don't have friends," he replies.

"So Professor Ayodele the prowling dildo is not your friend?"

"You're my friend—or the one I need as a friend."

This faux avowal, to his surprise, is greeted with a narrow-eyed inspection. He types a message and sends it to Professor Ayodele.

The great Yoruba man of our time, please don't bother. . . I've called off the party. Chinenye has a waist pain; she fell from a refrigerator. Thanks for your understanding.

He doesn't want Professor Ayodele near his house and his daughter: it's rumoured that Professor Ayodele's cheating on his fifteen-year old maid with his neighbour's fifteen-year-old maid. Can Chinenye possibly be safe around such a dog?

Chiamaka sets the bowl down on the desk and says, grinning, "I'm not taken aback because you're an infinitely irresponsible man. Some students told me they spotted you in a club with Ifenna last night, drinking, smoking, breakdancing and shouting until 4: 00 p.m. I'm sure you haven't gone home, Okonkwo. I pity your wife. Where did you tell her you were going?"

Okonkwo: is this the name of her secret lover, or has another vital vein been disconnected in her brain? He ignores the wrong address and informs her, in a solemn but insincere tone, that when his wife enquired he replied that he sang to Professor Israel's pastor friend's crusade.

"And she believed you?" she asks, with a hint of a smile.

He shrugs and hands her a polythene bag for his tomatoes. "My son also lied to her because I guess he was at the party too. A thoroughly useless boy."

"You think it's funny to call your son useless, Okonkwo? You're lucky to have one." She bends down, picks a fallen tomato and begins putting the fresh ones into the bag. "I want your wife to cook luscious stew for your daughter's birthday, yes. But when is your son's birthday? You're so lucky to have a son, Okonkwo."

Stop calling me Okonkwo, he thinks, and gives her a wincing frown. For Christ's sake, what the hell are tomatoes doing in a lecturer's office? What are fresh tomatoes doing in a lecturer's office? It occurs to him that he sells Nez toothbrushes and Nez toothpaste in his own office and he smiles at his hypocrisy, asks her how much her vegetables cost, how much he has to pay as a friend, as a colleague.

"I haven't told you, Okonkwo? Forgive me, yes. It's 1,500 naira only. Very affordable, no doubt. And let me tell you, Okonkwo. Tomato business procures both money and bliss, yes. I don't even know what I'm doing in this university. Customers would phone you for a supply of tomatoes worth 50 thousand naira and one serious-looking student would open your door, put his or her stupid head into your office and say, 'Madam, are you not coming to teach us?' It stirs all my evil instincts. But it's their right, isn't it?' I shouldn't have taken this job, Okonkwo."

He takes the bag from her, peers into it with a quick laugh, and then at his ringing phone. Oh God, Professor Ayodele. Does Professor Ayodele see him entering this mentally unstable farmer's office? What does Professor Ayodele want from him? He clicks on Answer Call with a reluctant hand and says, "I'm not in a beer parlour."

"Really, the great Igbo man of our time?" Professor Ayodele says.

"Sorry, Papa Kayode. Chinenye has a waist pain as I mentioned in the text. I'll see you later."

"Ah! Are you pushing Ayosky away? Okay, you're busy? Give me her phone number, so I can sing her a birthday song."

He makes salt-licking-imbecile face. He wishes a crate of beer, or a loudspeaker, would drop on Professor Ayodele's head wherever he is. Something really needs to bang and injure that large head.

"Who's that?" she asks. "It must be *your* Ayosky, yes. Birds of a feather. Fat, evil drunkards." She squawks, her saliva flying into his face, and he steps back and tries not to scream in disgust.

Professor Ayodele calls again. It's on the tip of his tongue to tell the sex-crazed caricature, who is probably dashing to a drugstore to buy condoms, that Chinenye has no phone, but recalls that he has continually phoned his daughter in the man's presence. This recollection burns his heart.

He gives Professor Ayodele the phone number of his hunchbacked cobler with yellow teeth, ends the call. His phone beeps almost immediately with a text message from his wife: *Humanizer, yuo don't want two teke my colls, write? I've being colling yuo sinse monin. Your not at ofanage home. I've goten the infomachon!*

"Infomachon", he thinks? What's "the infomachon"? With a knife-like finger, he kills the message, clicks off his phone.

Chiamaka has been watching him with inquisitive eyes. Now she opens her mouth into the shape of a funnel to pour further unfiltered words into his ears, but he hastens to say, "Thank you so much. I'll give you a cheque before I leave. For both today's tomatoes and the previous ones. I don't have money in my briefcase. No student has given me money since Wednesday, and I don't know why. What's wrong with them?"

"They're all tightfisted devils," she replies with a maniac's smile. "I wasn't joking when I said I regret coming here, Okonkwo."

A loud knock sounds on the door and he starts.

Chiamaka says, "Who the devil is that? If you're a student, back off! I'm preoccupied."

"I'm not a student, thank God!" a tiny girl's voice says. "It's Miss. Cecilia from your farm. The daughter of the woman who weeds your gardens."

"I've paid your mother, yes," Chiamaka says.

"I know. I was asked to inform you that Fulani herdsmen are pooing on your farm and their cows are eating your vegetables."

Chiamaka bats her eyelids, then lurches out from her desk with a nervous chuckle but walks sluggishly to the door and plucks it open. Sweating and looking over his shoulder like a thief, Ifenna hurries in with a pleasant odour of a cologne. Almost immediately Nkem appears, perspiring like his roommate, but his face is creased with anger as though he's tracking Ifenna to stab him at the back.

"I'm tired of your trivialities, Umbrella Boy," Chiamaka says with an unexpected laugh. "You're running away from Semicolon who wants to break your coconut head? You want to hide from him?"

The boy is smiling, the woman is smiling, and he, Okoye, is baffled by this affability, baffled and unsettled. He'd like to know what's hidden in the pocket of the Unbrella Boy's friend. A shortgun to blow up his stomach, blow up Ifenna's? A hunting knife belonging to Chioma brought in to slice their tongues? But this is not a movie, not a drama, and the heartbroken lover cannot be that wicked and dummy.

"I'm sorry, madam, but I swear, Nkem was not chasing me to break my coconut." Ifenna giggles because Chiamaka seems amused by the word "coconut." "Blissful morning, Professor."

104

He shakes Ifenna's outstretched hand. "Chief, you and Nkem came to check on me? On us? Nkem, isn't it?"

Nkem bows his head, opens the novel in his hand to annoy him, but he considers the snub a rubber bullet from a toy gun.

A lizard scurries across the desk, scattering files and papers, frightening him and Chiamaka. It jumps down and flashes under the shelf. A fly, yellow-belied and nut-sized, buzzes round the desk, buzzes round his head, leaves through the window. I wish I were the escaped bee, he thinks. What's in Nkem's pocket?

Nkem adjusts his Harry Potter glasses and approaches Chiamaka. "Blessed wine, we're told you reported ill. . . Sorry. Could you be kind enough to give me a lecture note? I want to photocopy it and teach the class since you've malaria and our exams are imminent. I can lecture them perfectly well like a professor, obviously. I need to help myself by helping them."

It's common here, students taking the duties of indolent lecturers, and so he's surprised to see Chiamaka roll her eyes as though Nkem has just ordered her to get on the desk and dance on her head for him. Surprised to see her suddenly let a grin creep across her face. Surprised to see her peek into her wastepaper basket and speak in a satirical tone that annoys everybody: "The cleaner probably swept it away. Or did she sell it to any of you?"

Ifenna brings his mouth, which is rosy and glossy with lipstick, to Nkem's ear, and whispers something, but Nkem brushes the suggestion off with a flick of his finger, brushes Ifenna aside with a ferocious hand and out of the open window. Outside, the air is hazed with smoke from burning grass and the noises of several engines are deafening. A car honks, poops, honks, and they hear the explosive laughter of lawnmowers. Blue-winged birds abandon the purple petals of the white flowers surrounding the building and scatter, like a baby's torn clothes, into the lavender-coloured sky.

Chiamaka says, "What did you tell Nkem, Ifenna? That it might be on my farm, yes? And remove that maddening gum from your mouth!"

"But I'm enjoying the chewing gum, madam!" Ifenna says, stepping backwards.

What an exciting children's drama, he thinks with juvenile cheerfulness. We two lecturers and these two students perform like amateur actors, following the instructions of an incompetent director woodenly. May this rehearsal never cease to be thrilling.

As Chiamaka watches Ifenna watch her, he, Okoye, fusses his alcohol-filled stomach, then takes off his spectacles to polish the lenses with a white handky his daughter gifted him when she found that all the ones he had were rumpled, smelly and stained with pepper soup and beer. Thinking of her daughter makes him think of his son, and thinking of his son makes him think of insults, broken chairs, flying unbrellas, karate and shirt-tearing fights.

He finds Nkem, as he shakes his head gloomily and puts the glasses back on, saying something presumably imperative, but his attention is not on the boy, not on his friend, but on Chiamaka, who's sidling towards Ifenna as though she wants to wallop him. But her wig, tattered and weak-looking like his wife's overused black sponge for washing pots and pans, tumbles off her rocking head of a horse, and she pauses to stare at it with amused embarrassment. He visualises Nkem cleaning their pots and kettles with the sponge-like wig, disposing it into a dustbin and shouting that it's shamelessly imported from China. He says, looking at smiling Ifenna, "Pick it up for her, chief; it doesn't bite. And, Amaka, don't hit the boy; he might be right. A bricklayer once found my lecture note in a beer parlour. We all misplace things because we are only human."

The amusement vanishes from Chiamaka's face and she picks the wig and forces the mess back on her head. "Earnest ambassadors, go and ask the students to disperse," she says. "Hopefully, I will find it today. I'm not saying it's on my farm . . . don't ever say that. It's probably in my. . . my . . . I'm sorry for the inconvenience, boys. Goodbye!"

Her eyes are wide and wild, and yet they, the boys,

do not move. He detests their aplomb, detests their seriousness, and yet he's silent. Silently he dusts his briefcase. Silently he watches her watch them. Silently he listens as Ifenna says, in an impassive tone: "Professor, your wife's combing the campus. She wants to see you. She said you switched off your phone."

"Goodbye," he says in a dismissive tone, waving Ifenna away as if the lad were a poorly trained dog. And, like a poorly trained dog, Ifenna refuses to withdraw without eating a bone. But which bone does this dog, this drag queen, want now? Is the drag queen's stomach, like his own stomach, a beneficiary of a breakfast beer?

Chiamaka approaches her wastepaper basket, peers into it and shakes her head in mock hopelessness.

Nkem stuffs his hands into his pocket and heads to the door, Ifenna and a brown moth following behind, flirting with their heads as though they were lit lamps, and after the two friends, or two enemies, are gone, Chiamaka leaves the wastepaper basket, bolts the door and returns to her desk. "We all just behaved like children, yes?" she says, dodging the bee, which has returned. "I despise the two boys. The clownish one is inevitably cracking silly jokes and chewing gum politically. The handsome one is conceited, but he reminds me of my younger sister's brilliant son, who's unfortunately the only son by the way, and who's studying medicine in Scotland now. A son, Okonkwo, a son . . . My sister is lucky, yes."

"What led you to take up this job, if I may ask, Mgbeke?"

"Mgbeke? Mgbeke? Let me pretend you didn't call me Mgbeke deliberately." She suspends the tomato business, watches the bee buzzing round his head and hits it with a file: it drops to the floor. She crushes it with her shoes and gazes at him.

"Thanks for saving my life," he says with dissimulated joviality.

Other female colleagues of his would be delighted to see the bee sting his nose. Why is she suddenly different, suddenly kind? Has she fallen in love with him? Is she giving him a green light signaling he may approach her, tell him the golden three words, take her, fuck her? No wonder she always visits him, always jokes with him, always confides in him. It'll not end well for her.

"My husband's friend," she says. "Nzube is his name, yes. He noticed I was bony because I was eating only cheap bread and *abacha* and swore that he must get me fat with a job in this university. So I took this despicable job just to improve my diet and save money for my tomatoes. . . It's a *despicable* job, Okonkwo, and you're aware. I'm wasting the students' time; they write protest letters to the HOD every week, but the so-called man of God doesn't listen to them because some of the girls among them wear trousers, which are against his God. The students hate him . . . Well, some of them also hate me. I'm wasting their time, honestly."

"They're also wasting your time. Go on."

Someone knocks at the door, identifies himself as a student, and asks if he might come in.

Chiamaka says, "No, sod off!"

"God bless you," the boy replies in a sarcastic tone, and leaves.

She glances at her wrist-watch, perches on her deceptively clustered desk, her oversized legs dangling. "Well, I took this job five years ago after I was unjustly chucked out from one provincial boarding secondary school in Ondo State where I was working as the chief cook. I'm not here at Heineken University of Education because I love to teach, no. Money, Okonkwo, money. I needed to splurge it on my farm. I still need it, yes. My soldier husband, a friend of the then Vice Chancellor, phoned me one morning when I was watering my tomatoes and told me I was now a lecturer. I was astounded. I didn't apply for the job. I had told him and my husband that I hate teaching the way I hate the devil, but they forced me to accept it. In the end, I felt happy because my paltry salary helped. It still helps. . . Don't feign surprise. You know I don't like this place. Just like you. No, you like it because of the pretty girls."

"My dear, I prefer pretty girls to ugly women who are married." He takes a nearby vacant chair and packs himself in it.

"Oh...yes," she says.

I prefer pretty girls: Isn't this obvious to her, obvious to every rational being? She's staring at him with disbelieving eyes. But he's glad his savage reply to her offensive joke stung her, stung her very well. "I'm enjoying the story," he says. "Go on."

"Fast-forward to the day I came to collect my appointment letter, the Vice Chancellor said he was ill. He wanted me to buy him malaria and typhoid medications and bring them to his hotel room. I foolishly jogged to the place with Amalar, Amozil, Paracetamol and blood syrup and saw that fat sheep lying in bed naked, chewing ripe bananas and smiling at me seductively like a pig in a cartoon. I was mad; I nimbly removed one of my high-heeled shoes and hit him over his bald head fifteen or twenty times with them until his eyes rolled and he wanted to faint. Then I seized his clothes and shoes and spun round to escape, but he knelt down and began to cry. Or made noises that sounded like cries. Two weeks later, I was called for an interview. He had insisted that I would be interviewed because I didn't suck his thing. He thought I'd fail, but I didn't. I phoned him and laughed for almost thirty-five seconds."

He's appalled. "You passed the interview? You used any *juju* from a native doctor?"

"Listen. I've not finished." An urgent knock comes at the door. She wheels around and snaps, "Get out if you're a student! Can't you see I'm very busy this morning?"

"Madam, the lecture?" a girl's voice says. "We've been waiting for you since 8: 00. Is it still possible? The lecture."

Briskly and awkwardly, he takes off his reading glasses, puts them into his breast pocket and wears his sunglasses; if the girl enters now, he can watch her breasts and bottom without moving his head.

But Chiamaka gets down from the desk, lumbers to the door, and pulls it open. A short-legged girl in a red gown smiles at her, then steps back. Chiamaka wallops her on the head, slaps her pimpled face, throws her out, not away and locks the door. "She-goat," Chiamaka says, blowing wind into her hand as she returns to her desk.

He removes his sunglasses. "You should've let her come in." His voice, he fears, sounds suspiciously low, suspiciously wounded. Is that why she is blinking, blinking and snickering?

"I knew you wanted to see her large breasts very well," she says. "I know why you bought those Godless sunglasses."

"I'm a shameless fool."

"I know." She fondles her beard, watching him. "Listen, Okonkwo. As I was saying, I submitted my credentials for the interview. We were three fighting for this job: Mr. Yusuf Obafemi, a bright Yoruba man with one ear; Dr. David Effiong, a very nice man of God who couldn't stop looking at my breasts from the corners of his eyes; and myself. I flunked all the breezy questions they were inclined to shoot at me. I couldn't even explain the law of diminishing returns, yes. Maybe I was nervous, but – don't laugh, Okonkwo—I landed the job because I'm Igbo. They told the Vice Chancellor that I did brilliantly well, then asked the two poor men to run back to the regions from whence they came. . . Please tuck in your pocket-flaps and zip your trousers."

He's alarmed to discover that his pocket-flaps are not tucked in. Up he jumps, and twirls round, ignoring the cigarettes flying out of his pockets, and hurries to the door, while zipping his dirty trousers. Did she see that his trousers are open and kept quiet so she would enjoy the sight peacefully? He cannot stake his one naira on that, but the mischievous smile on her face grills him. He returns to her, gives her a bounced cheque, thanks her, and faces the door again.

"I enjoyed your company, Okonkwo." She pauses, and clears her throat. "I'd love to see you again today, yes. Will you be busy with your students by three?"

He does not turn, but he answers her in a surly tone: "Mgbeke, you know I hate academic work and once it's two-thirty, I'm invariably rushing off to a beer parlour to enjoy myself. So why are you asking me a useless question?"

"I'm awfully sorry, my one and only darling," she says, her voice so fetid with manipulative tenderness. "I forgot that. Are you angry with me, philanthropist?"

Now he's sure she has feelings for him. He turns to her in slow motion, feeling, for the first time in his adult life, like a complete human being, a super model, a celebrated movie star, a Greek god. "I beg your pardon?" he says.

"Christ!" She jumps down from the desk as if a soldier ant has just stung her bottom and starts tying the lace of her flat-heeled alligator-coloured shoes with swift hands. "Stay behind for me, please . . . I didn't remember to gather the second-year students' papers which I kept on that shaky lectern after a test this morning. I forgot the papers because you were wasting my time on the phone. . . I was persuading you to buy these tomatoes for your daughter's birthday but your stinginess couldn't let. . .Jesus, I'm not really a careless woman." She circles her office, searching for her handbag, searching for her keys.

He gives sudden uncontrollable shouts of laughter; it's not because she's being clownish, but because he has just discovered that her left breast is bigger than her right breast. Why didn't he notice the dissimilarity of her breasts all these years?

"Forget the bag and the keys," he says. "Hurry…"

"I will be back shortly. There's no lecturer in that hall. The students must be laughing at me and rewriting the trash they have written and submitted. And it's too late to catch them. I'll be back, Okonkwo. Don't escape."

After she's gone, he takes seven tomatoes from her

bowl, puts them into his polythene bag, ties it up with a rubber band. He wants to take another seven tomatoes because, in his mind, she's obsessed with him. Because she's in love with him.

A familiar but distant female voice brings him to the open window: Chioma, he sees, is strolling towards a classroom with a lanky boy carrying a guitar.

What's she up to? Has she shown the boy the photos, the videos? He pokes his head into the window and bawls, as he usually does in pubs for more beers, "Hey! Chioma Chioma Emenike!"

The girl stops, whirls around to face the disturbance. Her companion does the same. She mouths, *leave me alone*, and clutches the boy's hand. He bawls her name again, but it's too late: they have strolled into the Music Department studio. Sudden panic flutters at the base of his throat. So his student can now dismiss him without an iota of fear? So this is how far he has fallen.

With a wistful shake of his head, he twirls round, and his legs buckle: he falls backwards, his briefcase flying to the door, and he lands on Chiamaka's tomatoes, squashing them and the bowl.

Oh God, he thinks, and struggles to his feet. On his trousers, on students' exam scripts, there are dripping tomatoes. What should he do? Flee? Apologise? No: Chiamaka will definitely suspect him, find him and wring his neck. Chioma, oh Chioma: Does she have diabolical powers?

He's cleaning his trousers with his handkerchief when his eyes fall on a blue pen and an eye pencil lying on the desk. He picks the pen, tears out a sheet of paper from a file and writes a frantic letter, imitating one demented boy he once taught in this university.

DEer mRs chIaMakA,

wHen i wAs A stUdaNt hia, you maLltreated me. so i hav To PaY U bak. OkOyE haZ gun ouT off Your Ofise so I desTroyed yUor tomAtoes and Stained yUour sTudEnts scripts Becos I hAte U anD want U sackEd. donT luk four Me Becos i hav rAn Away.

My regardS, idiOt.

YUor's fatefooly,

AbuBakaR Lanalana

He rereads the letter: the spellings are consistent, so he sticks the department's stamp on it, signs it with Chiamaka's eye pencil. Into his briefcase, he stuffs his bag of tomatoes and escapes without shutting the door.

CHAPTER 6

IFENNA adjusts the peacock-feathered hat to conceal his hair, a pixie cut deftly half-loosened by Rose, and crouches behind a peach-coloured jeep to eavesdrop on Okoye and Chiamaka. The body of the Toyota feels too cold like the inside of a refrigerator; he instinctively withdraws his hand and surveys the Campus Road, an untarred curve browned and soaked by a short-lived rain this morning, and the petals the winds threw along it. He likes the dersertedness of this path. He likes the air, heavy with water and winged insects, delicious with the faint scent of blossoming flowers. He likes the rinsed sky, flooded with birds and primary colours, and and it is here, under the inspection of nobody, he will watch his lecturers fight to entertain him for free. He feels his heart quickening with an odd mixture of childish excitement and a vague sense of foreboding. The gushing winds blow off Chiamaka's carrot-coloured scarf, but she's too angry to notice.

He stifles a laugh and hears Okoye beg her not to incite Chioma to open any drawer of secrets. Okoye wants her to forgive the petulant behaviour, forgive him for the bowl and the tomatoes he squashed accidentally, forgive him for the reddish stains on her students' scripts, forgive him because he didn't know how to tell her. "I didn't know how to tell you because it was the action of a spoilt child and an adult cannot behave like that," Okoye adds with false joviality.

"But you're not an adult!" she bays, shielding her eyes from the callous brilliance of a westfacing lamppost. "Junior, my youngest sister's two-year-old son, cannot play with those tomatoes!"

"I'm not mature like other children, but forgive me. Forgive me for the bounced cheque as well. I presume you haven't discovered that yet. I recalled that the bank account is dormant the second you left. I'll sign a genuine one."

She brushes an insect off her beard and says, in a lowered voice, "Listen, Mr. Philanthropist: you may have a son and some published books, but I'm more wicked than you. The devil will shed tears of joy if our colleagues and the students set their prying eyes on those photos and the pornographic video Chioma showed you to appreciate, yes."

"Appreciate? God, I pleaded with her. . . See, Amaka, I'm awfully sorry for what I did to your fresh tomatoes. Aren't you, as a Christian, washed with the blood of the Lamb?"

Flippant. Can Okoye bear the effect of his flippant tongue? He wills Chiamaka to slap epilepsy into Okoye's head, so he can have a barbaric laugh at them, video them, watch them with his friends, upload them on Facebook. But she is, it seems to him, unprovoked by the joke. Masculine women: he would like to go to bed with one, see how it feels to be kissed by a face carrying a beard. But not now, not with a married woman like Chiamaka.

She has folded her arms, watching him with the scary eyes of a cat. "What did my tomatoes do to you, Okonkwo, to deserve such a wicked treatment?"

"I'm not Okonkwo," Okoye says. "Interesting, how you treat tomatoes like human beings; and human beings, like tomatoes."

Chiamaka dips around and says, "You find this funny, yes? You find it funny? Well, the Vice Chancellor will find your pornography funny. I can imagine his laughter, yes."

"Sorry about my tone. Kindly tell me the cost of the fresh tomatoes – and the bowl. I will pay you instantly."

"The tomatoes you purchased cost 5,000 naira and the ones you annihilated with your buttocks cost 7,500 naira," she says. "The bowl costs 3,000 naira. Can I have the money now?"

"Yes, you can."

After Chiamaka's gone with her colleague's money, he, their Ifenna, does what he thinks a nice student should do: he coughs, and Okoye jumps. "Oh, I am so sorry, Professor," he says. "It was like a gunshot? I swear, I'm sorry!"

"Rosie told me you have sold the old handouts to the students," Okoye says. "Give me the money immediately!"

Immediately, he thinks: what a way to talk to one's agent! Does Okoye suppose it's easy to inveigle students, or threaten students, into buying tedious books, into rubbish handouts, from an apish fellow who's meant to teach you? Does Okoye want to sting him because the tomato woman stung him? He will not, cannot, let Okoye succeed. Let Okoye phone the police if he wishes and ask them to arrest him for squandering his money on sugar-filled chewing gum. He smiles as he remembers that the police station in the town was razed down by unknown people a day after they invaded an effeminate boy's twentieth birthday party off campus, shooting randomly, killing the celebrant for "homosexuality", arresting the tomboys for "lesbianism", and swigging their remaining beers for "helping God and the government to clean the country." An unforgettable party: that's where he,

Ifenna, squandered Okoye's money. That's where he almost lost his life, almost lost his scarf, but he was quick to fly under a table, crawl away and into a hole in the fence like a huge insect. Okoye does not deserve this captivating story, this truth.

Without a word he hands Okoye some of the money and scrutinizes his face. No trace of resentment, no trace of suspicion: glory be to God!

Okoye puts it into his briefcase without counting it and takes his hand. Together they trudge to the tree where Okoye's car is parked adjacent to a gleaming black Volkswagen that reminds him of turtles. He says, chewing his gum noisily, "I think a lecturer who gives his students beer is better that the one who gives them the knowledge of economics or such snobbish rubbish."

"Life without beer is unbearable." Okoye pulls the door open, and gestures to him to hop in. "But university education isn't about beer, chief."

He hops in, and as the car farts and jerks off, says with seriousness, "Yeah, I know university education is about free sex, but we must acknowledge and appreciate the kindness of beer-buying lecturers. They should all be promoted."

"May God bless you for that kind proposal."

"And may He protect you against any sack letter."

"Amen."

Off campus, at Children of God beer parlour, they

settle behind a Hero beer chair ridiculed with ashes from several cigarettes. Okoye leans forward in his chair and, over a bottle of Gulder beer, tells him about Chioma's trouble, and about Chimaka's trouble, and about Nkem's trouble.

It's possible, he says, for a lecturer in such a sizzling frying pan to be helped if Okoye is willing to come back with a basket of good grades for every Ifenna that once assisted him, every Nkem they wronged, every Chioma they exploited, every student who will lend a helping hand, every Rose that knows about this business to seal their lips.

"I'll bandy around As and Bs like ripe mangoes to all your girlfriends if you help me get those nudes and porn video," Okoye says. "Now, I don't care if my As and Bs are shared like mangoes, oranges, bananas or any other sweet fruits. I need to be safe."

He refills his glass, refills Okoye's, and looks up with a grin. "You're safe, Professor. I know bad guys who know bad guys."

"Thank God for bad guys," Okoye says, with enigmatic insouciance, and swiftly steers the conversation to the subject of discrimination. His friend Professor Ayodele cannot be the head of the Psychology of Education in the evening, Okoye says. The Yoruba man is not from here, and the argument that he's not from here, which is not aired, is saddening. The Yoruba man might be a womaniser like many of them, but he's the most qualified person, the most deserving person. The only good person.

Yes, Ayosky is good, he agrees. Good in bed.

To his surprise, Okoye laughs so hard his stomach shakes, and he laughs too. The subject of discrimination continues until the sun, a half-eaten orange in the sky, dissolves into the grey clouds.

He totters back to Else-Shall-Die hostel, telling himself that he isn't tipsy, telling himself that the hostel is his equally his. It's 50-50 because I, the gum-chewing son of Nzekwu, paid too. I cannot continue hiding in Uncle Elijah's church. Let Semicolon fight me if he can. Boys who chew gum can fight, too.

Inside, he finds Nkem mosquitoeing like an anxious husband whose wife is in a labour room. "Who died, homeboy?" he asks with a dim smile.

"Blessed wine, Chioma has just bombed me," Nkem says. "She wants to get married since I'm not interested in her anymore. Because her body is her body, and not my body. That was her vocabulary, not mine, obviously. I'm still interested in her, blessed wine. But I cannot. . . God, what will I do? I cannot let her marry that lurid turd who cannot even spell his name, let alone use a semicolon."

The new curtains, crimson and delicate, billow and flap, and then drop, blessedly, like the stone in his chest.

Does bringing to him, Ifenna, these tidings of heartbreak and disappointment entail Nkem has forgiven him? Gradually, carefully, he sits on the book-littered foam, pops new gum into his mouth, and removes his nose ring to acquire a temporal look of earnestness. "Who's the beer-filled turd who cannot spell his name and use a semicolon?"

"Chief Orikaobuo, obviously," Nkem says, and the sunlight winks on every sweat beaded on his forehead and turns them to tiny rainbows. "The illiterate ignoramus who supplies toothpaste to Okoye. I wonder how a dullard like that got to know a girl like that. I will interfere. A man like that is not healthy for a girl like that. I must disrupt that! Their wedding must be crashed!"

Just then, Chioma wades out of the slippery toilet, her eyes moist and disconcerted: she has been sobbing. "Sugar, you've to understand me," she says. "I still fancy you, but I have to marry Chief and save my patriarchal family from poverty. Do you think I fancy that primitive chimpanzee? You must be mad to think that. I don't like his wide nose and his big lips and his big stomach."

"But you love the money in his pocket?" he asks in a note of derision, and chews an imaginary gum. "His pocket is a darling?"

"Shut up, Princess!" She spits the word into his face like saliva, and turns to Nkem with with those glassy eyes of hers. "Frankly, Sugar, I don't know this man who will marry me very soon. The other day, Rose was plaitng my hair and telling me about him. You know, I go to Rose to know about a man who wants to marry me? The man who, according to Rose, lost two teeth, his front teeth, when he was playing football in primary school. Rose said he quit school instantly and that's why he cannot spell his name or mine. I know that disappoints you, Sugar. Right? That I could make such a choice."

"I'm not interested in the biographies of ignoramuses," Nkem says.

"I'm sorry, I'm sorry," she says. "It's my parents; they want to alleviate our poverty by marrying me off to a very wealthy ancestor. I've already apologised to my feminist friends. I wouldn't want my own daughter to marry a chimpanzee with a mouth odour if I finally become a mother, his wife. My marriage wouldn't affect our relationship, Nkem. I'll visit you every weekend and we will chat and drink and probably make love. God will understand; He's a merciful God. I read that in the Bible this morning when I was crying in that chimpanzee's mansion."

"Chioma and Nkem, I swear, I would rather laugh in hell fire than cry in heaven," he says, and pops real gum into his mouth. "In other words, it's better to cry in Dubai than to laugh in Onitsha."

Chioma waves him away, peers into her handbag on the reading as if she's searching for her hunting knife, and then faces the one she fancies. "Don't cry, Sugar. We're still together. We're still young and Chief is old. He may die tomorrow, who knows... Hug me, please."

"Stop!" Nkem says, stepping backwards. "Caution her, Ifenna!"

Has Nkem, unbelievably, shifted his wrath from him to Chioma? If so, he, Ifenna, will drink to it. He may, finally, get a girlfriend and celebrate this victory with her. But who will agree to be his girlfriend? Will she, like many other Nigerian girls, expect him to take care of her like an orphan? No: he will not have a girlfriend. He will let people continue to be curious. He will let them continue to be stymied. His lifestyle should not be anybody's business.

But one languorous Friday afternoon, on his way from the Department of Fine and Applied Arts, where he wanders to admire painted portraits and sculptures, he bumps into a group of whiskey-smelling boys wearing yellow berets, yellow belts, yellow socks. "Homo!" one of them says, slaps him across the face, and innumerable diamonds fly out of his eyes into the air that's now thick with the odour of marijuana. "Why you choose to be gay? Why you dey behave like woman? You think say this place na America, abi?"

They tear off his yellow turban, take his nose ring, take his wallet. They fling him into stagnant water and passersby pretend not to notice. He knows it's not only because they are afraid of The Yellow Boys, but also because they detest his non-conforming lifestyle. *My Oscar Wilde*, Nkem would probably say in a tone interspersed with gloom and vexation, if he tells him; but he will not tell him. He will not tell anybody. He will try to pretend to himself that it is just a dream. He will pretend to himself that he doesn't need a girl. He will pretend to himself that he's not curious about this popular thing called sex.

But one familiar voice of a girl phones him the following day, declaring herself ready. "Boy, I will be in your house in the next fifteen minutes to copulate with you," she says. "If you are not strong enough in bed, you better start running away from your hostel now because all my six condoms must be used in your bedroom this hot afternoon."

He remembers her now: Boss Lady. Her real name is Aisha, but all the students from her class call her Boss Lady. He finds her refreshingly fascinating: tattoos on her fingers and tattoos on her toes, eyes green and beautiful like a watered leaf, light-skinned, Fulani, Muslim. Not the best artist in the Department of Fine and Applied Arts, but not the worst either. He has known her for weeks, amused her for weeks, but has never been bold enough to hold her hands. "Boy, you make me laugh but you have no tactile experience with me and that proves you're one of *them*," she told him in her enviable English in the studio five days ago, the last time they saw each other. "It's in my bucket list to fuck one gay guy before I return to Allah in heaven. Wanna help me, boy? How much will I pay you to use you, boy?"

He's not a prostitute, not yet, but this is what he does: he brushes his teeth with Okoye's Nez toothpaste. He shaves his pubic hair. He puts a pink flower in his newly plaited hair. He perfumes his foam and dusts his pillows. He then phones this strange girl with a singsong voice and an infectious smile and asks her to visit him at Else-Shall-Die hostel.

She is usually in a hijab, but she arrives twenty minutes later wearing a soldier's polo, navy jeans that's ripped at the knees, and a pair of throwback sunglasses that is reminiscent of Shaggy in his prime. He takes off the sunglasses, offers her borrowed tea and half-expired bread because her eyes are hollow and reddened, takes her round the room, showing her his water-colour paintings of Okoye's stomach on the wall.

"I know you're a terrific artist like me, boy," Aisha says, giggling, and gives his buttocks three playful slaps. "But can you stop this irrelevant nonsense? Boy, I'm only here to fuck. Take off your clothes."

Take off your clothes: is this a line from a nasty movie she has watched? However, he removes his singlet and boxer shorts in silence, wears a stolen condom, slides into bedclothes. Humming a melodic song in Hausa, nodding to the rhythm, she takes off her clothes, flings them to the TV. He wants to rise because she's begun to laugh at him, but she strokes his failing erection, spreads him on the foam like a small bedsheet, climbs on top of him. The noise of a generator starting to life downstairs drowns the humbling *pah-pah-pah* sounds of her swift movements on him. He closes his eyes, for her own eyes hold a teasing amusement, and thinks about the First World War. Which country dropped the first bomb? And that Adolf Hitler guy: was he in the First or the Second World War?

Afterwards, she says, smiling, "Boy, you remind me of Edet."

Edet was a boy in his class, a boy in his life. Edet had breasts but there was no beard. There was no moustache. Everybody, it was said, gasped on discovering Edet was a member of Black Axe confraternity. During the last war between the Black Axe and the Vikings, the red-eyed capon of the Vikings nicknamed Scorpion caught him at night and gunned him down. The Vikings painted his breasts red with his blood, cut off his fingers, beheaded him and played football with his head. He liked Edet, and does not like that Aisha finds the boy's tragic end funny.

"I heard Scorpion, who's still missing, constructed a goal-post and kicked Edet's head into the net like a ball," she continues. "It was a bicycle kick. People say the goal was so good they wished it was nominated for Puskas Award. You look like him, though you have no oranges on your chest. The two of you are soft – you can't even fuck well. But I will pay you for the sex. How much, boy?"

"Go, Boss Lady," he says, wearing his boxer shorts. "The sex is free. It's a promo. Go with your money."

After she's gone with her money, he stumbles to the window and thinks: What's wrong with me? I didn't come. I couldn't come. So this is sex everybody is singing about? So this is that thing that makes men behead themselves, burn communities, go to war? Isn't sex, like university education, highly overrated?

He returns to the foam, picks the used condom with two fingers as if it were a rotten mouse tail, enters into the bathroom to flush it down, soap his hand and do *something*.

SECOND YEAR

SECOND YEAR

CHAPTER 7

NKEM peers up at the iridescent sky as he trudges d Chiamaka's office with her.

It's a dew-soaked Monday morning: there's dew in the electric-blue air, dew on whispering grass, dew on parked cars, dew on lampposts; and the red sun of this glorious dawn has appeared behind a gap in the freshly green branches of towering trees, setting the silver-coloured rooftops of buildings on fire.

Today, unlike the previous days, he glances at Chiamaka and turns up his nose. This woman, she has shoddier clothes this session, each one stained with tomatoes, each one has the odour of onions, each one washed-out, each one rumpled and parched. But her secondhand gown, silky and lavender-coloured, is liberally perfumed today. Undesirable perfume, an assault to the nose, but it's much better than the whiffs of different rotten vegetables. He recalls, with a crying-baby face, that he sat in the first row of chairs in the classroom and observed that she smelt faintly of garlic. Now her body is giving a nauseous odour of a criminally made perfume. They overwhelm him, this smelliness, this gracelessness, and he's on the cusp of humming a fable of boys whose girlfriends are lost at sea to distract himself from her, but Okoye's BMW roars past, enveloping them with black smoke from the exhaust.

Okoye the dog, she says with an adolescent shake of her head. The dog has slept with Jamike, Jamila, Jane, Janet, Jennifer, Jessica. The dog prefers to go to bed with his students whose names start with the letter J. But does Nkem know why the dog had an affair with Chioma whose name starts with the letter Ch?

"I don't think I'm keen on the subject of Chioma," he says.

"I gather that her parents have no male child. How unfortunate. Is her father looking out for a second wife?"

He waits for a horde of boisterous students to saunter past them before he replies that their family's problems are none of his business. "But nobody should feel remiss in not having a male child," he adds.

"You talk weirdly like you went to drink beer with Okoye." She grasps his wrist with a hand that causes him to shiver with its reptilian coldness, and steers him away from a blue puddle of water into which the morning sun falls and shines. He takes him down the leafy road leading to a tortoise-shaped building hidden behind a hissing bush, where her present but wood-paneled office and a burnt toilet share a shaky wall. "There's something I want to discuss with you and then we'll head to Okoye's office to extort an apology from him, yes. I don't want you to continue being cross. It makes you appear inelegant, and I want you to remain suave. You've such a chewable beard every female student would like to play with."

He has to change the topic. "What's my grade? My grade is the best, right? Obviously. No?"

"You passed, yes. Fine boys don't fail." She gives a quick awkward cackle, scratches her beard and her monkey-brown hair, which the afternoon sunlight is burnishing. "Your mother is the luckiest woman in Nigeria. I envy her."

"Did Chioma pass? And Ifenna? And Izu the class leader?"

"They all passed, I suppose. We've to wait for the irrational HOD to publish the results to be sure. As I was saying, your mother—"

"Izu passed?" He halts and stares at her with unwavering confidence. "Izu did not fail? That dullard didn't even know Lionel Robbins."

"Who's Lionel Robbins? Is he a friend of yours?" she asks without slowing her pace.

"Professor Lionel Robbins was an Argentinian economist. But the popular Adam Smith was Scots. Smith studied social philosophy at Balliol College, Oxford. After graduating on John Snell's scholarship, he delivered a public lecture at Edinburgh. Have you heard of Edinburgh, blessed wine?"

Her lips tremble. "Edin who? Edwin is a student here?"

"Edinburgh is a city in the United Kingdom, and not a man." He lifts his face to the cloudy sky so that his Harry Potter spectacles, which are sliding down his face, will return to the bridge of the nose. "Smith, I feel I must stress, published *The Theory of Moral Sentiments* in 1756 in Glasgow. His notable ideas are classical economics, division of labour, modern free markets, and so on. His major influence was Aristotle. Or would you say Hutscheson and Mandeville?"

"I think it was . . . it was the last one, yes."

"Who?"

"I'm enamoured with him. . .or her? I love economists and economics. We in this department are lucky, yes. The knowledge of this subject helps me a lot in my business. A proud fruitarian, yes. When things are cheap in the north, I travel to Sokoto, buy all the tomatoes, and back here in the east, my colleagues and students and common people dive the tomatoes like mad dogs over bones. But perhaps this is basic knowledge, yes?"

He's practically running after her. "Obviously... Please slow down. I just want a clarification on something. Could you throw light on Alfred Marshall's criticism of Smith's definition of economy and why there. . ."

"Economics is a nice subject, yes." She pauses, then lets out a mechanical cough he instantly resents. "As I was saying before you interrupted me, your mother is lucky to have you. How many are you in the family? Excluding the females."

He holds his tongue but continues trailing her with economics-related questions despite the mounting risk of kicks and blows.

In her office, he says, "Why am I here?"

"Chioma gave me Okoye's funny photos and videos last semester," she says in an annoyingly roguish tone. "Many of them, yes."

"May I see them? Are they family photos and videos?"

"Please don't pretend; it's not your talent." She shifts in the chair, yawns, scratches her itching hair with soil-stained fingers. "Okoye's fallen into a deep well, and I'm excited. The pictures are his. The pictures show him and your Chioma naked in bed."

"Have they gone viral? I haven't seen them. Well, it's understandable: I'm always busy in the library, obviously."

"What do you suggest we do? If I burn the photos

and the videos, Okoye will celebrate and begin to bite Chioma. He'll begin to mark her exam scripts harmfully. I know that devil very well. What should we do?"

He tingles with amazement and frustration, but words fail to pour out of his mouth. He's anxious of the Okoye-Chioma farce because his name is entrapped in it; he wishes all of them— Chioma, Ifenna, Chiamaka and himself—could expose Okoye, discipline Okoye, shame Okoye, and his name will not be thrust and muddled in the madness. But this dream of reputational disassociation, he thinks, is simply chimerical: There are people who know most of the chapters of the story. These people who know that Chioma is his girlfriend. These people, as if they are jobless, desire to know about all the missing chapters, all his adventures, all his misadventures. These people will definitely guffaw if these chapters are opened to the public gaze. These people: gossips who yearn for a public horse-kick on his face.

"Nkem, your mother is lucky, so lucky," she says, and gives him a queasy grin. "I don't want to see you looking crestfallen in this world because sorrow will erase your angelic smile. Keep that smile for your lucky mother. . . and for me, yes. You're my son, yes. Won't you be my son, Nkem?"

"I'm not dull, obviously, but I don't understand. . ."

She tilts her head, flashes him a provisional smile,

scratches her beard with slightly trembling fingers and speaks in a doggish rush he finds oddly poetic. She says she wants to take care of him as Christ advises Christians to love their neighbours as they love themselves. She says she wants him to be her son as she has no son but only daughters. She says she's not saying he has to follow her to her house and live with them as that is not what Christ preaches in the Bible. She says they can be chatting, they can be laughing, they can be sharing their problems as they walk at sunsets. She says she will be helping him in her courses after examinations as Christ wants Christians to be the merchants of lights in the Times of Darkness. She says she has no gold and she has no silver, but she will be buying him books, she will be protecting him against bad men like Okoye. She says she must punish the "Stomach" for him and he should just wait a minute so she can phone him. The Stomach must apologise to you for calling those idiotic security guards who dragged you to their office," she concludes with a note of pompous hostility he finds immature.

He leans forward to discourage her, but her beard, twitching and amusing, renders him speechless. So he lets her extract her scratched Tecno from that creased handbag that looks like the skin of a dead animal. He lets her phone and ask Okoye, in a tyranical tone, to run to her office right away or she'll give Nkem Obi the hidden truth, the pornographic video, the titilating photos.

He takes off his Harry Potter glasses and contemplates at his ringing phone. Prophet Elijah. Another grammar lesson? He rejects the call and looks up at her. "As I was saying, Lionel Robbin's theories. . ."

"As I was saying, you're a blessed wine," she says with a fierce frown. "Please no Lion Rabbit's nonsense this afternoon. I don't know him. You don't know him. He doesn't know us. He shouldn't interfere in our lives. Let him go to hell."

Fortunately, someone knocks on the door, and Chiamaka falls silent. After a few seconds, a female voice says, "I'm your student. The girl whose yellow gown reminded you of carrots in a lecture hall last week. Or was it tomatoes?"

A smile of petty mischief brightens Chiamaka's face. "The girl who pines for a visit to my farm to buy tomatoes for her traditional marriage?"

"No, ma. I'm Christiana Ekaette. The tall, beautiful girl who has been begging you to explain econometrics, fiscal economy and utility to her since. . ."

"Get out immediately!" Chiamaka says, stopping suddenly as if she had just seen a cobra at the door. "Sod off and never come back here again! Nonsense!"

"Madam, please. . ."

"Get out!" Chiamaka pushes back her chair and springs up: one of her fake-silver earrings drops to the floor, but she doesn't know. Lifting his eyes from the jewellery, he hears the girl run off and fall with a thud on the stairs.

"I want to go to the library to study my books," he says, glancing back at the schoolbag on his back. "Obviously."

"Don't go yet, blessed wine," she says, tilting her head like a little girl with a pink flower in her hair. Funny, he thinks as she rises. Smiling, shaking her head, she circles the office, closing the windows, turning off the lights. "I want to tell you a story, yes."

The story is a cliché: A woman she knows gets married to a man she knows. They both have jobs. They both have flaws: he whistles to a brothel, he smokes weed, he beats his wife; she drinks alcohol, she frequents her gardens and farms, she cooks late at night. The marriage has been dragging on for twenty-two years now. The first child is a girl, just like the third, the fourth, the fifth, the sixth. She has cried to bearded prophets, to famous pastors, to native doctors, to medical doctors, to spiritual rivers. But she's not pregnant with a male child. Her husband gave her twelve months to put a "bouncing baby boy" in her "cursed" womb or she will be shown the door. This crying woman is her best friend. What would Nkem do if he were this woman?

"Divorce him," he says.

"No, I...she. She says that divorce shouldn't be an option. Any other suggestion? She does not want to remarry."

"Okay." Prophet Elijah has sent him a text: *is these sentenz corect? Blessed are dose who pay there tithes for they shall evaporating into heaven?*

He deletes it and returns his attention to Chiamaka.

"Say something," she says. "Not 'okay'. You're a brilliant student. Do answer questions brilliantly in my class. So I want a brilliant answer now. Do you suggest she sleep with another boy...man? Do you suggest she sleep with another man to solve this problem in her marriage?"

"I don't give unsolicited advice, madam. Let her meet me, or go to someone else. I'm not married; I am young: I wonder why she needs my advice. Is she in a roundabout way, asking you to beg me to sleep with her?"

She stops lumbering in the office and stares at him for half a minute. "Nkem..." she says.

"Yes?"

"I will call her. I meant you. I will call you." She drifts to the window and opens it with a wet hand on which a leaf sticks like a green tattoo. "I . . . I will phone you. We shall see later. Go. Go to the library and read your books."

He puts his Harry Potter glasses back on, murmurs his farewell, and leaves with a grey thud in his chest.

CHAPTER 8

OKOYE rubs his belly and belches. He emptied two bottles of Satzenbrau and two cans of Turbo King into his stomach at home. He even drank one Trophy in his car while en route to an orphanage home to give the kids a bag of beans. Now everything he sights shifts, everything sways, everything swims. He should be in bed sleeping and not in his office, he knows, but alcohol is a dogged propeller.

He picks his fountain pen from the desk, gloats over his quarter-finished lecture note, which is stained with sweat and beer, and begins writing the last second paragraph of his new article for publication.

The high rate of poverty in the country is alarming. Over 38% of Nigerians cannot afford a packet of cigarettes, a bottle of beer on a Sunday evening, and a catfish for their soups. The far-

sighted Professor McCarthy Carr—he invented this invalid American academic colleague last semester—*opined in his book* ("Economics and West African Animals," *page 56) that the hungry masses in Nigeria might be tempted to return to "roasting and eating innocent lizards, frogs and toads if the federal government fails to slash the alarming price of petroleum." Eating these animals is not the distressing danger, but what will happen when they finish? In 2001, when Obasanjo was president, Nigerian children in the east—* he crosses out "east" *and pens "north"—* ate several toads. If this cruel inflation repeats, somebody is going to eat their daughter literally and figuratively.*

He stops writing as the sounds of approaching footsteps increase in volume and then a knock comes to the wooden door.

It's Chiamaka, he tells himself. Chiamaka has come to tell me that the Vice Chancellor has seen my pornographic photos and my pornographic videos. Chiamaka has come to tell me that I will be fired. Or, maybe, this is Rose? He exhales and says, "Come in."

The door opens with an unusual creak and reveals Ifenna, one of the students he's not prepared to meet or engage.

"Magnificient morning, Professor." With an unfathomable grimace, the boy ambles in and leans on the shelf, perspiring and studying him, as if he's contemplating painting him with crayons or in cheap charcoal.

"Painter, you're not wearing your nose ring today," he says. "You're not even chewing gum. I like it. Sit down, chief."

Ifenna does not obey. "I failed your course again. I came from the notice board."

Such effrontery. The Umbrella Boy must have the videos, the photos, the story: what else could have given him this incredible courage? He, Okoye, must be incredibly friendly and tolerant in order to cross this wobbly bridge or else he will fall off into the waters and drown.

"Nzekwu, you're not the only student who failed," he says.

"But they did not buy your handouts, Professor. They didn't even buy those books of yours that talk about cigarette importation and cow dung. They did not buy you beer. They did not give you girls. They did not give you shoes. They did nothing for you, but I did all these for you."

He half-rises, then sits again. "Have you discovered if Chioma has shown the video and the photos to any student or lecturer?"

"I helped you, Professor, but you allowed me to fail your course. Maybe I will give my life to Christ and stop selling your toothpaste and toothbrushes. Maybe I will stop buying shoes for my lecturers. Maybe I will begin to read, although books are nonsense."

"Crying? Stop it: you're not a girl!"

"Give me my shoes, Professor. The shoes I bought you for an A. Thank God you're in them today. Please remove my shoes and hand them back to me. I want to give the shoes to another lecturer."

"You're drunk." He rises, sways backwards and forward, tightens his tie-belt and rubs his baldness. "Who gave you the beer you drank?"

"Give me my shoes, Professor. If you don't give me my shoes, I will tell everybody. I will tell them you had sex with Chioma. I will show them the videos and the photos. I will print the photos and paste them on all the doors in this university."

"My boy, my chief," he says, with a lucidity of enunciation that sounds pathetically nervous, and shoves his hands into his pockets because they have begun to tremble. "My chief, the results have been published, as a matter of fact. There's nothing I can do about it. There was nothing I could do about it; the HOD, I heard, vowed to scrutinize all the scripts. I was scared. But I will help you after you resit the examination."

"Resit a course? A big boy like me?"

"Or a big girl like you? You know you behave like a pretty girl."

"I'm not joking with you, Professor. Give me my shoes, or I will shout and tell everybody what you and Chioma did in bed and show them the evidence."

In a split minute, the shoes are in Ifenna's hands and the Umbrella Boy is gone.

He imagines the boy standing in the midst of gum-chewing female students, the photos and the videos in his hand, and in their hands. He sees him telling the implausible story, cackling with his unbelieving audience, giving their backs jovial slaps. He sees the HOD limping by with a mighty Bible, wagging his head like a happy puppy, humming a song. The students scurry to the HOD with the videos and the photos, hold his hand, tell him the story, show him the evidence. These images are so real that he gasps like a character in a play, and draws nearer to the wall as if to hold the open window for support when he falls.

The air, as seen through this open window, is grey with fumes from a lorry carrying bags of cement. Its incessant honking sends students running or dipping out of the way. Retreating from this window on unsteady feet, he phones Professor Ayodele and unburdens himself.

"So you're you telling me that the greatest Igbo man of our time is barefooted in his office right now?" Professor Ayodele asks. "And probably naked. Did he run away with your trousers, too? But I guess the trousers are yours, not his. This is hilarious. Rose is already howling here…"

"I'm also howling." He ends the call, phones

Chiamaka and tells her his problems. "Your students buy you shoes?" she says.

"And singlets," he replies in annoyance. "And bread. But there's none now. Not even biscuits. Can you be kind enough to help me with shoes? Any shoes. I can't phone my family; you know why."

He ends the call and hovers in the office, pondering. What will he do? Keep his head up and go to his car barefooted? Will the students look at his feet and laugh? Or will they, surprisingly, cry or scream wondering if something has shifted in his brain? From Chioma, from Nkem, he has escaped like a rat in a weak snare. Or thinks he has, and now there's this sissy, this problem.

Minutes later, when he's seated behind his desk annotating his students' essays, the doorknob shakes. "Open the door, my dirty baby," Rose's amused voice says.

"Hope nobody's near. Nobody's listening?" He cranes his neck and listens. "Are you with someone? You've the shoes?"

"Only me, baby, so open. Open the door. . . Baby?"

"Can you stop using that stupid word?"

"Which stupid word, baby? I snatch Ayosky's wallet and runned to a boutique, baby."

Is this kindness an indication of her love for me, he thinks? Or perhaps it's a reward for the risk he took in giving her an A in the course Ifenna failed, failed woefully. "Who says stealing is not a beautiful thing?" he says with boyish exhilaration, and rises. "I'm coming, my dear."

The shoes look like twin toy boats, but he thanks her and wears them. Together, they arrange the scattered files and books on his desk, and creep out of the office and down the stairs. At Christ the King Hotel, she eats pepper soup and he drinks Baron de Valls as they discuss the threats that are the nude photos.

"Please, baby, don't kills Semicolon or Chioma or Ifenna or Mrs Chiamaka," she says.

He's already feeling splendid; the wine is good. He should leave the bottle alone, but he empties the alcohol in his mouth. "What do you suggest I do to make them annihilate those dangerous photos?" he asks.

"Pray to God, baby. Sleep with your Bible."

"I would rather sleep with you."

She laughs with him. She is still laughing when he takes her up the stairs and into his Room 18. He's removing her clothes when something happens to his brain and his eyes begin to swim faster. He sits on the bed, but the bed, in his swimming eyes, rises to the ceiling. *God*, he hears himself scream. *God Almighty*. He lies on the bed: it returns to the ground and then starts rotating him like a child in a merry-go-round. He struggles to stand, but some wicked hands he cannot see have suddenly tied him up with an invisible mosquito net. He spreads himself like a butchered animal. The bed continues to spin and spin and spin.

"Baby? Are you drunk?"

He screams, straightens up and holds the swimming wall: the bed stands still. But the curtains are cackling in Rose's voice.

Where's Rose? Perhaps she's behind the curtain. Perhaps she's in the curtain. The noisy TV leaves its wall, buzzes round the room like a giant bee. He struggles to catch the flying TV and crush it, but his right hand has been filled with stones. Good. But where's his left hand? Who fled with his left hand?

He moves his eyeballs laboriously upwards and finds, to his mute amusement, that the ceilings are descending like bedclothes as if they're intent on covering him like a freezing baby abandoned by its mother. He holds his eyes with his fingers, hears Rose's giggle, and decides to shut his eyes till morning.

At the first cockcrow, he wakes to find the rising sun has turned the window golden. Rising and frowning at invisible madmen's whistle noises in his pounding head, he kisses Rose's breasts, gives her three thousand naira and leaves without a word.

Downstairs, he notices it's a frosty day and men are smoking. He drives home smoking his last surviving cigarette and worrying about the nude photos.

He should bathe first because he reeks of alcohol

and cigarettes, but he installs himself in his battered cushion, lights a cigarette he finds on the side stool. He likes the breeze that lifts his curtains from time to time, likes that he's alone in the house: Ebuka has been kicked back to his boarding school, Chinenye is in Abuja for an essay competition. His wife travelled to Nsugbe, their hometown, to fight one Mama Sopuru, a chubby widow, who sends him poetic texts and nudes on WhatsApp.

He takes out his phone because he wants to call Chioma. He will call the girl and beg her forgiveness again. He will call Rose, invite her to his flat, take her into his bedroom and do to her what he failed to do to her in the hotel room. Scrolling through his contacts, looking for Chioma's number, his phone rings.

Chiamaka, the unguessed caller, fills him with rage. Why is Chiamaka, a married farmer, a frigid farmer, calling him this romantic evening? Still, he takes the call, asks her what the matter is.

"Not about your nude photos and blue films," she says. "The HOD and the VC have not seen them yet. . . yes."

His cigarette has split in his hand; he lights the surviving half and leans back on his cushion. "You're still hiding them for me? God bless you!"

"I saw your wife entering a commercial bus. She told me she's travelling to the village to stay for a few days since you prefer motherless babies…"

He knows what she is hinting at, but he'll not allow that. "Can we forget my wife today?"

"You talk as if she's a celebrity, an exceptional celebrity. A pretty celebrity. You talk as if you love her. I'm coming whether you like it or not, yes."

He's drinking his third beer and smoking his thirteenth cigarette when she arrives with a pleasant scent of an expensive perfume that astonishes him. He finds, with bitterness, that she's dressed in a biscuit-coloured gown that fails to conceal her large legs, her blemished legs. He finds the orange scarf around her head carries no fallen leaf, no fallen seed, and no bit of grass from her bushy farm. Does this cleanliness, this carefulness, indicate that she has just come from her office in this perfect weather, in this agricultural weather, as she likes to put it?

He lowers his glass to a side stool. "Welcome, Amaka, but…"

"No buts, Okonkwo," she says. "Show me your kitchen."

"The university sent you to supervise my kitchen?"

She pads to the refrigerator, returns to him with a bottle of milk. "I'm behaving very strangely, Okonkwo? It's me being myself. Now come. Show me your kitchen or I'll search for it myself."

He rises. "But am I not the one who should dart into the kitchen to cook for my guest? You're my guest."

"I know, but I'm a woman." She drains her bottle and keeps it on the sapphire-coloured carpet. "If I were a man, you should do the cooking. Where there are men and women, a woman must do the cooking. Force her to do it if she refuses."

"That's a backward opinion. I can't believe you said this."

"I can't believe you let a seventeen-year old girl in your class hold your thing like a microphone."

Her outburst of invective unnerves him. "Come and see my kitchen," he mumbles.

In the kitchen, he notices with embarrassment for the first time, that the ceilings have been covered with cobwebs, covered with smoke from the stove. "Very neat kitchen," she teases. "Where's your matchbox, smoker? You also gave it to the orphanage home?"

He gives it to her, returns to the living room, where he finds himself wishing for a Portuguese beer and wine. Is her irreducible ugliness and nastiness the cause of this sudden longing for another booze? He knows she will try to cook better than his wife, knows she will try to feed him, seduce him, sleep with him. He knows it well. But why she needs that, why she needs him, he does not know.

The sizzling of oil brings him to the door that leads to the kitchen and to the toilet. So she can cook, he thinks? So ugly women know how to cook beautifully?

He licks his lips as he returns to his cushion, as the smell of groundnut oil wafts into the living room.

"Food's ready, yes," she says, coming in with a tray containing a plate of fried yam. "After eating this, you will forgive me of all the horrible things I've done to you." She lowers the plate on a stool, and gives him several jovial kicks. "You like fried yams, yes? I will feed you. Your wife will not scream if she finds me feeding you?"

"You expect her to applaud you?"

She tries to spoon-feed him, but he seizes her hairy hand. "Because I are not your baby, baby?" she says, mimicking Rose's accent. "Eat, baby, eat."

Eavesdropper, he thinks. Has this woman been eavesdropping on him and Rose, peeping through the hole on his office door, savouring their adolescent joviality, their fabulous romance? Or has Rose been telling her things?

"Okay." He feigns a simpering smile, and lets her feed him. "Mmm…So delicious I feel like shedding tears of joy."

The sudden sounds of gunshots startle them. He suspects cultists, the Black Axe and the Vikings: these two confraternities have been gunning each other down since last month. Rose told him that a dozen boys has been killed, six Vikings members and six Black Axe members. A draw match at halftime, some students like to joke. Perhaps the boys are grappling for a "winning goal", as they call it. The winning goal is a cut-off head of the enemy that will be kicked into a net like football. He aches to describe the blood-covered head of his student named Edet, which he once saw in a net, but Chiamaka is saying something about her husband.

"Cultists are truculent like soldiers, Okonkwo. My husband is a soldier, yes. I want to tell you about him. Do you want me to tell you about him?"

"He's still in Borno fighting Boko Haram terrorists?"

"If he's still alive, yes." She feeds him again, cleans his mouth with her tomato-smelling handkerchief. "He's good in bed and all that, but he has scant respect for me. After fifteen years of marriage, he began hopping into bed with other women because I could never bear him a male child. He wants a male child desperately, yes. If I asked him to stop sleeping with those women, he'd kick my bottom and hit me with the head of his gun. Soldiers are a bunch of dunces, Okonkwo."

"They're worse than dunces."

She pinches his stomach. "But better than lecturers, yes? You're an abysmal drunkard, aren't you? An abysmal drunkard with an alarmingly mighty stomach."

"I'm glad you find it funny."

"It's rather depressing". She offers him a bottle of water and searches his face. "We're still hoping that a male child will grace my womb. Nnaemeka will start respecting me if our dream comes true."

"Nnaemeka?"

"My husband. He's a soldier, and a coward. When he sees me, he remembers that he's a soldier. Throw a live fowl at Nnaemeka, he will yell and flee, but I'm his punching bag."

"A chocolate cream soldier. That's what soldiers like him are called."

"What about lecturers like you?"

"Thanks…my stomach is filled." He brushes crumbs of yam off his beard, pours himself a glass of beer and lights a cigarette. "We're both adults, Amaka. Be forthright. Do you want me to be your boyfriend?"

She scoffs, slaps at the smoke curling towards her face. "Don't feel so important. You're not a boy, fat old man. You're not a musician or a politician. You're just a common man, yes. I only need you because I need a male child. I can't get myself pregnant, can I?"

"I'm certain you drank whiskey or one of these Portuguese wines. Very strong. Down the stomach and straight to the brain to do marvellous things."

"I'm extremely serious, Okonkwo!"

"You're serious and you don't even know the name of your future son's father." He takes his lighter and packet of cigarettes, and rises. "But I'm not the only man in this university. There are many bad men with bigger stomachs who are looking for a merry opportunity like this."

"You're pretending as if you'll not enjoy it."

"Enjoy what exactly? Your body? Yes, of course. What wouldn't I enjoy? But it's not right."

"But it's right to undress sixteen-year-old girls who are entrusted into your fat hands? It's right to put your forewood into somebody's girlfriend's mouth and ask her to lick it like a lollipop? Don't induce me take a ruthless action."

His packet of cigarettes drops from his trembling hand. "Are you blackmailing me?"

"Yes."

"God, your husband will find out and bomb us."

"You're a thoroughly funny philanthropist, Okonkwo. My husband is in the north. He'll not find out, yes. We made love before he left. Let's do this and save my marriage. That coward is impotent, I suspect. Remove your clothes fast. Don't be shy with me. Countless women have seen you naked and even brushed their teeth with your philanthropic penis."

He glances at the door as though he's desirous to escape, but he's actually trying to hide the effect of the sordid joke. "You're commanding me as if I were a suddenly repentant prostitute you hired."

He sees her clench in annoyance and leans back.

She has looked around the Department of Economics, but could not find a man or a boy who could do her the favour, she expalins, and then gets up to take his hands. He withdraws it with the word "no!" as if he were a kid and she snaps, "I'm not insinuating that you're irresponsible and easy to catch, you childish philanthropist."

"Only those who behave like children go to heaven: isn't that what the Bible says?"

She stares at him for a long moment and sits. "Okonkwo, if you sleep with me and get me pregnant and I find it's a baby boy, I'll burn all your nude photos and videos," she says with insuppressible sadness. "I will call him Okasigomobi."

The Igbo name, *he has consoled me,* amuses him with its sound and meaning, with its unabashed originality. He sits up to ask, "What if the baby turns out to be a girl?"

"I'll flush the rubbish away and you will sleep with me again. We'll keep sleeping until I find a baby boy."

"But you were once a baby girl and your parents didn't flush you away? What you solicit is dreadful, Amaka. It's barbaric."

"I am not a very nice woman, Okonkwo. Hope you know what I can do."

Show them the videos, he tells himself. Show them the photos. Show them they can sack me. I know what you can do, I know it well. "You want a boy?"

"Obviously, as Nkem would say," she says with a hint of humour, kneels and begins unzipping his trousers. "My baby, as Rose would say. My baby."

He removes her scarf, removes her clothes, and spreads her on the couch; they have sex. Despite her bearded face of a serial murderer, despite her smelly armpits, despite her animal noises, he still finds her surprisingly satisfactory.

"You fucked the hell out of me," she says, wearing her clothes. "I don't think I will be able to walk in a straight line again. . . God, so fat men are not big for nothing!"

"We're big for nothing."

"Wear your dirty clothes and drop me off." Laughing loudly, awkwardly, she helps him pick his trousers, helps him put them on him. "I will name the boy you've just ejaculated into me Okonkwo, after you."

"I'm flattered. Hope the young Okonkwo will take after my wonderful stomach." He stops suddenly, for she has wrinkled her nose in distaste, and retracts. "Our son will have a smaller stomach. Thanks for today."

CHAPTER 9

IFENNA increases his pace on the Campus Road because there are ghostly voices trailing him this moonless night.

The road is eerily quiet, deserted, and faint moonlight falls on its tea-coloured surface, weaved by the shadows of the leafless trees and flowers that line the path. Some of the streetlights have been felled by gushing winds, some faulty, some curiously disconnected, some stolen. The surviving ones, three or four of them, are turned off. Still, he can go most places here blindfolded. He knows there are potholes filled with mud water on this road. He knows snakes from the bushy football field sometimes slither to this road and bite students returning from night studies with their torchlights. He knows the signposts by the roadside have been repainted because of him, and because of a few students like him. The words, MEN WITH PLAITED HAIR ARE NOT ALLOWED INTO THE UNIVERSITY, appear on all of them. So his plaiting business with Rose has come to an abrupt end. So her voice, shrill and peevish as she apprised him of the new rule on the phone, was truly sincere, and not mocking, not playful. Now, he has loosened and cut the hair, but his heart still quickens whenever he glimpses the written law on the signposts.

I shouldn't have stayed longer at Children of God beer parlour, he thinks: while in the lecture hall no female students seemed keen on abandoning her books and rechargeable lanterns for him. No female student's face beamed as he cat-walked up and down, lampooning the exaggerated gaits of some of them who have refused to look at him as if he were a mere mannequin. No female students asked him why he's wearing a pair of pink trousers that stick to his thighs, a nose ring, and a turban the colour of a fresh onion. The turban now drops from his head, but he does not stop to pick it.

"Stop there!" someone shouts behind him. The voice is rough, masculine and familiar. The voice sounds like trouble.

Oh, God, not today, please, he thinks, but a stone hits the back of his head. He screams "Jesus!" in agony, drops his half-empty bottle of whiskey and scuttles off. His assailants follow him in what he can only describe as

Olympic pursuit, ordering him to stop or a dagger will be thrown into his "abominable arse." Yet he continues to run. He runs past chatting students leaving the university with their books. Past a boy and a girl kissing on a pew surrounded with purple hibiscuses. Past two male security guards snoring on a blanket spread on the field, their torches clarifying his leaf-carpeted path. Past wandering sheep under the whistling frangipani trees that line the track leading to the gate. Past the slightly opened gate and drops into mud water as though he's tired of running. Tired of dodging. Tired of being tired. But the eerie noises of owls, and not those of his assailants, cause him to rise hastily and continue his run. He does not stop until he reaches the first hostel off campus. The hostel is called Safe Haven. Aisha lives on the first floor.

He knocks on the iron door, speaks his name, and a sombre voice within says, "Ifenna? Go, no food."

"Aisha, it's true that whenever I wear my brown shirt, I always want to eat your brown beans, but my desire to see you today is not about food."

He purses his lips and waits for her to come out, but she does not. The sound of her feet moving in the lightless bedroom to the moonlit window, which is busted and slightly open, and the plaintive bleating of a goat, begin simultaneously, and then cease as she begins to question him. "You remember I have been begging you to visit me? You remember I have been sending you the location to my room? You remember I wanted you to be my lover? Why do you suddenly remember me today? Why do you want me now?"

There's no light in her bedroom, so he cannot see her face. "It's because you're the only girl who understands me," he replies. He does not say: it's because unknown hooligans are chasing me, trying to kill me. He does not say: it's because I need to have a girlfriend to prove to my assailants that I like girls and not boys.

"Boy, I wish I were a dog," she says after a lull. "Dogs are treated better here. My lecturers asked me to stop wearing my hijab to the studio. My fellow students say they will not give me any fucking mandate and I will never be the president of the department because I'm a Muslim from the north. And Professor Felix Nwachukwu, the Head of our Department, is not fighting it. Nobody is on my side. An Igbo Christian is slaughtered in Kano, and they come at me as if I'm responsible. Two weeks ago, *your* Igbo boys barged into this room, poured fuel on me and tried to set my entire body on fire. I hit them with my kettle and bolted away, my hair burning. Luckily for me, there's a stagnant water downstairs and I threw myself into it. But the fire had already burnt off all my hair and my eyebrows."

He turns on his phone torchlight, brings it close to the window to see her face. Jesus, he thinks with a shudder. The face staring at him cannot be Aisha's, or any human being's. The face is a mask of horror. The face belongs to a beast, or a demon, or a vampire, in a horror movie: the hair is gone; the scalp is a grilled egg. The eyebrows are burnt off; the nose is a roast pear. The ears are like beef prepared by a sleepy chef. This new appearance now makes him think of scary cartoons he used to draw and paint with crayons when he was in primary school.

He turns off the torchlight, returns the phone into his pocket of his dripping trousers and says in a quavering voice, "I swear, I'm deeply sorry about this cruelty, Aisha. Switch on your lights. Cry. Stop acting strong and tough and bossy. Show your emotions. Let the world know about this cruelty."

"Wallahi, nobody here will see my tears!" she says. "The cruelty, as you rightly call it, simply proves that this place is not meant for me. I have called home. My parents are soldiers in this state, but they will not be on this campus tomorrow for war. They will be here for me. Dad just wants to come here tomorrow and take me back to Katstina, our state. We Fulani people have universities like you Igbo people, don't we?"

"Stay with me, Aisha. Don't leave Heineken University. Don't throw away your two years of dedicated studies because they hate you. Boss Lady—"

"Don't call me Boss Lady. I'm not a boss here. To

you Igbo people, I am an enemy in your country Biafra. I will be returning to Nigeria *my* country as soon as the sun rises in the morning, insha Allah."

"We are all Nigerians, Aisha. We are one Nigeria. Don't do this to me, please. I swear, if you leave I will drink yoghurt and die—I meant cement, not yoghurt!"

But she closes the window. He feels a mosquito arrives on his left ear as if it's its home, humming, circling, trying to suck his blood. He slaps his ear in irritation and turns to a moon rising from behind smoky clouds. As his mud-coated shoes touch the first step, he hears Aisha, this burnt girl who will never be his, sobbing in her darkened, lonely room.

Back in his own room, he lies face down on the foam, listening to a self-pity song from Sam Smith. "What's the matter, blessed wine?" Nkem asks him.

He gives Nkem no answer, but the Semicolon Boy continues probing him until he switches off the singing phone. Closing his eyes, taking a deep breath, he prays that sleep will settle inside his head like a dew. A thousand masquerades barge into his sleep and pursue him from the east of Nigeria to the north of Nigeria, where herdsmen beat him up with planks. After handling him, they chase him back to the east of Nigeria, where tigers round him up, try to eat his head. He miraculously wriggles out of their claws, but they chase him from the east to the west, where gum-chewing policemen catch him running on the Third Mainland Bridge, arrest him, beat him up with a cudgel. Beside him, Nkem is snoring softly, Oscar Wilde's *Lady Windermere's Fan* resting on his hairy chest.

At sunrise he wakes Nkem and unburdens himself.

"A depressing incident, obviously," Nkem says. "You say her name is Aisha? Why do we Africans take Arabic names when people in the Arab World don't give a fuck about ours?"

"But, Semicolon, I swear, I like the name, I like the girl, I need the girl. I can't continue living without her. Should I commit suicide?"

Nkem disregards the question, wanders into the bathroom. Perhaps Nkem does not believe him. Perhaps he thinks it's one of his jokes.

After Nkem is gone to the campus, he lights a stolen candle and prays to God for protection, for understanding, for love, for peace of mind, for a lover. Then, rising with his stolen Bible and an erection, he pops gum into his mouth and smiles at his successful crimes at Uncle Elijah's church.

At the reading table, he drops the Holy Book on the top of Nkem's novels and gazes at his work-in-progress in a trance of reverence. The work is a pencil caricature of a girl. Her name is Chinelo. She's a light-skinned girl in his class. She likes him more than her parents and her siblings, or so she says. He likes Chinelo too, but told her he's a homosexual because Rose says the girl is HIV positive. Does Chinelo, like most students who know him, think he's truly queer? Does Chinelo, like most students who know him, think he must match like a man, roar like a man, harass women like a man: to prove his masculinity, to prove his sexuality? He is not going to do that. He is not going to tell her he likes looking at women. He's not even going to tell Nkem. Let every deluded fellow continue in their delusion. Let every deluded fellow remain chained in ignorance.

His phone rings. It's Okoye, the caller says. Ifenna? Yes, I am Ifenna, he answers. Is Nkem awake? How is the Semicolon Boy? He replies that Semicolon is awake, peevish, hopeless. Lots of apologies: tell Nkem that he, Dr. Ezinwa Okoye, is awfully sorry and remorseful, tell Nkem that he will appease him with a good grade; tell Nkem that Chioma is safe, Chioma will not be touched again; tell Nkem that it is imprudent to continue fighting his lecturer because of a girl; tell Nkem that their stay at the university is at risk and so they need to be civil. Is Ifenna less busy with economic textbooks, so they can visit Chioma and entreat forgiveness?

"Have I ever been busy with books in my life?" he says.

"My apologies."

The house in which Chioma and her parents live is a dilapidated bungalow surrounded by lemon flowers and thick with the smell of pond water. BEWARE OF DOGS says the open gate, the door says WELLCOME.

They can't spell, he thinks. Is Chioma the likely speller really home? Where are her parents? Where are her dogs, her guitars, her trumpets, her drums? Where are all the things she boasts of? The things she says that fill this grass-carpeted compound, this gritty passage, this concrete bench littered with soil-stained Chelsea jerseys that reek of sweat.

Filing these questions for future probing and teasing, he knocks at the metal entrance, speaks their names, and pushes the door open.

The stench of sour beans rushes into his nostrils, and he sneezes.

From a worn-out sofa, a lithe woman in a rumpled Manchester United jersey rises with the red, football socks she's knitting. "Who're you?" she demands in Igbo.

Dialect: Owerri, Orlu, Mba-Ano, Mba-Ise? He cannot place her dialect, cannot remember her hometown, their hometown.

"You must be Mrs. Emenike, Chioma's mother," Okoye says. "I'm Dr. Ezinwa Okoye, from Heineken University of Education. The boy with me, Ifenna Nzekwu, is my student. Just like your daughter."

"What am I to do with this useless information?" she asks, her voice rising. "And you say this girl...this boy is a student? I wonder what they learn there. . . Will you stop chewing gum in my house!"

He blows the gum and gives her a faint smile. "But I'm enjoying it, madam."

She stares at him, her forehead creasing with annoyance.

Like mother, like daughter, he thinks: always tough, always unbending, like iron. An unfailing snappiness to their tone.

"You're enjoying the gum?" she asks, still staring at him. "In *my* house?"

Mba-Ise: he remembers her dialect now. She's from Mba-Ise, her husband is from Mba-Ano. Elegant dialect, inelegant woman. Inelegant home. Inelegant attitude. Isn't their inelegant visit already hopeless?

Okoye intervenes. "I suppose you've heard some disgraceful things about me and your daughter. I beg forgiveness."

"Madam, please forgive him, for he knew not what he was doing," he says.

"Leave my house, Mr. Ezi," she says in hostile English. "Right now. Or I will unchain Satan."

Unchain Satan: is this a figure of speech, or did she speak literally? Who in her right senses chooses, among innumerable fancy names, this ridiculousness that is Satan? Perhaps she has mispronounced an unfamiliar word, an unfamiliar phrase. But which unfamiliar word, which unfamiliar phrase? "Please, madam," he says.

She tosses her socks and niddle under a wooden

chair, where there are football things: a whistle, a glove, a net, a pair of boots.

"Is Mr. Emenike home?" Okoye brings his hands together like he's praying, goes on his knees. "I don't know who told you, but forgive me. Beg her to forgive me. It will never happen again."

"Forgive him so that he will not lose his job," he says, unwrapping another gum. "I swear, he has children. He has children to feed, madam. Please."

From somewhere, a dog growls, frightening him. Like a child, he edges closer to Okoye, holds his left hand which, he notices, is shaking slightly.

"What will you guests drink?" she asks in an astonishingly velvety tone. "I have Life beer, Coke, Pepsi, juice, ice cream…"

"Ice cream," he says.

"No ice cream, Mrs. Emenike. We like beer, but don't worry." Okoye rises with uncharacteristic effortlessness as though his popular beer belly had been depleted like a balloon, dusts his trousers. "We should be the ones offering you something for your kindness."

"I must offer you something." She navigates to the door, bolts it with a gloved hand, gives them wooden chairs. "Back in a jiffy."

After she's gone into the room, Okoye says, "I didn't know she's good…"

"In bed?" he asks.

Okoye glares at him. But he smiles and thinks: Stop being too serious, Professor. We are just having fun here. I can't believe we are having fun here. This scene is surreal, unreal, but thank God.

He licks his lips, rubs his eyes, and watches as Okoye scans the walls, which are lined with Chioma's framed photographs: Chioma with a birthday cake, Chioma and Tiwa Savage smiling on a stage, Chioma playing a piano, Chioma playing a guitar, Chioma in her matriculation gown. On an old TV, near a plastic crucifix, sits the black-and-white wedding photograph of her and her husband. So Chioma is right, he thinks. She's their son and daughter; they only have her, and of course the dogs. No other daughter, no other son. Are they happy like that?

"Now, enjoy," Mrs. Emenike says.

They turn and, glimpsing a tan-coloured dog on a leash in her hand, scream in unison. "Catch them, Satan!" she says. "Eat them like doughnut. Drink their blood like Champagne."

The dog growls and surges forward, but she doesn't let go of the leash.

Okoye dashes to the door, but finds it's locked. So he knees and raises his trembling hands.

He, Ifenna, is already in tears. The window, he discovers, is broken, open. He runs to Okoye and tries to carry the fat man to the window and throw him out like a bag of rubbish. But the stomach is too big for him. The woman and her dog bark almost at the same time, and the leash in her hand drops. He leaves Okoye like he's a bomb that's about to explode, runs to the window with shrieks and flies out.

The rain-soaked plank on which he lands slits. Okoye either finds the idea of escaping through the window farcical or he simply cannot, so he runs to the latched exit and screams for help. Seconds later, he finds the fat man running toward the sunlight. Did Okoye break and escape through another window, kick down the door or the woman drifted smilingly into leniency? No time to puzzle this out; he stands, dusts his trousers and darts off.

CHAPTER 10

NKEM lies on his prickly foam in the dark, facing the invisible ceiling of squeaking and scurrying rodents, and turns on his smartphone to compose a text message.

Dear Lonely Room:

In my heart there's a Chioma-shaped hole.

So deep, so dusty.

So sad I am.

Chioma, my room is empty but full of your shadows.

Are you not that girl in a white gown,

Roving under the moon like an angel across my open window?

I'm here, Chioma: Won't you stop to say hi?

After rereading the message, he clears it, stares at the wall whitened by the light from the night sky, and thinks: another day, another day. But when?

There's power outage, as usual, and the room, as his deleted message conveys, is shadowy in a depressing way, shadowy and chilly; he leaves the window open for the stars and the moon, for the delicious smells of whispering trees, of flapping flowers. Bullets from gunshots are like nails pouring down from heaven. But there's nothing frightening about that: when last did he, or any other student of Heineken University of Education, spend a night without the earsplitting sounds of gunshots from cultists? Or, maybe, these ones are armed robbers?

He will not hammer his mind with that problem now. He wants to think about Chioma, not about gunshots, and yet it hurts to think about Chioma. He will always think about the singing girl but will not send her any message professing his love. He will not let her feel that Nkem the Great of all people is homesick for her body. He can find a better girlfriend, a prettier girlfriend, and she knows it. She knows he's not cheap. She knows he's beautiful, strikingly beautiful, and is a connoisseur and reader of Great Books: he reads Oscar Wilde, reads Achebe, reads Dickens, reads Austen. Let this sink into her head and sizzle like hot oil.

The prepaid metre cries like an evil bird in agony. The iridescent light from an egg-shaped bulb on the ceiling brings the room to life.

He keeps the phone on the foam, saunters to the reading table, dusts his classic novels and lies on the cold marbled floor with a pillow. He rises after a series of rapid slaps on the inanimate company, returns to the foam, returns to his phone. But, Christ, my heart is swollen with burnt birds, he tells himself: me disgraced, me deprived, me chastised, me sleepless, me without the voice of Chioma, without the presence of Chioma, me with nothing but the gloomy shadow of my drowning self on the wall. He bites his lips three times before he phones her.

"Mistaking me for your new girlfriend, Nkem?" she asks in an embittered voice.

"A mistake? Me? What makes you think I made a mistake?"

"Because you're a human being and we all make mistakes. Stop seeing yourself as a demigod or some supernatural being from the blue sky just because you read Oscar Wilde and know how to use a semicolon. You're just a human being; you're not Harry Potter, even though you wear his stupid glasses."

"Chioma. . .!" He pauses, and shakes his head. "This isn't the real you, obviously. What's biting you, blessed wine?"

Chioma is pinched-lipped; then, to his amazement, this usually stoic warrior begins to weep. Her songs are not doing well at all, she says. Her money has finished on several studios. Her mother is still forcing her to disconnect from him. Her mother has promised Chief that she's his. And as for her father, he's indifferent as usual, foolish as usual. He goes to Yoruba herbalists to enlarge his penis, goes to brothels, sleeps with prostitutes, staggers in and out of beer parlours. He has an Akwa-Ibom girlfriend who he wants to marry. He threatens to arrest her mother because she beats the girlfriend, beats him when he's drunk. She, Chioma, is also afraid of being arrested by the police because she beats his girlfriend, beats him when he's drunk. Why would a sacked school driver, a haggard drunkard, who now sells bush meat want to have a second wife? If he has a second wife in their house, will he allow his wife to have a second husband in their house? Isn't one wife enough? Isn't one daughter enough? Must everybody have a son? She will dismantle this patriarchy, mess it up, fuck it up.

"Calm down, blessed wine," he says. "Destroy the patriarchy, but don't destroy Dr. Okoye's pornographic photos and videos; they will be very important to us. I will explain some other time. Are you composing any other song at the moment?"

"I would rather talk about you, Sugar. My life is upside-down and boring. How are your parents? Rose said she sighted your father near the university basketball court, telling a group of students a joke. She said they laughed without cessation. Should I tell you what Rose said the joke is about when she was plaiting my hair in the hostel?"

Does his father, sitting with undergraduates, forget his age, forget his job? Does the balding man think he's seventeen years old?

He makes no attempt to hide his curiosity from Chioma. "Please tell me everything about his joke. Hope it isn't very disgraceful."

"I will tell you if you come to my hostel to see me tomorrow in the morning."

There's no student in her room when he arrives at 8: 10 the next morning.

"The only decent man at Heineken University," she says, enfolding him, pecking him, and he breathes in her delicious smell of body lotion.

There's no smell of cigarette today. There's no smell of beer. There's no music going on, only the rhythmic roar of the campus.

Chioma closes the door behind him, leads him into the spring bed covered with a mosquito net, and offers him a can of Guinness stout.

"Thanks, blessed wine." He drinks the stout in silence, his eyes on the flapping almanac on the wall artistically painted dark grey, watery white, fading blue—the colours of clouds promising an imminent downpour. He deliberately fixes his gaze on the wall, for she is dressed to ensnare: a white brassiere with the picture of a burning microphone, black but transparent boxer shorts that expose her pubic hair, a string of multicoloured beads around her waist. The tattoo of a hand playing a piano on her breast has been erased and his amused face drawn. He wonders why she chose to have his face smiling on her breast as he slurps his Guinness and rubs his mouth with a knuckle. After draining the can and tossing it into the wastepaper basket near the door, after adjusting his Harry Potter glasses and offering his thanks again, after stealing a second look at her left breast, he leans against the wall, glances at his Rolex watch and says, "Blessed wine, you haven't told me what my father's joke is about. Tell me now."

"Are you in a hurry, Sugar?" she asks in a voice fetid with hopelessness, and the evening sun, as he watches, etches her hair red. "Don't go yet. Teach me Microeconomics I and Intermediate Mathematics for Economics. I don't want to waste my money on any hungry or frigid lecturer."

He offers a rather vague background of the two courses, and rises to go. "I have to be on my way to the library, blessed wine."

"But you haven't told me about your siblings. It's been long." She pulls him down on the bed again, wraps her arms around him. Now he perceives a faint odour of cigarettes. "Please don't sleep with Mrs. Chiamaka even if she gives you one million naira to offer her a male child. I can exploit Chief, my suitor, and give you one million naira so you will not yield to her temptation.

Chief is fifty-one, but he obeys me. Men are childish; once they're in love with a girl, they become unbelievably childish. I wish you could be childish for me, Sugar."

"That's your keyboard on the reading table?" he asks.

"Yes, *obviously*," she says, aping his accent.

Together, they amble to the reading table and admire the musical instrument which is, surprisingly, a podium for the great Mozart's albums. A slanted flash of sunlight falls along *For my wife*, *Chioma*, the white words embossed on the instrument's cocoa-coloured side, and turns it to liquid gold. A learned hand wrote this message, he thinks: a hand that is definitely not Chief's, a hand that was hired or implored to work.

"I'm not that chimpanzee's wife," she says, clicks on the keyboard and strikes the eight sounds: do, re, me, fa, so, la, tee, do. "Let me play and sing for you."

He sits on a red plastic chair, crosses his legs and watches her strike the keys and croon Onyeka Onwenu's "You and I."

He wills his eyes to remain dry, emotionless, as the words fill the room: *You and I will live as one...*

"Why do you always sing other people's songs better than yours?" he asks after her short-lived entertainment.

"Not always. I just love Onyeka Onwenu. I love Brenda Fassie. I love Nickie Minaj." She clicks off the keyboard and takes his hands. "But I love you more than the three of them put together. Sugar, you and I will live as one someday."

He takes her into his arms, closes his eyes and, in this surreal universe where he finds himself, white flowers drop like rain from the bluest sky he has ever seen. He opens his eyes and bends his head so that their foreheads touch, their noses touch, but their tremulous lips do not.

From the mango tree whose branches are brushing the closed windows come the songs of birds. The sun, visible through the spaces in the browning leaves of the mango tree, is a burning orange in the sky that blooms red. When the winds shake the branches, the half orange breaks into a million splendid suns through the holes in the leaves. Car honks somewhere. Someone, a girl or a girlish person, giggles.

As if disturbed or jealous of these distractions, she steers him away and takes him back to the bed. A call from Prophet Elijah startles him. He blocks the disturbing man's number, pockets the phone. He will unblock the contact after savouring this glorious moment with Chioma.

"The so-called man of God is obsessed with the English language," he says, and her eyebrows go up in confusion. "I remember you asked me about my siblings Joseph and Josephine? They are fine in their boarding school, obviously."

"Rose says Mrs. Chiamaka admits she wishes she

had two twin sons like your mother. I know you are shocked that she knows about your family. That woman can go any length just to discover the background of any man she wishes to sleep with for a male child. Rose says she is anxiously looking for a student, or a lecturer, who can get her pregnant and give her a male child. I wonder how Rose gets to know everything." She pauses, and edges closer to him. "Touch me, Sugar. Make me happy. My two roommates are students of Political Science and they have gone to class for their lecture. The door is locked."

He gets out of the bed and goes to the windows to close them. Returning with what he fears is an excited smile of a child whose mother has promised chocolates, he sings one of her songs, the only one he truly loves:

Broken boy, broken girl, when will you be happy?

It's afternoon in the town, but where's the sunlight on your window?

Broken boy, broken girl, why can't you hold hands and count the stars?

Chioma does not allow him to finish the music: she pulls him into the bed and kisses his nose and his mouth, her tears trickling down her cheeks, staining his face. He kisses her back, first on her forehead, and then, on her lips. The tastes: cheap cigarettes, cheap sweets. The rise and fall of her chest accelerates as he pulls off her shorts, as he loosens his belt, as he slides into her.

Later, in his own room, he phones her and reminds her that she hasn't told him what his father's joke is about.

"It was a moment of endless pleasure in the mosquito net, Sugar," she says. "With you, it's always wonderful. How my legs stuck out in a V shape and vibrated like a phone. How I clawed and bit and screamed like a demon. How I crawled backwards like an octopus, tearing the innocent mosquito net. Why didn't you laugh then?"

"The only show, which I desired to laugh at, is my daddy's joke. You're being evasive, obviously. Tell me."

"Seriously, Sugar, I wouldn't call it a joke. Rose said he said he will barge into our lecture hall one day and cry and tell your lecturer that you shirk from him on the campus because he doesn't know how to use a semicolon."

There's a small truth in the accusation. "You played really well on the keyboard today, obviously. And you sang well."

"Is the joke a mere joke or a fact? That you dodge Daddy because he cannot use a semicolon?"

"That song you sang is, to me, Onyeka Onwenu's greatest composition. I pray you get to her level. Or eclipse her. What song are you working on at the moment?"

There's a long pause. "Sugar, I'm irreversibly in love with you," she says instead. "Chief just phoned me: he has paid my school fees. He has bought my mother a sports car. He'll marry me, but I will marry you. Will you marry me?"

Before he can comb through her words for a trace of insincerity, before he can relinquish his pride and reply that he will be the happiest man alive if she marries him after graduation, she ends the call.

Mysterious. Did her mother, out of the blue, appear wherever she is, carrying a plank or such a weapon? But her story, her proposal: what does this all mean? And that part about irreversible love: what does it aim to achieve? The poignant song of her heart, or she's simply, experimentally, voicing her piece of music titled "I'm Irreversibly in Love with You"? He can forgive the piece of music if it's actually a piece of music, he can forgive the abrupt end of the call, but he doesn't think he can forgive her for bringing Chief into their conversation to depress him.

Chief pays her school fees and buys her mother beautiful things, but he hasn't even bought them any great thing except Cecelia Watson's *Semicolon: The Past, Present, and Future of a Misunderstood Mark*. When will he have money, big money, so that he can compete with this wealthy Chief?

He moves to the window and looks out. A rich-looking overweight neighbour holds his attention: a black suit, a black cap, a black staff. He's probably a trader in the market or a land agent in the town or a ruthless robber at night. The fat man is opening the gate to escape from the compound because a hen with chicks is at his feet, attacking, sqwarking, flapping.

He closes his eyes and, to his surprise, finds himself imagining one million naira dropping from the chubby man's back pocket.

At sunset the next day, he strolls to a drugstore in his neighbourhood and asks the young woman behind the desk to check his blood pressure. "Someone broke your heart?" she asks after testing him. "Your BP is normal. But, again, did someone break your heart?"

He gazes at her in a trance of revelation and respect, but makes no comment. Slim, tall and light-skinned. Twenty? Twenty-one? "Yes, she's beautiful like you," he says, touching her cheek.

He does nothing but watches as she half-smiles and closes the door with her back heel. He does nothing as she pulls him to herself, nibbles at his neck and strokes his strengthening erection.

Minutes later, after the first and only bout of lovemaking, she says, "My name is Catherine. And you're Nkem, believe me. That's your name, remember? Don't forget your name, please. And don't forget me, too. Will you come to see me tomorrow?"

"Yes," he says, but thinks: No, you're ridiculous, like Oscar Wilde's Gwendolen.

After that day, he blocks her phone line, avoids the road leading to her shop. Each time she glimpses him, she gives him a wounded look or looks away. He feels sympathy for her, but he cannot date someone out of pity.

A week after their encounter, he has sex in his room with another girl also named Catherine, blocks her line as she combs her hair, sees her off in the icy rain, their breaths floating above them. On campus, he avoids her, avoids her cliques, her friends. He knows she has wealthy parents, wealthy suitors. He knows she's more brilliant than Chioma. He knows she's the former Miss English and Literary Studies. But she's not Chioma. She cannot be Chioma. With Chioma, there are things he feels which he cannot feel with Catherine Number Two. Catherine Number One was the worse: he couldn't even come, he hardly got hard. The name Catherine is not the problem, he tells himself. The problem is his love for Chioma, his addiction for Chioma's bad music, Chioma's politics, Chioma's cigarette-smelling mouth. Oh, Chioma, his Chioma. Will another Chioma solve this problem? Will this question, to Chioma, to any thinking person, even make sense? Isn't this question asinine?

At night, after dinner, he surprises himself by telling Ifenna that his love for Chioma is affecting his health.

"Your love for Chioma is affecting your health?"

Ifenna asks, chewing his gum on the foam. "Is she a cigarette? How can love affect one's health? I don't smoke, so the only thing that can affect my health is chewing gum made with excessive sugar. Do you think Banana chewing gum is good for my health? Prescribe your preferred chewing gum for me."

"You have to leave this room. I am sick of your childishness." He sits up on the foam. "When will you get out? Must you stick to me like a lover? Are you?"

"I'm not sure, sweatheart. I need to go to bed with you before discovering if I'm one."

"No. No, you haven't touched me. Humility aside, I'm the cutest guy in this university. My beauty, just like my intellect, is extraordinary. Anybody who sleeps close to me without touching me is either blind or she's a lesbian—or he's a heterosexual folk. You haven't touched me, blessed wine. So you're straight. Go and get a girlfriend. Leave my room." He pauses, for Ifenna has put out his tongue at him. "Sorry. But I want you to leave this room, leave this town. Rose apprised me of some cult guys' plan to murder you if you don't stop being gay."

Ifenna wears white gloves, twerks to the P-Square's 'Danger', a new favourite playing on his smartphone, and titters. "I will forever stick to you, like adamant chewing gum."

"I want to go back to America. I'm sick of this campus. Almost all the lecturers are mad."

"And we students are mad too." Ifenna scrambles out of the foam, pads off to the television and increases the volume.

Professor Eziokwu, the voice of the generation, he thinks. The most respectable lecturer at Heineken University of Education. He's worries that the professor is saying something about the Minister of Education, who will be visiting the university the following day. He worries that the professor's distinct, fearless voice will cause troubles:

Why are we incurably pusillanimous? The barefaced Minister of Education once junketed to this very university without meeting the Vice Chancellor. Imagine! The students should've burnt that maniac's car because he and his fellow fraudulent politicians fly our girls to Europe and America and molest them there. They pay these girls with the money they siphon from the government, money we should be investing in education. I hear he'll infest here tomorrow. I don't want to see that psychopath on our campus, or anywhere near our campus. He's not coming for anything but immorality. We intellectuals should stop being cowards. We shouldn't continue to fold our arms while these maniacs make fun of education…

"Nothing will happen to Professor Eziokwu, obviously," he says, rising and edging closer to the radio. "He's safe?"

"I swear, his party members will slaughter him like a Christmas fowl."

"This is not a military regime, you ignoramus. We're a democratic state. There's freedom of speech."

"But there's no freedom after speech, as we say here. And you know it. I know you like the prof, but stop pretending. Pretense makes you look like a pastor, and I don't like it."

"I heard he's building a hotel in this town. Is it true? The students should burn it down."

"Why? Because he bangs the girls our lecturers want to bang and our poor lecturers bang the girls we want to bang? Darling, don't be jealous. Work hard so that you will be a corrupt politician in the future. Me, I want to rule Nigeria. A lot of things have gone wrong. And if I become the next president of Nigeria, the first very important things I will change are my clothes."

"You'll change your clothes?"

"And yours, sweetheart. And Chioma's, of course. How's she, by the way?"

Nkem looks away, at the TV. Professor Eziokwu's furious voice has not softened:

The problem in this country is not only religiosity, but also tribalism and nepotism. It hasn't died. It'll not die down any time soon, unfortunately. An Igbo man or a Yoruba or even a Hausa man in office would always desire to appoint his brother whether his brother is competent or not. If you ask the denegrate opportunist why, he'll shamelessly say, "In the last administration, it's his people's turn to eat the national cake. That's why the dumb Alhaji Musa was appointed the Minister of Education. That riffraff is apparently ineptitude; I'm sure he cannot write a manageable informal letter, but he's the Minister of Education, Federal Republic of Nigeria. Shame on him. Shame on that stoic robot who appointed him. Shame on any Nigerian who's not ashamed of him.

"I'm not ashamed," Ifenna says, lowering the volume of the TV with a remote control. "I'm rather excited. Darling, I can't wait to see him tomorrow; he'll open his hotel, and drinks will be free. We'll go to drink beer?"

CHAPTER 11

OKOYE straightens his glasses and scans the audience in the hall of the Minister of Education's hotel on the dusty hill. They are surreal, he thinks, this gold-painted hotel, those gold-painted motels—the Paradise, the Angel—and that diamond-studded tree that towers on a neighbouring green hill where his favourite white-walled orphanage home sits under the radiant sun. Beside this orphanage home, which he watches through the open windows, there is a gleaming roof of a Pentecostal church called Poverty Bye-Bye Ministry and there's a tea-coloured river flowing behind it. The tiny figures of the fishermen rowing their boats on the waters make him think, fleetingly, of his late father who's said to be a popular fisherman and carpenter.

On the wall, in this hotel, a red light in a digital font

says "Alif Standard Hotel and Suites", reclaiming his attention. Above it, multicoloured lights dance around a blueish light blinking *Welcome, welcome!* in italics. Below these lights are the audience: pot-bellied politicians, fat-necked senators, eccentric clergymen, state governors, British expatriates, pressmen and presswomen, professors from the university's various departments, top businessmen, hired prostitutes, Heineken University students. The girls among these students swarm all over the place, looking for politicians' pockets with eyes wide open like windows. The boys among these students cluster every entrance, cluster every window, like weed. The pleasant odour of perfume, the unpleasant odour of armpits—they compete in the freezing air.

Beer, he almost says. Where did the ushers pack the beers? He looks from Chiamaka, who talked him into coming here, to Professor Ayodele, who, without being a moron, is listening to the Minister of Education's speech.

"The Almighty Allah knows I'm really, really glad you lecturers lept your pine oppices in order to attend my hotel-ofening farty," the minister says, revealing his kola-stained teeth in an awful smile. "I'm really, really honoured, *wallahi*! And your clothes are surfrisingly pine! Who says lecturers are so foor they hardly eat pood? He or she's a pool, *wallahi*... My feofle, thank you, and welcome!"

Through susurrus of mutterings, through sycophantic applause, through whistles and shattering glasses, he looks back and says to Chiamaka, "These mischievous ushers don't want to give you and me beer? Why don't they want to give us beer? See Professor Okafor, Professor Okereke and that nasty students' patron drinking Heineken beer. Why are they treating us like dustbins? If my beer doesn't come to me in the next five minutes, I will. . ."

"Sssh," she says, her warning finger across her lips. "The Minister of Education expects decorum, yes. No noise, please. Behave very well. Don't disgrace us."

But that muppet is an arsehole, he wants to say, but cannot: Two red-eyed hefty soldiers are strolling by with double-barreled gums, looking for noisemakers, for troublemakers. The reddish tattoos of tigers on their biceps remind him of his son, who has a new tattoo of two horses drinking water at a river drawn on his chest. One of these soldiers glares at his rumpled trousers, another smiles at his dirty shirt, and he looks away. The craving to gulp beer, get drunk and march out has become almost unbearable to him.

Slapping Chiamaka mentally for her rudeness, he rises and leaves to empty his bladder.

But the Convenience Section is, to his surprise, quiet, smelly, and noisy with the buzz of flies. He will endure it. He will not back out because he has to give the Minister of Education his urine. Slowly, carefully, he loosens his tie-belt but does not step into the open lavalatory. This hesitation is not caused by the offensive odour, and not by the noisy flies, but by the approaching figure of a girl called Nneoma. Religious and dull, this girl, but she's the one whose skirts he often takes off with his roaming eyes in the class, the one whose heart his son says he has won. How did that louse do it? And with what?

In this deliciously prolonged silence, he ties his belt, runs his tongue teasingly round his lips like a dog sighting a bone, and the girl hisses and wends towards the ladies' toilet, her lemon skirt billowing at her feet.

What a nice arse, he thinks, and rushes after her. What a glorious nice arse. Oh Lord, what a glorious, decorous, marvelous, superluxirious, nice arse. Unnice flies follow his uncombed hair, buzzing to the rhythm of the savagely loud music his son's girl's curvatious backside is playing in his head.

Inside, he says, in a tone fetid with lust, "Hey, isn't this toilet meant for men, and not... No, don't scream!"

But the girl screams, pulls up her white pantie and her skirt. "Jesus, you followed me to my toilet, Daddy! This is madness!"

"I'm not your daddy, Nneoma, and this toilet is not yours." He locks the door and kneels on the tiled floor. "Let's have a quickie here, my good girl.... I have a condom. Or do you suggest we escape to another hotel?"

"Leave my toilet, Daddy!"

"I'll give you anything you want. I'll even give you an A. One hundred marks, and all the students in the department will give you a standing ovation. It's not easy to make an A in Comparative Economic Policies. I'll give you one hundred marks, not ninety-nine. One hundred. Imagine that. You'll be applauded by all."

"But I'm a virgin, Daddy… Get up, first, please!" She tries to lift him, but his stomach is a full bag of cement. "Your son is my boyfriend, Daddy! He wants to sleep with me, you want to sleep with me, but I'm a virgin. I told Ebuka I want to marry as a virgin so that my husband will respect me."

"Rubbish." He rises, slightly irritated. "Your future husband's probably in a hotel having a threesome with prostitutes. Your private part is not where your worth lies. Think like a feminist and let's enjoy ourselves. I thought you're a feminist. Show me you're a feminist by turning for me. You need it. Stop pretending. Let's do this fast and go back to know if we can drink one or two beers before exiting this despicable hotel."

"No, sex is a sin. In the Book of Exodus…" She hesitates, listens for footsteps, for voices. "Open the door, Daddy. I want to go…I will shout o!"

"Jesus, sorry. I was only kidding."

Back in the hall, he whispers to Chiamaka, "That's a crate of Guinness under the so-called high tablet? It's childish and unfair to deny us beer. . . and food. Take me out of here. Stop doing this to me."

"The minister has not recognised me yet," she whispers back. "Sit down, Okonkwo. I told you I want him to take me out of this bushy university town and fly me to Abuja. Don't destroy this golden opportunity. Sit down, or do you want me to get angry and show the VC and the HOD your pornographic videos and photos?" She smiles and pulls him into his cushioned chair.

A playful threat, he is aware, but he feels something watery and boiling fills his chest, rise to his throat.

Before they came here, she told him the Minister of Education knows his husband's friend and many soldiers in their barracks. He promised to help their wives, help any of their children. But does Chiamaka, this unsightly nonentity, seriously think that the minister can notice her, single her out? How can he, Okoye, get out of this place without provoking her? Bondage: he is living in bondage. He'll probably live in bondage until he retires, or until the videos, and the photos, are stolen from Chiamaka, from Nkem, from Chioma, from Ifenna, from anybody who's in possession of them. Who can steal all these videos and photos from these enemies? This blackmail is sapping him, drowning him, and he cannot swim.

At the end of the party, he takes her aside and says, "I hardly sleep these days, Amaka."

He says, "Some of my students want me disgraced and thrown out."

He says, "Tell me the truth, Amaka: Have you burnt those photos and videos? All of them?"

And she says, "I don't know, Okonkwo. Okoye."

It tears at his heart, this unfeeling comment. He waits a few heartbreaks before pouring questions on her: How long does she want him to beg her before she can help him? Can't she kindly take him to her office and burn the photos and the video? When will she burn them and bring the ashes to him? Does she enjoy seeing him distressed?

"I'll set fire to them when I get home, yes," she says. "I will persuade Chioma to burn hers, too. Hers are the last ones. I will only do this because you've really toiled for me. But you'll keep toiling until. . . Would you stick to me until I gave birth to a male child, Okonkwo?"

"If you mean will I continue having sex with you until you're delivered of a baby boy, the answer is an emphatic yes."

At the Car Park, they see Rose wear sunglasses and put gum into her mouth, see Rose sneak into the minister's Murano jeep, see Rose kiss the minister's forehead or nose. Is the man's mouth odour that bad? He, Okoye, would like to burn that mouth, burn the owner of that smelly mouth, burn the moving car tyres, burn the car's gleaming blackness, burn its unabashedly open window from which Rose, his departing rose flower, waves and waves, and then puts out her tongue at him and laughs.

He'd like to burn her, too, and all the "honourable" men in the car. But Chiamaka finds it hilarious: the laugh that pops out of her mouth is that of a hyena. He ignores her, and continues staring at the vehicle that is carrying his girlfriend away. A tinted glass rises, concealing his departing Rose, and he feels his neck tighten into a knot.

"A Minister of Education is going to sleep with an eighteen-year-old girl," he says. "No wonder the world is laughing at us."

In his car, she says, "The minister noticed me, but pretended. I used to cook for that goat. I was his best cook. Do you think he noticed me?"

His throbbing forehead is bowed to the steering wheel. "Rose is a toilet," he says instead. "She's men's public toilet."

"You're taking me back to my flat, Okonkwo."

He lifts his head, turns the key in the ignition: the car farts, shudders and roars to life. "Your flat?" he asks. "But there's a little fuel in my car."

"You'll not take me to my flat?"

"The roads leading to your house have dangerous potholes and there's no fuel, you see."

"So you're refusing to take me to my flat?"

"No fuel, little engine oil. Deplorable roads. And the car tires are leaking."

"For the love of God, are you taking me to my flat or not, Okonkwo?"

"Yes, yes, Amaka. I'm taking you to your flat."

The flat is, as he expected, hilariously untidy. He tries to smile at the tea-coloured carpet with razor cuts presumably performed by a food-deprived rioting member of the family. The sofas are a playground of a hundred moths. The leaf-coloured curtains are torn and stained with palm oil. The tablecloths, which are collecting dust on old-fashioned stools, are shaped like aged turtles.

He looks up at the wall and finds the clock is broken and its hour hand is missing. The photographs are covered with cobwebs except one on which a stone-faced man captioned *Major Johnnie Nnaemeka* is smoking a cucumber-sized cigar, grinning, nursing his AK-47 with a shriveled hand.

"Where are your daughters?" he asks. "Do they look like Major Nnaemeka, your handsome husband, or like you?"

"Can we discuss anything but ourselves?" she says in undisguised annoyance. "I don't know why you enjoy reminding me of my husband. I know I've a husband or something like that, but don't mention him in my presence again. If you don't want to talk about ourselves, you can sod off. You're the one to lose, after all."

He mumbles the word *sorry*, and his gaze drops.

At his feet is a cat with orange stripes. The curled cat frightens him, but he doesn't scream. "I love your pretty animal," he says with a stimulated smile, wishing the filthy pet an untimely death. "A very pretty cat."

She chases it into her bedroom, returns with a bottle of Gulder beer. "Do you want this?"

"Do I want the beer? Yes, of course. Everybody knows I like beer."

He hands it to him, sits beside him like a lovely wife. Her heavy perfume fills his nostrils.

Oh God, he thinks. God Almighty. This woman had to perfume her armpits for me? How long has she been perfuming her armpits for him? Has she perfumed her armpits for lecturers like Professor Ayodele? What about her handsome students? Has she perfumed her armpits for Nkem?

She scratches the armpits before she speaks. "Of course everybody knows you like beer. You love beer the way my husband loves vodka, yes. We were madly in love, my husband and I, but I'm not sure now. In fact, he hates me. He's mad at me because all our children are girls. I love my girls, mind you, but I will gladly exchange all of them for a male child."

He gulps his beer. "Any male child? Even a one-eyed bearded baby boy with a tail?"

"Are you deriding my preference?" She nudges him, spilling his drink. "You're reducing my problem to a joke, yes? You're deliberately annoying me, Okonkwo?"

"No, Jesus!" He empties his bottle and lowers it to the ground. "I'm so sorry. Jesus, I didn't want to provoke you. Why would I want to provoke my colleague who's incredibly kind to me? If you were selfish and malign, you'd have run to the Vice Chancellor's office with the videos and the photos. But you're an immeasurably good woman. So why would I set out to annoy my best friend?"

"You're not handsome, Okonkwo, but I think I'm getting fond of you. Do you like me? Do you find me attractive?"

He cannot afford to be sincere. "Well, nobody's really ugly," he says, scratching his baldness. "Beauty, they say, is in the eyes of the beholder. To some men, you're a queen. To other men, you are. . . a king. I mean, you're a. . . I don't think you're ugly, that's what I mean."

"Thanks for your kind lies." She leans back and stares at the ceiling. "My husband and his people threatened to throw me out of this window if I don't produce a male child before Christmas. I was pregnant seven months ago, yes, but Nnaemeka forced me to abort the foetus because it was a girl again. He does that each time it turns out I'm carrying a baby girl. I didn't plan to tell you this, but I couldn't help it. God hates me, Okonkwo! He hates me!"

"Don't cry, my dear." He goes to the fridge and

returns with a cold bottle of Star beer. "I'll phone that soldier and tell him why a female child is as good as a male child."

"Call him? Oh, don't be funny, Okonkwo!" She sits up and strolls to the window. "Don't laugh if I tell you that in one of my melodramatic moments, I think of ringing up one of those chaps in our department to come and get me pregnant. I'm always ready to pay them, yes. I can do anything just to have a boy in my womb. This problem is driving me crazy. My life is messed up."

He sips his beer. "No, you're lucky! God blessed you with six girls."

She turns to face him. "Something tells me you can give me a male child if we sleep together again, Okonkwo. But maybe you're no longer interested because my breasts are not firm like Rose's and you're not enjoying me. I'm telling the truth. Am I not telling the truth?"

He lets the question float in the glacial air between them.

"My son is coming!" she says, pulling at the curtain and tearing it, as if it were the demon withholding her male children. "Come and see my son, Okonkwo! He's coming! It's a bouncing baby boy! Jesus reigns! He answers prayers! Come, Okonkwo! Dance round that table, sing hallelujah!"

The bottle in his tremulous hand drops, shatters on

the floor. Is Chiamaka pretending to be mad to probe the genuineness of his affection for her? Or, perhaps, she's truly going off her head? Whatever it is, he cannot stay here to witness it.

He takes his car key from the sofa and races to the door, his shoes crushing dropped pens, crushing dropped carrots. Remembering his unfinished beer, he hurries back, finishes it in one gulp and slips out of the house.

CHAPTER 12

IFENNA is studious tonight; he's in Economics Department, revising a stolen textbook and a stolen handout because three of his lecturers will administer quizzes the following day. This day, this night, most students seem mysteriously unserious. He lifts his head, gazes at the Economics students in the classroom who are nattering or snoring, idling or flirting. He tells himself they know their lecturers intimately, these unstudious students. They know the lecturers will help them. These helps consistently go to the pretty ones, the dangerous ones, not to him, not to Nkem. He knows Nkem is not here, but he's sure Nkem's studying his books wherever he is.

The door opens with a sigh: gushing winds, as he watches with tired eyes, chase waterproof and bits of paper into the classroom, chase noisy Chioma and noisier Rose in. He cannot guess the subject of their heated argument, but he wagers that it must have something to do with hairstyles.

"It's funny that you two come to read your books," he says with feigned levity, and sipped his whiskey. "It's mighty funny."

"Professor Eziokwu and Mr. Chijindu doesn't take bribe," Rose says in a mournful tone. "They're foolish. Look at the old cars they drives. Why can't they sell As and Bs to us and makes money like the nice men like Mr. Okoye? A customer whose hair I always plait telled me their bedsheets is old."

"Professor Eziokwu's bedsheet and Mr. Chijindu's are old?" Chioma asks, toying with her cigarette lighter. "You speak as if you've been to their bedrooms?"

"She said her customer *telled* her," he intervenes. "So, Rose, how is the Minister of Education? I heard he paid you in dollars."

The two girls spread their handkerchiefs on the mahogany bench and perch. A bespectacled boy seated behind them raises his orange-painted head, studies them with contemptuous eyes.

"The minister's horrible," Rose says. "After drinking and talking dirty, I ask him to open an enviable hair saloon for me and punish one or two of my lecturers for me, but he want to undress and suck me first. But I don't want to sleep with him and he get mad and begin to tear my pantie and bra. He force his wrinkled body on me. I pick his half-finished bottle of champagne from the bed and bursted it on his shoulder and runned away without my pantie and my bra. . . And my shoes. I'd have breaked his little head, but I'm afraid he'll die."

"Where's Nkem?" Chioma asks, and scans the classroom.

Her earrings, Rose's earrings: four glinting beauties in the brightly lit classroom. The delicious perfume on one of them reminds him of fresh apples, of glorious Paris. Paris: a city he relishes drawing, painting, eulogizing. He wants to say: Which of you girls are wearing this expensive perfume? He wants to say: The Minister of Education bought perfume for you, Rose, and this intimidating iPhone on your palm? But he does not say these.

"Why didn't the Minister of Education pick you?" he asks Chioma. "Are you not sexier than Rose?"

"Shut up," Rose says. "I'm prettier, because I'm light-skinned. I'm gold-haired, and my arse is curvy. How many professors has touch Chioma's arse in their offices? Do you know how many professors who has touch my arse and press my breasts? If I'm not a very fine girl, why are they pressing my breasts anyhow? Please don't compare me with any girl on this campus. I don't like it."

Three girls who are seated in front—one tall, one short, one average and pregnant — turn to glare at them. He rises, takes them to an empty row of chairs where no one can hear them. "We've to count the professors who have sucked you girls' breasts in order to decide whether one pair of breasts is better than the other pair." He closes all his books and pops gum into his mouth. "How many professors have pressed your breasts, Rose? And you, Chioma. How many professors have pressed your breasts? I know you're a feminist, Chioma, but we *need* to count. This very controversial debate must be settled once and for all."

Chioma's eyes redden; she unzips her handbag and peers into it. Her hunting knife, is that what she's searching for? Fear grips him.

"Only Okoye and maybe Professor Isiokpo press Chioma's breasts last semester," Rose says. "Me, the lecturers is up to twenty. Or thirty. Even the great Reverend Father Titus Mbah has touch me. He press my breasts this early morning. He's not my boyfriend, honestly. He's my roommate's boyfriend. I go to submit my term paper in his office and he closed his big bible on sighting my impressive boobs. He say it's unfair that he haven't seen any of my nipples, and I laugh and throwed a blob of chewing gum on his holy head. He laugh too and come to hold my waist. I bites his hand and he say he'll not accept my book and I'll fail. I have to let him raise my shirt and bra and play with my nipples. Immediately someone knock at his door, we both starts saying the Angelus. Later, he phone me and say I have the finest nipples in this university, and I don't think a Reverend Father can lie."

Chioma abandons her search and touches Rose's shoulder. "I feel like knifing every woman who encourages men to objectify women," she says. "You've to stop competing for the attention of men. Physical beauty is not a trophy every woman should strive to acquire. It's not bad if some of us wear asexual clothes to discourage all these lustful he-goats from objectifying us like sex toys."

"You're advising we girls to looks ugly?" Rose asks, her cheeks turning tomato-red, as though she's has been slapped. "So I will stop plaiting my hair and my customers'? Me, I feels like knifing you. I feels like knifing every woman who do not looks beautiful for our men. I hates ugly women."

He blows his gum and titters.

Women, he thinks. Women: the greatest enemies of women. It's on his lips to speak this sentiment, to let it fly, but the door is flung open.

Three tall, muscular boys in black appear with axes and machetes in their hands. Also in their hands, in their rope, is Nkem; they carry him into the classroom, drop him to the floor. The lights, except for one energy bulb, go off. Something crashes to the floor, a glass shatters somewhere. Everybody screams. Through the windows, through the back doors, the students escape without their books.

"You be Ifenna, abi?" says the tallest of the boys.

He's too scared to respond. Behind him, behind the assailants, Nkem slumps. Nkem's nose and eyes, he notices with a shudder, are coated with blood. On his white polo, HOMO is scribbled with blood. GAY is scribbled on his brown chinos, with blood. Blood is on his hands.

"Lie down like agama lizard," the tallest boy thunders, and pulls out a gun. "You…yes, you the homo! Here no be America! Here no be Europe! This is Africa: we no be faggot! Why you go leave sweet pussy come dey fuck yansh? Evil spirit dey your head, abi? I say, Lie down like agama lizard!"

The boy is rebuking only him, commanding only him, but Rose, promptly, humbly, joins him on the floor. Her eyes, he notices, are lustrous with trepidation. Her arms are shaking violently, uncontrollably. But Chioma is, unbelievably, unafraid. She stands with her arms folded across her breasts, gazing at the unknown assailants with daggers in her eyes. From the chilly air comes the stench of Chelsea dry gin, marijuana, cigarettes.

"Don't kill us!" he begs, his forehead on the sandy floor. "Please don't take our lives…take our money, take our books, take everything but our lives. Rape us...I mean, rape Chioma or Rose, but don't kill us! Please! Chioma, allow them to rape you... Rose! Rose, please allow them to rape you!"

"This guy abi girl na confam homo," a deep voice says. "See how 'im mouth dey run like woman's!"

They snatch his smartphone and Nkem's, they snatch Rose's expensive iPad; but Chioma refuses to relinquish hers. So they call her a bitch, slap her face, push her into a wastepaper basket. And rushing back to him, they demand he close both his eyes. But he closes one, his left eye. His right eye sees Chioma struggle out of the wastepaper basket, sees her escape through a busted window. Rose's sudden cry seizes his attention, seizes their attention. Her urine, he finds, has soaked her mini-skirt, soaked the sand on the floor. The boys laugh with a demonic glee, and fear makes him close his other eye.

Both eyes remain closed as they kick his head, stamp their feet on his hands, spit on him, interrogate his ears: Why did he choose to screw men's arses? Why did he choose to let men screw his arse? Does his bottom drip with water, with blood, or with shit? Does he wear napkins or Pampers? How long has he been possessed with this white people's evil spirit? But he does not answer, he cannot answer: from his mouth, from his nose, blood gushes, like a fountain. Darkness descends on him.

The following day, he wakes in a spring bed in the University Medical Centre that smells of antiseptic. Next to his bed is Nkem's, rusty and creaking. A hawk-faced nurse in her mid-forties stands watching them. The fluorescent light above glints in dabs of light of sweat at the corners of her inquisitive eyes. "The students say the cultists assailed you because you initiated Nkem into homosexuality," the nurse tells him in lyrical Igbo. The word *homosexual*, however, is in English. They stare at her without saying a word, but she continues. "Dear bad youths, why is your generation learning bad things from white people? But you can't learn science and technology from them? *Tufiakwa*!" She pauses, retches theatrically and shakes her head. "Those cult boys are heartless. They raped a girl called Rose. But are the two of you homosexuals?"

"Yes, obviously," Nkem replies, anger wrinkling his face. "Where's Chioma? And my parents? My parents are not aware, I hope?"

So they raped Rose, he thinks. Of course they would. But did they use contraceptives?

He shifts his gaze to the nurse, and finds her eyes are popping out because Nkem said they're gay. The popping eyes amuse him, but he hides his smiles on the Dettol-smelling pillows. Everything here smells of Dettol: the bedclothes, the buckets, the sea-blue curtains, the hand towels, the bandages on their noses, their mouths, their hands. "Chioma was here most nights, but your parents weren't," she says, shaking her head. "Maybe they don't know. Chioma paid, you know? Is she your girlfriend, Semicolon? She calls you Semicolon. Do gays have girlfriends? You're gay?"

Nkem nods, pulls his blanket up to his chin. Abomination, she probably says in her mind. Abomination. The world has come to an end. God should send the angels to blow the trumpet for Rapture. Let God blow a whistle if there is no ready trumpet.

He hisses as the nurse retreats with her drugs, shaking her head, wagging her fingers.

"Your friend says you two are homo," she says the morning they're expected to be discharged. "I think he's right. Look at your nose ring. And your pockets, which are filled with chewing gum. Remember, God destroyed Sodom and Gomorrah because…"

"Thank you, blessed wine," Nkem says, interrupting her, rising from the creaking spring bed. "We've to leave."

Back home, under the patter of rain on the roof, they moan and groan into their pillows. Impossible: that's the heavy word in his head. Impossible for Nkem to bribe lecturers for a fake make-up quiz, for unmerited marks; impossible for them to pass their examinations: they've missed all their quizzes, missed all their lectures. Impossible for them to recover the things that are lost: their phones, their time, their pride. But is he going to stop chewing gum, stop buying powder for his face, stop wearing nose rings? Not feasible. He's not even going to get any girlfriend to prove to the unknown ruffians that he's not possessed by an evil spirit. He's not going to prove anything to anybody. Let them all go to hell.

CHAPTER 13

NKEM examines his face in the cracked mirror nailed to the wall. Healed, clean, and dazzling like Oscar Wilde poetry: this is the look he has been waiting to see. Now he's waiting to forget it's been three weeks since they were attacked, forget it ever happened. He's waiting for Ifenna to see the note on his ink-stained hand, and watch him glue it on the reading table. Waiting for Ifenna to read it after he has gone for his morning lectures, waiting for a change in the boy, waiting for peace in the town.

Blessed wine:

I don't think we can continue being roommates. Not because you once betrayed me by giving my Chioma to Dr. Okoye for bread, Cabin biscuits and an A. Not because you're not a serious student like me. Not because you're not intellectually enriching like me. Not because you eat foreign rice and do not know how to use a semicolon. But because your Oscar Wilde appearance and mannerisms will continue to attract enemies to me. The other day, you wore a pink skirt and high-heeled shoes to Mr. Heineken University's birthday party off campus. Nothing wrong with being you, but can you afford this risk? Can we afford this risk?

I wish you good luck in getting the fuck out of MY bedroom.

Nkem the Great.

PS: This, obviously, is in writing not because I'm afraid of shouting the truth into your powdered face. It's because I don't think I can stand your girlish tears.

The sound of water running in the bathroom where Ifenna is showering brings him to the door. "What are you doing, blessed wine?" he asks, peeping through the keyhole but seeing nothing. "Still bathing?"

"No, darling," Ifenna's voice replies. "I'm masturbating. But this soap… God, I should've bought Joy soap. Lux soap, this Lux soap, is not the best for masturbation. Kindly give me another three minutes. By God's grace, I will eventually reach orgasm."

"I will not give you three minutes. I will give you nothing but three sex-starved girls." His towel slips from his trembling hand, but he makes no attempt to pick it from the wet floor because he's irritated. He knows his tone is hostile and knows that Ifenna knows. Because Ifenna remains silent, he goes to the reading table, takes the note, reads it out in his hearing, and pockets the paper.

"Hope you used some nice semicolons in that *letter?*" Ifenna asks.

He leaves the flippant question in the air and turns to leave.

But the door is locked. The key, where is it? In the bathroom? Forcefully, awkawardly, he pulls the door open and, for the first time as an undergraduate, leaves without taking a bath.

The lecture hall, when he reaches the building, proves to be locked. Why is it locked? Who locked it? Lecturers, dispersing students say. Lecturers: the ones who are aggrieved. The reasons for their grievances, the students say, are clearly these: Lecturers have not been paid for four months after the ASUU strike. Lecturers' cars are stolen every day by current students, by ex-students, by expelled students, by some non-academic staff members, by the villagers. Lecturers' quarters have no electric light, no clean water, for weeks. Lecturers are murdered every day by cultists, by failed students, by jealous boyfriends, by jealous girlfriends. Lecturers' girlfriends migrate to the Minister of Education's new hotel to brush their teeth with his penis.

Christ, he thinks, and turns to the blinding sun.

On the Campus Road, his new phone rings, startling him with its loud ringtone, Idris Abdulkareem's "Mr. Lecturer."

He takes the call. "Who's this? —Good morning."

"You deleted my number? Why did you delete my phone number?"

A deep voice of a disgruntled woman: Who is she? The students' patron? One of the security women? Chioma's mother? Chioma's untalented musical friends? Mrs. Chiamaka? Yes: it must be Mrs. Chiamaka. "I was attacked, obviously," he says. "And my phone was stolen. I lost all the contacts. . . Mrs. Chiamaka?"

"Yes, blessed wine," she says, and giggles. "I'm sorry about the attack. I suspect Okonkwo...Okoye, sorry. I suspect that fat pig. He had the guts to tell me that if you, Chioma or Ifenna leaks any of his sex videos and photos, he will make sure the two of you are booted out of this university. We need to keep the videos and the photos out of his reach until we get what we want. That man's a very bad pig. I'm sure he was the devil who sent those boys to brutalise you, to kill you. He wants all the people who have those videos and photos to be destroyed by all means."

Liar, he thinks. You're telling lies, you bloody liar. You have an ulterior motive. But what is this ulterior motive? What does this vegetable-obsessed trollop want from him?

"I cooked *moi-moi*," she continues. "And I still have beer in the fridge, yes. You can come over."

"Madam, I'm a very busy guy, obviously. I'm at the moment studying the early lives of Oscar Wilde's grandparents in Ireland. And Chinese Economy. It was interesting, the economic reform of Deng Xiaoping in China in 1978, during the Boluan Fanzheng period."

"Yes, he tried. But please come over. Let's discuss China and . . . and . . . What's his name again?"

"Deng Xiaoping."

"Come. I've fried plantains and fish, yes."

"The economic reforms, unfortuanately, stagnated after the crackdown in 1989 Tiananmen Square protests."

"Oh God, that's sad, that's so sad. But, Semicolon, do you like plantains and fish? I'm eating fish now."

"But after Deng Xiaoping's Southern Tour in 1992, the reforms were revived."

"Really? Wow, the nice fish tried. . .I mean the nice man tried."

"Eight years after, in 2010, China overtook Japan as the world's second-largest economy. Do you agree that the leadership of CCP General Secretary Xi Jinping, who frowns upon the restructurings, ended this reform era?"

"Yes, yes, and I like his recent book, which is his *magnus*. . .*maganus*. . . *magazine open*. And talking about magazines, I want to rush off to the market to buy yams. Do you like fried yams?"

"It's *magnum opus*, blessed wine. But which book?"

"The magazine? Maybe it has run of of prints or. . ." Her voice trails off. Something crashes to the ground over there. A ceramic plate containing fruits? A tomato-filled tray? A glass of wine? Is she drinking wine for him? Is she drunk?

Turning to say hi to a rough-voiced person hailing him the Perambulating Semicolon, he hears Chiamaka say, "I'm only inviting you to my life because I enjoy your company, yes. I want you to come. There are ripe bananas in my bedroom."

The rough voice belongs to a one-eared boy in his class whose name he always forgets, who says that men who read novels are lazy idiots. He ignores the boy. "You'll give me bananas in your *bedroom*?" he speaks into the phone. "But I'm not a monkey, obviously."

"I eat bananas, yes. Does that make me a monkey? It appears Ifenna has infected you with his irksome playfulness. Be serious. Stupidity doesn't look good on you. You're a smart boy who knows about great economists' maga. . . magazines, maga-something, whatever, and I believe you'll be greater than Adam Sniff or even Afraid Marshall. I wish you well because I like you. I love you, and I want you."

"But you're married."

"No. Yes. . .no. I mean yes. Yes, I'm married, but a little bit. I'm a little bit married. In other words, my husband is not in this town. He'll not find you, yes. He shouldn't be the reason why we shouldn't be... Do you understand?"

"I'm a homosexual, Mrs. Chiamaka, remember?" He shifts the phone to the other ear, bites his lips. "Ifenna and I, obviously. That's why we were attacked. Remember?"

There is a long pause. "I'm shocked and disappointed that a child of God like you'd prefer to go to bed with his fellow men. That's a sin. That's an abomination. Have you forgotten that God destroyed Sodom and Gomorrah because of homosexuality?"

"Mrs. Chiamaka, you're married and you're courting me. Adultery is a sin in the Bible, obviously."

The call disconnects.

Splendid, he thinks. Splendid: Now my ears can rest, my mouth too. Now my heart can slow down, settle down. I'm breathing, for my head is above this water. But how long can my head be above this water?

Off campus, at the muddy market, he quarrels with traders selling imported commodities like rice, oil and noodles, shouting that they are stabbing Nigeria's economy in the chest, shouting that they are watering other countries' economies like flowers and crippling Africa.

With a tattoo of slaps on his face (his face again!), he leaves the market without finding any Nigerian butter for his Nigerian bread, trudges homeward to see if he can take a siesta. *I can't sleep in this state and in this world,* he sings Chioma's song as he nears his Else-Shall-Die hostel. *My love's using my heart as a toilet and I can't sleep in this state and in this world…*

But lying on his foam and rereading Kingsley Amis' *The Old Devils*, he catches himself dropping off to sleep. The novel is saturated with alcohol and not at all boring, but he'll close the thing and nap. He needs to doze and forget both the fictional and the real worlds, but his phone rings and it's Chioma. "Come to our house, Sugar," she says. "Not to my hostel: our family house. Rose says she hears the cultists will attack you this evening. I don't want you to be attacked again."

"Hope your parents are home: I want to beg them to let you leave Chief."

There's a long pause. "Come, Sugar."

The door to their flat is locked when he arrives. There's a photograph of a gap-toothed white girl, or a bleached African girl, advertising "a skin lightening soap made in India." What happened to soaps made in Nigeria? he thinks. Why are they watering the Indian economy at the expense of the Nigerian economy? He knocks on the girl's left eye in a muddle of annoyance and shame, speaks his name, and waits.

"Chioma, it must be Chief," he hears Chioma's mother's voice within. "Nobody knocks so violently on our door like a wicked landlord. Now, run into you're the bedroom and wears your mini-skirt!"

"Mum, are you sure it's Chief? I think it's my…"

"Run into the bedroom fast! And you, Ogechi, go and hide somewhere: you're dirty. Run! But, God, you're foolish, Chioma! Why didn't you tell me Chief is coming today? Don't answer: run! Mary, remove all these bottles of beer your pathetic father emptied into that tireless stomach of his!"

The sounds of hurrying feet frighten him. "It's not Chief," he says.

"I'm coming, Chief… Oge, I said, Hide in the bedroom or toilet! Chioma, wear your sweetest perfume. And let your top be transparent because those breasts will play a very important role."

So Chioma's breasts now play roles? What kind of woman is this? He imagines her unhooking Chioma's bra to show a frog-eyed Chief those pointy bossoms. He sees Chief enfolding Chioma's mother in gratitude and shedding tears of joys. The vision, painfully pellucid and real, makes him ache to horse-kick the door, but the knob turns and it creaks open. "Who's this thing?" Chioma's mother asks, stepping backwards and crinkling her face as though she has seen a bespectacled goat at her door. "What are you and how may I help you?"

"I'm here to help *you*," he says. "I want to protect your family from evil men."

She arches her eyebrows in disbelief, but keeps her lips sealed. Perhaps she's contemplating where to hit him with one of her many boots.

She's the coach of the town's women's football team who always wears a jersey to announce her rare talent, but today she's dressed in a blue gown bearing the head of a white woman titled Mary Sumner. Chioma appears behind her mother with eyes blinking rapidly with trepidation, gesturing him to go, putting a shaky finger across her lips for him to conceal his identity.

But he cannot let Chief win. "My name is Nkemdilim Obi, blessed wine. Your daughter's friend, obviously. I'm delighted to meet you."

"I'm *not* delighted to meet you," Chioma's mother says. "And if you don't take your broke arse out of my house, I will unleash my dogs."

Chioma mouths, *Go, Sugar. Go, please!*

But he will not go. He will not go until he destroys Chief's reputation with the information Rose gave him few days ago. "Are you aware that Chief is a ritualist?" he asks Chioma's mother. "Everybody says he throws stolen newborn babies to his crocodile. It's a sacrifice that helps him in his shirts and shoes importation business. How can you allow your daughter to marry a ritualist and importer of shoes? Nigerians make shoes in Aba, but idiots like Chief are bent on destroying Nigeria's economy."

She pounds his chest with her fist. "You come to my house to lecture me? You come to my house to accuse my son-in-love of blood money? You come to my house to insult my daughter's husband? How dare you?"

With a surprisingly steady hand, he takes off his Harry Potter glasses, cleans the lens with his white handkerchief. Again she pounds his chest, tears his shirt and shouts for her dogs or daughters. Her dogs bark. Her daughters rush to the door, but he has already turned for departure.

Waiting for him on his new foam is Rose. "Welcome, my Semicolon," she says, rising to hug him.

"No, no...!" he says, brushing off her hands. "Who opened the door for you? Ifenna is still bathing?"

"He leaved here a few minutes ago. He say he's going to find a girlfriend. He say he will find a girl before 12: 00 a.m. I advise him to go to the library. That's where boys finds girlfriends now. And girls finds boyfriends. Rose find you. . . finded? She finded you there in our first year, right?"

He wants to ask her to go, but his phone beeps with a WhatsApp message from Chioma:

Sugar, am so sorry. Mummy thinks am a product to be sold to men for money. I will talk to her. Don't worry. Remember you and I will live as one?

Balderdash, he thinks. You and a ritualist will live as one! You and your ridiculous mother will live as one. He drops his phone and his books on the reading table, perches on the chair. "What do you want from me, Rose?" he asks. "I heard they raped you."

"Yes, they rapes me." She pauses, gazes at the ground

in a preoccupied way. "They rapes me, but I have abort it. Emeka say I'm lucky to be alive today."

"Emeka?"

"The handsome drug-man who remove it. . .Thank God I doesn't die. Don't die...doesn't...don't doesn't." She pauses, frowns at the fuddled verbs locked in her throat and continues in fluent Igbo. "But, oh my God, Emeka is handsome! He's so handsome. I almost kissed his curly beard, *maka Chukwu*! But you're more handsome than him." She returns to the foam, her legs slightly open. "Let's be lovers, Nkem. Chioma is almost married, so let's get sweaty."

The door creaks open, welcoming whistling winds and the dazzling sunlight that bronzes her startled face. Welcoming Ifenna, the Umbrella Boy of his life. The Umbrella Boy comes with a strange umbrella that's short and crooked and yellow like a ripe banana, a strange odour of rum, a strange girl in a sand-coloured T-shirt that says *Praise Me, Please!* Thick-lipped, long-necked, short-legged. How old is this caricaturish teen? Seventeen? Eighteen?

"This is my...my...a girlfriend," Ifenna slurs, staggering forward with the girl. "A girlfriend. She's a first-year student of English, though she cannot recognise a subordinate clause, a noun phrase, prepositions, and such grammatical nonsense because she's not intelligent at all. Of course I know she's dumb and too ugly for me, but I like her because...because she likes herself. I met her fifteen minutes ago near the library dustbin. We talked about dustbins and other interesting things and started dating immediately. We have dated for nine minutes...almost." Ifenna brushes a crawling insect from the "girlfriend's" unkempt hair, inserts chewing gum into her mouth. "Darling, meet Nkem, my Semicolon. Semicolon, meet...meet... Jesus Christ, I haven't even asked her what her name is! Please who are you?"

The "girlfriend" looks from Ifenna to the door with frightened eyes as though she's desirous to escape. "I'm...I'm...I'm Adaku Nwaku," she stammers.

Bush dialect, he thinks. Where did Ifenna, this drunk Ifenna, pick this semi-imbecile? Why is he, a boy, carrying an umbrella when it's not raining? To protect his skin and powdered face against the sun? He shakes his head, opens an anthology of African poetry to puncture conversation. But Ifenna snatches the book, asks him to rate Adaku as though she were a mannequin recently purchased. The girl covers Ifenna's mouth, which is busy with chewing gum, and titters.

"An English and Literary Studies student?" he asks Adaku. "Enchanting, enchanting. Is Oscar Wilde in your life? His poetry is magnificent, but I can kill any critic who criticizes his plays, or his only novel, *The Picture of Dorian Gray*. Your boyfriend, Ifenna, is like the narcissistic Dorian Gray, obviously. One can imagine that Ifenna will kill himself if he isn't smooth-skinned and sexy at eighty. The first day wrinkles will appear on his face, he might kill himself."

Ifenna acquiesces with a quick nod, a broad smile. "I don't rike novels," Adaku tells him. Then, to Rose, in English: "Good afternoon, pletty girl...solly, hi first. I mean herro, not hi. Hi? No, it's herro!"

"I knows. . . know you," Rose says, smoothing a pillow. "You're the girl Kalu use and dump? And Kelechi use and dump. And Kabiru use and dump. And his brother Mohammed, too? Franklin, the guy in Physics Department, also use and dump you?"

"Yes," Adaku says. "And his fliend, Flankrin. They all bloke my heart."

Rose's gaze shifts to Ifenna. "You're lucky o! One: You will start eating vegetables because Adaku cook vegetables for all her twenty or thirty ex-boyfriends. Two: Her parents has money. Three: People will stop calling you homo. Four: you will have sex for the first time. Congratulations!"

Ifenna faces Adaku. "I swear, I never wanted any girlfriend, especially in the sun. Girlfriends always demand money from us boys and what do they shamelessly say they offer in return? Sex. As if they, too, don't enjoy sex. Don't you think that plywood is more useful than a girlfriend? Plywood can be used to construct furniture. Plywood can be used as firewood.

226

Plywood can also be used as a weapon in self-defence against thugs. But girls only take, take, take. But you look different; you look like a giver. You'll be as useful as plywood, Adaku. Or more. You smell money."

You smell money. A conciliatory compliment, but Adaku coughs and closes her eyes as if the words were cigarette smoke curling into her face. Then, like a child who's miraculously stepped out of a burning house unscathed, she spreads her arms with a triumphant joy, wraps her arms around Ifenna. Despite Ifenna's warning glare, despite the finger across his lips, despite his furtive winks, Rose still gives a yelp of laughter.

"But, Ifenna, never hurt or exploit the heart that sings of you." He gathers his books, shakes hands with the delighted couple. "Today's a historical day in your lives, particularly Ifenna's. Rose and 1 will allow you both to have a nice time." He snaps his fingers at Rose as if she were his dog. "Let's go on a walk, blessed wine."

Rose stifles another laughter, rises from the foam, and follows him.

CHAPTER 14

OKOYE pulls his car door open and a cockroach flies off, almost getting into his beer-filled mouth. He swallows the alcohol, drops the emptied Star beer can to the browning grass and, with unaccustomed meticulousness, puts the key into his briefcase since the pockets of his grimy trousers have holes. From behind him, he hears a phlegmy cough, hears heavy approaching steps. Are these confident footsteps not the footsteps of one of the breathing problems in his life?

He makes three guesses: Chioma, the fearless one? Nkem, the studious one, the upright one? Rose, the nomadic, the dramatic? Making a mental sign of the cross as if he were a Catholic, he turns to find Chiamaka marching toward him with the confidence and sturdiness of a Major General. This morning, she's wearing a long gown that conceals her undesirable large feet. Her brows are penciled and her beard shaved. Her body, which consistently smells unkindly of farm produce like tomatoes and pepper, fills his nostrils with the smell of a discreet perfume.

Mrs. Chiamaka's still unpresentable, he tells himself. This attempt to minimise her hilarious ugliness is a welcome development. But does this desperate shot at prettiness mean she's trying to make herself attractive to *him*? He imagines them sharing a flat, sharing a foam, sharing food, fruits, water. The vision actuates his nose to widen like two toy funnels, but he's able to stop himself from throwing up.

"Where are you running to, Okonkwo?" Chiamaka asks without greeting him.

What a question! Everybody from the Department of Economics knows he habitually drives to a pub at ten every morning to drink his breakfast beer. Everybody knows this and everybody says this. Everybody will undoubtedly wonder why this woman is asking him where he's going to. Why on earth is this woman asking him where he's going?

"Good morning," he says, his eyes following Ifenna who's passing by with a girl. They seem to be in love: his hand round her waist, her hand round his waist. Finally, Nzekwu, he thinks. But this is a girl romancing another girl: isn't this lesbianism?

Chiamaka looks away from the couple and coughs to get his full attention. "I want you to drive me down to The Lord is Good Farm," she tells him. "Some of my students phoned to tell me that my tomatoes are ripening quickly and they're keen to purchase some of them. Start this car, yes. Start, start, start. I need to speed down to that farm before the students will change their minds and begin to buy from Christiana, whose tomatoes are also ripening quickly."

"I'm engaged at the moment." He hopes she didn't detect any hint of irritation in his voice, in his facial expression. "I have scripts to annotate and grade. And I have a seminar to supervise. And I want to send another bags of rice to the orphanage home."

"You're just being inimical and callous," Chiamaka says in Igbo, her language of antagonism, and he's frightened by the wild shine in her eyes. "This may sound childish, coming from a grown-up, but I will show the HOD, the VC and everybody your porn if you don't drive me to my farm."

Before his sternly tenacious colleague can blink, or spew another puerile nonsense, the car is in motion. Through the thinning engine and the rattling wheels, Chiamaka says, "You've been looking at me from the corner of your eye and driving in silence. Why?"

"I was admiring you."

"Oh…But how do I look, Okonkwo? Be honest."

"You look like Mrs. Chiamaka."

"I'm Amaka, yes, I know. I mean, how is my... Forget it."

"You'll fuel my car at a filling station, won't you?"

"Okonkwo, you're not happy that I'm in your great car, yes?"

"Who said I'm not happy you're in my car?"

"You want me to get down, don't you? I will get down!"

"No, no, please... Sorry!"

"Be careful."

They arrive on the farm in silence. *"Welcome to I-Must Eat Farm"* says a signpost on a path. *"If you dare steal any of these fruits here you will die, and it will not be well with your family!"* says the warning below it. Before them, behind them, there are crowds of students: sweating students, smiling students, frowning students, flirting students, eating students, drinking students. At her summon, he helps her gather the ripe tomatoes, helps her stuff them into waterproof, and helps her sell them to the students. But the money goes into one pocket—her pocket.

"Madam, we will pass your course now we have bought your tomatoes?" he hears one of her customers, a big-nosed boy in sunglasses, ask in a whisper, following her.

Chiamaka gives the boy a surreptitious nod, waves him bye, waves the others bye, and faces him with an expression of faint annoyance.

Back in the car, she shouts, over the noise of the engine, "Animal! The boy is an animal. He wants an A because he bought one tomato from me. One tomato! Can you believe this, Okonkwo? Let him go and buy me a bag of manure or fertilizer. Or just give me his money, for Christ's sake!"

"My name is not Okonkwo!" he bleats. "Who's this invalid Okonkwo character, by the way?"

"Take me back to my flat."

"But there's no fuel in this car and I'm late to work! And there's no money in my pocket. I have no money because I don't have a tomato farm."

"Take me back to my flat."

The wild shine in her eyes scares him into obedience. "All right, all right," he says.

Upstairs in her flat, Chiamaka says, "I will burn your porn today if you want me to burn it."

Burn it, bitch, he thinks. Burn the damn thing! "Yes, please," he says.

Chiamaka unbuckles his belt, unbuttons his shirt, pulls him towards her bedroom where he'll be used. "I know you'll run away from me if I burn these important embarrassments for you," she says after doing it with him on the creaking bed. Under the bed, there are squeals of mice, there are smells of fruits. The black-and-white carpet is littered with torn clothes. On the wall, the red eyes of her husband on their wedding photograph stare at him as if he's mad at him for doing it with its wife behind locked doors. Why isn't she, like him, worried about this affair?

Ignoring the odour of rotten eggs filling his nose, he dons his clothes. "Where's your matchbox? Let's burn those pornography things."

"I'm not happy yet." Chiamaka uphoulters herself in her own clothes, flounders to the window. "I've forgotten how to dance. God hasn't answered my prayer. But I trust He'll eventually give me a baby boy."

"Or a baby girl?"

She wraps her hand round his waist and leads him back into the living room. "Haven't I told you I conceived twice? You put two female babies into my womb, yes, but. . . I exorcised them. I pray the sperm you just released into me this month will form a baby boy."

He removes her hand and stops. "So I impregnated you twice? You aborted the foetus?"

"Do you expect me to go ahead carrying the female things in my womb when I need a bouncing baby boy urgently?" She sits on the sofa, shifts away from him. "You must be mad, Okonkwo. My husband and his people want to bayonet me out of his house because I gave them six girls and no boy, and you're advising me to. . .I've seen that you don't like me. You don't like me at all."

"That's ridiculous! I'm shocked that you, an intellectual, also think like all those illiterate people in the market." He goes to the refrigerator and takes a bottle of Gulder beer. "A female child is a child. You were once a female child and now you're a famous supplier of tomatoes, bananas and other vegetables and fruits, and I'm sure your parents are proud of you. And I'm a man, but I'm not as good as you; I'm fat, ugly, poor and slothful. I can't even differentiate between a tomato and a banana. I'm a smoker and an irresponsible alcoholic. I'm sure my parents are ashamed of me."

She rises with a crinkled face. "Goodbye, Okonkwo."

CHAPTER 15

I FENNA tears out the *Proudly Fruitarian* sticker pasted on Chiamaka's door before he knocks. But there's no answer, and there are no footsteps, no windows, no human to ask for help. He empties his whiskey into his mouth and Adaku disposes it on the sandy stairs.

Here on the stairs, he can see the kites hovering in the sky of enameled blue. The schoolbag he carries has holes. One of the holes exposes a white hen he stole at Else-Shall-Die hostel for Chiamaka; the bird watches Adaku, who now follows him virtually everywhere he goes like some nice puppy, and squawks as if that's a greeting.

Adaku steps forward, gives the door three timorous knocks, and retreats for him to reclaim the front position.

From within Chiamaka's voice says, "Who's that

indolent idiot?" and the door opens to reveal her in a white silk gown with tomato stains. "Ah, Ifenna! What are you doing here, reptile?"

I'm here to apologise for not following the students to your farm to buy tomatoes, he wants to say. I swear, I have nothing against your tomatoes or tomatoes generally, but I was literally sleeping with Adaku that morning. He wants to say: In my pocket are naira notes. Take them and help me in your course. Take the hen breathing in my schoolbag and help me in your course. But what he says is this: "I'm here to...to...wash your toilet."

"Who's this girl that can't greet her elder?" Chiamaka asks.

Adaku's lips sag: she has nothing to say. He hands Adaku his umbrella, wipes sweat from his face, and wonders why she hardly greets, and hardly responds to greetings. He wonders why she hardly reads. At home, Nkem is rereading *Macbeth* for her assignment. Nkem the book maniac: always rereading books for Adaku's assignments, always glowers at the "farcical idea" of buying good grades from lecturers with a stolen fowl, always tells him that Chiamaka is mentally unstable. But will Chiamaka really think that he, Ifenna, and Adaku are high on marijuana, or playing a prank, and hit them with a plank? How wrong Nkem was. This woman, this incredible woman, might look weird and scary, like a masquarade, but she's not mad, not yet; she

236

understands the value of money. She can accept a crate of eggs in exchange for a good grade. He likes her for her cheapness, for her madness, but he does not like the way she looks at Adaku. Maybe she thinks: Which avaricious uncle or auntie used this girl's brain for money rituals? Maybe she thinks: Why is Ifenna interested in this girl?

He unburdens himself to inquisitive Chiamaka. "Madam, many people threatened to kill me if I didn't stop being a homosexual, so I looked round our university and Adaku seemed to be the only girl who could solve this problem for me. I was afraid of them. And I was worried that Semicolon would throw me out of our room. He, too, was suspected of having a romantic affair with me. He asked me to get a girl or get out. So I got Adaku. I swear, I reveled in my singlehood, but those guys wanted to murder me. Adaku was never my choice. But she's not a very ugly girl, and she can cook. She's very obedient. . . Watch. Adaku, clean my shoes."

"Yes, sir," Adaku says, and crouches to clean his dust-coated shoes with her handkerchief. "Vely crean now, sir?"

"Adaku, say I'm very sorry for not greeting you, Mrs. Chiamaka, and then stay outside here to wait for me," he says.

"I am vely cholly for not gleeting you, Mrs. Chiamaka," she says, and starts retreating.

For a long moment, Chiamaka watches Adaku's

unkempt hair with wonder-filled eyes as if she were an almost extinct animal escaped from a zoo; then, without a word, she waves her bye, lets him in. "I noticed you now go everywhere carrying an umbrella in the sun like a princess, yes," she says. "And you think the amusing umbrella will make me to help you in my course? You're here to bribe me, aren't you? Don't deny it, I won't stop you. But I don't encourage bribery, yes. But do you want to bribe me?"

"Yes," he replies without thinking. "I mean no."

The fowl squawks suddenly in his bag, but neither of them is startled. Neither of them makes a comment. Perhaps she's engrossed with something, something that has to do with agriculture. Perhaps her suspicion that he's keen on bribery has transported her into another world where he and the fowl are not present. Perhaps she did hear the fowl and is pretending not to have heard.

"You're dating a mad girl?" she asks him in the living room. "You're afraid to ask a presentable girl out, Ifenna? Or an older woman who's employed. Single or married. How can you fall in love with an imbecile?"

He knows what she wants and is encouraged to encourage her. "Your new hairstyle is amazing, Mrs. Chiamaka," he says. "Was it plaited by Rose? Rose used to paint my hair until the authority prohibits boys from entering into the university with girls' hairs, whatever that means. God, I swear, your hairstyle is absolutely amazing!"

"Thank you, darling." She scratches her tangled hair and her beard. "I had to pay Rose to change the old one because we will receive supposedly learned, fat old men and women here next week for the accreditation of some laughable departments. The hairstyle was much more beautiful in the morning, but my colleagues' noisy arguments ruffled it. You should've seen me in the morning before the boring academic staff meeting, yes. I slept almost throughout the two or three hours of nonsensical debates about the forthcoming Students' Union Government elections."

"I'm sure the professors stood up and applauded your new hairstyle."

"No. We, or rather they, were busy shouting and parroting about ballot boxes, ballot papers and candidates' agents."

"So no one talked about your hair? The professors didn't rise to applaud your hair?"

She shrugs one shoulder like an amateur actress playing a hypertensive patient. At her feet, there are two emptied bottles: one of Guinness, one of Heineken. Was she drinking, or did she host Okoye the King of Alcohol?

"This is unbelievable, madam!" he says, turning his head to a wall, so that she cannot see the smile spreading on his face. "I swear, I'm furious right now! People are so acidic and envious. What would it cost them to rise and praise your gorgeous hair and applaud it for ten or twenty minutes before continuing the meeting? I'm very angry with them. A pretty hairstyle like this should be complimented at every very important academic meeting."

There is a long silence. "You suddenly forgot I am your lecturer, yes?"

"You're my favourite lecturer, and I always strive to study your notes and write convincingly in your exams."

She gets up, circles her living room, returns to her sofa with a half-emptied bottle of Guinness. "I have a family problem," she says in a deceitfully slurred voice. "My husband is…I mean, we have no male child, yes. Things like this make women do sinful things. Not because they are in love, but because they have to. Do you understand me?"

They have no male child: how does that concern him? How does that concern his learning, her teaching? Let her say, Ifenna, I want you to impregnate me. Let her say, please give me a male child. Let her say I have been pretending to be drunk and I'm sorry. But no: he cannot swallow such a henious confession, he cannot go to bed with her, he cannot do that without a protection. "No," he says. "I don't understand."

"You're not intelligent, Ifenna?" she asks.

"I am proudly unintelligent, madam." He pops gum into his mouth, chews it for a few seconds in silence, and then blows it: the hen in his schoolbag squawks and Chiamaka jumps out from her sofa, startled.

"What's that?" she asks in a tremulous voice.

"Ma, don't run; it's only a well-behaved hen."

"A hen? A hen? What's a hen?"

"A hen is a female chicken, particularly the one that keeps its eggs." He carries the bag from the floor where he kept it, unzips it, takes out the fowl. "Madam, you know, Easter is around the corner. I bought the hen for you so that you'll celebrate Easter with a delicious meat-filled stew. Don't ask me for its eggs; they're still in the hen's abdomen...or kidney? I want to bring the hen out of this bag before it lays eggs in my textbooks. Should I?"

She squawks. "But the hen is not weighty."

"Perhaps the politicians in her country stole all their foods and flew away to London or France. Corruption is everywhere. Thank God for corruption . . . And here is one thousand naira. Take it? You don't want to take it? I know the money is too small, but don't worry; I'll amaze you after Easter. Use the token to buy some bottles of Coke or Fanta for Easter."

With those muscular hands that remind him of yams, she takes the flapping fowl and the money from him, goes into her kitchen, returns with a crestfallen countenance. "God bless you, but I want something better." She sits close to him and puts her hand round his trembling shoulder. "Something more important. Something that isn't tangible. Do you understand?"

He removes her hand, rises to go. "I will send my registration number and name to you on WhatsApp."

"Of course, yes. But don't be in a hurry. I am not busy today, I want to chat as if I were not your lecturer. I'm not the kind of lecturers that draw lines. So, tell me a bit about yourself. The most courageous thing you have ever done. Like fighting a lecturer, like falling in love with a lecturer. A lecturer who's a married woman, yes. Start with this, a delicious adventure with a married woman."

"I'm a coward, madam. So I have never been bold enough to commit adultery. I know adultery is the sweetest thing in the whole wide world, after fornication of course, but I am a coward."

She removes something from his cheek. "But cowardice has a solution. An overly willing woman sinks the cowardice of an interested man. Rose says you have slept with Dr. Sunshine Nwakaego."

Dr. Sunshine Nwakaego: why did this very bad woman remind him of this very good woman? This good woman is an improbably flirtatious eccentric who taught his class Introduction to Economics Statistics I in their first year. A divorcee with hair dyed the colour of the rainbow. Some students think they are in love, but they were never tactile: he has no romantic interest in her. He told her, playfully, that he did not know why he, unlike most boys in the class, did not have a crush on her. She, too, had no romantic interest in him and told him, with a dimpled smile, that she knew why. *I'm your teacher, my queer boy. Your teacher, your mother, your community.* His community: what a choice of word. He laughed then, but he knew she was serious, he knew she was having an affair with one grim-faced policewoman who routinely visited her in the university. He remembers peeping through the keyhole on her office door one rainy evening, remembers seeing them kissing by a window adorned with a fluttering curtain the colour of sunrise, and remembers that he left with insuppresible giggles: he liked them and wished them well. But last week, to his mild surprise, the university terminated Dr. Sunshine's appointment with no stated reason.

"I must admit, I'm dating that 52-year-old woman," he says. "But her 30-year-old son and 32-year-old daughter don't respect me. I'm eighteen, but these kids don't respect me. They wouldn't call me Dad, and when I asked the 32-year-old daughter to go to the kitchen to make me tea, her brother, who's now my son, slapped off my bottle of whiskey in anger. I swear, nowadays kids no longer respect daddies, especially their step-daddies."

She rises. "Goodbye."

Outside, he finds Adaku snoring on the steps, her handbag an improvised pillow under her head. A head that looks like a hairy coconut, he would like to say. But this is not the time for this hostile levity. "Baby?" he says, shaking her. "Baby...I mean, Adaku!"

Her prompt reaction to this high-pitched call is frightening: shivering like a soaked mouse, she yawns wildly, coughs and coughs, stretches, blinks her beady eyes open: then, farting like an old lorry struggling up a hilly road, she totters to her feet. "I was eating blead in my dleam," she says. "I saw a vely big cow clossing a main load. It saw my blead and chased me flom this prace to Onitsha. Flom Onitsha to Ragos. Flom Ragos to Ghana, then Engrand, then Portugal. I think the cow is hungly."

"I think I'm hungry, Adaku." He takes her handbag, peers into it, whistles excitedly at the crumpled naira notes he can see. "Take me to a restaurant. Buy me food and meat. Buy me clothes. Buy me ice cream. Buy me chewing gum. Then go home and wash my singlets and boxers. Did you hear me, Adaku?"

"Yes—Sir!"

Sir: the word is shot out like the bullet of a soldier on the alert; but, if he's asked to describe it, he will say it lands, gently, on his impatient ears sounding like a musical note filled with a million tiny red roses. He will say it spills into his mouth tasting like honey. He will say he's so delighted that when he puts her handbag on his arm as women do, takes the opened umbrella from the floor, kisses her nose, spits fretfully over her shoulder, honey spreads in his chest. "What a perfect girlfriend God gave me near that dustbin!" he says, and turns to go. "Thank you, Jesus!"

"Thank you, my Rord," she says, closing her eyes.

Whistling happily, arm in arm, they stumble down the stairs under the umbrella.

THIRD YEAR

CHAPTER 16

NKEM sees the engagement ring glistening on Chioma's finger and clucks. Chioma who will never be mine again, he thinks, and shakes his head, or imagines that he does, before adjusting his Harry Potter glasses and stepping into the HOD's office with the musical girl.

The sun, a huge orange radiating in a sky soaked with watery palm oil, lights up the glass window like a lamp, blinds him momentarily, and then it is swallowed by the branch of a frangipani tree lowered by rising winds. The smell of incense is faint in the air.

Behind a clustered desk sits Sir Israel, his left hand anointing his forehead with olive oil, his right hand fingering his rosary. The name pennon on his desk says Professor Israel Owen Abraham, Ph. D. No Igbo name

247

yet: one day, he will mock this little bastard's preference. But not today. A man whose house is ablaze does not chase fleeing rats. He ignores the water that boils in his chest every time he recalls that there's no native name; that Sir Israel flaunts the foreign names; that Sir Israel allows students to pray to the Christian God before examinations but rebukes boys who raise a kola nut to heaven and attempt to pray to Chineke before their own examinations; that Sir Israel's tenure has expired, yet the Vice Chancellor reinstated him because they're both Knights of Saint John. He punched the air in celebration when deserving professors threatened to drag Sir Israel out of the office and frowned when several students of Economics intervened; they warned the professors to let Sir Israel continue because he does not force recycled handouts on students, does not sleep with students, does not collect money from students for better grades, and does attend his lectures. The only problem, they all agreed, is that religion has fried his brain with onions.

The last time he visited Sir Israel the office was almost empty and fresh with the smell of new paint. Now the white paint is fading, peeling, and there are so many odd things: the Holy Bible (King James Version), a dozen New Testament Bibles arranged like toy houses on the desk, bulletins, church flyers, envelopes, candles, glossy photographs of Jesus Christ and His twelve Apostles nailed to the wall, a gold-coloured crucifix, a statuette of Virgin Mary on a clean but rickety shelf burdened with books, a stapler, a dictionary, a stamp, a laptop with a sticker that reads *Proudly Catholic.*

Sir Israel gestures to them to sit and they obey with smiles he hopes the HOD will not think insincere. All around them: the voices of students coming from the passage and the voices of students coming from the floor below, or the one above, and down the stairs are like the buzz of a million bees. From the open window, a light breeze comes, upsetting the fountain pens and the papers on the desk. Blinding sunlight streams in from the same open window, glowing on the silver clock ticking noisily on the wall, glowing on Sir Israel's oily face, radiating on the swivel chairs. He imagines himself transforming into Harry Potter, floating in the air like this wizard, shouting unprintable insults and hitting Sir Israel on the head with a hammer.

"I'm glad your sister is dressed in a skirt, and not in trousers like most Heineken girls," Sir Israel says, studying her for the second time through his magnifying glasses. "And how may I help you, Son and Daughter of the Most High God."

After clearing his dry throat, he tells him about Okoye's sex business with Chioma in a hotel, and about the videos and the photos that are the evidence, and about Okoye's allies' insane struggles to get their hands on these objects, damage these objects, and flee.

When he's done with his stories, he leans back and watches Sir Israel, who's staring at Chioma as if she has just insulted the Pope, as if she smoked terrific weed. But she finds it hilarious: she brings her hands to her mouth and giggles until the noise of a typewriter comes from the secretary's office next door.

He wonders what has happened to the computers, wonders if Sir Israel sent them to his church for their crusade, and then wonders if Sir Israel is wondering what he's wondering. He shakes off the thoughts and gazes at Sir Israel who has shifted his gaze to him.

"Mr. Obi, it's my frank prayer that you're not here to grumble over one lecturer or another," Sir Israel says. "I'm tired of your incessant complaints. You're not the only student here, but you always. . . How many times have you taken your troubles to God in prayer?"

"Blessed wine, how can I carry Dr. Okoye and other bad men and women we have here to God?" he asks in wan irritation.

"Sir, Okoye is *fat*; my boyfriend cannot *carry* him to God in prayer." She shifts in her chair and, with her army-green boot, covers the cigarette that has just dropped from her handbag. "Physical strength, like intellectual strength, belongs to women now. The fictitious story telling us that God took one rib from a man and created us women is patriarchal nonsense."

Sir Israel's forehead creases in impatience, and he

hits the palms of his hand on the desk with vehemence: pens, papers and the stamp fall off. "Please leave my office," Sir Israel tells Chioma; and then, to him: "And you, too. Follow your sister. Quick!"

In an unhurried but inoffensive manner, he rises to pick the fallen things but his Harry Potter glasses drops from his face and into Chioma's quick hands. She puts it back on his face, collects the things, sets them on the desk, and sits.

She still loves me, she still wants me, he thinks. If she isn't in love with me, she wouldn't have followed me to help me. She wouldn't have dropped her guitar to come into this office that smells of Olive oil. Why did she allow Chief to put that bloody ring on her finger? Why can't the God Chioma's mother serves intervene by sending thunder to paralyse him, to kill him? Why hasn't Chief died in a plane crash to make him happy?

He shakes off his unkind thoughts and settles down to bare his heart. He says payers cannot be the needed insecticide chasing weevils out of the wood. He says prayers might be reasonable but it cannot quench this fire that is burning him, burning every student in this weevil-ravaged department. This weevil-ravaged department has students who have been praying for a very long time and it is still a marketplace. To be a student here means that you must buy lecturers beer, buy horrible books from lecturers, buy pirated handouts from lecturers or give them girls. To be a student here means that you must endure Mrs. Chiamaka who is monomaniacally obsessed with vegetables. Mrs. Chiamaka who, constantly, fearlessly, compels her students to go to her farm, weed her farm, or buy her bananas, her tomatoes, her garden eggs. To be a student here, you must have to steal the campus dustbins, sell them, and use the money to bribe lecturers, some of whom collect even fowls.

"Fowls?" Sir Israel asks.

"Chickens are given to lecturers in exchange for good grades, obviously. Our girlfriends' breasts are being sucked by our male lecturers. Dr. Okoye should be removed from this department because he's a virus."

He expects Sir Israel to react to this report, but the man is only blinking, blinking and fingering his rosary. As if he's consulting God, he thinks. This is becoming dramatic. This is becoming infuriating.

He gives Sir Israel the two photographs and says, "These are Dr. Okoye and Chioma, naked in bed. You can see him sucking my girlfriend's breasts. You see it? A man who's paid to teach the students is more interested in breasts."

Sir Israel jerks his face to the window. "I cannot look at a pornographic content, I'm sorry. . . I'm convinced they are both doctored."

"Doctored, you say, blessed wine? But you didn't even look at them. How could you tell?"

"What do we do, then, Sir Israel?" Chioma asks.

"The only solution is prayer, my daughter…and my son. Songs and prayers. When Paul and Silas were in trouble, they prayed and they sang and the Holy Ghost came down. Keep praying like the Pharisees. And don't stop singing His praise. He knows all about all your troubles." Sir Israel hesitates, wrinkles his forehead as if he's irritated again. "And besides, your sister cannot sleep with the philanthropist, Mr. Nwoye. It's not possible. She's not a prostitute. Quit insinuating that Chioma your sister is a whore."

"Sir Israel, Chioma and Dr. Okoye had sex, obviously." He scratches his head, walks to the door, and returns. "They had sex. They had sex, obviously. The photographs are our evidence. And there are videos, too."

The wrinkles on Sir Israel's face deepen. "Relinquish this unrighteous facetiousness, Obi! No lecturer has ever slept with Chioma. Stop it!"

"Sir, are you calling Nkem a liar?" Chioma asks.

Sir Israel's left shoulder slumps; he tightens his grip on the rosary, gapes at Chioma. "So the man has slept with you?"

"But I didn't enjoy it," she says.

Sarcasm, he thinks: is Chioma being sarcastic? Well, the man deserves it. And why isn't Sir Israel using his bombastic words today? Perhaps a student has called him out on that pretentiousness, that ridiculousness. Were he to write a short story for the campus literary magazine, *Pen Magicians*, Sir Israel will inspire one of his characters. But will this tiny cartoon in glasses strike the supercilious chief editor as convincing? The students would be glad to read this farcical character, but he will not write it.

In annoyingly slow motion, Sir Israel leans back in his swivel chair. "Please go. I'll pray over this and decide on what to do. The Holy Spirit will direct us. Have a heavenly day, Nkem. And take a special care of your sister."

"Thanks," he says. He takes Chioma's hand and, whirling to the door, adds: "She's my girlfriend or ex-girlfriend, and not my sister."

Alone at home, with the shouty music of Tupac on the CD, he pens an acerbic letter to the Vice Chancellor, telling him that Economics lecturers are sucking the breasts of boys' girlfriends, collecting fowls from students, compelling students to buy lecturers' fruits and vegetables, give them beer, give them girls. But he has great news to share: he, Nkem Obi, and his classmate Chioma caught one of them on a tape naked with a girl. The lecturer is no other person than Dr. Ezinwa Okoye. He suggests the university sack such a lecturer. He suggests the university buy video recorders and share to the heads of the most corrupt departments to fish out the old devils. He suggests they use students, male and female, and begin without delay. There's no "thank you for your understanding." But he includes his phone number, his email address, his home address.

One week later, the Vice Chancellor frightens him with an unexpected call. "The Vice Chancellor, Heineken University. I believe this is Obi, Nkemdilim. Correct?"

"Correct, blessed wine," he says in a voice graceless with tremors. "Sir, I mean."

The Vice Chancellor is habitually playful, habitually childlike. But today, he is different. In a solemn voice, he thanks him for his fearlessness, his thoughtfulness, and then informs him that the university has provided one hundred video recorders to twenty decadent departments. He asks him to go to his HOD to collect one because they're designed for students with the boldest voices.

He calls Sir Israel. "Good morning, sir," he says, and when no reply comes, he continues. "The Vice Chancellor sent some videos to you?"

"I'm on my way to a mountain for prayers, Obi. I will call you back. Give me only seven hours. God bless you. Bye!"

But Sir Israel does not call.

The next morning, he picks Ifenna's stolen Bible, takes Chioma's hand as if she were his wife, and they traipse to Sir Israel's office in connubial silence.

"Beautiful, beautiful," Sir Israel says, looking at

his Bible with sparkling eyes. "I'm happy to see that you and your sister actually read the Word of God." He gestures to a seat, turns to Chioma but averts his gaze instantaneously. "Young girl, promptly withdraw that fragrant display of your. . . your. . . chest."

He faces Chioma's biscuit-coloured T-shirt: two buttons, he notes, are left undone. He buttons them for her and says, "She's no longer dangerous, blessed wine—Sir Israel."

"Are you certain?" Sir Israel says. He opens one eye, then two, like an infant cartoon. "The both of you are Catholics, I hope?"

He and Chioma were born into Anglican families, but he says, "We're Catholics, obviously."

"Best decision," Sir Israel says. "Now, what can I do for you?"

"The question should be this: Nkem, what do you want to do for this putrescing university?" he says.

Chioma nudges him before she speaks for the first time. "Nkemdilim Obi, my Sugar: the epic hero. Spiderman. Harry Potter. Black Panther. The Warrior and Feminist. Chioma's Future Husband. The One who was sent from heaven to save our campus, we hail thee."

"It's about Mr. Nwoye?" Sir Israel says in a bored tone. "My son, those photos look fake."

He bites his lower lip. "That's why we're here to have the video recorder which the judicious Vice Chancellor has provided."

"We'll use the video to shatter the shells of all the bad men in this department," Chioma says. "And bad women, if there are bad women. Women are better behaved. Except Mrs. Chiamaka. But is she really a woman? She has a beard. And maybe she has...a pe...a pe... pencil."

Sir Israel isn't paying Chioma any attention; he's searching his drawer for the video recorder. A candle drops from the desk, but they all ignore it. Sir Isreal says, after a few suffocating seconds, with incredible fervour, "Hallelujah, here it is! Thought I left it on the mountain. I prayed for it. It is, my son and daughter, covered with the precious blood of our lord Jesus Christ. Have it, Obi."

The device changes hands; but the shriveled one that gives is hesitant, unwilling, and the fresh one that receives is hungry and rash. This video recorder: new, black, portable, and shaped like an avocado pear. And above this electronic solution, his tongue: reflexively out of the mouth like a small pink snake from a hole, circling and circling the lips with babyish excitement.

Before they depart from the office, he fills and signs a form which the Vice Chancellor gave to Sir Israel.

Downstairs, the clouds are whitened whales pursued, languidly but gracefully, by blue-grey smoke: a heavy rain will soon pour on the campus.

CHAPTER 17

OKOYE half-stumbles into the classroom. Not a desirable place to be, he thinks: this classroom is teeming with the third-year students, and the third-year students, he is convinced, are mostly blockheads, romantics, eccentrics. He should have driven to one of the orphanage homes to be with those little orphans.

The students' greeting, to his surprise, is free of irony, free of laughter. He returns it in a slurred voice, opens his beer-soaked lecture note, and hopes they can't notice he's drunk. He's drunk because Rose told him that Chioma has resolved to use the photos and the videos to shatter the door behind his secrets. Drunk because he is tired of begging her for forgiveness, tired of plotting how to exterminate the videos and the photos from the surface of the earth. Drunk because Chioma is not taking his calls, Ifenna is not taking his calls, Nkem is not taking his calls. Drunk because he suspected that there was something anxious and fishy about Chioma's trips to the bathroom and to the wardrobe in the hotel room that regrettable Monday night three years ago, and yet he fell into her trap.

He scans the class for these three betrayers, but they're not in attendance. Perhaps they have shown the HOD, or the Vice Chancellor, those objects of defamation, and are now dancing and drinking celebratory beers at Children of God beer parlour. He, too, was drinking beer at Children of God beer parlour: why couldn't he see them? Did they see him and escape to another beer parlour?

"The lecture today is on the Concept of Value," he informs the class in a slurred tone and staggers forward with the lectern. The students scream with laughter. "To a layman—some of you here are laymen—the term, value, is the want satisfying quality of a thing when we use or consume it. This is related to the concept of utility. Utility, however, is the ability of a commodity to satisfy needs or wants. Take, for example, cigarettes and beer make us happy. When your wife or husband finds you in bed with another person and leaves forever with your TV or stove, you feel depressed. But you drink beer and smoke cigarettes and, before the yellow sun sets in the east, you see yourself laughing with genuine felicity.

When you're laughing because you cannot remember that your wife has run away with your TV or stove, it is the value-in-use of the beer and cigarettes. Clear?" He has hurried his speech because the words on the flapping book are now swimming in his eyes, some sentences slithering like tiny pythons, some paragraphs swelling like a balloon in the mouth of a not very nice little boy. He cannot stop the essay from turning into balloons. He cannot stop his ears from hearing invisible elephants, or mischievous students, trumpeting. He cannot make out the students' questions, only noises. The sixth free bottle of Guinness stout from Kofi, one umbrella-sized Ghanaian rascal who was expelled from the university on the grounds of examination malpractice and who lives down his street: he shouldn't have downed the alcohol. Now, it is clear to him that Kofi filled his stout with Ghanaian marijuana when he staggered into the Gents to empty his bladder. Now he believes what Rose had told him: that a boy called Kofi often put Ghanaian marijuana into the drinks of all the people who contributed to his dismissal and into the drinks of all the people who once taught him at this university. Now he cannot read further, he cannot even see the students clearly. Now everybody is rising to the ceiling with their chairs like supernatural characters in a speculative movie. The stone-filled head on his plastic neck seems to be jumping off on its own. He wags his head like a puppy and waits. The ground morphs into a river, the students return to the waters. Their chairs transform into boats, carry them like fishermen on a sea to him, returns. He staggers backwards so that salt waters from this sea will not drown him, and almost lands into a paper-filled dustbin: the students scream with laughter again.

Very good, he thinks: my students are enjoying themselves. But his head is rotating like a twirled football. He tightens his tie-belt and waits stubbornly, wickedly. This pause is unbroken until his beer-filled stomach propels him forward: he screams and dances drunkenly with the lectern. *Somebody call his wife or hire a wheelbarrow,* he hears someone bellow near him, and steady his still-dancing body. Maybe there's nobody close to him, and he's just imagining it. Maybe he's imagining these farcical manifestations. But the voices coming from the book in his hands are real, so real. He peers at a specified paragraph where the noises seem to have emanated from, but they grow louder, making him itch to tie his flapping red tie round his ears. Another noises, similar in rhythm and in volume, come at him from the white ceiling, which is gradually transforming into a blue sky. And what next? What next will his sleep-burdened eyes see in this lecture hall? A fish, a shark, a dolphin, or an antelope playing lawn tennis with a banana-eating Kenyan monkey? Only a loud cry for help will save him from this embarrassing situation, but he's too drunk to shout, too weak to walk.

"He has gone to a generous beer parlour," someone says to general laughter. The voice is virtually distinct from the noises: a proof that his ears have not been carried away by the whistling winds.

He touches both ears to make sure, says "Testing microphone: one, two…", although he has none in his hand, and reads on in an Oxford-accented voice that sounds suspiciously urgent and aggressive like that of Major General Odumegwu Ojukwu's when he was declaring war on Nigerians with a Biafran flag in 1967 and then as Osama bin Laden's and then as Nkem's, shouting his words, mispronouncing his words, repeating his words, ending each sentence with phrases like "blessed wine" and "obviously, obviously".

This horror continues uninterrupted until dust-laden violent winds from the busted windows snatch the flapping book from his hands. Holding his dropping trousers with his left hand, he tries to rush after the note flying towards the howling students, but trips and falls with the lectern. The students scream in horror. Several students rush forward, or is he imagining that too? The voices of ghosts, or students, ask him what the matter is with him, ask him to open his mouth, to retch, to do something, and seeing he's incapable of performing any of these actions, they try to bring him back on his feet. Darkness descends on him.

He wakes on his verandah to the earsplitting sounds of generators downstairs. The watch on his hand says 12:44 a.m., but he does not trust it. Moonlight clarifies his path as he stumbles into his living room. He does not know who took him home, does not know what means of transportation was used to carry him home like a full bag of beans or cement. A wheelbarrow, most likely, he thinks, blundering into his flat to put his noisy head into his Star Beer refrigerator. Today, like most days when he's heavy with alcohol, three hundred tiny children laugh into his head to whistle nonstop and three hundred tiny horses gallop. The chilly ice from the fridge will drop on his baldness, stopping the horses, collecting the whistles from the naughty children. Chilly ice from a fridge: it's one of his antidotes to hangovers. Professor Ayodele taught him that the first day they met and drank themselves into near insensibility.

The next day, he does not appear in the university for his lectures. He does not take his students's calls. He does phone his HOD to apologise for that unsolicited stage performance. He tells himself that the tiny man is on some mountain shedding tears of joy and glorifying the name of the Ancient of Days. He waits five days before he resolves to return to work.

A hilarious mystery, he thinks as he drives on the Campus Road. God, I hope the students will not laugh at me! I hope the HOD has returned to his mountain with a Bible!

Suddenly he brakes, but it's too late: he has knocked off the campus smelly dustbin that says "Please Do not Keep this University Clean." The words "Do not" are new additions by Ifenna Nzekwu or such gum-chewing nemesis.

Taking his toothbrush-filled briefcase, he steps out of his BMW and closes the door.

Of all the branches of the trees leafed in bright green and shedding parked cars, only the tiny coconut tree full of ants sways in the sudden gush of dust-laden winds: the branches shudder and the leaves spiral to the earth, fly up again, swirl with petals blown away from pink flowers, swirl with bits of papers, and then descend gently, teasingly, on his head. He exchanges greetings with a white-haired woman who has driven close to his car to park hers. A sparkling silver Benz, new and clean: when will he own this kind of car?

In a flash, he drops the depressing question as if it's a hot plate, faces the sun that hangs on the gleaming roof of a decrepit auditorium like a yellow ball, and trundles away.

On the busy veranda leading to his office, he finds Professor Ayodele exiting the building through another route, a newspaper in his hands. Behind him, a short girl slaps a tall girl on the cheek, hits her head with a handbag, pulls at her blond wig; four students, two boys and two girls, and Professor Ayodele rush to separate them. Because he's already late to his morning lecture, because he's not in the mood for a bearded man's childishness, he tries to dart into office to avoid meeting Professor Ayodele, but it's too late: their eyes have met.

"The greatest Igbo man of our time," Professor Ayodele says with annoying mirth in his voice. "The students say you delivered the greatest lecture in the university's history."

"I am glad they enjoyed it."

"You avoided all Ayosky's calls for five days. Where have you been? Jesus, look at your shirt: rumpled and stained with food. No laundry services in your neighbourhood? Your girlfriends don't comment on this dirtiness?"

"You ask too many questions, Papa Kayode. There are more important things to do than washing shirts and ironing trousers. Besides, dirty, parched trousers don't discourage learning, do they?"

"Of course, they do."

"Let the students drag me to a river and wash me with detergent, then."

Professor Ayodele follows him into the office, hands him the newspaper. "I no longer see you at Children of God beer parlour. The manager chased you out because you didn't invite him to your sensational lecture? You know his eyes are on Rose your property. Did Rose tell you that Ayosky was the kind guy who hired a keke-napep that drove you home?"

"Oh, thanks, Papa Kayode."

"On reaching the university gate, the tricycle galloped and the greatest Igbo man of our time threw up on the trousers Ayosky had just collected from the laundry. Rose and I held your beer-enlarged stomach as the teethless driver laughed. Rose also laughed."

"I'm glad you all enjoyed yourselves."

Three bespectacled girls approach and Professor Ayodele falls silent. They stroll past them, point at him, stifle a laugh. He does not know their names, but he's certain they are his students. He turns to look at Professor Ayodele and finds, to his small amusement, that the man's mouth is wide open and the man's eyes are following the swinging buttocks of the three pretty girls. He himself likes those buttocks, but he'd like to spank them with a plank: why are they amused at their lecturer's fainting in a lecture hall?

"They are some of the people you regaled last week with your fabulous lecture, the great Igbo man of our time. It was a memorable entertainment. The three girls, like all your students, will never forget that brilliant lecture."

"It's nice to know they are some of my fans," he says, and peers at his faulty watch. "Papa Kayode, I—"

"Of course I see you're busy, and I have to free you. But when should Ayosky expect his money?"

"I owe you?"

"The cyclist charged me two thousand naira. He said your stomach is weighty. His tyre actually burst on the way."

Your stomach is weighty: can't this short-legged nonentity take care of his so-called friend's heavy stomach without demanding his money back? "I will pay you tomorrow," he says, but thinks: I will not give you even one naira. You have drunk countless beers bought by me. You have used countless condoms provided by me. Why can't you take my stomach home for free?

"Tomorrow?" Professor Ayodele asks in a skeptical tone, turning to stare at the backside of a passing female student in a mini-skirt. "Are you sure, the greatest Igbo man of our pink pantie. . . Time, sorry. Of our time. Later: see you later!"

When the door bonks shut behind Professor Ayodele, he glances at the newspaper with a little interest.

"A Trending Controversy: Sacked Igbo Lecturers in a Yoruba University.

Professor Christian Igbokwe was allegedly murdered yesterday in his house by Yoruba students seven hours after his appointment as their Vice Chancellor. The few Igbo lecturers protested, the few Igbo students rioted, and the brilliant, solomonic state governor has fired all the Igbo lecturers "for encouraging violence in a citadel of learning. . ."

An unexpected knock on the door interrupts him. "Rose?" he asks, folding the newspaper.

"No," Nkem's sharp tone replies. "Respectfully, Dr. Okoye, we have been waiting for you, obviously. Are we to go home or stay?"

"Come in."

The door opens and Nkem steps in with Chioma. "Oh, I left my phone in the class," he says after greetings. "Be back, blessed wine. Be back, Dr. Okoye."

"One of the nice, God-fearing students must have stolen the phone," he says with his eyes on her chest. "Rose or Chizoba. Let him search these two Christians."

"And what about boys, sir? Boys don't steal?" Chioma shifts uncomfortably in her chair. "Aren't boys equally bad? When will lecturers stop this hatred of the female gender?"

Stop this hatred of the female gender: the tone is a sharp razor sliding down his skin, but he cannot rebuke her, caution her, walk her out; she still has the videos, she still has the photos.

"Yes, the boys are just as bad," he says. "Everybody. Everybody is looking for what to steal. Without money, how can they buy Mrs. Chiamaka's important tomatoes?"

"And your toothpaste. And your toothbrushes. Men do the worse." She runs her hand through her new Afro. "We have all bought the tomatoes, so nobody needs to steal and sell my Sugar's phone. I'm surprised that I also bought the useless tomatoes."

"They're not useless. Use them to cook jollof rice

for me." He touches his breast pocket for a forgotten TomTom, but it proves empty. "My wife is gone. I helped her pack. So come. Come with the photos and the videos. Won't you like to come to my house with the photos and videos and tomatoes and cook jollof rice for me?"

"I didn't know men like their jollof rice cooked with tomatoes, nude photographs and porn. Men…"

He will not let her fire another shot. "Yes, we eat everything. Thanks for reminding us."

"If men like their breakfast cooked with pornography, they should enter the kitchen and do the cooking. We women don't know how to cook blue films showing naked fat men and a very pretty girl."

"How may I help you, Chioma?" He rises and takes his briefcase from the desk. "I want to go back home. I have already missed my lecture."

"Sit down, please," she says in tender voice that astounds him. "It's about the photos and videos. We want to settle this problem once and for all. Rose, your sweetheart, needs to be here. We really need her presence."

He settles down. "And Ifenna. I suspect he also has the videos and the photos. We need him?"

"No. I prefer the hairstylist, Rose. A girl is better. Boys don't know how to resolve conflicts."

"But we know how to do *it* in bed."

"You're a bald old man, Mr. Ezi, and not a boy."

"I may be an old man, but I'm a boy in bed, as a matter of fact."

"Write it on your CV."

And he laughs with his shoulders and stomach, as though it's the funniest joke, and she laughs too. The door, as if waiting for their laughter to die down, opens with a startling creak. Ifenna appears, smiling and chewing gum.

"The fact that you didn't knock before coming bespeaks you were well brought up," he tells Ifenna. "Come in, well-behaved boy."

"Good afternoon, Professor." Ifenna shakes his hand with both hands, touches Chioma's Afro, settles down. Sunlight from the window glints on his nose ring, on his necklace, and on his anklet. There's no gum in his mouth, which is very unusual. But his hair is relaxed and combed, like a girl's, and his eyebrows are darkened with an eye pencil or *otangere*. Is this funny clown, wearing a girl's pantie?

He shifts his gaze to Ifenna, who is fanning his powered face with a file like a lady. Chioma is sweaty, but she's not bothered. Her eyes, he notices, are fixed on Ifenna with unconcealed curiosity, or faux curiosity. When he inspects Ifenna's swollen trouser pocket for money, for the videos and the photos, or for anything at all, he pops gum into his mouth and launches into the subject of corruption on the campus. There are lecturers who collect money from students for As and still bang them in their cars, he says. These men are found in Physics Department, found in Guidance and Counseling Department, found in Political Science Department, found in English and Literary Science Department. Adaku, his girlfriend in English, forgot to submit her term paper and her lecturer compelled her to buy Christmas clothes and shoes for her breastfeeding baby in exchange for thirty marks. Adaku obeyed and yet her result was incomplete. Her friend, a girl also named Adaku, is angered by this breach of contract. Both have twenty Fs or more. Frustration made Adaku Number Two to steal the lecturer's baby and run into a bush. No one has seen her since then. The woman cried, phoned the police, put it up on the radio. Eventually, Adaku Number Two sent a text message to the woman, informing her that she sold the baby and has used the money to buy cream, a big umbrella, a crate of eggs and a frying pan.

"I suspect she used the money to buy another JAMB form," he says.

Ifenna eases back his chair, crosses his slender legs and asks him surprising questions: he asks him how much his A's cost. He asks him how much he will take from them. He asks him if he wants a Portuguese wine.

Portuguese wine: who told Ifenna that he loves

Portuguese wines? He cannot remember sharing one with him, he cannot remember asking him, or any other student, to buy one for his stomach. The last Portuguese wine his tongue tasted was provided by Rose. That was last year on his birthday. Where she got the wine he did not ask. Perhaps she told Ifenna about it, and the sissy is now using it as a material for his comedy. Will he be glad to accept any wine sent to Ifenna from Portugal? Yes, of course. Will he accept ordinary beer? Absolutely. The nude photos and pornographic videos are a rope around his neck and he's prepared to help any dumb student who's capable of tearing off the rope. He's prepared to tolerate all Ifenna's jokes, all Chioma's jokes. But he will try to make them raise the amount of money they are offering him. "Never appear cheap to your customers", his economics textbooks teach, and henceforth he will follow the philosophy.

"As Rose intimated us, Mr. Ezi's A is sold at four thousand naira only," Chioma is saying. "Or have you multiplied the price, sir?"

Five thousand naira: that is what he charges his favourite student, his close students, his sexy students. Not eight thousand naira, not ten thousand naira: five thousand naira "only". He accepts cash, he accepts cheques, he accepts payments into his bank account. That is his custom. His custom is not going to transform into a shark because he's suffocating in life's bottle. His custom, like the Holy Book, is unchangeable, inflexible.

Ifenna pays and delivers one of his tireless jokes. "By God's grace, more students will buy your As and Bs, and we will use the money. We will be drinking beer and eating catfish every Sunday evening with pretty girls."

"The Umbrella Boy is an improbable character," he tells Chioma after Ifenna is gone. "But I don't have his time." He waddles to the door, locks it with his left hand, and returns to his chair rubbing his stomach. "I'm writing a paper I want to submit to a journal, but each time I remember the photos and the videos I drift helplessly into incoherence. I will, however, fill it with jargon and complex sentences. Imponderable papers flatter us learned idiots. I bet you my complete nonsense will be accepted, published and celebrated. But do you think the videos and the photos will be destroyed for me?"

"Why are you looking at me with romantic eyes?"

Romantic eyes: what does that mean? His eyes, according to his wicked mirrors, are bulbous and bloodshot. Flirt. This girl is flirting with him. For money? For future helps in his courses? Whichever is her motivation, he's prepared to flirt with her and see if he can cross this wobbly bridge and into her heart once again. Love and friendship, he read somewhere, can make people build a fence. This fence that insulates them, he swears internally, must be demolished now. She started the demolition with that flirtatious comment, didn't she?

"Your own eyes are more romantic," he says, going to stand behind her. While he approaches, she giggles and says something about men desiring women's body all the time. Yes, all the time, he thinks, blowing air into her ear, kissing her neck, fumbling her breasts. A curious result: she does not smile, she does not glower. Why? He repeats the action, backwards.

"Leave me, Ezi!" she whispers.

With throbbing hands, he covers her mouth in haste. "I will start giving you As and Bs and bread and butter again. Please let's be friends again."

She tilts her head backwards, stares into his eyes. *Sir, you're funny,* her eyes say, surprising him, reassuring him that she's merely pretending not to be interested. *Okay, I am willing to submit my boobs to you for another good grade.*

Thank you abundantly and exceedingly, he wills his eyes to reply. *May God bless you, darling.* He frees her mouth. He smiles. He waits. Her eyes, those lovely eyes, wait too. Slowly, tremblingly, his hands approach her breasts again, take possession of them, rub, squeeze, honk.

"But leave my breasts first," she says, struggling to tear them out. "I will bring out my hunting knife now!"

"But there's a smile on your cute face," he says, but frees her. The smile dries up on her face and perches on the desk. "Burn the remaining videos and all the photos, Chioma. Persuade your Semicolon and that drag queen to burn the ones I suspect they have. I can handle

Mrs. Chiamaka. Help me. Let's return to being friends, darling."

She unzips her handbag, pulls out her hunting knife and his heart jumps. "Don't touch me!" she warns, edging to the door. "Just raise your hands, shut your mouth and stand still. Like a statue."

But he cannot be still; his hands and his legs shake so bad that his swaying shadow on the wall resembles a masquerade dancing to the ringtone of a phone.

He waits for the door to close before he stumbles to his feet, takes his ringing phone from the desk, peers into it and furrows his brows because it's his wife. Why are some women adamant about coming to those who objectify them, cheat on them, beat them? He has deleted her phone number, but he knows it ends in 779. "Who's this?" he shouts.

"Dorothy," she says. "Ebuka's our son is upturning everything in the house, throwing tomatoes at your clothes and shouting that you prefer bastards in orphanage homes to him. I will tame him for you, Ezi. This marriage of ours will work... It's Dorothy, your wife. Can't you recognise my voice?"

"I'm not married! I don't know you! I don't want to know you! Get out and stay out!"

Dramatic, he knows, but he's not prepared to take any risk. He will not welcome her in his life again, nor welcome her in his house. Let her get out and stay out.

Let everybody get out of his life and stay out of his life. Now they can go ahead and expose the videos and the photos to the whole world. Now he's prepared for a disgrace that will surely hit him, a disgrace and a sack letter. Or will the committee recommend a demotion with no salary for one year, for six months?

His briefcase is on the ground. He takes it with a surprisingly steady hand, throws the door open, and slams it behind him. Hurrying up the staircase is Rose. He knocks her out of his way with the briefcase and continues his clumsy descent.

Downstairs, the evening sun is a pale rose and trees are swaying and whistling. He ignores the waving Professor Ayodele, the sad-faced Chiamaka, and two white-haired male lecturers whose names and departments he invariably forgets, and strides to the mango tree. *I have your pornographic property*! is written on the dust-coated bonnet of his car. Below it, the word, *HA-HA-HA-HA-HA*, slopes downward.

He drives home with slightly trembling hands, honking like a lunatic, frightening fowls and sheep out of the road, splashing green-coloured waters at pedestrians, shouting insults at sluggish schoolchildren crossing.

At the corridor, he meets his wife washing his clothes and listening to a Radio Pastor, or a man with the phlegmy voice of a pastor he suspects he knows, saying something about marriage and how to make it work on her portable radio. Who the hell gave you the key, he wants to snap. Mention his name or I else I will kick you and that despicable radio to the wall. But he recalls that he has done so many dramatic things today.

Slowly, silently, his wife dries her quivering hands on her worn-out *lappa*, rises to give him a welcome hug, but he brushes her aside and stumbles into the house. To his daughter's unfailing greeting he does not respond, does not return his son's, and goes into his bedroom to phone Izu.

Izu is the class leader of the third-year students of the department, and one of those who sell his Nez toothpaste and Nez toothbrushes. "I suppose you've heard about my videos and the photos," he says without a preamble. "I want you to help me destroy them."

"Here I are," Izu says in his unmistakable terrible English before reverting to fluent Igbo. "Use me, sir. But my reward? Just give me A after the exams because. . . Or B. I can even accept C. Not a vitamin C, because that was what Rose once asked you to give me when. . .I remember the day I first got an A from you, it was raining and the door opened and Rose. . ."

Shut up, he thinks and scratches at his baldness as Izu continues chattering. "Meet me at Children of God beer parlour tomorrow at 4pm," he says after a pause on the other end.

Izu produces squeaking noises akin to a farmished

monkey sighting bananas in the hands of his approaching owner, and he ends the call in annoyance; then, after a series of head-shaking and restless hovering in the bedroom, he bolts the door, takes off his clothes and shoes, and switches off the light.

CHAPTER 18

IFENNA kisses the two video recorders, sips his whiskey and looks smilingly from Adaku to Rose to Chioma to Nkem. "We made it, Semicolon!" he says, and leans forward in the Gulder Beer chair at the tranquil bar of Children of God beer parlour. "I swear, I didn't believe that Okoye could think we actually came to bribe him."

A sudden rush of anger in his chest: for their silence, for the shouting voice of a girl behind their table, for the interrupted blues on the loudspeakers, for the startling sound of a shattering glass. A shattering glass that dropped from whose hand? From the hand of the pretty girl who's tearing her pot-belied elderly lover's hand off her shoulder? From the hand of the elderly lover himself? Shamelessly, the girl slaps him and marches out; but, shamelessly, the oldie follows her, pleading for her understanding. Nobody makes any attempt to disguise their curiosity.

A hawk-faced barman standing close to the shattered glass sighs. He sighs again, dramatically this time, as he saunters into a store and re-emerges with a broom and an Indomie noodles carton.

He, Ifenna, drops his drained bottle of whiskey and sips his beer in silence as the barman packs the shards of glass into the carton and shuffles out of the bar to dispose them. Another barman, long-necked and short-legged, staggers in with an empty crate of Hero beer, carries an empty crate of Guinness stout and returns to his grass-roofed shelter.

Multicoloured disco light dance about his bald head. Beside him, at the next table, sits a uniformed couple: a bearded young man pushing a glass of beer teasingly into his pregnant wife's face, and she's leaning back in her seat, shaking her head, giggling like a teenager. From a loudspeaker positioned close to the exit comes the chorus of Chioma's latest song:

Be warned, men, for my hunting knife is sharpened.
Can't you learn that a woman's body belongs to her alone?
But my body also belongs to my Sugar
'Cause we are one…

What a hilarious joke, he thinks. Is the DJ, or whatever he's called, playing this unharmonious rubbish to amuse every listening drinker? Perhaps the DJ doesn't even know the singer is right here. Perhaps the DJ knows but longs to discover which of the girls is the joke.

He turns to Nkem with blinking amusement to see how the song is received, but Nkem says, "I feared you would venture to Dr. Okoye's office and start chewing gum instead of recording his doings. You and Chioma did a terrific job, obviously."

"This music is funny," Rose says, his shoulders shaking with laughter. "Ifenna always laugh at Chioma's music when I used to plait his hair. He laugh yesterday… He laugh in the lecture hall when someone play it…He play it to Adaku and laugh… He like funny music!"

Chioma neither looks at him nor at Rose; she takes a Benson and Hedges cigarette from her handbag, lights it, closes her eyes and inhales deeply. "Sir Israel na one kin' insensible man," she says in unusual pidgin English. "I suggest we bypass am and meet the Vice Chancellor. VC will surely protect me. He always protects me, but he doesn't want to drag me into his bed like all these foolish men that litter this campus. As we planned, we go give am these ones Ifenna and I recorded, and the old ones. And the photos. Okoye is out already. Let's drink to that, abeg!"

Chioma refills her glass and Nkem's with her left hand, asks him ("Umbrella Gum-chewing Princess") to refill his and other empty glasses if he pleases. He ignores

Nkem's apologetic eyes and leans forward to inquire why she has chosen to discriminate some glasses, but she blows cigarette smoke into his creasing face.

At his summon, Adaku refills his glass, shoos away flies from the table and adjusts his new pink scarf, which he bought from Rose to annoy some people. With an unsteady hand, Adaku readjusts the scarf, slaps at the cloud of cigarette smoke Chioma has blown into her face, coughs. Chioma blows smoke into her face again. He blows the smoke back to its owner and turns to face Adaku, who's got up from beside Chioma to sit close to him.

"Take money from your handbag and go and buy more drinks and meat," he says. "Be fast, like a sports car."

"All light, sir," Adaku says, and leaves coughing.

"Some guys say you are still gay because you have not fuck Adaku," Rose tells Ifenna. "Have you fuck Adaku? Semicolon, some guys also say you are gay because you lives with this homo, and they'll kill you like dogs. You know this, Semicolon?"

There's no answer. Can't these guys mind their business? Do they want him to kill them by coming to school dressed in a G-string pant? He has eyeshadow and eye pencils, he has pants, he has mini-skirts he bought when he was acting bourgeois comedies in the university's theatre. There are many high-heeled shoes in his wardrobe, many purple leggings, many boxes of body lotions, lipstick, eyeshadow, lip gloss. If only the security guards will let him cat-walk into the university, chewing his gum happily and unapologetically!

The return of Adaku fills him with with a ridiculous joy. Blinking and licking her upper lip like an infant, she staggers to the table, carrying a Life beer crate containing six bottles of Hero beer and two bottles of Maltina. Sweat trickles down her cheeks, trickles down her hands. He claps encouragingly, and Nkem gives him a warning frown.

"There's no meat reft," Adaku says, and sits. "Should I lun home to bling that goat reg, sir?"

Nkem intervenes. "No, Adaku. We don't need meat, obviously. And stop calling your boyfriend Sir! He's your equal, not your boss!"

Adaku blinks, blinks again and embraces him. Nkem shakes his head and sips his beer. Rose laughs; Chioma blows cigarette smoke into her face. Another song, 2 Face's "African Queen", spills out of the silver-striped loudspeaker, exciting the couple at the next table.

"When does you want us to see the chancellor?" Rose says, and winks at Adaku to run home for the meat, but she's busy cleaning the beer bubbles on her oversized cream gown. "I wants my face to appear in a newspaper, so that my parents will be proud of me."

Nkem drains his glass, lowers it to the table. "None of your business, obviously."

"I really wants to impress my parents," Rose says, and makes a crying face. "Please don't kicks me out. I wants them to see my face. If they sees my face in the newspaper, they'll show it to some of the people in our neighbourhood and they'll die of envy. I wants Mama Eloka to see my face in a newspaper."

"Your parents read newspapers?" he asks, coughing. Chioma's cigarette smoke is becoming unbearable. But nobody wants to rebuke her. Perhaps nobody can rebuke her. Not even Nkem, not even her parents. It is remoured that she blows cigarette smoke into her father's face whenever he refuses to pay her school fees. Is this kind of girl what Nkem is prepared to settle down with after graduation, after NYSC?

"Mrs. Chiamaka is pregnant," Rose announces. "I'm plaiting Jennifer's lice-filled hair when she pass with a stomach that look like football. I suspects Okoye. They are always going to her house. They are always going to his house. Yes, I suspect my baby…I mean, Okoye. They do it, *did* it. And she's pregnant. Her stomach is getting big. Let's look at the stomach on Monday. Who look at the stomach on Friday?"

Nkem straightens up, his eyes ballooning behind his Harry Potter glasses. "Male or female, blessed wine? She needed a male child, but I wish it were female. Is it a female child? Is it? It's a female, obviously. Because I haven't seen the madwoman running round the campus with a triumphant flag shedding shameless tears of joy."

284

"Can somebody slap that foolish woman for me?" Chioma asks, and lights another cigarette. "The first day I heard she wanted to birth a male child by all means, I visualised myself knifing her stomach."

Nkem stands. "So it's settled? We will be going to the VC's office to show him what we videoed?"

The door bursts open and a voice screams. In steps a boy in a black polo and black jeans. In steps another boy in a black polo and black jeans. A scream on the cliff of his tongue, but gunshots shatter the ceilings and the two black-clothed boys become three black-clothed boys. Three becomes four. Four becomes five. Five jumps over six and seven and eight and nine and becomes ten. Dangerous-looking boys: all unsmiling, unshaved, unfraid. The couple are hiding behind their table, shaking, watching. The barman is a wet mouse making his quivering retreat into a box-shaped uncompleted building that is another bar. A female voice screams inside. A male voice shuns it inside. Another gunshot, another screaming. He looks at them, ready to die. There are tattoos of skulls on their bare shoulders, necks, hands; Nkem grasps the video recorders from him, stuffs them into his pockets, grasps Chioma's hand and jumps over an empty crate of beer. Together, they run past a beer-filled refrigerator nearby, past trembling waiters and trembling waitresses, past tables and crates, past a sliding door and into an uncompleted store that usually smells pungently of urine. The female voice screams again.

"Where that homo?" one of them roars, pulling out his gun from under his polo that says *Me Against the World*. Like his fellows, there are tattoos on his shoulders, on his neck, on his hands. "Where the homo make 'im collect!"

"See am here!" another one says, tearing off his scarf. "Na so una they convert innocent people to homo!"

They collect his gold ankle, they slap his mouth, they boot his bottom. They whisper among themselves, stop momentarily as though they want to ascertain whether he's still breathing, whisper among themselves once again before tearing his shirt and dragging him like a bag of palm nuts to the door. The huge one among them pull down his trousers, tries to force a dry stick into his anus, but he stops him with a twitching hand. "But na wetin you do your fellow man?" asks the huge one. "Why you choose to be homo, man?"

I will burn all my girl costumes, he would like to say. But he cannot speak; he can only watch them; his mouth is full of blood. Behind him, he hears Adaku cry in pain, hears her call his name. He closes his eyes as they take his phone, take his wallet, and escape through the front door, through the back door, and through the windows opened to welcome the steep sunlight.

Adaku takes him to the Medical Centre, where he

receives treatments for two days causing him to miss a test. Nkem and Chioma also missed the test: they were hiding in his Uncle Elijah's church, they tell him on the phone. They thought the thugs would attack their hostels, snatch the videos away from them, rape Chioma as they once raped Rose. "My consolation is that nobody took the recorders," Nkem says.

"But you and Sugar have missed a lot of tests because of your flowery outfits, Ifenna!" Chioma says. "Can't you change? Please!"

"The only thing I want to change right now is my nose ring," he replies. "I want a new one. This one no longer glitters. Do you know where I can buy new nose rings? And scarves? They tore my scarf, God!"

Uncle Elijah calls him last. "I'm not happy with you, Ifenna," he says in Igbo. "Sister Kate complained to me that you came to this church last week and escaped with their scarves. Seven headscarves belonging to seven women in this church."

He took six, not seven, but he says, "I stole *two* scarves, not seven, Uncle Elijah. You heard I was attacked by ten handsome boys? And I am in this beautiful medical centre."

"The Lord is your strength," Uncle Elijah says in surprisingly good English, and ends the call.

Adaku takes the phone from him, dries his sweaty face with her handkerchief, fans his neck with it. From the mango tree he can see through the open window come the songs of birds. The sky is turquoise and burnished, and the air is thick with the delicious smell of flowers.

"How often do you read your Bible?" a blemished, middle-aged albino nurse with chicken legs asks him as he wears his shoes for departure. "Can't you stop being gay, embrace Jesus, and have peace?"

"I wanted to embrace you to have peace," he says, heading to the exit with Adaku who carries his drugs in her handbag. "But you're not attractive at all."

Wrathful curses and insults from workers and patients follow him and Adaku out of the Medical Centre.

On the Campus Road, he glimpses Okoye strolling with Izu, chatting with Izu. A dog, brown and emaciated, trots behind them. Does the dog think they own him? Or hired him. Hired him to help them in their hunting. Are these semi-mad fellows really hunting? Hunting for what exactly? He, Nkem, Chioma, or the videos and the photos? Or the video recorders? No: Okoye is not aware that he was videoed in his office. But he'll soon hear it. He'll soon fall from his present frying pan and into the Vice Chancellor's fire. As for the thugs who continue to attack him, attack them, he will buy a local gun and wait for them. "Go to my hostel and cook *ofe nsala* for me," he says. "Thank God those boys didn't rape you.

Sometimes it's good to be ugly. You were lucky… Who would be cooking *ofe nsala* for me if they had raped you to death?" He pets her cheek, laughs with her. "Please, remember: enough fish, enough meat. After cooking, wash my clothes and iron them. Leave the socks. Stop ironing my socks, please."

"All light."

"Then bring the soup to Uncle Elijah's church. Be fast, like a sports car."

"All light." She takes his hands, presses herself to him. "Sir. All light, sir."

He wriggles out of her pseudo-embrace because she smells of onions, waves her goodbye. Then, popping gum into his mouth, he turns, takes another route, and leaves the campus.

CHAPTER 19

NKEM cannot get himself to believe what Rose is telling him about Chioma. Chioma the newest married woman on campus, Rose says under her breath. Chioma's feminist friend Jewell and Rose's customer, an Ivorian stripper in her hostel, came to plait her hair and told Rose that Chioma's mother seized her phone so she couldn't invite Nkem to her wedding. Chioma and Chief got married five days ago in Abuja. Top businessmen and top businesswomen, top actors, top musicians: they were all in attendance. The stunning photos are on Chioma's wall on Facebook. Stunning, too, are the smartphones and the iPad Chief bought for Chioma in London where they are honeymooning. "I know you feels like fighting," she adds.

"Hold on a minute," he says in a disembodied voice, and ends the call with a quivering hand.

Of course Rose is, to him, to many people, a personification of honesty; but can Chioma be this heartless?

On her Facebook wall, there are hundreds of colourful photos of the wedding. They show that Rose is right, he thinks. But it's in Paris, and not in London. Some of the photos that show the new couple drinking coconut with straws at a seaside are captioned "The Surreal Paris, Finally!"

He scans the wedding pictures, lingering on one: Chief bending to kiss her in a heavenly reception hall overflowing with applauding attendants. He has already imagined Chief as a white-haired, frail man of sixty-five or seventy with short legs, but this balding man in a black suit who's kissing white-gowned Chioma in this photograph reminds him of Okonkwo in *Things Fall Apart*: intimidatingly muscular, huge, hairy, dark, wide-nosed. He cannot be older than fifty-five. He clicks on comments with an increasingly quivering fingers. The word, "congratulations", litters most threads. Of all the 97 commenters, he knows only four. It's obvious she didn't invite the class. The boys must be disappointed and the girls envious.

Ifenna Nzekwu: I cannot find my earlier comments here. I commented ur husband's eyes are already on ur breasts and his wedding trousers are swollen at the centre because he has an erection, but you deleted it? Jesus

Christ, what's wrong with the comment?! It's clear that Chief ur horse-band has an erection. Congratulations to HIM.

Dr Okoye Ezinwa: Congrats! Kindly send your account number. Want to send you money. Not because of those things, if you know what I mean. See it as a wedding gift.

Rose Eloka: I wiLL TelL nKem.

Izuchukwu Junior: You doesn't invait us. So your deleting anger comments from us from economics depathment. Am impresed.

She must also be impressed, he thinks, if I send her a stroke-inducing comment embellished with curses, but pauses on the brink of a fall into pettiness, and logs out of Facebook. This is unfair, he thinks, fighting tears. This is so unfair and so wicked. How can love be so wicked? How can he, vertiginous with this problem of Chioma-lessness, possibly stumble across this campus and across this life without falling and breaking like a glass?

Rose calls again. "Since she have get marry, you will take me?"

"Take Ifenna," he replies. "Take any guy of your choice in this university, but leave me alone. I'm tired of love. I hate love, Rose. I hate love. Look at what it has done to me?"

"Don't cry. You're not a girl or Ifenna. And stop asking me to take him…her. Ifenna is a girl and I cannot sleeps with a girl." She has spoken rapidly in Igbo, so she now pauses for him to ponder her suggestion, and then continues in unbelievably grammatical English. "Semicolon, I have another breaking news. Disconcerting news."

"I don't want to hear about Chioma again, obviously!"

"No. Not Chioma. It's Izu. As soon as you and Ifenna the Chewing Gum leaved your apartment for our morning lectures, the albino fool enter into your room through the broken window and take away the video recorders. Maybe he drinked your milk and tea before escaping."

"Are you insinuating that you're omniscient?" he asks. "You don't understand me? I mean, you weren't there, obviously. So how did you find out?"

She opens up: a week ago, she offered Izu some money to buy her a good grade from Chiamaka. She suspected the well-hidden textbook from which she copied during the examination was for a different course, which meant she failed the course. She could not accept an F or an E, so she slept with Okoye again for the money. But Chiamaka told her that "the albino" did not give her the money, not even one naira, and she, Chiamaka, noticed the boy bought new shirts, new caps, new shoes. Maybe Izu slurged the money on shoes. Maybe he gave it to another woman lecturer thinking it is she. Now, she and Chiamaka are tracking the "criminal." They will tear him like a cloth. They will slap his face and watch him turn red or pink. They will arrest him with the police. They cannot fold their arms and watch him get way with their money. "May God saves us," she adds with an exasperating sigh.

"Amen." He murmurs his insincere thanks and ends the call.

Far-fetched, though it seems, but he will approach this matter with the seriousness of a professional inspector. He will knife anybody who tries to stop him. He hurries out of the bedroom and finds that the sky, which was packed with clouds so white and shaped like snows few minutes ago, is now tainted with startlingly brilliant red—the colour of war, of spilt blood.

On the pothole-filled road that leads to Okoye's house, he finds Izu. He grabs the foe's waist from behind and kicks his bottom. The boy yelps like a puppy, but he gives him another kick. He slaps his back, his neck, his head, and the boy falls to the soil, groans in agony, rolls away from him and begins making convulsive noises.

Funny. It surprises him that the recorder-criminal think that he, Nkem of all people, will be fooled by his fake convulsive noises. "Give me the video recorder or I will kill you!" he shouts.

"You're spitting into my face," Izu says in rural Igbo.

He bats Izu's mouth with George Eliot's enormous

novel, *Middlematch*, which is his current read after his temporal break from Oscar Wilde's *The Ballad of the Reading Gaol*.

He hits Izu again, and again. The criminal cries out as he scrambles to his feet, dusts his brown trousers, dusts his Liverpool jersey. "I collected the video recorder, but I have lost it. I was blowing dust off the thing and one fat boy from nowhere pushed me from the back and I fell into a bucket of water with the videos and ugly girls screamed, Jesus! One of them is Adaku, who is Ifenna's and Noisy Beans my roommate's crush. Noisy Beans used to tell me that the girl snores while sleeping and he used to cover his ears with two pencils. . ."

"Enough of that digression! And listen. If you don't produce the devices in the next two seconds, I will strangle you to death." He pauses, clucks over a skinny old woman limping by with a basket of crayfish and stockfish and staring at them with disapproving eyes. "Now, for the last time, where's the video?"

"It's in the bucket—a blue, plastic bucket with a shiny cover. I wonder why it has no handle. Chidi, my roommate, says he likes buckets with a shiny cover. . . He's the sheep that threw away the video."

"But you said it was in the blue, plastic bucket with a shiny cover, obviously. Didn't you?"

"It was a slip of the tongue. I've lost the video recorder, but the bucket is still in my bathroom. Should I go and bring it?"

You bloody bastard, he thinks, and shoves Izu with both hands. The recorder-criminal dances backwards, falls into tea-coloured dust. From his under his polo, the video recorders drop. He kicks Izu again, and again, before marching out.

The next day, Okoye phones. "I'd like us to settle once and for all over a bottle of beer and a plate of pepper soup," he says. "You have all my dangerous videos and the photos and I have a woman at the Exams and Records who have all your dangerous Es and Fs. You deserve better grades, but you don't want to help yourself by helping me. Climb down from your dangerous pulpit of uprightness: This is Nigeria. Come to my house and understand me better. Come with Nzekwu, will you?"

"No, blessed wine!" he replies.

He says no with vehemence, but the truth is, he likes what he heard. Surprising, yes, but he likes what he heard. And Okoye likes that they are both in need of something: he an impressive grade, Okoye his job safe in his hands. Of this, he is sure. He is sure, too, that Okoye heard in his voice a promise of a compromise, of a yielding. He tells himself he needs to relinquish his pride and principles, and see what can be done to his crumbling grades. He tells himself he has missed a lot of quizzes, missed a lot of lectures, and their assailants might still prevent them from taking future tests, from attending future lectures. He tells himself that his dream, oh his dream, of making First Class, or at worst a 2:1, is drifting away from him, like a soap bubble in the wind. He knows he needs to be wary. He knows he needs swiftness of decision, of action, or this floating bubble will, tragically, burst to the joy of the enemies. So he will seize this opportunity. He will not let his final grade point to mock him, shatter him, and send his pieces to your grave. Bribery: he will have to resort to bribery. But who would have guessed that he, Nkem the Great of all people, would ever consider bribery? How the mighty have fallen!

At night, amidst the sounds of gunshots from cultists or robbers, he unburdens himself to Ifenna, who chuckles without mirth but suggests they visit Okoye. He thanks Ifenna and pulls his blanket to his chin, but knows he cannot sleep: the gunshots are now close, now frightening.

As the sun rises in the morning, he and Ifenna get out of the foam but do not knock on their neighbours' door to check if any boy was killed and if any girl was raped.

Downstairs, they glimpse a small gathering: five or six students saying something about cultists raping innocent Ginika, robbing wretched Lotanna and Jidenna of their phones, dragging asthmatic Samuel and epileptic Frank into bushes for initiations into their confraternity. He and Nkem glide past them without a syllable. They do not eat beans and plantains at the Eating Mall as they usually do most mornings, but make their way through herds of boisterous students to Okoye's office, knock on the door, and enter.

The reception: a plastic smile, tattered seats, apologies for the untidiness of the living room. There are empty bottles of beer under stools, beside a refrigerator, behind their sofas. There are bawdy clothes strewn across the floor. On the centre table are an ash-filed ashtray, an empty packet of cigarettes, a pile of books. Okoye clears the table, carries them into his bedroom, returns with an excuse: "My children are at boarding school. And I have been busy writing, so pardon my embarrassing flat. My wife? She threatened me with a divorce, then threatened that she'd leave me. I smiled and I helped her pack. So nobody helps me at home now. Dorothy still comes and goes, though."

"You smiled and helped her pack?" Ifenna asks, and throws gum into his mouth.

Okoye nods and murmurs something about philanthropists being easily charitable. And rubbing his stomach, Okoye pads off towards the refrigerator, re-emerges with three bottles of Life beer. But they do not accept the offer. Without a word, Okoye leaves the bottles on a stool close to them, goes into his kitchen. In half a minute, he returns with two plates of pepper soup, sets them on the stool, and looks at him.

The noise of a faulty generator starting somewhere downstairs splits the silence. "Dr. Okoye, you sent a young thief to break into our house to steal our property," he shouts over the noise. "Stop celebrating; Ifenna and I have overpowered the dubious ignoramus and reclaimed our video recorders."

The generator noise dies down. "Let me see who's toying with that gen," Okoye says. "A minute, please."

After Okoye's gone, he says, "We will not touch the pepper soup, blessed wine."

"Why?" Ifenna asks in a faux mournful voice, his eyes on the pepper soup. "Why, Semicolon? Why? Don't do this to me! Is it because Chioma left you for a Big Nose in France?"

"I'm not in the mood for your habitual drama." He pauses, looks into Ifenna's melancholic eyes. "I suspect he poisoned this pepper soup. Have sense."

"No, no, no," Ifenna says, rising. "We're Christians, Semicolon. At least I am. But let's kneel down and pray."

"You must be joking!"

"Only a fool jokes when there's a plate of delicious pepper soup before him." Ifenna goes to the stool, takes the bigger plate and returns to his seat with his eyes closed. "Jesus, protect me. Remove the poison in this pepper soup. I want to enjoy it without dying. Heavenly Father, cover your son with your precious blood. Baba, we are really Christians, I swear. So protect us. We're serving nobody but you the God of Abraham, David and Daniel. If you could make lions not to eat Daniel like bread, why does the devil think you can't save us from poison in pepper soup? The Bible says we shall trample upon serpents and scorpions and they shall not harm us. Thank you for what you've done in this pepper soup. Amen."

Ifenna is eating the last meat in his plate when Okoye returns. "Delicious, right?" he asks Ifenna; then, to him: "Chief, you are not eating. Why?"

"I'm not here to eat pepper soup, blessed wine," he says.

"I'm here to eat pepper soup." Ifenna lowers his spoon, washes his hand in a bowl. "And do business, *obviously*."

Obviously: it's my accent, he thinks. How dare Ifenna mimic the accent, mock the accent? Why is this gum-chewing guy chasing a rat when the house is on fire? The pepper soup: it must be the sweetness of the pepper soup. Perhaps Okoye cooked it to oil his way into their hearts, take the video recorders, sneak away. Who told him that two plates of pepper soup can do it for him?

"You invited us, Dr. Okoye," he says.

Okoye clears his throat and sits up. "First, I apologise for paying that albino to go and get me the video recorders from your room. Now, what will I do to make you keep the videos and the photos out of the Vice Chancellor's reach? I don't want that sissified man-child to throw me out. Help me, chiefs."

"There is a friend of mine at the Exams and Records block. Mama Nkechi is her name. Not my friend exactly, but with money there's nothing that beautiful idiot cannot do for me. Your grades are falling. She can transform all of them to As and Bs. Last year, she made so much money from altering students' poor grades and now she drives a Benz like a Yahoo boy. Do you want her to help you chiefs? Remember she once told me you want to make a first-class? Let's contact her, okay? Say yes."

He does not speak because this grade alteration business has suddenly seemed hopeless. This grade alteration business goes against the university rules, goes against his own rules, goes against everything he believes in. This grade alteration business, if discovered, will certainly collar his God-fearing mother and amuse his father who relishes absurd jokes. He opens his mouth to say no, but his lips tremble and his heart begins to thump.

Into the sullen silence Ifenna blows his gum. This act of childishness stiffens his face; he glares at Ifenna, then his gaze falls. "This thing we want to do is not good, it's not right," he says. "Altering our grades is the action of a corrupt soul. But those poor grades I have are not mine; I deserve better but..."

The door flings open; they all turn to see the ill-mannered intruder.

Ebuka, Okoye's son. Of course it has to be the Facebook addict, he thinks, and watches the boy enter with a swagger and scan the living room. The boy is shirtless, sweating, panting and nursing a soiled football.

"Close that door!" Okoye shouts in Igbo. "And where were you? Downloading another Facebook app in the market? Playing football, drinking and chasing little girls up and down the street like a good Christian boy that you are?"

His son doesn't touch the door, doesn't greet his father and his father's visitors, but does take the untouched plate of pepper soup. "Exactly, Dad," his son says, chewing the meat and strolling into a bedroom. "I can cook better than you. Maybe it is because it is no longer hot. On Facebook, Zikora hinted that cow meat is the king of meat. But...mmm...! Too much maggi or curry!"

The door closes behind him. From the curtain a gecko drops, scuttles under his dinning table to hide in a pile of decaying books. Pig, he thinks. A pig in human clothes.

"I'm sorry about my son's. . . the boy's awful manners." Okoye scratches his baldness, scratches his armpit. "I will discipline him later."

"Like father like son," Ifenna says with a smiling joviality.

Okoye jerks toward to Ifenna with a rumpled face, but words do not drop like stones from his mouth. The faulty generator starts again, dies, restarts teasingly, and then roars to life.

"So, Dr. Okoye, when do you suggest we see Mama Nkechi for this humbling business?" he shouts over the noise.

Okoye lights a cigarette before he answers. "Tomorrow. 4: 00 p.m. Maxi Hotel. Not Children of God beer parlour; I don't want to run into Professor Ayodele. Is tomorrow convenient, chiefs?"

Downstairs, a deep, masculine voice of a furious man bawls the name of Nnamdi, and the generator dies down again. *Taaaaah!* comes the sound of a slap. A youthful voice shouts something about old fools always suspecting fine boys of stealing their fuel, stealing their engine oil, stealing their plugs. *Taaaaaah!* comes another slap. Something crashes to the ground.

Okoye cranes his neck to listen to the fight, but Ifenna blows his chewing gum, startling him.

"Phone Mama Nkechi today, blessed wine," he says to Okoye, and rises to go. "Tomorrow's convenient to me and Ifenna, obviously."

CHAPTER 20

OKOYE drives to the Exams and Records block with his windows rolled up.

Waiting for him at the crowded entrance is Mama Nkechi. "Come outside," she whispers, and takes his hand. "Walls have ears."

Beneath the whispering neem tree where his car is parked, she says, "Business, Ezinwa? Do you want me to lose my job? And who told you I still do this type of thing?"

Beautiful, pretentious fraudster, he thinks. But she used to go to orphanage homes with him. Big sensual mouth, big Indian eyes, big pawpaw-like breasts, and a big, curvaceous waist. How old is this distracting Aphrodisiac and ex-philanthropist called Mama Nkechi? Forty? Forty-five? He cannot remember. What he remembers, however, is that he has made love to her in his office, in her office, in a hotel room. She likes it fast, she likes it rough: like Rose, like Chioma. But she's much better: because she writhes and screams, because she eats this fruit they both know they shouldn't be eating and cleans her mouth, because she always asks for more. He would like to enjoy another bout of reckless fucking with her, but let her upgrade Nkem's grade and Ifenna's grade first.

"It's been long," he says, his eyes on her magnetic chest. "It has been really long I see... I seen... I saw. I saw you at the bread where I ventured to buy a loaf of market."

"You ventured to bread to buy a loaf of market, Ezinwa?" She takes off the *Have You Been to Jesus?* bonnet she's wearing over a silky lemon gown, scans their surrounding with eyes radiant with panic. "Your mind isn't here... Let's discuss this grade business in your office after work today. No, tomorrow. I have a meeting in my church at 5: 30. You may come, the ministering man of God, Pastor Elijah, once raised a dead girl."

"I didn't know I am a dead girl." He dusts his briefcase and turns to his car. "Tomorrow, then."

At exactly 4: 30 p.m the following day, she comes to his office carrying a large Bible to meet him, Nkem and Ifenna. Without a preamble, he says, "Mama Nkechi, these are the boys...the chiefs. Turn their Fs, Es and Ds to As and Bs. How much?"

"Pastor Elijah said you're his nephew," Mama Nkechi tells Ifenna. "And he allows you to wear a ring in your nose?"

"And earrings," Ifenna says. "He also allows me to wear earrings in his church. That's the kindness of a true Christian."

She looks at Ifenna with unblinking eyes, and he bets her reaction to this improbable will be a self-righteous reprimand, but a knock at the door breaks the silence, preventing, or postponing, the possibility of an absurd episode.

Rose stumbles in like she's pushed. "The HOD have die!" she announces with glee, and closes the door behind her. "He die this morning in his office! Go and see his corpse before they'll takes him to the mortuary. I hear he die because he is fasting and praying. He want to fast and pray for forty days and forty nights. Now look at what he have done to hisself. He die with his head in a hymn book. Maybe he is singing 'Rock of Ages'. That's very funny. I can't stop laughing!"

Before she completes her speech, the cries of mourners come from the floor below and into the office. I can't stop laughing too, he thinks. And the students, perhaps. Now every student, every lecturer, will go to a funeral, eat meat-filled jollof rice, drink beer, and urinate on a fence. Or will Sir Israel's staunch Catholicism forbid the intake of alcohol at his burial ceremony? He, Okoye, will disagree with his people and make sure every booze-drinking person has at least one bottle of beer. He will drink five bottles of chilled Gulder beer, if he has no appointment with one of the pretty girls in his class in a hotel room.

"Rose, you mean Sir Israel died?" Nkem asks, and she nods and smirks. The head of the department is dead: is this supposed to be funny? He folds his arms, swallows, and watches Nkem, who's shaking his head and gazing at Ifenna. But the Umbrella Boy is chewing gum with unapologetic indifference and looking out a half-opened window in silence. From this window, an incredibly bright and fierce sunlight streams into the office and makes the beads of sweat on Rose's bleached face glisten like some strange pieces of gold jewelry. She moves drunkenly closer to Nkem and, with some difficulty, wears a green cap that says *Students' Union Government* on her blonde wig. The breeze from the window brings the odour of alcohol into his nostrils.

Oh, Rose my girlfriend, he thinks. Which despicable blockhead in the students' union government has been giving his girl beer and caps and making love to her?

"I hope the late Sir Israel didn't owe any of us," Ifenna says. "I suspect he owed Chiamaka. He bought her tomatoes on her farm and he hasn't paid her. That woman will cry out her eyes. Thank God, he didn't owe me. I would have marched into his office to slap his face."

Downstairs a female voice lets out a shrill cry and frightened fowls begin a mutiny of squawks. Several voices, mostly female, murmur their consolations. His church members, he tells himself. Or our colleagues? Do they expect me downstairs? Do they expect me to shed a tear? Over my dead body.

He glances at Nkem, who seems indifferent, and then at Ifenna, who's chewing gum with smiling felicity. Mama Nkechi, as he expects, is being pretentious: her head is lowered in faux sympathy. He wishes she would lift that head so he could look at her breast-filled bra showing through her transparent gown.

"Let's go to Alif Standard Hotel," he says. "Soon my colleagues will start trooping in here. . . Rose, don't follow us. Go and plait hairs."

Alif Standard Hotel bar smells deliciously of rich perfume, but the AC is so mercilessly breathing out freezing air. At a Life beer table, they sit. He glances round the bar to see if his wife, like a police inspector, is hiding somewhere to observe his actions, and then looks furtively at his clothes. Food-stained, parched, and rumpled like a rag: he hopes the manager, who's obsessed with cleanliness, will not frog-march him out of the hotel.

"Beer," he calls. "And cigarettes—Benson and Hedges, or Oris. And three glasses, not these modern plastic cups, which make our beer look and taste like a urine sample."

After a bloated barman has offered them his orders, he says, "How much, Mama Nkechi? You have not answered us."

"You ask me how much as if you want to buy a TV or a carpet from me," she says, and sips her beer. "If my husband or my church members catch me here, what will I tell my God?"

Nkem, who sits quiescent in the only gold-striped cushion, now leans forward with giddy hopelessness. "Let's stop beating around the stupid bush, do this necessary but wrong thing, and get on with our lives. God, I didn't know I would ever succumb to this madness."

She stares at him for a long moment before she speaks. "Eighty thousand naira, Ezinwa. I would have collected seventy because I know you, but this boy is arrogant. He's arrogant, but he can't pass his courses. Nonsense!"

Nkem puts his head into his hand, sneezes, mutters something; but the crazed honking of a car somewhere submerges his words.

Is the anxious boy on the brink of tears? He knows Chioma has slipped from the boy's fingers. He knows she didn't invite him to her wedding and didn't inform him when she returned few weeks ago. He knows the boy needs something to cheer him up, something to rescue him from the darkness into which love has plunged him. But there's no good news. There will not be any good news: a Second Class (Upper Division) degree is slipping, or has slipped, from his fingers. And something tells him this woman is dubious, and cannot help this grieving scholar.

"I will give you fifty-thousand naira," he tells Mama Nkechi, and sips his beer. "I'm your…remember? I am your…."

"This is business, Ezinwa. Everything is expensive in the market now. A bag of rice is almost twenty thousand naira. Our barzar at church is around the corner and I have promised God that I will give Him a bag of rice. Give me seventy-five thousand naira, let me buy the bag of rice. And other things the church needs. Or are you still sending all your money to those stolen babies in the orphanage?"

Ifenna blows his gum as if to mock this woman, to mock this ridiculousness. "Sixty, madam? Reduce the price, because there's no capital in this business. Everything is your gain. It's not a bed that one has to buy wood and nails and start construction. This one is different. And there is no receipt to be issued to us your new customers. Just clean the funny Es and Fs and give us nice As and Bs."

"Your diction is admirable and worthy of emulation, Nzekwu," he says, and then, to Mama Nkechi: "I'm so sorry."

But she wrinkles her nose and rises. "I think I'm not the right Samaritan for this business."

"No, please, wait!" He clutches her hand with his right hand and drinks his beer with the other. "We will give you seventy-five thousand naira. Send your bank details to me on WhatsApp."

Nkem raises his head, his eyes percolating with shame and hopelessness. "How sure are we that you're going to do the job, blessed wine?" he asks Mama Nkechi.

Ifenna speaks for her. "She has been doing this for years. Very talented, Semicolon. If she isn't good at what she does, why does everybody keep crying to her to change their embarrassing grades to applaudable ones? I think she has built a duplex in this town from cleaning bad grades and creating good ones."

"You talk like a woman!" she says, and picks her Bible from the table. "Where did you pick this parrot, Ezinwa? No, no, don't answer: I am late to church. My money, remember? Goodbye."

In sullen silence, he drives Nkem and Ifenna back to their hostel; but they do not thank him, they do not even say goodbye. Returning to the university, humming Cristy Lane's "Try a Little Kindness", he finds Rose running after his car with her mouth wide open like a panting dog. He parks, plucks open the door, and she enters. "Good afternoon, baby," she says.

He restarts the car and it commences its drunken movement. "You have a lecture, Rosie?'

"Baby, I'm returning from plaiting the smelly hair of Chika, the girl Professor Efe once lick like stew in his car one night, when I see you and Mama Nkechi entering a hotel again," she says, rolling her newly fixed blue eyes. "You want her to change Nkem's results or what? Do the business, but don't do her. I don't trust you. She *climb* Reverend Pious, my first boyfriend. And Ifenna's uncle, Elijah. And my roommate's boyfriend, Papa Nwokedi. And your friend, Ayosky. But Ayosky have now. . . Do you know, baby? Your friend Professor Ayodele, or Ayosky, have die? They kill him today."

"Don't joke with death." He drives into the university, ignoring the haggard security guards who are waving, smiling, hoping for tips. "Your Ayosky wouldn't dance if he heard you used the word 'death' and his name in the same sentence. A very childish man, that Ayosky. He wants to be young forever."

Rose slaps his back playfully. "I'm serious, baby! He die! The killers say he can't destroy the private parts of our Igbo babes and return to his Yoruba state just like that. They write it on a cardboard sheet and glue it on his arse. His corpse is find…finded in that gutter in front of Children of God Beer parlour. Don't pretend you hadn't heard that?"

He drops her off at the department block and

strolls over to Chiamaka's office to see her. Or to see her imbecile baby boy, their imbecile. But her office is locked.

He phones her, calls her the newest mum in town, and waits. "Your friend is dead, yes," she says. "And if you don't come to see your baby, you will be the next, Okonkwo. Mark my word. If you want to see me, come to late Sir Israel's hometown. I am helping his wife. His burial is next week, yes. But you don't know. You only know your numerous girlfriends. Come and know your baby, Okonkwo. But keep your mouth shut. My husband is suspecting... Oh, Mrs. Israel is already here! Talk later, Okonkwo!"

So Professor Ayodele is dead. This tragic news is a reassuring proof that Rose can't be mendacious. He will never see Ayosky again. With whom will he be drinking beer? With whom will he be discussing pretty girls? Who will be inadvertently teaching him to wash his dirty shirts, to iron his rumpled, patched trousers? Who will be using his spare condoms and calling him the greatest Igbo man of our time? With a steady hand, he pockets his phone without ending the call, folds his arms, shakes his head. Ayosky. So Ayosky is gone, gone forever? Life: a borrowed butterfly in the hand of an infant, which can be blown away by the wind without any notice.

It's mid-day already: the sky is the colour of a placid sea and in it sits a blinding orange. Either his irises are failing him, or heavens want to torture the town with a burning sun? He does not know. He does not need to know. He closes his eyes to escape this universe, this reality, but he cannot breathe. He opens the eyes, rubs and rubs, but he cannot see the lit world he has left behind: Darkness has descended upon him and he feels the ground opening under his feet, invisible waters rising to his nose. A new education: Never did he know that the transition of any of his friends could make him feel weightless, like a kite released into the air.

He drives home and drinks five bottles of Hero beer, and yet his heart is still heavy with muddled feelings of sorrow and anger.

He is opening his sixth beer when a knock comes to his door. "Who is that?" he asks, lowering the bottle to his stool. "Ebuka? Chinenye? Who is that creeping being? Come in or get out!"

The door opens and a middle-aged man in shiny star-littered suit steps in. He is handsome with striking brown eyes, a striking straight nose, and curly hair that reminds him of a soaked rat he killed in his bathroom in the morning.

"My name is Papa Nkechi," the stranger says in Igbo.

"Okay."

The stranger installs himself in one battered cushion, leans back in slow motion, crosses his legs like a famous movie star who's not well brought up. "I'm sure you were expecting an older man with a bald head and perhaps a similar beer belly, but I am just a young guy. I married earlier than my mates because I am rich and smart and handsome. I'm responsible, God-fearing, but I can make your life miserable if you don't take your beer-smelling hands off the breasts that do not belong to you."

Breasts that do not belong to him: which breasts in this university town do not belong to me, he thinks. My hands are on your wife's breasts, and so what? His chest is swelling and boiling, but he will not fight. Is he afraid of the threatening stranger? In all things, no, he thinks he is not. He has the man's history with some married women, thanks to Rose. But he will not detonate one of the bombs on his bleached ears, not yet. He will let the man insult or threaten him again. The toy gun sticking out of the childish man's breasts-pocket triggers a crazed urge to wrestle him to the ground, stuffing him with food and toilet paper, until they both look nine months pregnant.

He decides to be rude. "Which animal chased you into my flat?"

"Look, look, Mr. Lecturer!" Papa Nkechi says, uncrossing those infuriatingly beautiful straight legs of his. "Look. I'm not here to argue or exchange insults with a man who's fat enough to be my father. I'm here for a decisive investigation, and you must comply. Rose your girlfriend and student told me she always saw you and my beautiful wife. I wonder what you're doing with my beautiful wife, Mr. Lecturer. Only God knows if you've kissed her. No, it's not possible. Angelina cannot stoop so low to touch an obese nonentity who sells toothpaste and toothbrushes to his students. It can't be possible; I trust Angelina. She has a high taste, and she's remarkably choosy. She can't eat a toad because every woman is eating a toad. She likes her men petite and neat and charming, and not like a bag of cement or a bag of foreign rice. Man, your hip and stomach and head are so fat; I cannot believe that the God I serve made these shapes."

"If you think it's impossible for your wife to cheat on you, why did you cry and venture to my house? Answer me, Papa Nkechi."

"Be warned, you beer-smelling pig—you lowdown chaff! Of course I trust my incomparable wife, but I cannot live to see any random squalor-personified nonentity with no reputable textbook. . . God, what will people say when the scandal begins to spread? A beer-soaked rag like this is having an affair with my wife. I can't stand this! What do you have to say, Mr. Lecturer? Are you sleeping with my wife?"

He lights a cigarette with shaky hands. "I'm not sure I've slept with your wife, Papa Nkechi. But don't say it's unfair; that I banged other men's wives, but I don't want to bang yours for you. Oh, my dearest, please forgive my laziness and procrastinations. If I've time this week I will make love to your wife in my bed or in yours to make you feel very happy, my dearest. I promise, because you do the same favour to other husbands. You're eating another man's wife like nsala soup. That God-fearing woman who sells goats and sheep in the town's main market. Isn't that correct, child of God?"

"It's not correct!" Papa Nkechi bays, and springs up. "Who told you that filthy nonsense? Mention his or her name. It's not true."

On his radio in the bedroom, a dog barks in a drama being enacted by schoolchildren and, down the stairs, the landlord's German Shepherd responds. Is the landlord listening to the radio with his dog or is this a mere coincidence? The dog, not the one on the radio, barks again and he says, "Now, Papa Nkechi, get out of my house before I report you to my bulldogs."

Papa Nkechi jumps out from the cushion, points the red plastic gun to his face with both hands. "Close your mouth, raise your hands. I will shoot you dead if you move an inch!"

"Go and return that Christmas plastic you call a gun to the baby from whom you hired it or I will look for his parents myself." He wears his glasses, stretches his neck like a zebra to see the toy gun clearly in the silenced man's trembling hands. The dog barks again on the radio.

"The bulldog barking is called Major General," he says. "Let me invite him to come and have fun with you?"

"Wait, wait!" Papa Nkechi says, stepping backwards. The toy gun slips from him, shatters on the ground. "Wait, sir. I am leaving, Lecturer—Sir! Yes, yes: it's a toy gun for Christmas. . . Leave the dog, please: I'm leaving, as you can see. Thanks, sir. Goodbye, sir!"

He reaches for his *Vanguard* newspaper on the stool as the man hurries out of the flat. The door bangs shut; his photograph on the wall swings back and forth, like a pendulum, drops and shatters on the floor. The coward will surely hit back, he thinks. Cowards always run to fight another day. Papa Nkechi will hit him where it hurts. Nkem, Ifenna, Mama Nkechi and himself— three big fruits that have dropped from a tree and into a burning bush. He has to do something fast and wise to quench this fire smouldering on the mountain, but he continues to smoke his cigarette.

CHAPTER 21

IFENNA strolls to the Department of English and Literary Studies to know why Adaku has not been taking his incessant calls for two days now. He wants to tell her that Mama Nkechi is having a row with Papa Nkechi; that their hope of working with Mama Nkechi is like a thread; that he needs two hundred thousand naira from her to bribe Papa Nkechi. But she isn't taking his calls. Why isn't she taking his calls?

At the entrance, there's an effeminate boy in a flowered shirt and flowered jeans who, like him, is chewing gum; he greets him, asks him to call a tiny girl named Adaku for him.

The boy winks, a timorous flirtatious wink, and glides into the noisy classroom with his mingled odour of Smart perfume and whiskey.

A girl in a flowing red gown approaching with a guitar absorbs his attention. Chioma. She looks prettier, healthier, but there's no smile on her face as she strides past him with no greeting. Maybe she also strides past Nkem with no greeting. Maybe all these unfriendlinesses and all these silences are her weird ways of demonstrating that she still feels guilty. Maybe she's just pregnant and ashamed of her pregnancy. Will she return to Nkem after she's been delivered of her baby? Can she and Nkem be bold enough to commit adultery? Well, it's not his business. His business is Adaku. As he waits for Adaku's appearance, he logs on to Facebook.

On Rose's wall:

Do anybodi knows Dat mRs chamaka is preGnent? okoye iz a philantopic so he's sharing sperm and iS respondsible 4 the Baby imbecile. De baBy is imbEcile. Is funnY.

He lets out a neighing laugh and clicks on the comments with fingers quivering from excitement. *And, oh my God, it is a lovely imbecile*, writes a stranger named Mhiz Fwesh. *I sospect my fathers generous Penis,* writes Okoye's son: *who else can produce an imbeside? Ha-ha-ha!*

He leaves a comic meme of a laughing elephant, logs out without reading other comments and looks up at the sky of enamelled blue. The sun is a big orange on fire, and he thinks: beautiful. So beautiful like a perfect grade, like a perfect cocoon of inexpugnable happiness.

But he does not like that the winds are hot. He does

not like that the back of his neck feels hot like a roast corn. He should have come with his umbrella. Or will these students of English in black and white, who are milling around with notebooks and novels, laugh at him? But they are funnier: some of them are discussing a linguist called Ferdinand de Saussure in a "British" accent. The "British" accent reminds him of cartoon cats with hot potatoes in their mouths and in their noses.

All around the turquoise walls: the painted photographs of Chinua Achebe, of Elechi Amadi, of Wole Soyinka, of Ngugi wa Thiongo. Below their solemn faces are their names and the titles of their books written in shiny red ink. No woman writer: an injustice that will certainly infuriate Chioma if she were a member of this department. Nkem might not be angered, but would surely harp on this unapologetic exclusivity. Or will he prefer to focus on the authors' profound quotes on the wooden frames of the noticeboards, scanning them for a wrongly used semicolon? Interesting boyfriend and his interesting girlfriend, he thinks. But where's my own *uninteresting* girlfriend? Where's that tiny, nice, rich, rash Adaku? Is she breaking up with me? I swear, I will not accept any separation unless she agrees to pay me off.

Right before him, near a discarded white flower, a shard of glass, sapphire and square, glints in the murky light of the mid-afternoon like a tiny piece of miracle.

He stares at it in a childlike trance of admiration and

thinks, almost sunnily, that perhaps this quick flash of light is a symbol of hope.

He's about to step into the classroom and suffer the ignominy of any lecturer's help or debasement, but Adaku stumbles out of the building, squinting in the sun, her hand cupped over her eyes.

"Adaku," he says, approaching.

She does not hug him. "I'm not interrigent, I'm not interrigent."

"What's wrong with being unintelligent? But you're very intelligent, you're a genius."

"But I cannot pass any examination."

"My dear, examinations are the only useless thing one should not take seriously in life. The only thing one should take seriously in life is friendship. To keep my friends, there's absolutely nothing on earth I cannot do except give up chewing gum, study to pass my examination, or obey my parents."

"I'm going to Kano to be with my palents. I can't pass any exam. They're in my hostel. They say I'm an imbecile. They say I will stay at home in Kano. They say I must reave you. People say Daddy used my brain to do brood money in a shline, but I will be with him in Kano. And Mummy. So I'm reaving."

"Only a fool would prefer her parents over her boyfriend. Can you have sex with your parents? No!"

"But we don't have sex. You don't rike sex."

"Okay, okay, let's go home and have sex. Let's commit *this* fornication once and for all." He clutches her hand, but she slaps it off. "So you don't want to commit fornication with me?"

"I'm bleaking up with you, sir."

He stumbles as if her words were blows. A *bleak-up*, he tells himself with her accent, and then makes an attempt to keep his voice steady. "But you know full well that you're my protector?" he asks. "If you leave me, bad guys will start attacking me, calling me gay. You know that will make Nkem to kick me out like bad football. You know all these?"

She begins tottering away. "I'm reaving, I'm reaving!"

He's saddened by the puzzling news of her departure, and yet he makes no effort to detain her. His feet feel too heavy like two oak wood, and they are glued to the ground. His life will never remain the same again, he is aware, and there seems to be no girl who will accept him with his eye pencil, eyeshadow, scarf, umbrella. He spits on the grass and walks away.

On the Campus Road, a new Toyota Camry slows down and Chiamaka's head says, "Come in, Ifenna."

This woman, he thinks. This wily woman. He would like to ask her why she pocketed his money and ate his fowl last semester, but could not remember to give him an A or a B. He would like to ask her why she could not apologize, and has not apologized? He advances to the car and touches the door like a baby because he is too sad to walk home, too lazy, too brittle.

Inside, Chiamaka offers him a ripe banana and says, "Taste the banana and then review it. I mean, tell me if it is sweet or not, yes. But, first of all, where's Okonkwo—Okoye?"

"Did he sneak into your farm to steal bananas?" he asks.

Chiamaka changes gear rapidly, the car lunges forward and his nose hits the windscreen. The result: a quick light, multicoloured and tiny, breaks into a million splendid stars in his eyes. He expects her to apologize straightaway, but she nods appreciatively and spits out the window; the saliva lands on one of the white-and-yellow petals of the daisies that line the slithering slope. "You males are lovely and charming when you were babies but once they have a beard and a firm *screwdriver*, they transform into monsters," she says. "You start prowling the street like lions, catching and screwing every living thing in a skirt and breaking their hearts. If women could get pregnant by eating, let's say, ripe tomatoes, all my daughters will not be found in any man's goddam house. Men are ruining us. Some men should be killed, or encouraged to die. I think the world will be a better place if the population of men is reduced to five percent all over the world. This country is littered with men, most of whom are rapists, woman-beaters, heartbreakers, killers, cheats. I'm prepared to encourage all the women in this university to leave their husbands. We women cannot be truly happy if we still remain in the houses of the enemy."

He is silent.

"Ifenna, I want to ask you an infinitely important question," she continues. "It has nothing, absolutely nothing, to do with me, but it's important. I'm asking the question to help a friend, yes."

Her eyes are focused on the bumpy alley, so he flings the bananas out of the window. "Questions?" he says. "But I'm not intelligent."

She smoothens her beard. "You are married, Ifenna. . ."

"I'm not married."

"You're married!"

"I swear, I am not married, madam!"

"An assumption, yes. You are married. You come home and discover that the child. . . that the son your wife says is biologically yours is another man's, what would you do? Remember it has nothing to do with me. I am just asking for a friend."

"If I discover that the son my wife said is biologically mine is another man's, I will whistle excitedly to her parents' house and tell them I will build a new house for them. I swear, they will dance, hug me, bless me. I will demolish that very house they have and then tell them my money has finished. I will render them homeless."

Silence. A bee, green-belied and swollen, flies into the car through her open window, buzzes round and round her head, frightening her, amusing him, and then it is gone. But she still does not say anything, and he does not care. The car continues to climb the dusty road leading to the exit.

Outside the university, she says, "It's quite unfortunate that most of the girls in my class will graduate and get married to men, make love to men, cook for men, wash for men, dress for men, abort for men, cry to God for male children for men, die for men. God will punish men. You men enslave women, and the prudent way to end that is through abolition of marriage. Women should thrash men, destroy their marriages, destroy the institution of marriage. Unless it is a marriage between a woman and a woman. Men are wicked!"

"Adaku, my girlfriend, broke up with me few minutes ago," he says.

"I talked to her. I'm looking for Chioma to talk to her too. I'm looking for Rose to talk to. All the girls in this university must break up with their boyfriends. All the wives in this university must leave their husbands. As far as I am alive, no man will ever enjoy a woman!" She hits the door. "Where's Okoye? Where is Okoye!"

"But I'm not hiding him in my school bag! He's

neither a book nor a pen. Okoye is not in my school bag, I swear!"

She grabs the collar of his shirt with the swiftness of the witches he sees in horror movies, her eyes fiery like those of an incensed tigress. "Where's Okoye!"

He pushes the door open, slaps off her hand and escapes, the sound of his shirt tearing and his high-pitched screaming riveting the attention of passersby.

He arrives home wearing only a wet singlet.

Nkem, bent at the reading table like the letter C and writing a letter addressed to "Dear Silly Papa Nkechi," suspends the action and rises. The stamp on the clumsy signature would have been comical, but the day has, in fact, been striped of its sunniness.

"Has Chioma left you, Semicolon?" he asks. "Sorry. I mean, has Chioma left Chief her suitor? Did Rose leave Okoye? Did any girl leave any guy in our department? Or in any department on this campus."

Nkem seems uninterested in his questions: he's busy scanning his anatomy with popping eyes if he were an imponderabble specimen in a laboratory.

"Adaku broke up with me, Semicolon," he says, sinking into the softness of the foam, which is littered with Oscar Wilde books, economics textbooks, and crayons.

Nkem lowers himself into a seat and crosses his legs. "Blessed wine, you fought, obviously."

He slouches up and down on the foam, splitting the orange and blue crayons, and then looks up to relay his encounter with Chiamaka to him. "That's madness," Nkem says. "Another madness: Papa Nkechi gave Rose a letter for you and me. I am writing a reply…take a look at the nonsense he wrote. No semicolon, obviously."

Why not a text, he wants to ask, but takes the A-4 paper from Nkem.

Dear Students:

How are you? Hope your fine. If your fine, thank god. Have you eating? Thank god. My aim of writting this formal letter is to inform you, Nkem(Semicolon) and Ifenna(homo) that if I see you around my beautiful wife, I will shoot you like dog. I love you, but I will shoot you like dog. I am not tryin to scare you, but I will shoot you like dog. Because I'm angry with that big stomach you call your lecturer(Okoye). And if I shoot you like dog and you die and run away, I will report you to your principal.

Good buy, my friends!

Papa Nkechi.

"Vice chancellor, not a principal," he says, folding the paper. "But why did Rose tell him I'm a homosexual. Am I a homosexual?"

Nkem rises, scratches his forehead with quivering fingers and paces up and down the room like a character in a tragic drama. "Your gaudy dressing, umbrella, eyeshadow, powder, scarves—all these have pulled me down from my mountainous greatness. Knowing you is the worst thing that has ever happened to me. I used to like you because you say funny things like Oscar Wilde and dress like him. But now, like Oscar Wilde, I am a ruined genius! I may even die before the age of 43, as Oscar Wilde!" Nkem stops to tear up his own letter. "The day I will find out that it has become mathematically impossible for me to graduate with at least a 2:1, I shall kill myself!"

For a long moment he stares at Nkem without knowing what to say to him. Look, Ifenna, it's about time, he tells himself, turns, and drifts to the wardrobe. With a quivering hand, he opens it, scans the housed items: his scarves, his eyeshadow, his tight jeans, his nose rings, his tight trousers, his packet of chewing gum. He collects all of them, saunters to the kitchen. Their abandoned stove still contains a little kerosene. He pours it into an empty Coke can, takes a matchbox, and walks past Nkem who's following him, trying to stop him with his left hand, and then he's out of the apartment.

Downstairs, under a leafless mango tree and near a narrow water channel where the pale sun shivers and gleams, he sets fire to the objects of beauty he has gathered. Never again, he thinks. Never again will I be an object of people's hatred. Their teaching practice is few weeks away, after all; he ought to look like a decent student teacher in the eyes of the management of

Heineken University Secondary, where he and Nkem have chosen. He ought to look professional. He ought to be a man, whatever that means.

He spits the gum he's chewing into the smoky fire, takes his can and matchbox from the grass where he dropped them, returns upstairs to their room.

FINAL YEAR

CHAPTER 22

NKEM glares at the screen of his vibrating phone at the end of a yawn-inducing lecture on Curriculum Planning and Evaluation. It's drizzling outside this morning and the air smells of dust, of stale urine, of animal excrement. There are hurrying students with umbrellas, there are speeding cars with blaring horns. Winged insects flirt in the air. *Aku*: that's what they were called when he was a kid. He wonders if people still fry and eat them now.

A false-sounding cough from the pregnant Chioma seizes his attention. She's seated beside him and has been telling him she still loves him, telling him she's considering leaving Chief who has already paid her bride price. Behind them sits a changed Ifenna: no nose ring, no scarf, no chewing gum, no powder on his face. Ifenna is now used to ripped jeans, ripped caps, basketball tops, soil-coloured Timberlands. But today, he's wearing sunglasses, biscuit-coloured chinos, a black Tupac polo, white sneakers.

When he turns back to tell Ifenna he's leaving, Chioma says, "Can I follow you, Sugar? Can I follow you guys?" as though his mind is a book opened in her hand and she has read it.

"No," he says, but thinks: Yes, Chioma, yes, although you hacked an axe at my heart by having an evening of reckless sex with a bloated toad who's married. You hacked an axe at my heart by marrying a prosperous ignoramus, someone you don't even care if his empty head is on a pillow or on a viper, someone who can neither read nor write, someone who is old enough to be your father. How can he pick the bleeding pieces of his heart and mould them into a song?

The eyes staring at him are unblinking and compassionate. Are his own eyes, which are also staring at her, equally compassionate? Or are they liquid, reddened, telegraphing his depression?

Two exquisite butterflies, yellow and purple, enter through a busted window and flit round the classroom and then leave through the exact window. The louvres emit such entrancing luminescence that sends his mind, right away, to rainbows.

To win back his attention, she says, "Why are you

always despairing nowadays, Sugar? Why are you always fretful? You've changed. And Rose told me surprising things you now do. Surprising things like hovering around the office of that very bad Mama Nkechi …"

"Shut up!" He rises, trembling all over. "Shut up and get out and mind your business! It isn't your business, obviously."

The classroom is almost deserted. One boy, one girl: the only humans here with them. One lizard on the wall, above the ink-dotted whiteboard, nodding, watching. One ceiling fan, swift and rattling. One bulb is switched on, circular and bright like the moon, shining on the two the lovers' faces. This couple are ten or fifteen rows of chairs away from them. Yet they heard his irate shout: they are no longer holding hands like adolescent lovers, but are on their feet, staring at them.

"How sad it is," Ifenna says. "You're fighting with your girlfriend, or ex-girlfriend, but I have no girl to fight. The beauty of a relationship is quarrels. A perfect relationship is boring. May God never give me a good woman who will always refuse to fight me and entertain our neighbours. It's unfair not to entertain our neighbours…and ourselves. Semicolon, never you marry a woman who'll not fight with you at least once a week."

Chioma hits Ifenna's face with her handbag and giggles. "You tse-tse fly! So I'm a bad girl?"

"You're neither bad nor good, which is worse," Ifenna tells her. "You're not good because you ignored Semicolon for almost a semester because you are a faithful wife. A wife who's bad to her boyfriend and good to her husband. There's no fight yet. God, how I love fights. God, please give me a bad girlfriend with a hunting knife and violent attitude! Don't allow my relationship or marriage to be boring by cursing me with a God-fearing girl, God! Hearken to my cry, Oh Lord!"

She takes his hand. "Sugar, don't be disquietened by my marriage. My heart is still for you. Nobody, not even the gods or my husband, can change my love for you. One day, I pray, you and I will live as one."

He gazes at her in a trance of reverence and gratitude, but she relinquishes his hands and jerks away her face: a puerile tear, he feels, has risen to her eye at his utter silence which is also an indication of his undying love. He has feared she would never be prepared to mention her marriage in their conversation. Feared she would never promise to love him, promise to live together with him as one. Feared she would never apologise for her silence, her coldness.

He moves closer to her for an embrace, but she steps back with a snicker and his phone rings. Without a word to either her or Ifenna, he leaves the classroom to answer this inquisitive person who has been bothering him with a hidden number. He cannot know who the caller is, of course, but can bet it's Ifenna's uncle phoning to tell him how much it hurts him that he has been ignoring his calls; how much he has missed him and his semicolons; how much he wants them to meet again and discuss the English language; how much he owes him for rescuing Ifenna from that hollow pit of madness that is women's costume.

But he is wrong. "This is Izu, the class rep," the caller says. "I want to tell you important something fastly before my airtime will finish. I remember that yesterday when I recharge my MTN line and phone my mother, who live in Abakaliki with my father, a Biafran soldier. But now crippled and almost blind, and the last time I saw him, he was playing table tennis with our landlord and the ball flies over the fence and into the big nose of a noisy old woman who happen to be…"

He has to stop the running mouth with piggish eyes. "How may I help you, blessed wine?"

Izu reverts to Igbo to escape the problem of fuzziness, to save time. Did Nkem see Okoye today? No, no, he says he didn't. Will Nkem be kind enough to inform him if he finds out? Because the mysterious disappearance of the man is worrying: the man hasn't been attending his lectures. He turned off his phone. He turned away from his girlfriend Rose. He locked his office. Nevertheless, there are places where they can comb for the missing alcoholic—the beer parlours, the hotels, the hospitals. But the hotels are not on his own personal coupon because Rose intimated to him that Okoye is probably at home, hiding from Chiamaka the radical "fenimest."

"What am I to do with this useless information?" he asks in English. "And mind you, she's not a feminist; she's just mad, obviously."

"As you saw, the *feminest* has made Amanda Eze the class rep," he says, still in Igbo. "I've lost that job, unfortunately. The way I lost the friendship of some of our lecturers. Okoye is still my friend and I don't want to lose him, Nkem. I don't want to lose him. Please don't expose the video. If you do, he'll be sacked and I will stop making money. Nkem, my illiterate parents are dying of hunger in the village; they can't pay my tuition fees. I pay my fees. I make money by working as lecturers' agents. We sell As and Bs, as you probably know. I pay my school fees from the money we make. So why are you and Ifenna conspiring to chunk Okoye, my only source of income, out of this prestigious university? Nkem, my friend, please don't expose Okoye. If you do, I will die of hunger and my parents' enemies will celebrate. Don't spoil my only business, Nkem. I'm begging you. Do you want me to kneel down?"

Izu's speeches, he has come to know, are only coherent when he's drowning. Does this imply that his characteristic fuzziness is fake?

"Cut this connection with immediate effect!" he says.

"Nkem, please! Be kind, listen to me. Have mercy on me and Okoye. Remember you're a Christian. . . Sorry I lied to you. Okoye's actually at home. He's almost crying at Alif Standard Hotel. I left him a few minutes ago. Meet him, please."

Blue and red lights disco-dancing on the walls hit his eyes as he strides into Alif Standard Hotel bar.

Okoye and Mama Nkechi are seated at an elegant glass table, drinking Black Label in defeated silence. He lingers at the entrance for half a minute before floating to them, his hands moist with anxiety, and his heart heavy with a vague sadness.

"The Honourable Chief Semicolon Hyphen," Okoye says with no mirth, gesturing to a chair. "Sit down and ask the waitress to give you something to drink."

Mama Nkechi refills her glass and studies him with undisguised inquisitiveness, her lips sealed as though speeches were prohited here. She didn't come with her Bible—or is it in her duffel handbag? He expects her to reprimand him for not greeting him, but she remains tongue-tied. Even Okoye has lapsed into silence. Their silences: an indication that something is wrong, that something is dangerously wrong.

From the windows, he glimpses people hurrying out of the hotel, while others hurry into it: it has begun to rain. Purple petals from tall, swaying flowers that line a broad track are everywhere. They are falling on people's heads, on people's umbrellas, on the heavenly blue roads, on car roofs, on lampposts, on trees painted green, white, green. Falling, drifting away in the crisp air like me, he thinks. Falling slowly, falling languidly, into the swimming pool, into the bar. They are falling, too, on the roof of the gold-striped gates, where two burly security men are examining their guns.

A new atmosphere, a new disappointment, he thinks. A new knowledge: to crave an impressive result is to embrace consistent restlessness and eventual heartbreak. It is the slow closing of a pair of moist eyes and praying to Jesus Christ, even though you are not sure you truly believe in Him. He prays, Oh Lord, let this short-lived congress not be a doorway into doom, let it be a hand moulding my past mistakes into grades that sing. Let Papa Nkechi allow his wife to be a torch we will use to search for these beautiful grades hidden in the darkness. Part this sea that is rapidly drowning me, choking me, so that I may rise and cross and glorify your name. He prays, Oh Lord, if you rescue us, bless us, forgive us, I will enter into a boat, sail to villages that do not know civilization and spread the Gospel.

He starts when Okoye lays a hand on his shoulder. "Chief, listen to me. A good result is not everything. A bad result cannot stop you from being a professor of economics, or a great writer, which, I conjecture, is your dream. Wole Soyinka, who I'm sure you know so well, made himself proud by graduating with a third-class."

"I'm smarter than Soyinka, obviously," he says without lifting his head. "But his was not a third-class. Mine must be a great result. Has Mama Nkechi erased those bloody Es and Ds from my file?"

"What you think happened really happened," Mama Nkechi says. "My husband asked me to discontinue any business I was doing with Mr. Ezinwa your lecturer. He's a Christian, you see. I am, too. We're a Christian couple. I'm just trying to help you and Ifenna. I am not like all these men and women at Exams and Records who collect money from any student who cannot even spell 'cat' or 'dog'. All is vanity. In the Book of Leviticus—or was in Exodus. . . ?"

"Apart from you, nobody else in Nigeria loves the Bible the way I do," Okoye says. "Every time a good Christian wants to offer me a Bible, it always drops to the soil and I always pick it up, dust it and give it back to them. I always dust the Holy Books because I love them. But let's return to the matter. Help Nkem and the one that chews gum so I can have a peace of mine. Are you being unkind to us because you are the only worker who computes the economics students' GPA? Ignore your husband's atrocious advice and command. Let's alter these boys' disrespectful grades. Reconsider your decision. You don't go to your husband and tell him who to business with. You don't police him around, so he shouldn't police you. Be yourself."

"There's a housefly on your nose," she says. "Two, actually. Male and female, maybe."

"Allow the couple to have fun on my nose. Maybe its their honeymoon."

Okoye's acidic tone makes him lift his head and speak swiftly with pathos: "Madam, please, please! Help me! Without a good result, I will kill myself!"

"Remember what the Bible says about killing?" she says, and takes a warm swallow from her half-full bottle. "My husband doesn't like Dr. Ezinwa your lecturer."

"And Dr. Ezinwa his lecturer doesn't like your husband," Okoye says with his brows knitted in annoyance. "Sorry…I like your husband. Kindly ask him to forgive me and allow you to help us. You're the only one who can help us. Not because others can't sell As and Bs, but you're the chief person who computes the Economics students' result. Compute Nkem's result and Ifenna's favourably. What will I do to make you change your mind and help us?"

She stares at the wall, where the rotating chandelier above them has thrown a trapezoid of primary-coloured light, and purses her quivering lips.

Outside, the leaves fall, grey and wet, across the sun-reddened window. "My husband is mad at you," she says after a while. "So it can't work." The glass in her hand drops and shatters on the floor. "It cannot work, and I have to go now!"

From the back door, the hotel manager, a corpulent middle-aged man with the tattoo of a vulture on his oversized neck and biceps emerges, drinking Gulder beer from the bottle, his eyes bloodshot from incessant smoking of cigarettes or weed, or both. The manager's arched brows and crinkled forehead reminds him what Rose told him on the phone two or three days ago. Rose told him she came here with Okoye to have fun and the workers threw her "boyfriend" out because he pressed the bottoms of one of the waitresses, told him the manager swore to assail Okoye because he usually lets beer bottles slip from his hand and crash to the floor and Okoye talks too much and disturbs other customers. She told him the manager is not sick in the head, but he threatened to kick Okoye out if he damaged any other thing belonging to the hotel or raise his voice to inconvenience "important personalities". Now the young man looks like he's prepared to do what Rose says he'd do.

Okoye stirs in his seat and glances at the door that says EXIT as though he's desirous to rise and walk away in peace; but it is too late: the offended manager is already upon them. "Now, get out, you noisemakers!" the manager bawls. "Get out quickly!"

They rise at once and begin shuffling out in embarrassed silence, drinkers' inquisitive eyes following them. "Run, run!" the manager bawls again, kicking Okoye on the bottom with a soldier's boot. "You dirty lecturer periodically come here to make noise, harass my female workers and break our bottles! Out, you grey-haired child! Out! Go outside and play! I don't want to see any of you here again! I don't even want to see your shadows here! Out!"

Outside, in the waning rain, Okoye says, "I'm sorry, chief. Mama Nkechi and her husband might change their minds. Can I drive you home?"

He remains silent, confused, shivering, his Harry Potter glasses in his hand. Before him, behind Okoye, Mama Nkechi is wearing her waterproof tarpaulin that says *I'M RIGHTEOUS, FOR JESUS' PRECIOUS BLOOD HAS WASHED ME CLEAN. Okoye,* too, is comically protected against the rain: the briefcase, an instantly improvised umbrella, is raised over that big bald head of his, like a labourer's pan of concrete. The scene is pure P. G. Wodehouse, he thinks. But this isn't a laughing matter; he is weightless with hunger, adrift with heartbreak, with hopelessness: it's impossible to be happy after graduation. So what will he do now? Abandon economics, sit for another JAMB examination, study English and Literature in a better Nigerian university? But aren't many of the universities just as corrupt? Uncle

Sobechi's America: this still sounds like a splendid idea that is also an improbable idea, an improbable mission. But he'll phone Uncle Sobechi anyway. He'll tell Uncle Sobechi everything about Chioma, Ifenna, Okoye. Everything about his grades. He'll tell Uncle Sobechi it hurts so bad he feels like sinking, sinking into the River Niger. Hopefully, Uncle Sobechi will volunteer to lift his burdens, and he'll fly to America again. He'll fly to Oxford and attend the prestigious Magdalen College because Oscar Wilde was an alumnus. But what about Chioma, his singing Chioma, his unsung Chioma? He would like to be close to her, to assist her in writing political songs, to sing with her, to practise with her, to watch her grow musically to the level of Simi, Teni, or maybe Rihanna. No: she's married; she is annoyingly married to a man who's old enough to be her father. Let her and that dumb ancestor go merrily to hell with her guitar!

"What are you children still doing there?" the manager bellows from the entrance. "As far as I am concerned, you're criminals, and I will not hesitate to shoot. Out!"

"May the Lord be with you!" Mama Nkechi tells him and Okoye, and rushes off to the gold-striped gate.

Okoye opens his car door for him to enter, but he turns away, throws his Harry Potter glasses into a nearby refuse bin, and faces the gate and the drifting rocks across the sky's horizon. God, my head is filled with boiling oil, he thinks. And there's a lightness in his hair, heaviness in his chest. There's moistness in his eyes. But he does not bring out his handkerchief in case of an embarrassing tear: he will journey home in the rain and nobody can know whether the liquids dripping from his eyes are the rain or his tears.

At the university bus stop off campus, he sights Chioma and his heart lurches. The girl, who is not his and will never be his, carries an umbrella that has his face drawned on it in sky-blue and is singing a song about *fighting for you, baby, bleeding for you, baby, laying down my life for you.* Immediately their eyes meet, the melodies falling from her mouth freeze in the air as ice cubes, and then dissolve and float away like colourful petals in the wind. "Sugar..." she says, blinking, blinking and smiling. "I know you must have heard, but listen: Chief bought me a sports car, but I can't drive yet. He's still teaching me. I want *you* to be teaching me. Do you know how to drive?"

He used to wear a black mask and escape in his father's embarrassing Peugeot to the university field, cruising round shirtless boys kicking football, cruising round their applauding girlfriends, cruising round whispering trees, looking for an idea for a poem in the flying egrets, in dust-laden winds blowing white feathers and combing green grass, in suns the shape and colour of a burning orange; but he will not disclose his driving experience. He will not comment on the car. He will not comment on any car bought by Chief.

She nudges him and asks, "Aren't you happy for me, Sugar? I will give you the car and tell him it was stolen by cultists. Do you prefer Benz or Lamborghini?"

He strokes his small beard, watching her. "Stop. Just stop."

"Your eyes are pouched," she says in Igbo. "You gifted someone your funny Harry Potter glasses?"

"I should have given the spectacles to your husband to make him look educated?"

She laughs, as if his bitter question is meant to be funny, and he laughs at her laugh. The hunting knife in her unclosed handbag, for the first time, makes him shift from her a bit. She laughs at him again, pulls him closer, and as they bustle down the stony road under the flapping umbrella, she says, "My husband, the rich idiot you've just insulted in my presence, built a mansion for me in this town. It's painted white and it's stunning, like the White House in America. Did you see the White House when you were in America?"

"Rose says your husband wants to christen the baby in your womb Nnamdi, after Nigeria's first president, but you insisted on Nkemdilim, after me. Is that true?"

"I wonder why he just concluded that our baby in my womb *is* a boy? It might be a girl. I want a girl first,

Sugar, but a boy is also beautiful. The name, Nkemdilim, is my quick and immediate suggestion and preference, and not even the gods can change it. Nkem is a unisex name, you know. Nkemdilim: *may mine be with me.*"

The soft drizzle progresses to a windy rain. Some young people, most of whom are students, open their own umbrellas and stare at them as they pass. Do they know Chioma? Do they know him? Do they know she's married and he was her boyfriend? *But they look and flirt like a legally married couple,* he imagines them telling one another in muffled tones. *What do you think these ex-lovers are up to?*

"Does Chief know you don't love him?" he asks. "Does this frighteningly immature millionaire know you married him to save your family and yourself from poverty?"

"He's a fool, so I don't know what goes on in his large head." She pauses, and looks him in the eyes. "Follow me, Sugar. I want to introduce you to him. I want him to see how a human being should look and taste: like a blessed wine."

"No: he's a fool and a chimpanzee, according to you, and I don't know what to say to zoo animals, obviously."

"You sound like you're still in love with me."

It's my grades, he wants to say. My bloody grades. "Follow me, and stay with me, blessed wine," he says.

Upstairs in his room, he unburdens himself. "Is that

why you are losing weight, losing your beauty, losing everything?" she asks with an irritating smile. "Those grades have humbled you. Who do you blame most? Dr. Okoye's wickedness or Ifenna's women's costume?"

I blame you, he wants to retort. I blame you for sleeping with Dr. Okoye. I blame you for renting my heart, breaking my heart. I blame you for marrying someone else because your mother is drunk with his wealth. But instead he says, "What will I offer you?"

"A blessed wine," she replies.

"I can go downstairs to buy you a wine, you know. Or cigarettes."

"Pregnant women, I read somewhere, are not advised to smoke. Besides, I have given up smoking. I don't really love cigarettes. It started one Christmas, this cigarette business. My three uncles were smoking their lungs off while my grandmother watched them with her toothless grin. But when Aunt Oge lit a half-finished cigarette to have her own fun, Grandma rose from her bamboo chair, slapped her mouth and called her a shameless harlot. To our surprise, Aunt Oge slapped back. The case flew to the ears of the kinsmen who banned smoking among women in our village. Men can smoke, but women shouldn't near a single cigarette. I was so mad, Sugar. I marched out in the village, bought a packet of Benson and Hedges from one ambitious Tiv guy and smoked the cigarettes round the houses of these old kinsmen. Each time I saw them, I blew the smoke into their wrinkled faces and watched them run, cursing and coughing. The ban was lifted, but I had already fallen into the habit. Chief couldn't stop me: I just quit. Do you want me to quit my marriage the way I quit cigarettes?"

"You told me you would not get married unless the idea of bride pride is abolished. You said men should stop paying girls' fathers as if they're buying a carton of Indomie noodles or a TV. You swore that no man can pay to have you because you're neither Indomie nor a TV. But your bride bride was paid, and you were taken home like a TV. Or Indomie?"

"I kicked my dad's arse thirteen times until he gave me the money. I returned it to my husband, who returned it to my mother, who returned it to my father. My so-called husband knows I am a no-nonsense girl. If he, or my future husband – there might be future husbands—tries to tell me what to do and what not to do like a boss in an office, I know where my hunting knife is." She takes her smartphone out of her handbag. "May I show you the photos of my husband?"

"He should come and see mine."

She hits him with her handbag and giggles. "You don't want me show you his face. You don't want me to tell you how we met."

"I don't want to hear it, obviously."

"You will hear it." She pauses, moistens her lipstick-free lips. "I was performing with my guitar at a hotel here. . . what's its name? Maxi. It's Maxi Hotel and Suites, I remember. So after my small show, everybody clapped, though it's titled 'Dismantle the Patriarchy.' Chief was drinking beer there with some of his friends. He watched my chest with his mouth wide open throughout my show. Later, he told me that the late Professor Ayodele, one of these drinking chums of his, was the hungry parasite who told him about me. Chief can't even spell 'cat', and I know you wonder what Professor Ayodele was doing with him, right?"

"I don't bloody care."

"You do. I can see curiosity in your charming eyes." She hits him again with her handbag, but does not laugh this time. "Professor Ayosky, I must tell you now, knew I conducted a brief affair with Okoye. He had my number because he thought he, too, could sleep with me. But that's a story for another day. So Chief phoned my mother and told him he would give her a sports car and she would give him her daughter for marriage. And my mother agreed. Later, my mother phoned me and informed me that I am married. I didn't know I was married. In a gold-coloured sports car, we journeyed to see my husband. I hated him immediately, but we were poor, Sugar. Will I ever love him? You're brainy and creative, Sugar: teach me how to fall in love with a man I don't love. You must have encountered unrequited love scenes in some of these novels and poems you read. So teach me, Sugar. How can I unlove you and love him?"

"Don't unlove me, Chioma," he says with a humility unsual in him, and finds himself moving towards her as if he's hypnotized. "I don't want to lose first-class or second class (upper honours) degree and still lose you. I still love you, Chioma. My master, Oscar Wilde, says: 'Never love anybody who treats you like you're ordinary.' But I will disobey him for you. You treat me like I am not extraordinary, but I continue to love you. You think I am ordinary, obviously, because you married Chief. But I can't stop loving you. I know that God, if there's a God, abhors this speech, this sin. But I can't stop chasing you. I can't stop, and I am not afraid of hell fire. Like Oscar Wilde, I don't want to go to heaven: none of my friends is there. I know you're a devoted Christian and I am leading you into temptation, but I can't help it. Take my hand. Sing me a song. You used to sing '*you and I will live as one* to me'. Sing, blessed wine, sing."

She turns away from him and faces the misty window, where an orange-plumed bird is perking at the glass, struggling to get in. Thunder booms; the window rattles, then glows with the startling reflection of lightning. "Sugar, I'm married, pregnant, hot-tempered, pimpled, plump, almost fat now, debauched, and do not know how to use a semicolon."

"I know, obviously. Even if you were mad, I would still come for you. Even if you were blind, deaf, dumb and crippled, I would still love you." He steers her to himself, lowers his head to hers but hesitates to kiss her quivering lips. "I want you to want me, even though you're married. Say you want me. Say you will want to want me. Say you will be mine. Say yes. Say yes!" He is kissing her neck now, and now her ear, and now her nose, and now her lips. "Say yes! I command you say yes!"

There are several worn-out romance novels he donated to the town's library of very nasty literatures and pirated textbooks as a punishment to its avaricious manager. Like most of the ridiculously written heroines in these novels of his childhood, Chioma dissolves in his arms, trembling, closing her eyes, saying, under her breath: "Yes, Sugar, yes!"

Somebody taps at the door, but he does not care. Let him or her injure their hand. Let him or her continue wasting their time: he will not open the door. With impatient hands, he unbuttons Chioma's silky shirt, which is painted the colour of seawater solidifying, tosses it to the wardrobe, and begins to caress her breast, to kiss her ears. Despite the increasing knocks on the door, despite the voices of people at the door, they continue kissing and touching, as if the world does not matter to them again. Nothing matters except he and

Chioma. These heavenly minutes that are passing in this room that seem suddenly filled with the delicious smell of flowers and the delicious strings of acoustic guitar music, will forever be remembered: It is a bold excursion into a garden surrounded by smouldering fires, a thrilling induction into adultery, a consolation for crumpled grades and crumpled dreams.

His tongue finds her nipple; she closes her eyes again and says, "Oh God, yes."

The knock comes to the door once again, louder, angrier, but she pulls him to the foam.

"Undress me, Sugar," she says. "Make love to me!"

Without a word of eroticism, without a sense of danger, he licks her nipple again and begins pulling off her underwear with gentle hands like a loveable poet he read in a popular French romance novel.

CHAPTER 23

OKOYE hurries to a whispering mango tree, where his car is parked, and where he expects to meet Rose. Here there's no perceptible being save for the purple butterflies flitting around sunflowers in a broken pot. A red sun in stagnant but clean water is setting his car windows on fire and a lizard is eyeing him, nodding, waiting for him to leave so it can chase after the butterflies. He waves the reptile away, extracts his car keys from his briefcase, and thinks: What a frustrating lecture that was!

With the single exception of Nkem, all his final-year students do not know what arbitrage pricing theory means. They don't even know what agency cost means. Agency cost, Nkem explained, arises when somebody (the principal) hires someone else (the agent) and the interest or interests of the agent conflict with the interest of the principal. Take this university and its lecturers as an example. The federal government, who's this *company's* owner, wants lecturers to teach and behave in ways that maximise the value of the investments in education, but these hired lecturers' priority is to sell bloody textbooks that aren't recommended to the students, sell pirated handouts, sell toothpaste, sell toothbrushes, sell ripe tomatoes, sell other similar delicious vegetables that improve the quality of education in Nigeria. Their priority is to sleep with the female students, sleep with the male students, sleep with themselves. Which, obviously, cannot centuple the university's share price.

A fragile yet interesting analysis, he tells himself now as he told himself in the laughter-filled classroom. The creativity of a frustrated student: subtle and sarcastic in turns, but I approve!

He unlocks the door, pulls it open and hears someone bawl his name from behind. The voice: a familiar girlishness, a familiar urgency.

Slowly, he turns, hoping it will not be Rose or any of the girls in his class with whom he moans under hotel duvets.

But he isn't lucky: the lanky woman who has summoned him is his postgraduate student and in fact one of his long discarded lovers. He tries but fails to remember her name. Behind her, to his mild surprise, is Izu. The file in the boy's hand is flapping in the chilly wind, making slapping sounds. What do they want from him?

"Good morning, sah," Izu says with a half-grin that betokens his anxiety. "You look like. . . like an important movie star today. Like my Uncle Graham who dressed like you and they thought he was the president of Nigeria or some eminent politician and shot him in Abuja, near a mosque that's painted, or repainted the colour…and the bullets, thirty-five of them, yes, were found on the zinc, but the newspapers or the magazines—"

He is about to interrupt the lad, but the woman beats him to that. "Beery morning, Doc," she says in jovial Igbo, and gives him a ridiculously overdone smile of a dim-witted sycophant. "The greatest Igbo man of our time, to borrow your late friend's phrase."

He remembers her name now. "How may I help you, Christiana Ojukwu?" he asks in English, which he hopes will remind them how infantile theirs is. "And Izuchukwu: What are your problems? I have paid your school fees, haven't I?"

The smirk on Izu's face reminds him of the sepia photographs the orphan once showed him, saying it was his father who drowned while trying to save his drowning wife who also drowned.

Again the orphan smirks, touches his left pocket, looks round like a pickpocket trying to rob a frail elderly in an isolated neighbourhood, but says nothing. He says nothing because there's a group of female students protesting against a new law that says only male students can be Students' Union Government Presidents; female students can only be encouraged with the post of Vice President and other lesser positions because "God made man the head over the weaker vessels and Heineken University of Education is God-fearing. "Chioma, the protesters' leader, holds up a sweat-soaked banner that says "Women are Not Half-Brained Humans", kicking things, uprooting things, chanting one of her ballistic songs against patriarchy.

After they have disappeared behind a dilapidated classroom, Christiana says, in Igbo, "It's about my thesis, Doc. How much do you want me to pay so you will be kind to me?"

He has to continue in English, a language which seems too complex for her empty head. "I no longer indulge in unscrupulous activities like that, my friend," he says. "Go and study your books and research. You should behave like a student. This is not a supermarket where you buy good grades like short bread, cakes and ice cream."

"Doc, you has change!" she says in English. "I are not saying this prace is ice cleam or blead, but. . . Jesus Chlist of Nazalet, this are not the Okoye that I knows."

"Yes, it are not the Okoye that we knows," he says, aping her infantile accent.

"Can we goes to a beer parrour and deezcoss this? Ahyam vely solly you hasn't quit dlinking. You can't. Or has you?"

What should I do now, he thinks? The only thing that comes to his mind is this: throw this empty-headed trollop out of your way. But how? By giving her seven or eight Mike Tyson punches on her left and right ears, on her neck, on her stomach? No: this is a university that prohibits lecturers from fighting with their students. But why does the university forbid lecturers from beating up some of their students? Who made such a stupid law?

Deciding never to hide his hatred for the woman, he says, "Stop showing off your *elegant* English, Christiana, and allow me to go."

"I will buy you beer, Doc. Stop pletending that you doesn't . . ."

He has to do what he has never done before: he slaps her mouth and pushes her back.

Upstairs, downstairs, students cheer with the maximum excitement of fans watching their favourite clowns dazzling them the fans on a stage. A white bus with its side embossed The Students' Union Government in green roars past, honking madly and throwing them clouds of dust and torn papers.

This recklessness startles him, but he's too angry to curse or insult. Izu, he believes, is equally angry with the driver, and the prying eyes of the students; the boy hisses, then fixes his gaze on Christiana, who's cupping her reddened cheek with a hand trembling from annoyance. When the students' encouraging voices die down, she whips abruptly to Izu and says, in Igbo, "Give me back my money!"

If he leaves now, this nasty woman will certainly accuse him of sexual harassment. If he leaves, she will accuse him of extortion. Stay, Ezinwa Okoye, he tells himself. Stay until the end of this episode. It's true the students do not know what the matter is because they are far away, but he will not take a risk.

She repeats herself and Izu says, "Okoye go change 'im mind. Wait, abeg. Let's beg am again."

"If you don't give me back my money now, I will murder you right here with my bare hands!" she says.

Reluctantly, Izu brings out a rumpled brown envelope from his trouser pockets and hands it to her. She looks at them with murderous rage, then flounces away, a handful of passersby staring with their mouths open.

Soon everybody I know will learn this, he thinks: soon it will be clear to them that everything that has a beginning must have an ending. Soon, the disappointed woman will share the story of her misfortune with her clique; soon the fat envelopes that usually pour into his deep pockets of his dirty trousers like rainwater will cease. Soon, hopefully, he will be as free and happy as the blackbirds he can hear chirping among the leaves of a cashew tree behind them.

He pulls the door open and asks, "What do you want? Speak English. And be fast: I'm in a hurry."

"I wanted to tell you that I have convinced some students to pay me for your course, but it appears you've changed," Izu says in Igbo. "Unfortunately. You remember asking me to get at least fifty students? That was the target."

"I remember."

"I wish you hadn't changed? Many of us will fail. Why did you change? It's not fair."

"I'm ashamed that at my age, I didn't know it's bad to be good. Shame on me. Thanks, Izu, for the knowledge."

"You're welcome, sir." Izu cups his hand over his eyes as he looks upstairs at the students who are watching them with unmasked curiosity. "You're my only source of income, sir. And I'm an orphan. If we stop this business, I will be depressed and probably commit suicide."

"So I should remain a bad man so you'll not commit suicide, Izuchukwu?"

Izu's head droops in sorrow. "I didn't know you'd give your life to Christ. But you're a philanthropist and I am an orphan. You help orphans. You can postpone your repentance. Repent next semester. Can't you wait till next semester, sir? Let's make some money before repenting.

It's not a big sin. Just a small sin. Our priest told us . . . I think it was last Sunday or two weeks ago, because it was raining and the congregants have umbrellas, which were many and their clothes. . . my clothes. . ."

He switches off his ears and opens his car door but does not enter. "Students should go and read their books."

"So we will continue our business? You said you've. . . What? Sir, please be serious. Should I go and start collecting money from those students?"

He enters his car. "Don't collect money from any blockhead. Let them go and read their books, if they have any."

"What about Olamma, the beautiful fair girl you promised to give free marks?" He looks back at the watching students again. "You will not help her?"

He inserts the key into the ignition. "Is it the Olamma in your class?"

"No, sir. This one is a second-year student. The one you promised to surprise with medium-sized underwear if she agreed to sleep with you. Have you forgotten?"

"Oh, Olamma Okeke. Have you given her the medium-sized underwear?"

"No, sir."

"I wonder why you, a respected Christian, haven't given her the underwear."

"Because she hasn't slept with you, sir. I detest selfish

girls. Why can't she satisfy her own lecturer in bed? We will never give her the pant. Let her call the police if she likes. I know you're a philantropist, but don't let her take the pant. It's not her pant. The pant belongs to you, sir. Don't help her. Stop spending money unnecessarily, sir. I love you; that's why I'm advising you. I really love you, sir."

"I love you, too."

"So I should go and collect the money from those students?"

"Sell those medium-sized pants and keep the money. I have retired from that kind of business, and I mean it." He closes the door, puts the car into gear and cruises off, his BMW tyre squealing on the desiccated mud. On the side mirror, he sees the boy covered with dust and the smoke from his exhaust pipe, and feels ridiculously happy.

At Children of God beer parlour, the only pub where he still has a good reputation, he sits on a surprisingly clean Gulder Beer chair and orders two bottles of Guinness and a packet of Dorchester cigarettes.

It's a Peacemaking Day, he thinks, savouring his cigarettes. Whom will he call first? Nkem or Ifenna? No, he has tried his best to help them. He has apologized for his inability to persuade Mama Nkechi to inveigle her husband to permit her to alter the boys' unwanted grades favourably. But what is whirling through their minds now? What next? What next will they do? Plot his assassination? That sounds melodramatic, sure, but Heineken University of Education is a very melodramatic institution. He composes a text message, inviting them here for The Last Peacemaking Conference and forwards it to them.

Time crawls and the daylight fades to gold, but neither of the boys has replied to the text. He thinks: next? Whom will he call next to apologize? Chiamaka, whom he impregnated and gave an imbecile, or Chioma, whose relationship he burnt down, or Rose, or Izu, who he once promised an A for his kind efforts to save him? He finishes his first cigarette and phones Chiamaka first.

"Are you drunk, Okonkwo?" she asks. "Of course you are. Things are hard, but you're probably calling from a beer parlour where you're filling your stomach with all sorts of alcohol."

Okoye is oddly flattered. "Yes, I'm in a beer parlour enjoying myself. You're a genius. Or did anybody tell you? Or are you here? Raise your hand or stand up and whistle or shout so I can see you."

I have told you I'm done with men, she says: because men are cruel and selfish and animalistic. Men are dishonest. She will hit men where it hurts. She will hit Okonkwo where it hurts. She will hit Okonkwo and hit Okonkwo and hit all Okonkwo's friends and any man who nears any of her daughters. She will live the rest of her life hurting men who lust after women and men who sleep with women. The richer she gets, the more she will invest her salary in the fight against men. She's glad the HOD is a woman, and not Okonkwo, not Okafor, not Okeke, not Okoye. She has said this before and she will say it again: Men should leave women's bodies alone!

"I have changed, Amaka," he says after her tirade. "Be kind to me. Forget our undesirable past. Please forgive me. Forgive us."

"Come and take Saul. He's your son."

"I don't like children."

There's a pause. "But you send countless bags of rice to motherless babies' homes."

"Well, I discovered I don't like babies, male or female," he says, quoting Ifenna. "Babies are wicked; they cry all the time to annoy us, poo and urinate on our bedsheets, drink all the milk in our houses without paying, and they cannot speak English or any other language well. I can't fathom them. Call me weird, but that's me. I don't just like babies."

"You're just dodging your responsibilities as a father. I'm not surprised, though. Which man is sensible in this country? A truckload of patriarchal dogs."

Okoye's hand have started shaking. "I don't like babies, including mine. Especially mine, I mean it."

"That boy looks like you. People have already figured him out. They open their mouths to tell me…"

"Throw rotten bananas into their mouths."

"Come and take him, so that when he grows up, the two of you will be dashing off to beer parlours every evening to drink beer and harass women. He's a perfect replica of you."

"Take the cute boy to the motherless babies' home."

"I expected this. Men are heartless."

Chioma is the next person he calls. "Chioma, I'm sorry for all the things I did to you," he says, and sips his beer.

"I've taken my revenge, but I'll never forget your wickedness," she says in a placid voice. "And why did you ring me up? Be snappy: I'm writing a song."

"I'm here, at Children of God beer parlour, drinking beer, smoking cigarettes and pondering about all the people I wronged in the past. Your name was the first that rose in my head. That's why I phoned you. Forgive me, please. I don't know how long I will last in this university. I wake up every day, thinking that a letter of termination will hit me. It hasn't come, but I'm now certain that it will come someday. Maybe I'll go to my village and become a farmer or a fisherman or die. I don't know. What I know, however, is that all my cruel actions against you and other students still haunt me. If you tell me you've totally forgiven me, I will be fine."

"I've nothing against you. I'm not your girlfriend. You know who your girlfriend is. You beat my boobs like drums once, played them like a guitar, and we did it once or three times. But I'm sure you've banged Rose seven hundred and fifty times."

"I don't think it's up to seven hundred and fifty. Six hundred, maybe. But I will not sleep with her again even if she's naked in my presence. I will phone her after this call and also tender my candid apology. I will call Nkem, Ifenna and some boys and girls. They are many."

"You really hurt a lot of people. You're very bad."

"I was even worse when I was an infant, but I have gravitated away from some bad habits."

"But you still collect our breasts? You still objectify women?"

"I've stopped that too. Even if your breasts are as big as a watermelon, I will not collect them."

"Unbelievable. Goodbye!"

He crushes a fly drowning on the beer-laden table. "All right. Have a nice time writing your great songs. I pray you become the next Celine Dion or Beyonce. You'll make it, my daughter."

"Goodbye!"

On his way home, his phone beeps with a text from Ifenna.

Professor, I got ur text. Semicolon and I are still down with depression. Let's meat tomorrow in another beer parlour; I owe the manager. I can only come their with Nkem, if you promise to pay the manager or slay him for me.

Let's *meat* tomorrow: so, in Ifenna's mind, this is a joke? Or is this some typo, just like "their"? Perhaps Nkem did not read this, did not edit this. Perhaps it was autocorrected by Ifenna's smartphone. Or was it truly intentional? If it's intentional, it means they are making fun of him. If they are making fun of him, it means they have shown the Vice Chancellor the videos, the video recorders, the photos. If they have given him all these, it means he will lose his job. Is he prepared for this disgrace, this descent into poverty?

Forget about all of them, he tells himself, and pockets the phone. Forget, forget, and if they please, let them expose me. I'm tired of this cat-and-dog fight, tired of plotting how to stop them. No lecturer has ever been hanged for having an affair with his student, for harassing his student sexually, for selling a few good grades to his students. He can only be demoted, suspended, or booted out. People will talk, people will laugh, people will throw a party—all these will happen for a few weeks and then everything will be blurry by time.

The following day, under drifting clouds of dawn and in golden air, he drives back to Children of God beer parlour to submerge his worries in alcohol. After draining two bottles of Gulder, after smoking half a packet of Dorchester cigarettes, after sending Nkem a text asking him to do whatever he wants to do against anybody, he phones Rose.

"Baby, how are you?" she says. "No, I know how you are. You're suffering. Amada tells us she saw you yesterday drinking beer at Children of God with tears in your eyes. Is it true? It's true! Everything is true, baby! It's funny, what Amanda say. And what Jamila say. Jamila say you are going round the campus apologizing to all the boys you has maltreated and all the girls you harassed sexually, but she is a gossip. I hate her. I heard she slept with the late Ayosky. And with you, maybe?"

"Rose, I called you primarily to apologise for everything we did, everything we shared." He lowers his half-filled glass to the plastic table. "I am old enough to be your father. We shouldn't be naked behind locked doors, laughing under bedsheets."

"Are you breaking up with me?"

"I am sorry, Rose. Sleeping with you, sleeping with one's student, is very appalling unprofessionalism."

"Baby, if you leave me I will show every human beings the photos and the videos and they will see your anus and . . ."

He cuts the connection and pockets his phone. There are five barboys hovering around him, picking emptied beer bottles, nodding to Eminem who's shouting on the loudspeaker, smiling at him. He tips only the dirtiest one and staggers off, every drinker and every object swaying in his eyes like a painting made blurry with water.

CHAPTER 24

IFENNA steps out of the bathroom with his bottle of whiskey and sits at the reading table to complete his drawing, to watch white dust drift in through the window, to listen as Nkem's new MP3 player amuses him with one of Chioma's maudlin love songs.

He has abandoned the picture of Okoye running across the campus naked with his briefcase covering his genital because the song is a distraction. He was painting the work when the song started.

But now Nkem has gone out with the phone, and to be here, in this room, alone and painting, without a being to amuse or to annoy: it's like bereavement.

But where did the Semicolon Boy go without telling him? To the library? To see his parents at the staff quarters? To Chioma's new mansion with a driveway, which is on the lips of most students? Well, that's none of his business. His business is to make sure the work is his latest masterpiece. His business is to use his art to annoy and to amuse, to satirise.

He finishes his drink and picks his paint-stained brush to commence work, but someone raps at the door. "Hope you're a sexy girl?" he says, opening the door to let in gritty sunlight. "Because I'm looking for a girlfriend…oh, Mrs. Okoye!"

Okoye's wife, together with her daughter, enters as he steps backwards. "My daughter said Nkemdilim lives here," Okoye's wife says. "Oh, good morning. Afternoon, Student? Yes, afternoon."

She's wearing a discoloured black polo that says ANIMAL LIVES MATTER, a huge cream neckscarf, a silky leaf-coloured skirt that fails to conceal her large legs, a rusty wrist-watch that has lost both the hour and the minute hands. Her daughter's appearance is acceptable: a white T-shirt, white trousers, white sneakers. Even the novel in her hand, *A Farewell to Arms*, is white. During his Teaching Practice, when he taught her Economics, she usually praised his purple clothes, his pink clothes, and once remarked to her classmate, a girl in gold-striped glasses, that she'd rather be shot dead than be seen in white. Why, then, is she all white today? Perhaps she *was* just struggling to draw his attention.

"Are you bringing your daughter for Nkem to marry

her?" he asks. "Or you want to reiterate the need for humans to stop killing animals?"

Okoye's wife lowers herself into a chair and a rising wind from the uncurtained window ruffles her browning hair. Her daughter remains standing, her eyes on Nkem's several novels on the reading table.

"Who's Oscar Wilde, Master?" Okoye's daughter asks in English. "Master Nkem used to pontificate about this man…"

Her mother cuts her short to address him. "Student, I don't keep fowls or goats. Or any domestic animal whose live I will terminate just because I love meat. I don't support people who *murder* fowls or any of these domesticated animals. Fowls, for example, are not eating us human beings, so why are we eating them? It's wickedness. We don't eat meat in my house, Student."

Student. Why is she throwing this rock-heavy cross into his face? The only English word she has used here and probably the only one she can pronounce without biting her tongue. She knows his name, and should use it. People who remind one what one is are the only creatures he does not want to have around him. No wonder Okoye her husband does not want her around him. No wonder Okoye is always running to restaurants and beer parlours with little girls. "Your daughter once told me you hinted that we human beings should allow mosquitoes to bite us?" he says. "Like, we shouldn't kill mosquitoes, Mrs. Okoye?"

"I'm in trouble, Student. My husband can sleep with a nine-month-old baby girl. He is having an affair with one of his students called Rose. I want you to do me and my daughter a favour: call the girl so I can beg her to leave my husband. She and babies in orphanage homes take all his salaries and allowances, and Ezi hardly gives me money for food. Some nights, he doesn't come home. He's sleeping with her because all his trouser pockets and his briefcase are filled with... with. . . This is killing me, it is killing me!"

He retreats because she reeks of sweat. "Get up, Mrs. Okoye. You'll scratch our carpet. I can't help you; your husband didn't help us when. . . Never mind. Get up and save your knees and our carpet."

But she remains on her knees, her sobs increasing in speed and in volume, the sunlight gleaming on her oily forehead. On a radio downstairs, people begin to clap.

"Please help us, Master," her daughter says in English.

Why can't this girl speak Igbo like her mother? A Western gospel song begins somewhere, and the girl repeats her last words. Funny, he thinks, but before he can say no to the girl's plea, Mrs. Okoye has thrust a Nokia phone into his hand. "I'm calling her," Mrs. Okoye says, mopping her eyes with the edge of her clothes. "Student, I stole her number from my husband's phone. If she takes the call, talk to her."

He steps backwards, away from her, as if she had just transformed into a tree on fire. "And say what?"

"Please invite her here, Student. I want us to have a meeting. . . Oh, thanks!"

When he brings the phone to his ear, Rose says something in Igbo about a hairdryer-criminal dying an untimely death. She has abandoned English because the foreign language, she admits, is like a fruit on an incredibly tall tree full of thorns: her hand cannot reach it and she cannot climb the tree. "Who's that? Francisca? Francisca, Oge told me you're the harlot who stole my hairdryer. If you don't bring it this evening, I swear to God, I will write a letter to the police headquarters!"

"The inspector is your boyfriend?" he says, scratching his head, struggling for an idea. "But I'm not Francisca the hairdryer-criminal."

"Oh, Ifenna the ex-homo!"

He ignores her laughter, and continues in a more serious tone. "There's this pair of shoes one of the members in my uncle's church gifted me. It's unisex, but I don't want them; they make me look girlish. Come and have them. Don't pay."

"Are you serious? Tell me you're not serious, Umbrella Boy!"

"Stop asking me dumb questions. If you're not interested, let me know so I can give the shoes to another girl. I think they'll fit Chioma."

She giggles. "I will leave this girl whose hair I want to plait, but if you disappoint me by giving that girl those shoes I'll assassinate you!"

It takes Rose only fifteen minutes to appear in the room. The amusing things about her: her blinking eyes, her sweat-soaked shirt, her unzipped jeans, her badly applied eye pencil.

"What's the meaning of this, ex-homo?" Rose asks him, but her eyes are fixed on Mrs. Okoye and her daughter. "What's the meaning of this nonsense?"

Laughing, he dashes to the door, locks it and puts the key into his empty wallet. Despite his loud laughter, despite her daughter's grimace, despite the triumph in Rose's eyes, Mrs. Okoye kneels before the girl who's enjoying her husband salaries and allowances, like a slave at her master's feet.

"Leave my husband for me, my daughter, please," she tells Rose. "You've enjoyed my husband for four years, Rose. Can't you be kind to let me have him for a four minutes? I'm begging you. Think about his family. We haven't paid our house rent because of you, and the landlord is threatening to throw us and our property out the window. Would you leave him, my sweet, kind daughter?"

Rose puffs out a sarcastic laugh and tosses her blond wig from side to side. "But he's my boyfriend, and not yours. Find your own boyfriend, madam."

"He's my husband," Mrs. Okoye says. "Ezi should be staying with me, and not with you."

"My ripe fruits are still standing because I'm young." Rose pushed up her breasts and puts out her tongue at her. "I'm young, I'm hot, I'm charming; he'd be staying with me, and not with an old woman who loves animals. Allow that man to enjoy himself. He's not the only man who has a girlfriend. Men keep girlfriends all the time, even in movies and in novels. Don't you read novels or watch movies? At least you read newspapers? You see how other married men enjoy themselves with young, fresh babes? Sleeping with young fresh babes like me makes men happy. It improves their health and they live longer. Life is brief, you know. Don't be selfish; allow that man to enjoy himself, and stop disturbing me."

A hushed silence falls.

Say something, madam, he thinks as Mrs. Okoye's eyes bulge and her chest rises and falls. A blink sends the beads of sweat on her eyebrows rolling down her cheeks. Like she's an exhausted athlete in an Olympic race, he would like to say. A marathon race, perhaps. Is this accelerated breathing a sign of a heart attack? Is this woman trying to feign a heart attack?

"Rose, leave this woman's husband," he says, and takes her hand. "If you want a boyfriend, take me. I'm cheap. Ask me out, I will agree. Men are cheap. We don't behave like girls. Let's start dating now; there's no time to waste."

Rose hits him with her handbag as Chioma usually does when he says something witty, and laughs, as though he it's a joke.

"Rose, if Ezi wants to enjoy himself, he should come to me his wife, not you," Mrs. Okoye says. "He's my husband."

"And he's my boyfriend." Rose folds the sleeve of her onion-coloured shirt, as if she wants a fight. "Okoye's my boyfriend. He loves and needs me, not you. I'm a Nigerian, but I don't have a Nigerian thing. My thing is an Italian, though Okoye my baby says it's French. Well, the point is that my *juice* is foreign, a young European, and yours is old and local. Thank God for that. Thank God I'm so sweet. Okoye my boyfriend said it with his own mouth. If you doubt me, I'll phone him and you will hear him kiss his phone and call me a sweet potato, honey, Tomato Jos. Leave us alone. You're disturbing our relationship."

"He's also in a relationship with me, Rose," Mrs Okoye says. "Ezi is my husband."

Rose looks Mrs. Okoye from head to toe, sizing her up. "Cheap clothes," she says. "You know what, madam? Okoye will stay with you on Mondays, Tuesdays and Wednesdays and stay with me on Thursdays, Fridays, Saturdays and Sundays. Especially on Sundays. I like to club on Sunday evening. He'll buy me wine and we will dance till five o'clock in the morning and I will dress him up and send him back to you."

He suppresses the laugh that is threatening to explode from his mouth. "I don't think you divided it well, Rose," he says. "Let this woman have him on Sundays; they need to go to church. Women like to go to church with their husbands."

"Young girls like to go to church with their Sugar Daddies!" Rose shouts. "I'll have him on Sundays. Okay, all right, I'll give her Saturdays. She'll have Okoye on Saturdays, but Sundays are mine. If Okoye were here, he would tell you that I like Sundays. Maybe you will go home and try to persuade him. . . he'll not listen to you because he enjoys sleeping with me because I'm young and fresh like a fruit. I'm young, and you're old and wrinkled, thank God." Rose laughs wildly into the collapsing face of Mrs Okoye.

He cannot help but join in her laughter. Oh Lord, I swear, I am enjoying myself, he thinks, and then his amusement dries up as the distressed woman stumbles to her feet, dusts her knees and leaves with her daughter.

Rose settles down on the foam. "Funny woman… but where you serious when you asked me to be your girlfriend, Ifenna?"

"Yes."

"But you're a woman, and I'm not a lesbian." She stands again, laughing, and goes to wrap her arms around him. "Of course, you're now an ex-homo. You're a man now."

"Let's have sex."

She pushes him away. "How you talk! Are you really from this planet!"

"I swear, I also wonder if I'm from this planet."

"The other day, Mirabel told me she said hi to you and you fell in love with her immediately. Or said you did. But she doesn't like you."

Mirabel is a big-nosed girl in English and one of Adaku's friends; he has never asked her out because he doesn't find her attractive. "She doesn't like me?" he says. "Of course she doesn't like me. That's why I like her."

"You like people who dislike you?"

"People who do not like me are the only people I like. And I can do anything for them. I hope you don't like me, Rose. Please don't like me. Tell me you don't like me!"

She flies back into the foam with girlish giggles. "But I like you, you funny boy. I like you, so it won't work!"

"You like me?" He slides into the foam, takes off his singlet and raises her skirt. "You like me? I like you, too."

She closes her eyes, kisses his neck, and then, delicately, peels off the skirt and the underwear and urges him on with a seductive smile of an experienced pornstar.

Afterwards, he gets up and screams. "Who's this on

my foam, please? Rose? Jesus Christ, I swear, I thought you were Mirabel!"

The joke, to his surprise, eludes her, annoys her. "Ifenna, in your mind, you think you're smart because I let you..." She pauses, gathers her clothes and gets out from the foam. "So, you have used me, right? I am cheap, right?"

He squawks. "Come back, darling. Just a joke."

When Nkem comes back, she runs to him laughing as children do when their parents return from a far-flung market. "Guess what, Semicolon?" she says in an excited voice. "I have fucked the last drop of homosexuality out of Ifenna. He and I are dating! You refuse to take me, so he took me. He and I will be building our surprising relationship with Okoye's salary, if the dirty man's not fired... And that reminds me, Nkem my love. I know everything about your grade and Ifenna's and Okoye and the video and Mama Nkechi and Papa Nkechi and the money paid which hasn't been refunded. I once wanted to go to the Vice Chancellor's office with you guys. That was when I wanted my *beautiful* face to appear in a newspaper. Remember? Of course you do. You're smart. And sexy."

Nkem removes her hands from his, turns to him with a letter. "From Okoye's daughter, blessed wine. She wanted to speak to me, but I don't want to stand with a kid like that, obviously. People might conjecture...

I compelled her to put it in writing. It's a depressing, error-free letter, though it lacks semicolons. I thought she knew how to use semicolons. Read it."

He takes the letter from Nkem, kisses Rose on the cheek, and saunters into the bathroom.

Dear Master Ifenna,

I'm flabbergasted at your insensitive behaviour in your room. You found my mother's excruciating tears hilarious? Anyway, I desire to inform you that Mama Nkechi came to our house crying: she was caught altering a student's grade and is now suspended. I discovered Dad wanted to use her to help you and my wonderful Nkem. I yearned to tell him myself, but Blessed Wine doesn't like to be seen with me as if I don't know how to use a semicolon. That's heartbreaking, but let's not talk about it. Tell him I love him and I sincerely wish something miraculous would happen to you gentlemen's results.

Chinenye.

Her pedantic diction, the unguessed virtuosity of spelling, the verb "suspended" – all these hit him with a ruthless force, and he is so shaken he nearly falls into the lavatory basin. A blessed wine has become a sour wine, he thinks. We were crying because we feared our results would be funny, but now we will not even graduate. Now we will face the panel for paying Mama Nkechi to alter our grades. Now we will be captured, questioned, disgraced, expelled. Now we will return to our people empty-handed. How have the mighty fallen! No, neither of then is mighty, has ever been mighty: how have the fallen *fallen*! But Nkem isn't worried. Nkem who makes his first excursion into corruption because his grades were falling. Nkem who says he will kill himself if his result wasn't impressive. Nkem who yearns to be an academic. Why is Nkem not shaking? Is his indifferent façade a shield to his despondency?

He rereads the letter, then folds it into a firm ball, and gets up from the bowl with the uneasy movement of a man who has suddenly grown old and frail.

On the marbled wall, a bloated cockroach spreads its wings, circles a leaf-shaped stain the colour of blood, pauses. He opens his mouth to blow it into the lavatory basin, but nixes the thought and removes his singlet and boxer shorts with trembling hands. The clothes end up in a bucket. He waits for the cockroach to fly out the handkerchief-sized window before he turns on the tap. The tepid water from the shower will wash away the tears in his eyes.

At sundown, he stalks Okoye's daughter, but does not find her. The following day, the search continues until he finds her on her way back from school. She is, unlike other returning school boys and girls, reading a novel in the sun and stumbling on the stony road. A neat sky-blue uniform, neat white socks, neat white canvases: how come a pig produced this walking photograph?

"Master, master." This is her greeting, her jovial

greeting. As his student, in his class, this was also her greeting, her jovial greeting. A boldness foreign to her classmates, foreign to her teachers. Does it mean she's used to men, used to sex? Perhaps she isn't, but she cannot be a virgin: a ripe banana in a tree cannot go a season uneaten in a land full of monkeys. Today, in his room, he will try to be one of these lucky monkeys.

"The beautiful reader of ugly novels," he says, smiling, hugging her. "I swear, Nkem bought new novels, ten new novels. One is called *Oliver Twist* by. . . by... by Cristiano Ronaldo. No, I mean. . . Let's go home so you can see the books yourself."

"Charles Dickens wrote *Oliver Twist*, Master. But there's no problem if one forgets the author's name. The problem is this: Will Mummy open the door for me if I don't come home before five-thirty?"

"Mummies are wicked all over the world! Can't those fucking bastards allow their daughters to follow fine boys and end up being useless in life?"

Surprisingly, she slaps her schoolbag and giggles. "Funny master!"

Upstairs in the room, he shows her Nkem's heaps of books on the reading table and under the reading table, shows her his own artworks on the wall, shows her his premature photos of big-eared cartoons making love on loaves of bread.

"Where's Master Semicolon?" she asks, roaming

round the chair she's been offered and averting her gaze from the comic pornography. "When the two of you were my student-teachers, he promised to teach me how to use a semicolon."

"Chinenye, I did not bring you into my perfumed room to talk about punctuation marks."

She blinks in surprise. She blinks again. "But to? To do what, Master? Oh, novels? Where are the novels? Hope you have Nicholas Sparks. Love his *A Walk to Remember* so much! Made me cry."

He pads to the door, locks it, returns with the key. "Nkem strolled to the library to read," he says in an intensified Onitsha dialect, and takes her confusingly feverish hands. "He and I, as you're aware, will no longer bag a first-class degree or 2: 1, partly because of those brutes' quotadian attacks on us, partly because your fat dad and other old devils dealt with us."

She brushes off his hands and whips round to the window to hide her face.

"Look, Chinenye, I don't want a revenge, but a consolation. My consolation is lovemaking. If you, Okoye's astonishingly beautiful daughter, sleeps with me, I will forgive him and forget my funny grades. Mind you, sex is not that sweet. I just want to experiment, to see how fornication tastes in September. I heard it's mind-blowing in the first week of every September, especially in West Africa." He edges closer and holds her waist. "Let me remove your clothes? Heat is doing you."

"'Heat is doing you' is bad English, Master." She caresses his biceps and fingers, stares at him with glassy eyes. "You want to do me, Master? Because you have a gun. You have a gun?"

"Not by force. Not with a gun. Just a peaceful fornication, my dear. God knows I only want to have a very brief fornication with you without harming you, as a good Christian child that I am. Just a consolatory fornication."

"Okay," she murmurs, and does what shocks him: she drops her schoolbag on the ground, climbs onto the foam, spreads her legs, and closes her eyes. "Do it, but don't harm me."

Amateur drama, he thinks. This is like an amateur drama. Nothing looks convincing, nothing sounds convincing: is she pretending she doesn't want to do it so that she wouldn't look cheap? Perhaps she's genuinely scared of him, scared of his nonexistent gun. But he will not softpedal. He will not let this opportunity slip from his grasp. He will try to see if he will, for the first time in his life, reach a toe-curlingly fabulous orgasm while thrusting a woman.

"You agreed, my sweet banana?" he asks her in a quavering voice, and takes off his clothes. "Hope I'm not raping you?"

She takes off her clothes, but does not speak.

"Chinenye?" he says.

Silence again. But he lies beside her, strokes her small breasts, kisses her ears and lets his finger travel on her thigh and locate what it seeks. The shudder she gives, the moan that escapes from her mouth, the silence that follows, the closed eyes, the heavy breathing: they interest and surprise him. The girl remains passive from the beginning to the middle of it, and now, as he shudders and says "oh, no, no!" like he's being electrocuted, she pulls him deeper inside her and calls out an unpronounceable German-like name exactly seven times.

Whether this unknown lover is a character in a love poem or in real life, he will never know. "For the first time in the history of Africa, Ifenna Nzekwu from the Federal Republic of Nigeria reached a leg-shaking orgasm!" he says, rising with his clothes, and floats to the door to unlock it. "Tell your dad that I am not a homosexual."

She wears her clothes in silence, combs her hair, and leaves with her schoolbag. As the door closes behind her, he drops to his knees. A sudden shadow of sadness engulfs him.

CHAPTER 25

NKEM beats his chest with pride: after several days of procrastinations and self-doubts, he has successfully written the outline of what he calls a groundbreaking novel.

This book will be my confession, he tells himself. This book will be my declaration of my greatness, my atonement for shattering my own heart. Perhaps there's nothing remarkable in that, he thinks as his eyes fall on Jack Kerouac's *On the Road* lying on the table: several writers and scholars before him, before Jack Kerouac even, walked this road. Oscar Wilde comes to mind first: *The Ballad of a Reading Gaol*, he suspects, was Wilde's coping mechanism, Wilde's literary therapy. And because he reveres this master, because he considers this master worthy of emulation, he will lock himself up like a criminal and write his own tragic account. He will write about his campus that swallows students' future and students' lovers. He will write about poverty and class and how they matter in romantic relationships. He will write about Chief and how he stole his girlfriend with "blood money", a fancy car, a fancy house. "But I will try to make it funny so that it will not resemble those depressing works of the eighteenth-century writer Thomas Hardy," he tells Ifenna in their room one day after the first draft has been written. "And there will be humour, blessed wine."

"May God bless you for free!" Ifenna is stirring cubes of sugar in his teacup, but suspends the action now and gazes at him. "If I were a writer, I would write a novel that would be so funny that my dear readers will fall off their chairs laughing and die. That'll be the greatest literary achievement in history. But, unfortunately for the very few people who read fiction in this country, I don't even know how to use a semicolon. I am a mere artist. I paint oceans, seas, rivers, fountains and, of course, naked women. My current work is an *impressionistic* portrait of our new HOD, though."

He strolls to the reading table, examines the painted photograph of the new Head of Department, and wonders if the woman will like it.

Professor Nwanyibufe, that's the woman's preferred name. Professor Nwanyibufe. She says she does not like her students addressing her as Nwokedi, her husband's surname, or as Otakagu, her own surname.

This painting he carries, a remarkable likeness: light-skinned, white-haired, gap-toothed. Leonardo da Vinci: that's what he thinks his roommate and friend deserves to be called by everybody, at least by the youngish HOD whom Ifenna has imitated so elegantly.

"This is your masterpiece, obviously," he says. "Will your whiskey allow you to send it to her as a congratulatory present for defeating all these men?"

"My whiskey advised me to send it to her. Very wise whiskey."

"We will seize the opportunity to ask her to persuade the university management to bring Okoye to the panel, shame Okoye, ostracize Okoye."

Ifenna chuckles. "I swear, you became wicked after discarding your Harry Potter glasses. But we will do that, *blessed wine*."

Professor Nwanyibuife is happy to receive the picture in her office. "This is beautiful, so beautiful," she says, holding the silver-framed portrait up in the sunlight streaming in through the open window. "So beautiful. You should have studied fine and applied arts! What are you doing here in the Department of Economics, this boy? Now, get out of this department before the count of three…!"

Ifenna laughs and she laughs: a tiny doorbell

competing with another equally tiny doorbell. He, Nkem, laughs, too, because silence from him will telegraph his mounting impatience. He likes the woman for her youngish manner, her Stage Behaviour, her approachability, her habitual friskiness, her sense of humour: but these characteristics sometimes compel him pick a pen and write an acidic essay, promulgating the ban of comedy nationwide. It's obvious they are merely here to discuss Okoye, he and Ifenna, to see how the video recorders have been received, to plan Okoye's removal. But this woman is palavering about her photograph, palavering about Fine and Applied Department, about Economics Department. About irrelevant things, he thinks. But she's far better than Sir Israel. Far better than most of her colleagues, but why does she seem disinclined to fight for the punishment of Okoye? Why does she appear to be in love with the Beer Belly, as Chioma once suspected on the phone when he brought up the issue? It's true she has no church, no mosque, no shrine, but she is, to his mind, the last professor on earth to be found in bed with her colleague. Is she afraid of Okoye, then? He hopes not.

A blue-belied bird flies into the window, pecking at its reflection or at an invisble insect, flapping, flapping, its yellow feathers dropping and drifting in the fruity breeze. He closes his eyes and hears Ifenna recline in the swivel chair. He hears Ifenna speak as if Ifenna had a supernatural power that transforms people's heads into transparent glasses through which he reads their thoughts. "Nkem and I are aware that you're better than the late Sir Israel, madam. Now every Okeke and Okafo is laughing happily in this department. No more 'go and pray to God' nonsense." Ifenna pauses, as he opens his eyes, and humid winds from the window ruffle Professor Nwanyibufe's hair and the files on her littered desk. "And our girlfriends are safe."

What an honest but puerile speech! Even Professor Nwanyibuife, he sees, is embarrassed: she lowers the artwork to the ground and glares at Ifenna, who's smiling. Foolish ignoramus, he thinks, and looks away.

On the wall, there are tiny ants crawling in a straight line towards the ceiling. The petals of artificial blue flowers in emerald pots quiver, the departmental almanacs slap the walls and the plagues threaten to drop and shatter. The office, he notices now, smells deliciously of Apple hair cream, and love, and freedom.

"I almost forgot," Professor Nwanyibuife says. She pulls her drawer open, retrieves two envelopes and hands them to him and Ifenna. "From the Vice Chancellor. It's about your video recorder that caught Dr. Okoye Ezinwa in the act. Chioma has taken hers. Don't bother reading it: they all contain the same message. They are all inviting you to a hearing."

The backs of the envelopes are marked

'Confidential', but he doesn't see why. "Okoye has been caught and it is clear in the video," he says, his voice rising. "Everything is in those videos. Why can't they dismiss him with immediate effect? The inquiry is not necessary, obviously."

"Maybe they want to have fun," Ifenna says.

Professor Nwayibuife grins, showing off her white teeth. "You tend to see humour in everything, Nzekwu. No, it's not for fun. I conjectured that they needed to hear a word, a spoken word, not a written word, from the criminal before showing him the door. I cannot give you videos, ask you to catch corrupt lecturers and accept everything you record as true. This is the twenty-first century: the computer can fake things, and the wrong people might fall victims. Dr. Okoye Ezinwa has answered their query (which, like videos, can be faked), but has yet to defend his actions in person. He deserves the few minutes he will be given to speak before his victims and you the heroes in this new and sensational Catch Corrupt Lecturers Tactic."

"I don't want to see that bloody termite who has eaten deep into our education," he says.

Professor Nwayinbuife, to his surprise, scowls at his vulgarity. "Don't forget to honour the Senior Staff Disciplinary Committee's invitation to the hearing," she says, rising with her laptop computer. "Have a wonderful day."

The Department of Religious Studies conference room, where the inquiry is scheduled to take place, reeks of books decomposing in water. The whir and rattlings of the cobweb-coated ceiling fans are the only noises he can hear. The doors and windows are locked against eavesdropping students and lecturers. The bright light of midday permeates the room.

Around the glistening gold-coloured table: to his right sit Professor Eziokwu, the chair of the enquiry or whatever it is called; Reverend Okenna, the parish priest of the campus Anglican Church and curious friend of the effeminate Vice Chancellor; Dr Nnedimma Rebecca, the Secretary Senior Staff Disciplinary committee. To his left, at the other table, are two other committee members whom he does not know. Both are female and white-haired. Facing these unsmiling men and women are he, Nkem the hero, Chioma the heroine, Ifenna the helper and, of course, Okoye the "defendant." They are asked to sit, but Okoye says he prefers to stand.

"First and foremost, Dr Okoye," Professor Eziokwu says, opening the case with a booming voice, "the committee does not converge here today to probe the validity of the video recorders and other materials that expose your undesirable secrets. Why? Because the man in them are no other person than you. You were caught, Dr Okoye, and you admitted that in your reply to the query we sent to you on the seventh day of July. Do you want us to proceed by reading out your reply to the query?"

"No," Okoye says. "No, my dearest. That will be time-wasting and pointless and childish. I don't see why I should be repudiating an obvious fact. I don't see why anybody who's not mad will doubt that I am not the fat devil dressed in those filthy clothes in the videos. I admitted that I am the criminal in my answer to the query. And I bet my kidney and a crate of beer that you nice people, you very nice people, have sent that excellent entertainment to the Vice Chancellor. And he enjoyed the videos. So why are we here to waste our time? Don't we, ladies and gentlemen, have clothes, pots or plates to wash at home? Am I to understand that we are leaving our house chores to our wives and husbands at home to do them alone? Is that fair to these people we married?"

The committee members exchange glances.

But this isn't funny, he thinks, as Ifenna bends his head to hide his amusement. He and Chioma throw the jolly fellow disparaging looks and the face, glistening with beads of sweat, turns away as the smile recedes.

Reverend Okenna straightens his black-framed glasses and leans forward. "Dr. Okoye, Heineken University of Education is unique," he says in a sympathetic tone. "We don't approach issues like other universities in this country. What you did was sinful and shameful, but we want to gauge the Vice Chancellor's ability to forgive. Of course you might not continue as a lecturer, but you will still be here. Demotion is not an unkind penalty. Perhaps you can be stationed in the library or in some nice place like that. Sending you back to the village will dampen your family. We are here to prevent that from happening."

"We are not here to prevent that from happening," Dr. Nnedimma says with a fierce frown. "We are here to make certain that the video isn't doctored. He has admitted that he's the man in the videos. So, as he rightly said, why are we still wasting our time?"

"Thank you, Dr. Nnedimma," Professor Eziokwu says. "You're right. Dr. Okoye is right, too: we are wasting our time because the case ended even before it began. But we must hear from the students." He peers into the file on the table, his wrinkles deepening. "Nkem Obi, Chioma Emenike and Ifenna Nzekwu: how was that plotted and executed? How real are these videos?"

He rises and, in a voice consciously cleaned of antagonism, explains in present tense. After he rounds off his speech with "Thank you all" and sits again, Chioma shifts closer to him, whispers the three golden words into his ear, squeezes his hand with affection. Ifenna writes "That's my Semicolon!" on his palm with a fountain pen, shifts away as thunder booms outside and the building shakes. Lightning brightens the rattling window. Soon this drizzle will quicken into a downpour and they cannot hear each other. Before five-thirty, he hopes, this hearing will be over. This rain that's threatening to fall will also be over. But why was this scheduled at five o' clock?

Okoye, not the chair, speaks first after his narration. "Thank you, Nkem Obi. Now, it is clear that I'm a criminal. That I did it. That we are wasting our time. Am I free, at this juncture, to say goodbye and return to my house? My wife's brassiere is spread outside and it looks like it will rain."

"Ezinwa," Reverend Okenna says, "please stop kidding. We want to help you. The Vice Chancellor is not an unkind man. We want to recommend that he remove you from your position as senior lecturer to… to… Would you like to work in the library? Not as a cleaner, but as. . . as. . . a book-keeper or something like that."

"Dear Reverend Okenwa, the case is closed. Let the Vice Chancellor do whatever he wants to do to me."

Dr. Nnedimma nods. "He will do whatever he wants to do to you. He knows that lecturers who play with the breasts of their female students deserve a round of applause and promotion. He knows that!"

"I think we will not achieve anything if we continue like this," Professor Eziokwu says. "So we have to call it a day. Thank you, Dr. Okoye. Thank you, Nkem, Chioma and . . . and what's the name of that smiling one? Oho, Ifenna!"

Outside, it is raining in slants. He folds his arms and watches as Dr. Nnedimma lends Chioma an umbrella and asks her to follow his boyfriend because her Volvo cannot help all of them: the car is loaded with books and scripts. Ifenna helps her with her carton of books, follows her to her car.

He unfolds his arms, puffs of vapour leaving his mouth in fanciful curls like cigarette smoke, and he edges closer to Chioma, leaves from the nearby mango trees drifting toward them. He peels off a browned one that glues itself on her wet cheek and she smiles up at him. The rain intensifies, but they remain here, on the sandy corridor, near a rusty pillar, cuddling, shivering, and watching as Ifenna and the lecturer hurry into the Volvo. As the metal noisemaker starts and moves after the departing cars of the other committee members, Chioma says, "I'm married, Sugar, but am going to your hostel to do something reckless with you again in your bedroom because today is a happy day."

"A happy day, obviously," he says.

Awkwardly, she kisses him on the lips, opens the umbrella, and they run into the chilly rain laughing like children.

CHAPTER 26

OKOYE does not deign to read his letter of dismissal when it's delivered to his office. He unseals the ink-stained brown envelope with swift fingers, tears the message enclosed in it, and drops the pieces into a wastepaper basket. Sipping his canned Star beer, he staggers into his Office Convenience, urinates liberally round the lavatory basin, then on the wall, then on the ground, and returns without flushing it, like a spoilt child. The red message on the door, clearly written in Rose's hand, says *Out!* The can-littered desk says *Out!* The book, *The Economic Importance of Cow Dung in West Africa*, together with six other publications of his, which he now packs into his briefcase, says *Out!* So he gets out of the office, his head bowed by shame.

Downstairs, there's an assemblage of lecturers in

conversation. Most these colleagues, he notices, are from Economics; they look away when he passes by. They do not look away when his students point at him and giggle.

Above his head, around his ears, green-belied flies: they follow him like he's a faece-coated madman, circling his head, buzzing with irritating regularity. He shakes his head, shoos them away, increases his pace.

The air is golden or perhaps it's because he's tipsy; he will trip and fall into stagnant water if he's not careful. The noises of the university, like the buzz of a million bees, disturb his ears and his concentration. Still, he manages to get to his car parked under a mango tree without tripping into stagnant water or on the stony earth, manages to enter into it, and manages to drive home without knocking any passerby or animal into a bush.

Back in his flat, he flings his briefcase onto the centre table, drops on the battered cushion, and puts his whirling head into his hands. Moonlight falls on his feet and he thinks: What next now? Go to the village and start selling firewood, go to a bottling company and start assisting in distributions of beer, or go to a far-flug secondary school and apply to teach Economics? Demeaning and depressing, all these options, but there's no other alternative. The least belittling is teaching, but school proprietors in Nigeria, he recollects with a start, are unparalleled in the business of slotting invisible straws into the heads of their workers as though these employees were mere bottles, sucking their fresh knowledge like milk or honey until these carriers of drinkables are dried up, fed up, and are promptly discarded with peanuts or nothing.

As the winds lift the curtain and a shaft of starlight slices in, the idea of bus driving flashes across his mind like a bus at a high speed, but he shakes his head. He'll not drive any commercial bus for any wealthy bull and he will not teach any human being, a blockhead or a genius, in any despicable private school. His wife offers no suggestion, no encouragement, but a letter informing him that her glowing interest in the marriage has been blown off like a lantern in a rough wind.

"I want to pack my bags and return to my father's house," she says when she's back, and waddles to the wardrobe to retrieve her property. "Thanks for being the best husband in Nigeria, Ezi."

"You're welcome, my love." With a gelid smile, he helps her dust her luggage and pack her clothes, and when she's gone, he pours himself a glass of beer with a slightly shaking hand. He does not know where his son is. He does not know where his daughter is. He does not know where he will go, what he will do to earn a living, but he knows how he will live the rest of his life: alone in this smelly flat until he is too hungry, too weak, to leave, like a bee caught in a spider web; dead and dried up like the bee, the wind will scatter his remains. He shudders at the thoughts and his phone beeps with a text from an unknown number:

We payed your sun Ebuka to help us get an A from you, but now your sacked. We may belong to the same confraternity, but he must COLLECT! Ask him to bye a gun or an axe because we're coming!

A rubbish message from Ifenna the joker, he thinks, and deletes it. Rose phones almost immediately. "I'm calling you with my customer's number, baby," she says in Igbo. "Ebuka's cult friends will kill him if he doesn't escape from this town. I wanted to inform you earlier, but you've been ignoring me. See, we're still dating whether you like it or not. After pounding my *honey* for four years you want to abandon me. I'm not saying you'll not cheat on me with your wife sometimes, but always call and check on me. How many times have you called to ask me if I need new bleaching creams and foreign panties and brassieres? You've stopped calling and it's not fair. I don't like it, I don't like it!"

"I'm sorry, Rosie; I've returned to my darling wife. My love for her has returned. So move on."

"Are you dumping me for that woman who's the size of a house? That thing you call a wife is bigger than this university's auditorium and library put together. Jesus Christ, she's so fat, baby! How can you forget a fine girl like me because of that house-shaped creature?"

"Yes."

"Send me money, Okoye! I want to buy more weave-ons for my customers. Send me fifty thousand naira. Okay, lend. Lend me fifty thousand naira."

"The university has finally dismissed me."

"I know. But you can help me. There's only fifty thousand naira in my account. Should I lend myself my money and when the government pays you your last month's salary you will lend me the money I borrowed from myself?"

"Have a splendid life."

The half of a moon has fully emerged from behind the beautifully solidified waters drifting across the grey sky when his daughter comes back home. Her hair is tousled, her knees are stained with sand, and there are tears in her eyes.

"I am sorry, Daddy," she says, and begins to sob. "I'm so sorry! I never wanted to do it, but Master Ifenna would not listen!"

"He attacked you on the road?" he asks.

"No, I'm pregnant, Daddy! I am pregnant! Will you ever forgive me? What will I do? Mummy has already disowned me!"

He is too shocked to speak. "I will write a great romance novel, Daddy, and dedicate it to you," were her last words to him.

That was only a week old, but now she's pregnant

by an undisclosed boy or man who's probably infected with HIV, sociopathic or psychopathic. He has no timeless book or any remarkable achievement to leave behind in this world aside Chinenye the girl who aspired to immortalize their surname. Chinenye the girl who planned to remain single and celibate until she has graduated from a British or Canadian university, published her masterpiece, built him a mansion. Chinenye who vowed to marry a prince and give birth a boy named Ezinwa, after his grandfather, in a garden lit with the sunlight. But now Chinenye has been raped, now Chinenye is pregnant. Now what will he do, what will Chinenye do?

He finishes his cigarette and totters into his bedroom to hide his moist eyes from the mocking windows.

His wife, or ex-wife, visits in the morning. "Where's Ebuka?" he asks her.

"I thought that Chinenye had a God-fearing private part, but I was wrong," his wife says instead. "I was so wrong. She has ruined her life. I blame her, and not the devil that put his sperm into her unchristian private part. Or a general part. God, Chinenye has been deflowered, stained and wasted! No man can marry her! She's finished! I'll throw her out!"

"Don't do that!" he bays, rising from the cushion.

But his Dorothy has picked an iron jug, swept out of the living room and into the room, where their daughter is. Or has she absconded? Locked herself up in the kitchen or store, weeping, sinking? Minutes later, Dorothy reappears, sweating and trembling. Chinenye saw her and escaped, she says. The sinful girl escaped through a broken window. The sinful girl is running down a narrow path leading to the town's stream.

"If any bad thing happens to Chinenye, I will buy you a car," he says in an irritated tone, and lights a cigarette. "Expect a car from me."

Dorothy hisses and leaves, banging the door behind her. Banging it at my bleeding heart in this crumpling family of mine, he thinks. My family is clearly crumpling, crumpling, like a heap of files on a rickety desk. What is he going to do?

Three cigarettes and three bottles of Hero beer consumed, he belches, sets his phone to Unknown Number and phones Ifenna. "Hello?" he asks in a quavering voice.

"Who's this?" Ifenna asks.

"The vice Chancellor of Heineken University," he says, assuming the man's accent. "I was notified that you got your lecturer's daughter pregnant. You destroyed her. See me, or forget your certificate. Where and when do you want to see me? I want to choose."

"You funny philantropist, Mr. Okoye," Ifenna says, laughing, and ends the call.

And ends the call, he thinks. The Umbrella Boy

ends the call because he discovered I was the caller. The Umbrella Boy is a green snake in my green grass. Will this green snake escape from the campus, escape from the town? He would be glad to hear that the little foe ran into a block-packed lorry barreling along a road and lost both his legs. But is he, Dr. Ezinwa Okoye, the newly sacked, prepared to face the depressing demands of the corrupt police officers? The SARS will need a bribe to kill off the boy for him, won't they?

With shaking hands, he changes his clothes, hurries into the university, and searches for Ifenna in all the classrooms belonging to the Department of Economics. He searches for Ifenna in the university halls where students receive lectures in educational courses. But there's no Ifenna.

On his way out of the campus, near the exit, the balding fat priest in dark-framed glasses, Reverend Father Benedict Okafo, honks for his attention.

He likes the cross-shaped scratches on the clergyman's vermilion jeep, the fewness of his teeth, the shortness of his legs. But he doesn't like the sound of the horn, the voice of the man, the wintry smile on his face, the eyes of onlookers, the delay in his movement. Does this man of God, dressed in an immaculate white cassock that draws infuriating attention to his own dirty shirt and rumpled trousers that reek of alcohol, want his banana-shaped nose flattened with a John Cena punch?

The clergyman is presently occupying his office and teaching the courses he was teaching. A ceiling fan will drop on his head one day, he tells himself. A ceiling fan or the ceiling itself. Why can't this white-robed, bead-thumbing nuisance leave me alone? Coming to mock me, or pray for me? He pouches his hands into his pockets until the priest approaches him with that elongated mouth of his that always reminds him of a horse.

"My brother, how are you coping outside this gruelling academic world?" Reverend Benedict asks in a tender tone. "I know it must be hard on you. But because Jesus lives, because the Blessed Virgin Mary lives, you shall face tomorrow, my brother."

"I'm *not* your brother," he says in his son's hostile tone. "And how may I help you? Speak fast, man: I'm in a hurry."

"There are seven packets of Gold Circle condoms my cleaners discovered on the shelf in your office… Now my office. Of course, the condoms are yours, not mine. There are empty bottles of Gulder beer, too. Even undrunk cans of Gulder beer and a packet of cigarettes. I entreat you to follow me to the office to collect all these things. And a few books belonging to you. That's all."

"I'm a generous colleague and a philanthropist, Reverend, so I will not break your heart by stopping you from drinking my forgotten beer, smoking my misplaced cigarette and using my abandoned books. Drink all the beers, my dear. Smoke all my beloved cigarettes, and use all my books. You can also use the condoms, Reverend. They are well lubricated for maximum pleasure."

Reverend Benedict's mouth is a shocked letter O as he marches past him and out of the campus that smells of dust and roars like a market.

Back home, he pours himself a glass of rum, but it drops from his shaking hand and shatters on the floor. He leaves the shards there and stumbles into the toilet, his feet crushing fallen onions. The tripping voice of a female newscaster on the radio follows him:

She ran out of her husband's house with the imbecile and into a bush. Since that Sunday evening, no eye has seen her. Perhaps she's mad now, some say. Perhaps she's abandoned the academic life for an agricultural life in the North. Which, according to her student named Nkemdilim Obi, whom we interviewed, is "Madness." Mrs. Chiamaka's husband is in tears as we speak: he admits he wishes his wife had disappeared with their five or six daughters, and not his precious son. The boy this man prefers, Mr. Fresh, is an imbecile. Isn't that madness?

Remain wherever you are, bitch, he thinks, and watches his Fanta-coloured urine splash all over the toilet bowl, which he imagines is Chiamaka's open mouth.

Back in the living room, he is surprised to meet his wife. "Where's Chinenye, Dorothy?"

"I don't know where the harlot ran to, and I don't

care!" she says. "As far as I'm concerned she's no longer our daughter."

"She's still *my* daughter. She'll always be my daughter. Stop acting like Virgin Mary. Before I got married to you, some people in your village told me you were impregnated twice, aborted twice and divorced twice. Yet I married you. Now you're throwing out our only daughter because of one single mistake. Can't you wait until she's pregnant again before throwing her into a dustbin?"

She covers her watery eyes with her hands. "I made those mistakes because I had dumdums as parents who weren't God-fearing Christians, but Chinenye has God-fearing parents, so she's not expected to be sleeping with useless boys."

"She's expected to be sleeping with useless boys!" he shouts, and she jumps back with such unexpected speed that is impressive in overweight women. "We both know that her parents are not better behaved. You only teach her the life circles of stupid cockroaches and houseflies and such nonsense, and I teach her nothing. I'm always shamelessly drinking and smoking at beer parlours with my girlfriends, and you know that. So she's expected to be having fun with useless boys. This is not the time to point accusing fingers. Let's find her and make her feel happy."

"Make her feel happy?"

"Sorry, I meant *excited*. Let's make her feel *excited*. She's not the first girl that enjoyed a penis, and she'll not be the last. As we quarrel now, other people's daughters are somewhere in this university town, sucking both small and big dicks with smiles on their young faces. "

"An adolescent girl like her should've nothing to do with male private parts. Girls, including female animals, shouldn't be seen running after males. They grow, mature and wait for male animals to come to them. Study the lifestyles of fowls, cows, goats and even sheep. But female human beings like Chinenye thought they're wiser than God. I don't like women who run after men they love. They should hide the feelings, keep them to themselves. Telling a man you love him makes you look cheap. It makes him to put his penis into your sealed dignity and get you pregnant. Chinenye is a disgrace."

"You're unbelievably unreasonable. I must find *my* lovely daughter today."

But he stumbles down the street, down the market, down the stream; but he does not see his daughter. He searches his church, her school, her favourite library: no Chinenye.

The next day is suffused with dust and flying insects. The winds whistle through trees and the sun warms the back of his neck. But he is not discouraged. He travels, under this fiercely glowing sun, to both radio and TV stations by bus and gives her name, her age, her hometown, her complexion, her ambition. He travels by yellow-painted tricycles to all the major churches in the town and does the same.

On his way home, the sun softening and retiring into shifting clouds, he closes his eyes and, for the first time in almost twenty years, recites Psalm 91 in a quaking voice.

That night the sky is brilliant with the stars, but he cannot spot the moon. He shifts in his bed with a laborious effort, his head trembling on his pillow as if he has suddenly developed Parkinson's, and wills his uncurtained window to close, shutting out the stars and the winds and the synchronous songs of nocturnal birds in pawpaw trees. The bedclothes smell faintly of beer and cigarettes. A mischievous mosquito descends to his left ear, buzzing and circling, and he shifts again, and again, trying not to think about blood, and about his daughter, and about his son. He is trying, also, to breathe fine and sink into sleep, but he knows he cannot: the voices of his children echo in every room he visualises, their faces appear on every shadowed wall he looks at. Even his own silhouettes are sometimes the ghost of his daughter and the ghost of his son, and sometimes of his wife who isn't even dead. How, then, can he possibly fold himself into sleep?

The morning is windy as the night, but is suffused with animal sounds and human voices. Before the usual

cockcrows, the aggressive barks of dogs, the plaintive
bleatings of goats, before the laughter of a new couple
honeymooning on the floor above his own, his son
returns from nowhere humming a Bob Marley song. He
welcomes the "Rastafarian" without questions.

"Chief, my chief!" he says, hugging the boy. "Don't
go again. Please."

"Jah will kill whoever raped my sister," his son says.

Together they lumber down the street and come
back without Chinenye. "Oh, Chinenye," he says,
flinging himself down on the cushion.

Moaning about Babylon and Redemption, his son
cooks breakfast—roast yam and oily stew rich with fresh
vegetables from their garden—and then dishes the food
in uncharacteristic silence and delicateness that instantly
brings Chinenye to his troubled mind. This means
he cannot eat now. This means he will perhaps not be
able to eat again. Chinenye: the name is a stone in his
throat, but he cannot chew it, swallow it. He will carry
it like a cross for the rest of his life. He glances at the
food again, follows the smoke rising gracefully from the
bronze-striped ceramic place to the cobwebby roof, and
hears his son mutter something about wasted efforts in a
damn kitchen. Fretful and touching, the boy's voice, but
he the father still cannot touch the meal. He can only
smoke and drink and watch himself drown.

He is sipping Guinness beer with his son and

planning the next step to take in search of Chinenye when gunshots are fired into the stillness of the night.

"What?" His son lowers his glass to the side stool and faces him with startled eyes. "Armed robbers?"

"It's the vigilante group on a parole, of course." His eyes fall on a crooked cigarette on the floor. He picks it, dusts it, lights it with his own lighter. "You dropped your cigarette, why?"

"Ezinne my ex-virgin girlfriend continually told me smokers would die young and go to hell fire, so I gave up smoking to avoid domestic violence. I'm glad I stopped, frankly." Ebuka takes his glass again and sips his drink. "Dad, what do you think about the Bible? I think it's an essential book, isn't it? I've been studying it since last month. It has changed my life."

"I'm not interested in any religious publication." He looks away from the new Bible his son has opened on the glass centre table, suppresses a desire to close it, and blows his smoke to the ceiling fan spinning noisily above their heads. "I'm interested in your sister. I can give anybody everything just to see my angelic daughter before I die. I feel convinced of my impending death today. I might die before finishing this one cigarette."

"Ezinne taught me a lot about Jesus Christ, Daddy. That was after I had raped her. Since I accepted Jesus, my life changed. The only bad thing I do now is beer. I'll stop after drinking this one, I mean it, man."

All the lights in the house, without any prior blinking notice, go off, and the sounds of cans being crushed under boots quicken his heartbeat. Before he can scream or hide, the door flings open. Four hoarse voices of presumably hefty boys echo outside and they storm in with guns.

"Lie down!" one of them bellows, and he and his son obey without a word.

Jesus, take the wheel, he thinks, wobbling on his stomach like a pig on a huge ball, perspiring and peeing in his trousers. "Please take anything you want in this house except our lives!" he says in a tremulous voice, his tear-filled eyes on the moonlit Bible open on the centre table. "I am jobless, wife-less, daughter-less, hopeless: have mercy upon me!"

But they put on their flashlights, take everything they like—his car key, cans of beer from the fridge, a carton of sugar, tins of milk and tea, bread and butter— and shoots his son in the chest: *tah*, *tah*, *tah*! – three times.

He lets out a hoarse cry as if he's the one who's filled with bullets, and then watches the armed robbers escape with their loots laughing like amateur actors exiting the stage. Before he can rise to his feet and blunder to the moonlit window, he hears his car start and fart, hears it screech off as it is often done in low-budget thrillers. The gate clangs open: frightened women cream the name of Jesus in their bedrooms, dogs start barking. Fowls, jerked awake in their trees and in their rain-soaked cages, raise their own voice in solidarity.

His neighbour, a lithe man in his late twenties or early thirties who's rumoured to be gay and whose hair and ears were burnt off, is the first person to hurry into his house. Others, twelve or fifteen of them, soon follow in sincere alarm. On their way to a mortuary, in the perfumed comfort of the ear-less man's Benz, he remembers that the man's name, just like the name of his son who's lying stiff at the back, is Ebuka. Another similarity: both are the only sons; both are interested in reggae music. Is this earless Ebuka doing this because of these similarities, or is he just a naturally kind fellow?

"Life is full of sorrows," the man says on their way home. "Reminds me of my own tragedy when I was a student on the campus where you are teaching...*were* teaching. One night, they poured fuel on me and Daniel my friend and threw a lit match on us just because we were always crooning acapella in the hostel. We escaped. But they later caught Daniel off campus, robbed him of his phone and his wallet, lynched him. Dan was a boy who sang ballads and donated bread at orphanage homes. Dan was a boy who dreamt to be famous, build schools, give free education to the poor. Dan was brilliant and kind. My Dan was. I was so depressed I couldn't continue my university education. His ashes are here in my wallet. I will never let him go. I will never let my Dan go."

Is this youngster, ferrying a bereaved oldie with no tears in his eyes, trying to weep on the highway, fly into an oncoming vehicle, kill the both of them? Or perhaps he is, by shedding these melodramatic tears, telling him that Life is cruel to the young and to the old, that it is raining in everybody's hearts. He knows the youngster expects him to comment on the poignant story, lay a consolatory hand on his shoulder or simply shake his head, but his entire body feels heavy, as if an invisible magician had hopped into the moving car through the window and miraculously filled him with stones and hot oil.

"Sorry about the loss, my good neighbour," the youngster says. "I didn't have time to offer my condolences and now there's another tragedy."

"What's the first tragedy?"

Is that his voice? It sounded like the voice of a goat that's being strangled by an impatient glutton on Christmas Eve. He clears his throat and asks the question again.

"No, I'm not talking about your dismissal from the university. I meant Chinenye. Am I to understand that you are not aware that her corpse was discovered in a gutter last night? She fell into a gutter and dirty flood carried her. Dirty waters carried her."

He has been shaking his head, but now stops. His heart stops. But the car continues moving, rattling, galloping, green trees and buildings and people flashing by. He leans back on the seat, closes his eyes and, in a voice quavering like a strummed guitar string, asks God why, why, why.

CHAPTER 27

I FENNA strolls over to Okoye's house with his half-empty bottle of whiskey to apologize for the pains he inflicted on Chinenye, "a beloved daughter taken too soon."

But the victim's father, to his pensive astonishment, does not seem to recollect who he is. "I'm Ifenna Nzekwu, your one-time student," he says, chewing imaginary gum to aid recollection. "Ifenna the princess, remember? Chewing gum, eye pencils, nose rings, Baby powder, whiskey…"

"Are you the boy whom I caught hiding a piece of paper in a woman's bra in an exam hall?"

He stimulates a smile, edges closer to scrutinize Okoye, who has begun to rub his stomach with his left hand, and pops another imaginary gum into his mouth.

The effect of this false cheerfulness, or this pseudo-chewing, surprises him: Okoye blinks three times, coughs three times, and then lapses into silence.

Everywhere: vivacious flies; they buzz round Okoye's face, round his chair, round the stool close to him. A packet of Benson & Hedges cigarettes, a lighter, a toothpick, a dozen bottles of Guinness bottles: the four companions of Okoye's that lay on this furniture. The despairing man has drunk nine already and this one is halfway down.

"I'm the gum-chewing dipsomaniac with nose rings who used to chew gum and drink beer with you and call you Professor," he says. "Remember?"

Okoye sits up, his eyes popping out with cartoonish excitement. "Chief Okoro! Okoro my good man! Chief Okoro? Yes! It's been long! I'm delighted to meet you after thirty-nine years! Or it is forty-nine years? But forget the questions first. Have a seat and tell me what you'll drink."

"I don't think my name is Okoro," he says.

Okoye turns to him with a kind of stupefaction. "Captain Abdulraheem Kamba, is this young man not Okoro Nwagbo, the kind cook whose wife we helped build a local orphanage home the year France won the FIFA World Cup? In 1898, I think. No, 1998."

"Professor, we didn't build any orphanage home in 1898. 1998? I was born few years after that thrilling

World Cup tournament. My dad told me that Nigeria won the silver cup."

"Shut up, Chief Okoro!" Okoye says, almost spilling his drink. "Nigeria didn't win any cup. We didn't even win a spoon. Oh, I remember you couldn't follow the tournament religiously like our agemates back then. We were watching the matches while you were watching the buttocks of those big-breasted philanthropists from Ethiopia. I thought I was the most horrible woman-user of all time until I met you in 1898."

"1898?" he says, and sips his whiskey. "Well, I admit I loved women when I was in the eighteenth century."

Okoye slurps his beer and belches. "Speaking of women, how's Mrs Chiamaka? Has the university found her? Or has she found the university? I don't know who is looking for whom. The whole thing is puzzling."

"Let's assume a hunter shot her in the bush, thinking she's a wild animal, and they eventually fell in love and got married." He spreads his handkerchief on the floor, goes on his knees. "Professor, I slept with Chinenye your daughter and she fell pregnant. I'm so sorry that three minutes of pleasure has caused so much pain to you and your family. Find a place in your heart to forgive me. The demise of Chinenye makes me feel like I'm floating away. Can you forgive me? Please."

"I'm one of the people who smeared the reputation of that university in their recent history," Okoye says.

"Always pray that a termite like me will never near your campus or any campus. Always wish me and pray for me because I wish you well and will always pray for you. Always study your books with the aggressive determination of the devil because knowledge is power and the exams is imminent. *Are*."

"Thank you, Professor," he says, rising. "May God bless you!"

In his room that evening, he lights a candle and prays to God to give Okoye the fortitude to bear the loss, prays to God to forgive him and Okoye their sins and their trespasses. He is praying to God to give him a good result, to give Nkem a good result, to give their friends a good result, and cleanse the university until tears fill his eyes.

That evening, still in his room, Uncle Elijah phones him after several weeks of inexplicable silence. Your mother is about to leave China, Uncle Elijah says. She and he, Uncle Elijah, have spoken on the phone. She will be back in Nigeria to see her family, but nobody should inform Ifenna.

"Why, Uncle Elijah?" he asks.

"She wants to admonish you with her unexpected return," Uncle Elijah says in English. "Sorry: it's *astonish*, not admonish. Or abolish?"

My mother, he thinks. Why did my mother turn her back on me, and on us, for four years, and then suddenly yearn to make a sensational reappearance when I'm almost done with my university education? And why is Uncle Elijah informing me in English? To show off his slightly improved English?

"Goodbye, Uncle Elijah," he says. "Thanks for the useless information."

This is what he does after the call: he moves to the wardrobe, pulls out his photo album for his luggage and flips through it, staring at his mother's big-eyed beauty. He dusts her two painted photographs on the wall. He captures one of them with his smartphone. He takes the phone to the chapel on the campus, kneels on the altar, which is a rug the colour of sunset, and prays for his mother's safe flight to Nigeria.

Back home, he finds Nkem writing his book at the reading table. "Semicolon," he murmurs.

Nkem raises a hand in greeting, inhales noisily, and continues writing. The only disturbance in the room is the tick-tock sound of the analogue clock nailed to the wall, right under the open window. Through this window he can see a sea-like sky of golden clouds drifting downtown where palm trees sway this way and that way in the evening winds, like drunk masquerades.

He draws the rose-coloured curtain, removes his nose ring and shuffles to the bathroom with it. He's till clothed, still standing and reviewing his life when he hears the door creak open, hears Chioma's voice greet

Nkem in an astonishingly melancholic tone. But he doesn't hear Nkem's reply. Why is Nkem tongue-tied? God, let it not be that Semicolon, this book maniac of a friend, has got an idea for a story or a poem and is leaving his girl to herself. Let it not be that he's counting the semicolons in his novel. Let it be a mere pause for a dramatic effect, or a passionate kiss, or noiseless sex on the chair, on the floor.

At the expiration of one minute of pornographic imaginings, he drops his Lux soap into the soap bowl, tiptoes to the door, closes one eye, and peeps: nobody is on the foam. Nobody is on the table. So where are they? Having experimental intercourse in the kitchen, behind the wardrobe, or *under* the foam? Jesus Christ. He presses his ear to the door and, almost immediately, Nkem's words rush into his ear: "Chioma? Look, Chioma, you've to tell me why you look so broken."

"Okay, I will confess, I will confess," she replies, pauses, and he imagines tears trickle down her cheeks and Nkem dabs her cheeks with a hankerchief. "I . . . I poisoned Chief, Nkem. Sugar, I poisoned my husband, but please don't hate me!"

"Lower your voice, blessed wine. Ifenna is in the bathroom. He might be wanking and listening at the same time. But are you serious? You poisoned your husband? Or a rat?"

"My husband, Sugar. I had to. You know it was my

mother who pushed me into marrying that patriarchal chimpanzee. He seized all my musical instruments, burnt all the books containing my lyrical compositions, said he was protecting me against the fame that throws married women into the hands of lewd men. I was so enraged that I shouted to his face that I am not his property and he hit me on the head with my guitar. The blood is still on our white curtains. . . I stopped opening my legs for him at night and he began to beat and rape me. So I poisoned his *nsala* soup; he ate it and died." A pause. "But I didn't know I would ever be a murderess. I poisoned the man whose child is in my womb. Can God ever forgive me? Can you ever forgive me? Hold me, Sugar—Please!"

"Stop it . . .! Where's his corpse?"

"In a mortuary, Sugar. His people came and helped me take him there. They thought it was his usual epilepsy and high blood pressure. I hope the secret will remain a secret. Only you and I know the truth. But you're the cause! Why did you allow Chief with bags of money and troubles to take me away from you? Why, Sugar? Why?"

"You knew he was a chimpanzee and yet you married him. You were not a baby. Am I to infer that you were a kid few months ago and could not make your own bloody decisions? What on earth do you mean?"

"Sugar, don't be vexed. I'm not saying you were wrong; I'm just . . . I'm just blaming you. . . sorry, I meant. . . God, I am confused! I don't know what I'm babbling. I don't know what to do. But you can help me, Sugar. Can't you?"

He retreats from the door, unable to endure the confessional speeches, and almost slips on the crystalline tiles and falls into the lavatory basin. But he grips the shower tap with his left hand, and loses his nose ring. He hears his bones strain under the weight of his adversities as he stands upright beneath the shower. He hears a rusty creak as he twists the tap, hears tepid water rush and hit his head, hears the door groan open again and footsteps leave the apartment. Chioma. That must be Chioma. Will Rose, like Chioma, ever kill somebody for him? The parrot cannot, he concludes, and is jealous of Nkem whose girl can. He thinks: why can't women kill for me? Why must I learn how to use the damn semicolon before women will joyfully kill their husbands for me? He thinks he needs to buy watercolour paint: he thinks he draws comic stuff best, and will draw Adaku stabbing a man's bottom with a breadknife for him.

He steps into the room after washing, drying and clothing himself and finds his phone ringing. He takes it, but hesitates to answer the call. The unfamiliar number signifies it's an international call. My mum, he thinks. It's my mother calling from China, isn't it? He takes the call and whispers his hello.

"This is Ifenna Nzekwu. Am I correct?"

His guess is correct: the masculine voice that asks this question is his mother's, unmistakably. "No, I am Tea," he replies.

"I'm awfully sorry, Milk."

Milk. That was his nickname when he was a tiny kid jumping in the rain. He was always sneaking into his mother's room to empty the family's tin of milk into his mouth. No one has ever called him Milk since his mother's elopement. Now her tone is thicker but friendlier. Mother had a stentorious voice with which she commanded everybody at home, including his father. Does this change imply that money deepens people's voices? Is she even rich now? He will find out.

"Mum?" he says, stops.

"Can I explain, Milk?"

He closes his mouth, closes his eyes. The voice that asks this question is a cold rainwater: it pours all over his body and leaves him shivering like a leaf in the wind. Because he remains speechless, because his intermittent sniffing bespeaks a promise of a fall into tears, his mother pronounces the word *sorry* over and over again and explains her mysterious life. She has been silent because she is ashamed of her "necessary" action, she says. Married Yagazie, the younger man who made her escape to China easier after hoodwinking the "fowl-brained Chinese", and Yagazie deleted all her contacts to discourage the temptation of reconnecting to her family in Nigeria, reconnecting to her. They lived happily in Wuhan with their adopted daughter and two dogs named Ifenna and Uchenna. They separated after she discovered he was cheating on her with one of the dogs.

"The dog, his lover, wasn't Ifenna, I hope?" he asks.

"No, Yagazie hated Ifenna. He didn't find Ifenna sexually attractive. He was only making love to Uchenna. And why aren't you angry that he named the dog he hated after you?"

He steers the conversation to his impecunious, tragedy-filled life on the campus; and she apologises for her silence, for his nights of hunger, for the frequent attacks, for the undesirable grades. "Anyway, I missed you, Milk!" she adds. "It seems you're now a big boy. I trust you are no longer mellow like fresh bread. Or you're still emasculated?"

"Mum, I wear G-strings now; ask Uncle Elijah." He spreads his handkerchief on a rock by the roadside and lowers himself into it. A bus speeds by, a boy's big head poking out of the window and his emaciated hand waving at him. He cannot recognize the boy, so he does not acknowledge the greeting. "Lest I forget, Mum! Uncle Elijah told me you'll come back to Nigeria next week."

"He's positive." His mother pauses, coughs mechanically. "I've purchased a helicopter in Nigeria. We'll fly straight into your university to pick you like a handbag. Of course Elijah told me you've taken your final exams. I'm indebted to Elijah for your education. We really owe him big things, not buns or bread. You learnt something at Heineken, right?"

"A lot, Mum. I swear, I have mastered how to wear a condom in less than one second, drink one crate of beer and chew gum politically like a harlot. We owe the great Heineken University of Education aplenty. Because, with this remarkable knowledge, I can work in a bank or in any corporate organisation in the world."

"You're incorrigible, Milk. You can sacrifice anything for a single joke. But I love you like that."

"And I was mad at her," he tells Nkem in the room that evening. "My mother, I mean."

"She has been discovered?" Nkem asks with no perceptible emotion on his face. "When?"

"Yes, she has been discovered like a missing handbag," he says in a subtly sarcastic tone before relaying his conversation with his mother to Nkem. But when he's done with his narration, Nkem mutters, in a grudging way, "Good, blessed wine."

The unfriendly writer is at the window, staring at the grey clouds. On the reading table, under the reading table, lie discarded drafts of his novel-in-progress. Can Nkem complete it before graduation? If Nkem completes it, will he dedicate it to him or to Chioma? No need to worry about that: when was the last time publishers looked at the dusty manuscripts of an absolutely unknown writer, particularly those who are resident in Nigeria? Living without Nkem will certainly be depressing, but he hopes his dearest Semicolon and the manuscript can find their way into America or, maybe, into the Great Britain.

He undresses and lies supine on the foam, pondering on his grade until he drops off to sleep. "I see your final result," Rose tells him on the phone in the morning. "Saw. I saw it. I saw mine. I saw Nkem's. Chioma's. Everybody's. The man who compute the result, Mr. Inyang, was my boyfriend. He shows me the results. Don't tell anybody."

"What's my grade point?" he asks, breathless. "It is funny, I hope? Funny?"

She titters. "I know, but I won't tell you. Just know that I am the best graduating student. Wow! I will be made a lecturer here! Oh God, I feel like dancing on a strict lecturer's bald head!"

He ends the call, pockets the phone and navigates to the window. Outside, the air is thick with the smell of things burning. Kites hover in the sunless sky, looking down on people, seeking the fire, seeking innocent chicks they will carry away. There are many chicks to carry away; they are circling the compound with their mother hens, peeping, flapping, perking at the rain-soaked earth for food. One of them, white and bloated, lies in stagnant water the colour of chocolate. He stares at it for a long moment and wishes, morbidly, that he were the lifeless bird.

"Blessed wine?"

He starts, and looks over his shoulder at Nkem, who's yawning and stretching on the foam with a novel. Beside him, on the wall, the purple-painted face of a peacock regards him the artist with its red-and-black eye.

"I will be back, Semicolon." He leaves the room in a white singlet, something he has never done, and wanders the neighbourhood. He looks at church buildings, circles one of them, returns with the afternoon sun without saying a prayer. He does not talk to Nkem until sunset. And Nkem does not talk to him. The silence stands between them, like a glass.

The following month, a period to forget, proves that Rose is right; it's the month Economics students' cumulative grade points averages are published. The month his mother finally returns to Nigeria with his father and with his brother, and checks, or says she checks, into one of the top resort hotels in Abuja. It is a month Rose and some girls in the class stamp their footwear on the floor and howl with laughter because he, like Nkem, could not make Second Class (Upper Division). They sing, teasingly, how his grade point is 3. 44; how Nkem's grade point is 3.47. Sing how Izu, "a bootlicking bubblehead" who cannot distinguish between utility and equilibrium, made Second Class (Upper Division). Sing how Chioma, who barely attended lectures in their third and final years, also made 2:1. Sing how Rose, who cannot define economics to a layman, is the best graduating student. Sing of Shedrack, sing of Meshack, sing of Abednego and other truants who know only two or three lecturers in Economics Department but made 2:1. Sing of popular guys like Ifenna and Nkem who did not, who could not. Sing how close they are to this Upper Division, he and Nkem, and how sad. How Uncle Elijah describes it over the phone in Igbo: "in the game of football, hitting the woodwork one hundred times cannot equate to one single goal." How close, how sad: how all those fired shots at Second Class Honours (Upper Division) could not find the back of the net. They have lost the match and are qualified to be called failures. They have failed themselves. They have failed their parents. They have failed all the people who respect them and esteem them far too highly. And failed the future, our future, he thinks: isn't it truncated already, like a shrub hit by a felled tall oak?

They sequester themselves inside their room, besieged by grief, and Nkem cannot read, cannot write. The silence floats in the air like a knife on water.

"It's more heartbreaking because Nkem the Great and every inconsequential know-nothing who ended up with 2.50 grade point average would have the same result: Second Class Honours (Lower Division)," Nkem says one downcast morning. "And the bloody rubbish that is the certificate will not bear the grade points, obviously. The certificate will not explain our problems on this campus."

"I've already resolved to give that comic paper to Suleiman, the Hausa guy who makes *suya* downtown, and focus on my painting," he says. "If I'm lucky, Suleiman will give me onion-filled *suya* in exchange for the certificate I'm offering him to encourage his *suya* business."

This flippant speech flies about in the air like a dagger; then, like a battery-powered robot, Nkem leaps out of the foam and dashes into the kitchen, and he follows him at once. "I'll slice Okoye's arse, kill him and kill myself!" Nkem says, grabbing the knife abadoned on the paint-stained cupboard. "I must butcher that malignant pig!"

Before he can part his trembling lips to talk Nkem out of his desire to murder, before he can clutch Nkem's shaking hand, the charged bull has pulled the door open and flashed into the starless night.

CHAPTER 28

NKEM arrives at Okoye's house lacquered in sweat. The electric bulb on the ceiling casts a faint light on the staircase as he advances. He can see that the door, which was presumably knocked down by some rioter or Okoye himself, has been neatly fixed, but not painted, not curtained, not locked.

He mutters the word "good", takes his knife out of his trouser pocket and boots the door open. Skulking into the scary darkness, he scrunches up his nose at the unignorable odour of mingled alcohol and stale urine, and listens for the heartbeats of the grubby man. The entrance he pushes open, gropes through the dark to a wall and finds a switch. He turns it on and squirms as varied coloured lights from bulbs flood the living room, the whistling windows a mosaic of glorious rainbows.

Snoring on a newspaper-littered sofa is Okoye; he's sprawled gracelessly, his eyes half closed, saliva trickling down his throat into his moth-eaten singlet the colour of mud, flies using his open mouth like their toilet. A packet of cigarettes and a matchbox lie on his paunch. The cigarette-burnt black trousers, which Okoye has been wearing since the last time he sighted him, are now so stained with food, alcohol and cigarette ashes that even a penury-stricken, filthy madman would be greatly offended and furious if anybody offered to hand the clothes to him free of charge. And under the centre table, an evidence of insanity: a pair of mud-covered shoes, a broken toothbrush, a pair of shattered reading glasses, a glass of water filled with cigarette ashes. The most disturbing ones are the evidence of incredible drunkenness: a Gulder beer opener, a Gulder beer pen, a Hero beer opener, a cracked wineglass, a dozen empty bottles of Heineken beer, whiskey, St Remy, Toma, Black Rebel. Big flies buzz musically round the plates of unfinished water-soaked garri and groundnuts, buzz round his head, buzz round his stomach.

The sight of the cheap food fills him with empathy and a profound sense of forgiveness, and his knife slips from his hand and drops on a burgundy-coloured rug.

How hopeless Okoye looks, he thinks: like a heap of folded rags, a dumped bag no one will ever pick and dust. Okoye has always been a dirty man, a man of dirty habits, dirty businesses, but not this dirty, not this hopeless, this useless. He throws himself down on the nearest sofa, puts his hot head into his hands and prays: Dear Lord, please forgive me, forgive Okoye the jobless man. Dear Lord, the jobless man is a bereaved man too, and is going insane.

There's an itching sensation on the edge of his eye; gently, quiveringly, he rubs at it, blows his nose into his white handkerchief, and steps forward as Okoye blinks his eyes open, sits up, coughs. He expects Okoye to start and dash off, but the man's eyes do not even register bewilderment – only a vague trace of restlessness. Clearly, he has not recovered from the sack, from the death of his children, from the marital separation, from the shame. Clearly, he is sinking at his own sea, sinking deep, sinking fast, but is not screaming for help. He will be glad to be tied to a tree and shot.

"Good evening, blessed wine," he says. "You remember me?"

"Mike? Mike the orphaned plumber?" Okoye asks, struggling to get up, but his stomach seems overloaded with liquor. "Who are you, chief? Are you Ebuka's friend? Did you see my son? What about my daughter? My wife, my job? Who carried them away?"

He drops to his knees. "I'm Nkemdilim Obi, obviously, and I'm so sorry, blessed wine. I came here to stab you to death, but I'm so sorry. Forgive me. I was mad to consider murder. I was mad, obviously."

"Of course you're mad." Okoye sways drunkenly on

his sofa and coughs again. "I thought you had come to tell me that corruptions have dried up in that university. I have been here waiting for you to come and tell me that bribery and corruption have dried up in Heineken University of Education. Go and check if bribery and corruption have dried up. I'll be right here waiting for you. Like I always say, I'll not bathe or brush my teeth until bribery and corruption dry up in all the universities in the Federal Republic of Nigeria. . ."

The door bursts open and Ifenna staggers in, panting and sweating.

Okoye regards this second intruder for a few heartbeats before interrogating him. "Who're you, young man? Have bribery and corruption dried up in the university?"

Surprisingly, Ifenna holds his tongue, staring wide-eyed from one face to another like a child just awakened in a strange room from a nightmare.

"This young actor came to kill me," Okoye continues. "But he's a coward. I wish he had murdered me. I'm willing to pay him to slaughter me. How much will I pay you chiefs to destroy me?"

"No, no, no," he says. "We're not murderers, blessed wine. I was vertiginous before, and spiteful: I couldn't make an impressive result because of your impishness, obviously. But I will not kill you."

Ifenna picks a broken gold-coloured figurine from the ground to admire its gleaming head, but it burns his retinas. "Yes, our grades are funny, but we'll not murder you."

"You must murder me!" Okoye snaps. "How could one visit someone one calls a friend and refuses to murder him? It's unfair. I beseech you to bury that knife in my stomach."

"No, blessed wine, please," he says.

Ifenna drops the figurine, picks the knife and puts it into his breast pocket. "Nobody's going to die today. It's not good to die on a Monday, especially on a Monday night; the angels don't like it."

The house is, for an infinitesimal moment, enveloped in silence. Outside, in the dusty orange trees that are lit by the stars and the moon, birds begin tweeting. A goat bleats as the wind intensifies. The windows rattle and the doors fling open: from the kitchen, from the bathroom, comes a bad odour of sewage.

"The pipes," Okoye says, scratches at his armpits and tightens his belt. "Don't worry about your results. Good knowledge is better than good grades. Good knowledge, like sex and alcohol, makes this world a better place, and not good grades. So Keep your heads up. If you believe in yourselves, you can do great things on this continent and even beyond. You can go out there and show white people that Africa is a land of gurus, and not the Heart of Darkness." Okoye stops to light a cigarette. "What was I saying?"

"You were telling us you'll not bathe and you'll not

leave your house until bribery and corruption dry up in all the universities in Nigeria," Ifenna says.

Okoye blows a cloud of smoke behind him and coughs. "Get over your so-called poor grades and move on. I lost my job, lost my daughter, lost my son, lost my marriage and lost my pride, but I didn't kill myself. If one dies one will miss the joy of sex. You'll stop enjoying sex: think about that. I wouldn't self-destruct in a world full of pretty women. Let your failure be your motivation. Self-develop aggressively."

Self-develop aggressively: what a nice phrase. Who would have guessed that Okoye, a mentally deranged man, could come up with such a nice phrase? Such a nice phrase in such a nice speech. "A nice speech, but Chioma hasn't moved on," he says. "She cries every day."

"Then go and reunite with her," Okoye says. "If the two of you don't get married in future, you'll be the most handsome fool in Nigeria. She has money now, and she can take you back to the United States, where you can write novels and find readers and make money and cheat on her once in a while. I hear you're writing a book. What's it about?"

He settles down on the nearest sofa. "It's tentatively titled *The Fate of an Incredibly Brilliant Nigerian Undergraduate*. The title has given you an insight, obviously."

"Semicolon, which comedian told you you're brilliant, or did you sip my whiskey?" Ifenna asks.

"It's a novel, you ignoramus," he says but thinks: Well, it's semi-autobiographical. Anybody who knows him must know that the experiences of the protagonists are his. The face of the protagonist is his. The girlfriend of the protagonist and his best friend are loosely based on Chioma and on Ifenna. The lecturers in the book are nasty like Okoye, but not as horny, not as dirty. The anxious need for believability softens the hostility of his pen.

He returns his gaze to Okoye and the man lights a crooked cigarette and says, "What was I saying? Don't bother; I've remembered. . . No, I can't remember. What was I saying? Oh yes, the orphans. Please always send them bags of rice and make sure…"

"No, not that," Ifenna says, and looks at the silver-coloured bar nailed to wall as if he's searching for whiskey. "You were advising us to remain alive in this world because if we die we will never enjoy sex again."

Okoye yawns. "Go and marry her. I have forgiven you, so get out of my house. I want to be left alone. I will never leave this living room until a student from Heineken University of Education, or any other decadent college, comes here to assure me that corruptions have dried up in all the universities in Nigeria."

"Is that possible, Professor?" Ifenna asks.

"Good evening." Okoye drops his half-smoked cigarette into a stainless vessel filled with ashes and closes his eyes. "Go back to the campus and check if corruptions have dried up, please!"

Upstairs in their room, Ifenna confesses to him that he's glad they reconciled with Okoye, glad they failed to butcher the broken man like a lamb, glad the rock that sat on his chest has been rolled off. "But this renewed friendship should not cause you to take his advice," Ifenna adds, stirring the tepid tea in a glass. "You're too small to ponder about marriage. We're still twenty-one. Marriage is a prison. If I get married now, my wife will come to the pub where I'm drinking beer with my homeboys and ask me to give her money for food, babies' napkins or such rubbish. Any writer who gets married is a fool. Babies are selfish and wicked. God, do you want them to spill milk on your printed manuscript? May none of my friends ever get married in Jesus' name!"

"Chioma still means the world to me, blessed wine." He lifts his head from the novel he's writing at the reading table. "I know she has a son for Chief, but I will accept the boy as mine. I'll love everything that comes from Chioma. That lady is beer: she excites me, intoxicates me, and I'm staggering with love."

This unexpected avowal amuses Ifenna and he laughs into his face and then gives his back a playful slap.

Nkem the Great cannot be deterred, he tells himself. I will take Okoye's advice. Of course it has always been my fuel, my dream, my everything.

The following week is memorable: he completes

his novel. He sends the work to the Vice Chancellor who solicits "outstanding essays or fiction exploring the Academic Life" and it's accepted for serial publication on the campus. He is invited to meet the Vice Chancellor. But he prefers to phone the man first.

"This is Nkemdilim Obi," he says. "The student whose novel is accepted for publication, blessed wine – Sir, I mean. Am I speaking with the Vice Chancellor, Heineken University of Education?"

"Come to my office," comes the familiar voice of the Vice Chancellor. "My secretary will be at the door to receive you first."

The Vice Chancellor's office is crepuscular. The man himself, blinking a lot and smiling appreciatively, calls him a literary hero in a delighted tone that gives his head an instant buzz and sends a vibrating sensation down his arms to his fingers. Excitement? Nervousness?

He folds his arms to hide the slight trembling, and looks out the leaf-smeared window at the horizon striped with gold. He's divorced, he remembers Rose saying in his hearing. A divorced good man: doesn't that indicate the wife must be bad? He and Chioma twitched and disagreed in shouty tones then; but now, looking at the man's kindly face and slender fingers, he cannot help but agree with Rose.

"Your novel's fabulously written," the Vice Chancellor says, smiling in his swivel chair. "It's too good to be published serially in this bush. It deserves wilder readership. Believe me, I stayed up all night savouring it. I cannot believe you're only twenty-one. At thirty-one, I sent my manuscript, *Sleeping on a Bicycle*, to British publishers and one of the racist editors sent me a message, advising me to quit writing immediately and go back to herding cattle. Or help my mother in the mud kitchen. I aggressively sent him another manuscript, *Laughing on a Bicycle*, which was my tenth unpublished novel, and he threatened to come to Nigeria from London to beat me up on *that bloody bicycle*. It happened, believe me."

What a very generous parrot. The man's sleepy eyes, the black-framed glasses sliding down his wide nose, the line in his dyed hair, the glistening stars on his elegant purple suit lend him a look of comic amiability. Behind him, on the wall, there are blurring photos of the state's governor officially opening a public toilet, the Minister of Education empowering northern schoolgirls with kettles and stoves, the Vice Chancellor receiving an award from a group of grinning students. *Half of a Yellow Sun*, opened and sullied with pencil annotations, flaps on the clustered desk like the wings of a decapitated fowl.

"You're an angelically handsome young man," the Vice Chancellor says, licking his lips and staring at him over his glasses the size of car headlamps. "You should advertise for Delta medicated soap."

"Thanks, blessed wine." He feels, to his amazement, coy like a bride under the lecherous eyes of a bold suitor. His awkwardness dissolves as the man abandons the childish business of lips-licking and drifts, blessedly, into literature. "James Baldwin's *Giovanni's Room* is the best queer literature you've ever read?"

"There's nothing like queer literature, Professor, because there's nothing like heterosexual literature." He stops to make sure none of his buttons is forgotten, looks up and finds the Vice Chancellor's eyes dreamy eyes roving around his bicep. He tries to give a wan smile of appreciation, but finds that his face is stiff with anxiety. The professor's predatory eyes clash with his, then the older man looks away, embarrassed. Why, he wants to ask, Why are you looking at me, sir?

"You look like a J. M. Coetzee man," he says instead. "His masterpiece is *Disgrace*. I read the novel ten times. Any aspiring African writer who hasn't read J. M. Coetzee's novel *Disgrace* is a disgrace. What do you think, sir?"

"I think I like your name, Nkem, and I promise to employ you after graduation." The Vice Chancellor pauses, searches his face for a trace of excitement. "You will take the job Dr. Okoye Ezinwa lost. He has a replacement already, I remember, and there's no problem. It simply entails you will replace his replacement."

Deux ex-machina, he thinks. Isn't this technique quaint and overused like a typewriter in an aged writer's room? Isn't this rounding off a little undeserving, a little unbelievable? Perhaps every ending, both in fiction and in reality, is undeserving. "This is unbelievably kind, sir," he says in a voice thick with insuppressible emotion. "Just like that?"

"Just like that." The Vice Chancellor moistens his lips again, adjusts his red tie. "Come around tomorrow, so I can introduce you to South Korean literature. Or should we delve into the North Korean literature first?"

Back home, he breaks the good news to Ifenna and asks his advice in an uncharacteristically modest tone.

"Now, you and Rose have finally got the opportunity to bore innocent children with economic terms," Ifenna replies with whiskey in his mouth, his voice shrill but solemn. "Congratulations, anyway."

"When will you discontinue from drinking whiskey and speaking disrespectfully of economics?" he asks. "Okay, don't answer the question. Thank you!"

"Can you say that without crying, darling?"

The question stings him, but he let's that slide: he knows Ifenna is not being jealous or envious. He knows Ifenna well. The funny boy has learnt to be good while pretending to be bad. This pretence is like a stain in milk: very obvious.

At sunset, Smiling Frog Press emails him. *Congratulations*, the message says. The manuscript has been read by a team of editors. The manuscript is the angriest, the loveliest. They will publish the manuscript. Can he kindly reply to the email, indicating interest?

He reads the mail three times, drops to his knees, and cries.

Later, after replying to the email, he phones his mother and then his father and shares the good news. He shares the good news with Chioma, then with Pastor Elijah, then with Professor Nwanyibuife, then with Ifenna.

"You chose to tell Chioma before me," Ifenna says, painting his mother on a canvas and listening to some distasteful Europhobic jokes on the radio. "That's funny. But I will not laugh. I can only say congratulations even though the book will be published by a smiling frog, and not by a human being."

After dinner, his mother phones him. He switches on the loudspeaker so his father can join. "We serve the God of Abraham, Dictionary," she says. "It's not by your might, not by your power, but God's. Dedicate the book to Him. Him alone."

"If you don't dedicate the useless book to me, I will swallow your mother's alarm clock and die," his father says, and laughs.

He laughs, too, but his mother's silent. His mother does not always laugh. His mother will not laugh now. Is his mother offended by the joke, or by his laughter, or by their laughter, or by his unwillingness to disclose his dedication? Perhaps she is, as she often does, merely kneeling on the sandy floor, kneeling and praying tearfully, silently.

I will dedicate the book to her God, he tells himself after the call is suddenly disconnected. I will dedicate the book to her. I will dedicate the book to her husband. He sits on the reading table, opens his manuscript, and writes: *Dedication: to my parents, Mr. Jude Obi and Mrs. Faith Obi. Thank you exceedingly for my tortuous education.*

Rose phones to register her excitement. "I knew you'd make us proud one day," she says in Igbo. "I can now go to people in the street and proudly tell them I've slept with a novelist. I've made it in life!"

Chioma sends a text: *Sugar, I'm sorry 4 the silence. My mother's people confiscated my phone and other things their chimpanzee bought for me before he was poisoned. I still have his money hidden in some banks. I'll send some money to you. Please don't try to phone me now. Congratlations, Sugar! This weekend, when you're free, do me the favour of coming downtown to out newest house. A white duplex. A black gate.*

What a spelling. Why can't people spell "congratulations" properly? To kill time after long hours of writing, he asks Ifenna why the youth can neither spell properly nor punctuate properly.

"Rose is still missing," Ifenna says, zipping his luggage. "I told you she's missing? Any way, I have moved one. And my people, are coming to the campus in my mother's helicopter to take me."

"Sorry: I forgot, blessed wine."

The football field is green and full of egrets. Kids are everywhere: kids are running and screaming, kids are falling and crying. Kids are jumping, laughing, clapping. Kids' eyes are skywards: they are fascinated with the helicopter. He is, surprisingly, fascinated with the helicopter, too. It is new, shiny, and the body is a celebration of colours: orange, white, green, blue, indigo, red. Its blades, which are chopping through the air, are elongated and silvery. "I will not miss you, Semicolon," Ifenna says.

"We both know you will," he says with a snicker, and Ifenna hugs him. "We will be great, Ifenna—at least I will. Take this from me. I will never forget you. Keep in touch. Now, I will free you. Need to see my girl's people."

"Tell Chioma that all of us—you Semicolon, me, my parents, your parents and her parents, and your uncle will dine tomorrow, I swear."

The helicopter has landed and the schoolchildren are running off, scattering in the field and laughing.

"Goodbye, blessed wine," he says. They unpeel themselves from one another, and he rushes off, the morning dews hitting his face.

It does not take him more than fifteen minutes to arrive at Chioma's new duplex. The black gate says *Beware of Dogs*.

Grey-haired fool, he thinks. Chief is a grey-haired fool. Why did Chief build a mansion for a girl who never loved him?

He raps at the gate three times and waits. The gate opens with a creak and Chioma's mother appears. Then she hisses, enters, bangs the gate shut. He sends Chioma a simple text—*I'm at your gate, obviously*—and raps at the gate again. From somewhere, a dog—the one they named Satan?—growls.

He steps backwards and Chioma's urgent voice makes him look up: "Sugar, come upstairs! Come upstairs, *biko*!"

She's upstairs on the balcony on the first floor, chewing *ube* and a roast corn. When their eyes meet, she drops the food and starts waving urgently like a little girl abandoned in a forest full of frightening voices of wild animals. "Open the gate and come in. Satan is chained. Sugar!"

Scared and unsure, but he takes her advice, for it has started drizzling, and stops before their pool, where the yellow of the many lamp lights quiver on the blue-green surface of the water. He looks up and glimpses her mother, who is now on the balcony. Beside her is her husband; their faces are creased so badly by anger that he remembers the battered old leather chairs in Okoye's house.

"Good evening, sir," he says. "And good evening, madam."

They stand there, glaring down at him. A mischievous wind comes, snatching the woman's hand fan, ruffling her synthetic hair. What is she doing with a hand fan in a cold wind?

"Let him come up," Chioma tells her parents.

"Please. He must come up! This is actually my house, not yours. I have the right to welcome anybody I like. Sugar, come upstairs!"

"You better advise the poor thing to get out or I will tear him up like an old newspaper," her mother says, her eyes wild, her chest rising and falling.

"Your name's Nkemdilim Obi, correct?" her father asks.

"Yes, blessed wine."

"What's the name of your hometown again?"

"I'm from Oba. A town of sweet palm wine in Idemili South, Anambra State. Chinua Achebe is also from Idemili."

"And so what?" Chioma's mother shouts as if the mentioned writer once wrote a war-themed poem on her birth certificate which he had mistaken for an ordinary paper. "I don't care if Chinua Achebe is from Idemili or Japan. Get out! Vamoose!"

Chioma, teary and agitated, looks up at her mother and begins shaking her like a tree whose branches hold irresistible ripe fruit. "Mum, this is sheer wickedness!" she says. "Let him come up; he's shivering in the rain. Can't you see he's shivering in the rain?"

Her mother raises her jeweled hand as if she wants to slap her, but restrains herself. Her father watches on. She watches on. The dog growls again, followed by the squawks of frightened hens, and his head bows in shame.

Be a man, he tells himself. You are Nkem the Great and you must always remember that. "I really love your daughter," he says in the most modest tone he has ever heard from himself. "Chioma is my everything. My book will fetch me money, and I will take her round the world. I'll equally take care of the baby in her womb as mine. Hasn't she told you I will be a lecturer at Heineken University of Education? Hasn't she told you the world is killing themselves because each of them wants my book? I'm great, obviously. I'll be greater. The world will celebrate me, canonize me. Give me a chance, blessed wine. Say yes to me or I will die in this cold rain!"

He has begun to shed fake tears. Chioma covers her eyes with both hands, tears trickling down her cheeks, the wind ruffling her long hair.

Her father whispers something into her mother's ears, but she arches her brows and shifts away from him. He wills the couple to say yes to him, to say something, but they stand there on the balcony staring at him. Thunder booms overhead, followed by lightning, and the dogs growl once again.

"You're really the son of poor parents they say the Vice Chancellor of Heineken University wants to employ because he wrote a great book?" her mother asks, breaking the silence.

Impatient and unreasonable with fury, he says what shocks himself: "Obviously. Who else can possibly write a great book there?"

She blinks, gazes at Chioma, in an exaggerated shrug of incredulity or perhaps exasperation, and drops her broadened shoulders. And Chioma nods, nods again as if to give her a transfusion of encouragement, and then waits. And waiting her father puffs a pointless laugh, but thunder gargles, shutting him up and sending him barreling indoors with the shout of "Jesus!"

He blinks out the raindrops on his eyebrows and looks up again.

"Nkemdilim Obi," her mother says after the rumble of thunder has died down. "Come upstairs."

Finally, he would like to say and punch the air in celebration. But of course he doesn't know if she has agreed or not, of course he doesn't know if the Vice Chancellor will remember to fulfil his promises. He hopes Chioma's mother will be kind upstairs and the Vice Chancellor kinder.

These thoughts worry him as he ascends the stairs, but his step does not lose its bounce: he's buoyed by the unexpected invitation into their house, intoxicated by the promise of a great career.

I feel like the incomparable Oscar Wilde, he thinks, pouches his hands into his trouser pockets, and heads to the entrance. He takes his hands off his pockets as he hears Chioma's mother shout cautions at the yelping and whining dogs. The noises make him pause for a moment. Write about this woman, he challenges himself.

Write about this woman's daughter, and this university. Nkem the Great, think of writing your second book: a memoir, Ifenna's and Okoye's complied in a single book. A single book in which his university life will end well. His university life should end well because he thinks he deserves the best. Because he likes to see his protagonists happy in the end. Because that is how stories, plaintive stories like his, should end.

He continues his ascent and an idea flies into his head: it is to visit Okoye every weekend with a bottle of beer or wine, interview Okoye, ask Okoye to narrate his version of their story. He, Nkem, will take notes. He will also take notes from Ifenna, from Chioma, from Rose, from everybody who's integral in their story on the campus. The questions will be via emails. He will edit the relevant submissions, polish them, fuse them with his. But will their accounts be sincere? Will Okoye remember the past? Can Okoye type on his computer? Perhaps he will have to visit Okoye and all the characters he needs; they will prefer to narrate their experiences face to face—or on the phone? That's good, too: whichever way, he cannot complain, he cannot suggest differently. He can only be grateful when it happens. Now he is excited, now he is impatient to begin his second literary project at his reading table. He can already see the book in bookshops, in libraries, in classrooms. He can see it at literary festivals where it is displayed, collected, flaunted.

He sees teachers in workshop rooms holding it lovingly to their chests. He sees children, bespectacled and clean, lost in it. Adults in a book club are lost in it. He sees a renowned author garlanding the book with a prestigious literary award. He sees himself, complacent and smiling, giving Ifenna some of the money, telling Ifenna to give Okoye some of the money. He sees himself asking them to change their clothes, change their curtains, change their bedsheets. That's what he's going to do.

He hears Chioma's mother's shouty voice and increases his pace. The barks and growls of dogs have ascended competitively into an insufferable symphony: his thoughts, anxious and excitable, begin whirling in his head like harmattan dust. But on the last marvellously tiled stairs, littered with dogs' furs and studded with innumerable button-sized turquoise lights, the book's tentative title floats to him like a miracle: *The Shameful History of Academic Madness.*

The End

ACKNOWLEDGEMENTS

My profound gratitude to my family who were so nice to understand my obsession with literature, told me I am good, and backed me to go for the gold in the UK: Andy Love (Daddy, the reader), Ngozi (Mummy,the prayerful daughter of God), Victor (a brother who was kind enough to drive me round the city of Abuja so that I could have the gold), Chuks (the Kind One), Edozie (the Wise One, the One Who Criticizes with Love), Somee, Precious (my first sister, a princess), and Olive (a pure heart).

My secondary school classmate and friend, Maduka Eze, has always been supportive with his kind words. He read some of my stories and told me that the sky could be touched. He read the first three chapters of this book quickly, and his honest comments were priceless. Thank you immensely, brother.

Other helpful readers include Carl Terver (he edited the early draft of the first chapter, and some of my stories), Chukwudera Michael (an unforgettable motivator and believer who read some chapters and spoke brilliantly about the book's strengths and weaknesses), Chinwendu Okafor(My dear friend, I still wonder how you succeeded in reading the entire manuscript when it was a huge eyesore and brought my attention to some mistakes and inconsistencies), and M. Hassan, my wonderful friend from Sri Lanka who criticized the work, edited some parts of the work, and told me what I needed to hear.

And finally but very importantly, Ugochi Iyiegbu (also known as Favour Bliss). Thank you, my darling, for opening the window of Life to let me see the rising sun.